GIVE THE
DARK
MY
LOVE

GIVE THE DARK MY LOVE

BETH REVIS

RAZORBILL

RAZORBILL

An Imprint of Penguin Random House LLC
Penguin.com

RAZORBILL & colophon is a registered trademark
of Penguin Random House LLC.

First published in the United States of America by Razorbill,
an imprint of Penguin Random House LLC, 2018

LIBRARY OF CONGRESS CATALOGING-IN-PUBLICATION DATA
Names: Revis, Beth, author.
Title: Give the dark my love / Beth Revis.
Description: [New York] : Razorbill, an imprint of Penguin Random House LLC, 2018. |
Summary: Told in two voices, seventeen-year-old alchemy student Nedra turns to dark magic when a deadly plague sweeps through her homeland leaving her new friend, Grey, to pull her from the darkness.
Identifiers: LCCN 2018013398 | ISBN 9781595147172 (hardback)
Subjects: | CYAC: Alchemy—Fiction. | Magic—Fiction. | Plague—Fiction. | Fantasy—Fiction.
Classification: LCC PZ7.R3284 Giv 2018 | DDC [Fic]—dc23
LC record available at https://lccn.loc.gov/2018013398

Printed in the United States of America

1 3 5 7 9 10 8 6 4 2

Interior design: Eric Ford

To my father,
who deserved more time

&

to my mother,
who taught me how to grieve.

Dei gratia.

I love you as certain dark things are to be loved,
in secret, between the shadow and the soul.

—Pablo Neruda, Sonnet XVII

PROLOGUE

THE WARSHIP CARRIED twenty good men and two cannons.

"Bit of an overkill, isn't it?" Captain Pasker said. The sun was to his back, casting a long, imposing shadow over the deck.

Captain Pasker was from the mainland; his ship had accompanied the Emperor on the short voyage across the Azure Sea to the small province of Lunar Island. Pasker had been in three wars already, "skirmishes," he called them, bloody little inconveniences that were necessary to remind the people of the might of the Emperor.

The sailor beside him was a local boy, a new conscript. He'd been raised with the old legends.

He wasn't sure that one warship was enough.

The sleek, red-lacquered vessel cut through the bay toward a small island that bore only one building. A hospital, its brick façade illuminated by the rising sun, the clockface built into the tower so bright the captain could not look at it directly.

"Get the horn," Captain Pasker told the boy. The sailor went running. By the time he returned with the large vocal horn, the warship was just a few meters away from the stone steps that disappeared into the blue-green waters of the bay. He tried to count them—fifty or so, leading up to a stone plaza and the massive doors of the hospital.

The captain raised the horn to his lips. "By order of Emperor Auguste, you must surrender your person for trial." His voice boomed

1

up the steps, and he was certain that those who lurked inside the large brick building had heard.

The doors, however, did not open.

"This is your last chance," Captain Pasker shouted through the horn. "You are hereby ordered by the Emperor's Guard to present yourself for arrest on the grounds of treason."

"And trespassing," the first mate added.

Captain Pasker set the vocal horn down. "Treason's quite enough. Can't hang the girl twice."

They waited.

"All right, boys, get ready."

The sailors used oars to bring the warship closer to the steps, then lashed it portside to the posts.

"I'll take five," the captain said, one foot on the gangway. The first mate selected five additional sailors to accompany him, and they followed his long strides onto the small island, swords at their hips and muzzle-loaded smoothbore muskets in their hands.

"Blasted sun gets in the way," Captain Pasker grumbled as he looked back at the ship. "Try the horn once more," he called.

The first mate repeated the captain's message, the words amplified and echoing over the calm waters of the bay. The captain and his five were already halfway up the stairs when the heavy door of the hospital creaked open.

A girl stepped into the light.

She was average in height and build, her hair black and neatly braided, shining in the sun as if it were still damp after being washed. Her deep olive skin was typical of people from Lunar Island. She wore alchemist robes that seemed a touch too big for her; likely she'd stolen the clothing from the hospital closets. The only remarkable thing about her was that she was missing her left arm from a point just above where her elbow should have been, but even that detail wasn't too strange. Many on Lunar Island had lost a limb or two from the plague.

Still, she was young enough to be Captain Pasker's daughter. Seventeen, eighteen maybe. He could feel the doubt welling in his men, the hesitation. The captain gazed up the long stone stairs toward her.

"We're here to arrest you," Captain Pasker called. "Best come quiet now."

The girl smiled.

"Girl," Captain Pasker said in a warning tone, as if even her gender was cause for offense.

The doors behind her opened wider.

The people who poured out behind the girl seemed unarmed. Most wore hospital dressing gowns; a few wore peasants' clothing. All of them showed some deformity of the plague—withered and blackened hands or feet, an inky stain rising up their necks, under their skin.

And they were quiet.

They did not speak or even look to the girl as they descended the stairs as if by pre-agreed formation. They showed no fear.

They showed no emotion at all.

Captain Pasker's stomach churned.

The rifles in his men's hands shook.

"Steady," Captain Pasker warned, but it did no good. One of the sailors popped off a shot, the bullet aimed true despite the man's nerves. A woman in the front, about twenty steps away, staggered, her shoulder snapping back, the force of the blow causing her to stumble and fall on the steps. Her head smashed against the stone, an audible crack of her skull followed by the crunching sound of broken teeth.

The others around her kept moving, completely ignoring her body broken on the steps.

And then she stood back up.

The woman showed no pain. She opened her mouth and let the splintered teeth clatter to the ground. She ignored the skin that dangled over her broken skull. No blood poured from her wounds.

She just kept walking.

She was ten steps away now. Five.

"Fire!" Captain Pasker screamed. "Fire! Fire!"

The guns blossomed in flame and smoke around him as his men fired shot after shot. Many in the crowd staggered, but none cried out.

None fell.

The dead could not die.

ONE

Nedra

I OPENED MY eyes at the exact same moment my sister did. A grin spread across her face, followed by a flash of sadness.

"It's going to be okay," I told her, sitting up in bed.

Ernesta flopped over in her own bed, staring up at the ceiling. "I'm happy for you, Nedra." I raised an eyebrow. "I *am*," she insisted. "It's just going to be strange here without you."

I swung my legs over the side of my bed, my knee brushing the edge of my trunk, packed with almost all my clothing and the mementos I couldn't leave behind. I took off my nightshirt and threw it at Nessie—it was one of hers, after all—then slipped into the tunic and leggings I'd set aside to wear today.

"Ugh, how can you move so fast?" Ernesta groaned. She melted out of bed and let her head thunk on the doorframe as she rooted around in our wardrobe, now much emptier without my clothes taking up space. She withdrew a dark blouse and an olive skirt, a combination that would make me look drab. Ernesta never looked anything less than glowing, even with her hair mussed from sleep and her eyes half-closed.

I glanced down at my own clothes. We were twins, and yet somehow we never looked the same.

I left Nessie to finish getting ready and followed the scent of bacon into the kitchen, where my mother stood over the stove.

"Nedra!" Mama exclaimed, sidling around the table and hugging me with the arm that still held a spatula. "Are you excited?"

Through the window, I could see Papa loading up the cart he used to sell books, but which today would carry me away.

"I think so?" I said. My stomach churned, but even though Mama slid a plate of fried eggs, a biscuit, and three strips of bacon over to me, I realized that it wasn't hunger that ached me.

Mama made Nessie's plate—no biscuit and extra bacon—and placed it beside black coffee already poured and cooling. She squeezed my shoulder, her hand slipping around my neck to read-just my necklace. "You'll be fine," she whispered. I couldn't help but doubt her.

Doubt myself.

Ernesta came in, stealing a piece of my bacon before turning to Mama and chatting excitedly about plans to meet Kava, the shoemaker's apprentice.

As Nessie rattled on, I watched our father through the window. Papa stood outside, checking the straps on the mule and inspecting the cart, going over the same old routine but with a scowl on his face, his eyes blazing.

He didn't want me to go.

Mama noticed my gaze and wrapped an arm around me. "It's going to be okay," she said.

"Of course it is." Nessie rolled her eyes. "They obviously want you."

"They didn't last year," I said, staring at my fork. Yūgen Academy rarely accepted students who weren't funneled through the private schools and the alchemical tutors hired by the elite. Last year, I'd applied to join the program and was soundly denied.

"Well, they're paying you this year," Nessie said. "Quit pretending to be humble."

I wasn't pretending. The scholarship that would take care of my room, board, and tuition at Yūgen this year was astounding, even more so since such scholarships were rarely awarded. But somehow the pride of it—of having my dreams not only come true, but also be financed—was buried under the fear and worry of leaving behind the only home I'd ever known . . . especially if Papa didn't want me to go.

"Besides, what would you do if you stayed here?" Nessie asked.

"Steal Kava from you," I shot back, smiling as Nessie pretended to have been pierced in the heart by my betrayal.

But my focus drifted away as breakfast wore on. I'd thought I wanted normal on my last day at home, but normal made me sad.

The next time I came here, it would be as a guest. After I walked through that door, this would no longer be home.

"You're *meant* to do this," Nessie said in an exaggerated whisper.

"I am," I replied immediately, and was somewhat surprised that it felt true, despite my reservations.

"So humble," Nessie mocked, but Mama gazed at me with pride. My eyes slid away from her beaming smile.

"You'll do important things," Mama promised.

"I'll try," I mumbled. I was going to Yūgen to become a medical alchemist, and once I'd mastered my craft, I would return here, to the north, to help the sick. I wanted to learn everything—not just about the everyday ills and injuries that needed healing, but also cures and treatments for the more obscure diseases, like the Wasting Death.

My stomach twisted. Despite the scholarship and my family's faith, I still wasn't sure I was good enough to go toe-to-toe with the other students at Yūgen.

Mama kissed the top of my head. "You're like your father," she said gently. "You never know what to do with your emotions."

Papa strode to the doorway, stomping the mud off his boots on the large flat stone in front of the back door. "Ready?" he said, his voice gruff.

I nodded silently.

"No!" Ernesta cried in overexaggerated anguish. She threw her arms around me, dramatic as always, but it was Mama's soft farewell that broke my heart. I gently pried myself away from them as Papa turned silently back to the mule cart. He already had the reins in his hands as I climbed up to sit beside him, and before I was settled, he clucked his tongue, and our mule, Jojo, lumbered toward the road.

My hand moved nervously to my hip bag. I fingered the cloth, identifying each item by its feel through the coarse material. My pen set, a gift from Nessie. Wrapped bread, from Mama. An old alchemy book, the binding cracked. I'd found it on one of Papa's many book-shelves. It was handwritten, part journal, part guide. My great-grandmother had died when I was less than a year old, but she'd been a potion maker for the village and kept all her notes inside this book. She passed it on to my grandmother, who'd given it to my father, who'd tucked it on a shelf and forgotten about it. I'd come across it three years ago, and soon after, I started dreaming of becoming an alchemist, using the herbs and techniques my great-grandmother detailed in order to help heal others.

There was only one main road in the north, curving around the center of Lunar Island's top arm, with dozens of little villages blossom-ing along the edge. Our village was beyond the carmellina gate. When we passed the church hall, Papa touched the three-knotted cord he wore around his neck. After a moment, I did the same.

Papa made his living traveling up and down this main road, stop-ping in every small village to distribute books and messages. When I was little, I thought I might join his trade, eventually getting a book cart of my own. Like him, I'd journey from village to village, passing out stories for others to read and meeting new and interesting people. Nessie never wanted anything more than to stay in our village and flirt with the same people we'd gone to school with, but I knew I wanted more. I wanted something bigger. I'd told myself that just going past the carmellina gate, just following in my father's footsteps would be enough. I'd tried to believe that.

It was Papa who told me I should read the books instead of sell them; it was he who first encouraged me to apply to Yūgen Academy, saying I'd taught myself more than that school could anyway, so I might as well show up and take the alchemical robes.

But it was Papa who now glowered at the road, disappointment evident on his face.

"I'm sorry," I said as Jojo plodded down the road.

Papa's eyes widened. "For what?" He turned his gaze from me quickly and clucked his tongue at the mule.

"For going," I answered in a small voice. My scholarship would pay my way, but it wouldn't give my father help when the cart needed unloading, or pay the butcher when Mama ran out of meat, or help Nessie with the chores I was leaving behind. The cost of an education like the one I'd get at Yūgen was far more than any scholarship could cover, and it was my family who would sacrifice for me.

Papa yanked the reins, pulling Jojo up short. The mule didn't care; she ambled to the side of the road and started munching on a low-hanging branch of tigga leaves.

Papa turned to me. "Nedra," he said, his voice softer and kinder than it had been all day, "I'm not mad at you for going."

"Disappointed then," I said, sliding my eyes away.

"I'm proud of you, my love," he said, turning to me, the intensity of his words palpable. "I'm *happy* for you. I'm mad at myself." He sighed heavily. "I'm sorry. I didn't want to worry you, and instead I made it all worse. But . . ."

"Why are you mad at yourself?"

"Because I'm selfish, Ned." He laughed bitterly. "I want to keep you with me always. But I know I have to let you go." He glanced back at the book cart, heavy and dusty, the wooden shelves unable to fully protect the texts from the dirt road. "You think I want this for you? You think I want you to marry a farmer or a butcher or a fisherman, that I want you to always wonder if you'll have enough to feed your own babes?"

"You always took care of Nessie and me—" I started, but he was having none of my words.

"I got this cart from my father, and he from his."

"I can still work with you on the book cart when I come back," I said quickly.

"No!" The words burst from him. "I don't want you to. That's my point, love. You can leave."

I watched the red-and-yellow-striped leaves Jojo hadn't eaten yet. "I'm not going to be gone forever." My voice was barely a whisper.

"I hope you are," Papa said, a fervent tone underlying his voice. I looked up at him, startled. "Or," he added, a small smile peeking from behind his mustache, "not forever. But Neddie, my love, your path has always been longer than this little road. You're meant for the city streets, for ships across the sea, for places where there are no roads. I don't want you to take my book cart. Maybe whoever Nessie marries will, but it won't be you. I'd never fold you up into books sold to strangers. You're going to live your own story."

Tears stung my eyes. "I thought—"

"Who do you think wrote the Emperor?" Papa said, and I heard the note of pride in his voice.

"You wrote the Emperor?" I laughed.

"Him, the governor before he died, the new governor after, that headmistress of the school, the chancellor of the city—"

"How many letters did you send?"

"When they rejected you that first time, I was a bit angry," Papa conceded. "I wrote everyone I could think of. I guess someone eventually noticed."

"Papa."

"Aye, I've been upset," Papa said, switching the reins across Jojo's side and getting her back on the road. "But not at you. I don't like being reminded that you're not my little girl anymore."

I dropped my head on his shoulder and closed my eyes. "I always will be," I promised.

TWO

Nedra

IT WAS GETTING late by the time we reached the dock at Hart. Papa waved to someone on a flatbed cargo boat as Jojo plodded down the path. Two people—a girl about my age and a boy probably a few years older but quite a bit larger—were lifting crates onto the boat. They stopped and waved back when they saw us coming.

"You've heard me talk about Oslow and Mae," Papa said, his eyes on Jojo. "Their kids took over the farm. Carso—the oldest one—he makes weekly runs to Northface Harbor. He agreed to take you over."

I tried to recall them. Papa traveled every week across the northern part of Lunar Island—from the tip to the forest—and he knew someone from every village, but it was hard to keep up when all I ever heard were stories about strangers.

"Room for her trunk right here!" the boy said cheerily as he and my father hauled my belongings off the cart, and I hopped down.

The girl stuck her hand out. "I'm Dilada." I noticed the dirt making crescent moons under her fingernails. She pointed to her brother. "Carso."

"Hi. I'm Nedra," I replied.

Papa and Carso wedged my trunk between two crates of turnips, clumpy red clay still clinging to the purple skins. Carso put a basket of carrots on top of it.

And then it was time to go. Papa looked at me, his eyes a little too watery, his hands on his hips until I threw my arms tightly around him. He dropped his chin to the top of my head. "Write us," he said, his voice a little choked. "And don't forget about us."

I squeezed tighter.

Dilada and Carso climbed into the boat. They weren't rushing us exactly, but it was time to go.

"You ready?" Papa asked.

"Yes," I lied.

"One last thing." He went back to the cart and withdrew a tube about as long as my arm, the kind used for carrying documents or maps. "This is for you," he said.

I peered at the package.

"Don't open it yet," Papa continued. "You're going to a new city, all by yourself. It won't be easy, and we won't be there to help you." His voice dropped low, just for me. "Open this when you need us, and remember that we're never too far away."

I wanted to thank him, but my throat was tight with emotion. Papa hugged me once more, then held my hand to steady me as I stepped from the dock onto the boat. It dipped under my weight, and I struggled to find balance as I wove between the crates of vegetables and sat down on a box behind Dilada. I settled my hip bag beside me and clutched the carrying tube in both hands, too nervous to let it rest on the wooden floor of the boat.

Carso stood, using a long rod to push off from the dock and point the boat south while Dilada set the sails. I tried to be as small and out of the way as possible, stuffing my shirt into my waistband so the wind wouldn't blow it around. Behind us, Papa had moved Jojo back up the hill and sat on the cart, shading his eyes with his arm, watching us until we were out of sight.

"He's a good man," Dilada said, plopping down beside me.

I nodded silently.

"Helped us out after . . ." Her eyes shifted.

After. Suddenly, the memory burst inside me. Papa talking about the farmer in the village beyond the chryssmum gate, his wife who baked better than Mama, their two children . . . a boy and a girl, left as orphans after the parents fell ill with the Wasting Death and died.

The ride to Northface Harbor wasn't unpleasant. The water was clear and blue, the waves gentle. Carso made one stop—dropping his sister off at the forest in the center of the island, where she had a job waiting for her to help cut timber. Carso and I lunched aboard the boat, snacking on produce from the crates and dropping the carrot stems into the water when we were done. I shared the bread Mama had packed for me.

"Is that where the governor lives?" I asked, pointing to a castle on a small island close to the shore. Gray stone steps dipped straight into the water, leading up to a tall brick building with spires on each corner and a giant clockface on a tower in the center.

Carso shook his head. "Nah, that's the quarantine hospital."

I stared up at the ornate building. It was a good idea, I thought, to put the hospital in the bay, using the water to separate the sick from the healthy.

Carso grew quieter as we approached Blackdocks at the base of Northface Harbor. He had to wait for the dock master to clear him a spot, and then he hopped down, waving over a man with a cart. The two clearly knew each other, and they started talking as I carefully made my way off the low boat and onto the dock.

"Your pa gave me coin to make sure your trunk got to Yūgen," Carso said, nodding to the other man. "You can ride with him while he delivers the produce. It'll put you at the school a little later. Or you can walk up on your own, and he'll bring the trunk tonight."

I looked up the hill. Everything about Northface Harbor was built on an incline; the streets wound their way higher and higher. Blackdocks bustled with activity, and the factories and mills that sprouted along the water spat out smoke that obscured my vision. But it seemed as if the houses grew nicer the farther uphill I looked, and I wanted to see my new city on my own terms.

"I'll walk," I said. I adjusted my hip bag and repositioned the tube from Papa—I wasn't willing to entrust those for delivery.

Carso grunted in a way that made it clear he thought I'd made the right choice. "Take that street," he said, pointing. "Go up—you'll run right into that school of yours."

"Thank you."

"I make deliveries every week." His eyes searched mine. "You need to come home, just meet me here. I'll take you."

"Did Papa . . . ?" I asked, patting my pockets, looking for my coin purse.

"You go on," Carso said, nodding toward the street.

"Thank you," I said again.

"Hurry it up!" the dock master shouted. "We need the ports!"

Carso and his friend turned back to unloading the boat, and I headed toward the street that would take me to my new home.

"Flowers for the governor!" a young female voice called. I watched as a girl with cropped hair and an apron full of red poppy-buds dashed up to a couple standing on the corner. They were well dressed; a hunter green suit for the man, a tailored dress with a sweeping skirt for the lady.

"Just two coppers," the girl insisted, thrusting the flower under the lady's nose. When she ignored her, the girl turned to the man. "Buy a bud for your lady," she insisted. "The governor's own flower, sure to bring luck tonight."

"Go away," the man said, not even deigning to look at her. He bore an accent I wasn't familiar with, and I wondered which of the fine ships in the bay he'd come from.

The girl turned, eyes hopeful, as she heard me approach from the dock. But I was clearly not a lady from the mainland waiting for a carriage. She gave me one glance from head to toe, taking in my rustic braids and homespun tunic, and turned her back on me, not even bothering to offer to sell me a flower.

Overhead, the globes of the streetlamps had been slathered with shining mercury paint to display the new governor's silhouette, and green-and-black bunting decorated the posts and many of the windows. In the bay, a ship with three masts stood proudly, the Emperor's flag flapping in the wind. Several other ships bore the insignias of nearby lands.

Already, I was composing a letter home in my mind. *The Emperor was in the city when I arrived,* I would tell Nessie. *The new governor's inauguration meant that the streets were decorated, and people from all different lands came to visit.* I would leave out how the rich couple awaiting their carriage were so rude, just as I wouldn't mention the stench of the docks, the hazy air from the smokestacks in the factories, the crowded throng of people that overwhelmed me.

I readjusted my bag and headed uphill.

"Out o' the way, out o' the way!" a man with a deep voice shouted, his wagon thumping on the cobblestones. I stepped off the main street. The man's cargo was draped in white canvas. He drew his horses up short in front of a whitewashed building a block away. Curious, I drew closer.

"Hey!" the wagoner shouted, clanging his bell in the direction of the building's door.

People rushed out, and the man turned, whipping the canvas cloth aside to reveal his cargo. About a dozen people sat in the cart. Their backs were hunched as if their heads were too heavy to bear, and two children lay on the floor of the cart, their eyes open but their expressions blank, as if they weren't aware of their surroundings at all. A man about Papa's age sat near the back of the wagon, weeping.

"We have no room here," one of the women who'd come from the building said.

"Whitesides has always taken care of Mackrunmik's workers," the man driving the cart said, frowning.

I peered closer, noting the clammy sheen on the people's faces, the hollowed shadows in their cheeks, the hopelessness in their eyes. The blackened limbs they tried to hide in their shirtsleeves and beneath the hems of their pants.

"The Wasting Death," a bystander on the street hissed, his accent like my own. My hand flew to the knotted cord at my neck, and I instinctively took a step back.

"We're full," the woman snapped at the cart driver. She didn't wear the dark blue robes of an alchemist, but she did have a crucible in the crook of her arm. "Take them to the quarantine hospital," she ordered, pointing down to the bay and the hospital on the island. The man grumbled but clucked at his horses and turned the cart back down the road.

By the time I arrived at Yūgen, I was exhausted from the uphill climb, and sweat had made my hair stringy. I noticed the school's gate first. It wasn't like the village gates in the north. Its wrought-iron doors had three runes running down the side, one in gold, one in silver, and one in copper, with the words YŪGEN ALCHEMICAL ACADEMY etched across the top. Through the iron bars of the gate, I could see a group of brick buildings forming a square with a grassy courtyard in the middle.

My battered trunk sat on the sidewalk, skewed and scratched on one side. Carso's friend had delivered my belongings sooner than expected, but he had merely dumped them on the ground and left.

I dragged my trunk to the gate. "Hello?" I called.

No one answered.

I tried the handle.

Locked.

"Hello?" I said again, the word coming out as a question. Surely *someone* would open the gate. I had been told to arrive today, but not given a precise hour.

My coin purse held sixteen silvers, the result of more than a year of saving. Would it be enough for a room at an inn for the night? I didn't have to eat . . .

My stomach rumbled at the thought of food.

And what would I do with my trunk? It was too heavy to carry for long, and it would be too awkward to juggle it with the tube from Papa.

A wagon clattered on the cobblestones and I jumped, recognizing the driver from earlier, when his cart was filled with the sick and dying. Now, though, his bell was silent. The cart was empty of everything but a single child-size shoe, bumping along the floor of the wagon.

THREE

Nedra

"HELLO?" I CALLED again, more urgency in my voice.

"What're you doing out there?" A gruff-looking man emerged from a small cubby built into the gate on the other side of the bars.

"I'm a student," I said, sighing in relief.

"No, you're not. I know all the students that go here. Go on with ya." The guard started to turn away.

"I'm new!" I said, taking a step forward so my body pressed against the iron gate.

The guard narrowed his eyes.

"I am," I insisted, aware of how childish and overdone my tone sounded.

"All students were supposed to be at the inauguration," the guard said.

"I just arrived." I indicated my trunk.

The guard looked at it with an expression that seemed to imply I held illegal contraband within my luggage. Then, without another word, he turned on his heel and strode back into the small gatehouse.

"Wait," I said weakly, but then I heard the man's indistinct voice as he spoke with someone I couldn't hear. He emerged a moment later.

"Right. You Nedra Brustin?"

"Brysstain," I corrected.

The guard rolled his eyes, then unlocked the gate. "Come in."

He didn't offer to help me with my trunk, so I dragged it behind me, the wood clattering on the uneven paving stones. As soon as I was through, the guard slammed the gate shut and relocked it. "You're to go to the administration building."

I looked at the tall brick buildings that towered over the grassy courtyard, my eyes skimming the façades for some indication of which was the administration building.

"That one," the guard added impatiently, pointing. "The one with the clock tower."

The clockface shone brilliantly. When I looked behind me, I could see the clock of the quarantine hospital was positioned directly across from the school's. They were a matching set, just like Ernesta and me.

"I'll take care of that," the guard added as I struggled to lift my trunk again.

"Thank you," I said, relieved, and that at least earned a bit of a smile from him. He offered to take my hip bag and the carrying tube from Papa, but I kept those with me.

The sun had fallen more quickly than I'd expected, most of the stars obscured by clouds. The courtyard was cut into four smaller squares by gravel paths lined with gas lamps. My feet crunched over the tiny stones, and I was grateful for my thick-soled boots.

In the center of the courtyard stood a statue or . . . I squinted up at it. Some form of art. It didn't look like much of anything but a lump of coal, so black I almost ran into it despite the glow from the lamps.

As I neared the administration building, I saw a man standing by the door.

"Nedra Brysstain?" he asked as I approached. When I nodded, he immediately turned and headed into the building. I followed him into a grand foyer, the walls covered in gilded paper and decorated by larger-than-life portraits of people I could only assume were the past headmasters of Yūgen Academy. The man turned sharply toward a door that led to a staircase and descended. I raced to follow him.

I watched his head as we went downstairs, my stomach a mess of nerves. This man was even more abrupt than the guard; was everyone in the city this rude?

When we reached the basement, the man opened a door with a brass plaque on the front and stepped inside, clearly expecting me to follow. The plaque was engraved with a name: PROFESSOR PHILLIOUS OSTRUM, CHAIR OF MEDICINAL ALCHEMY.

"The headmistress should have been here to greet a new student," the professor said, waving a hand impatiently at the chair across from his desk for me to sit. I did. "But," he continued, turning his back to me and going behind his desk, "the school was given a special invitation to the governor's inauguration, so . . ." He lifted his hands as if he were baffled that anyone would choose a sparkling party for the new governor over staying in a cramped office in the poorly lit basement of the administration building.

"It's okay," I said. Exhaustion had set in, and I just wanted a bed. And maybe a meal.

"Well, it'll have to be," Professor Ostrum snapped back.

My eyes scanned the office. Books and papers were crammed into every available space—the shelves were at least double stacked, with piles of leather-bound tomes littering the floor. I tried to read some of the embossed titles.

Professor Ostrum abruptly stood up and slammed shut a door behind the desk that I'd not noticed before, partially hidden by a bookcase. A closet, I assumed.

He reclaimed his seat and lifted a folder with my name on the front. "You're focusing on medicinal alchemy?" he asked.

"Yes," I said. "Sir."

"Transactional alchemy is easier," he said, almost to himself. "And transformational alchemy has more job openings. Medicinal is a competitive field."

Not in the north, I thought. Traveling alchemists went from village to village as they could, but one could never be certain to get a good one, if one at all. I remembered the fate of Dilada and Carso's parents. No alchemist had come to their village until two weeks after they were in the ground.

"Medicinal alchemy," I said with conviction. "That's what I want to study."

Professor Ostrum didn't look up at me. "So. A scholarship student."

I didn't respond. He didn't seem to want me to.

"That's rare." Professor Ostrum peered at me over the folder. "The benefactor isn't listed. You have a rich relative somewhere?"

I almost laughed at the absurdity of that idea, but I bit my tongue. I explained about Papa's letters.

Professor Ostrum tossed the folder on his desk, ignoring the way the papers inside slid out in disarray. "Probably the governor," he said. "It's not like the Emperor cares about anyone on Lunar Island."

The professor's decision not to attend the inauguration suddenly made more sense. I'd never met anyone who had any type of passionate feelings for the Emperor one way or another, but Professor Ostrum's hatred was palpable.

"You only went to village school?" Professor Ostrum asked, changing the topic.

I nodded. "But I read a lot, both Imperial and some ancient, as well as runes. Sir," I added. "My father is a bookseller, and—"

He cut me off. "There's only so much you can do with books."

This seemed disingenuous coming from a man whose office was littered with books. My fingers outlined the hard edge of my great-grandmother's text. Professor Ostrum's eyes followed the movement, and my hand froze. I felt my cheeks warming as I pulled the book out of the bag.

"This is a family heirloom," I told him, opening the pages. "I, um, have been studying it." I struggled to find the words that would prove I was worthy to be at Yūgen. "It has medicines, potions. Some basic practices."

"Alchemy is a science," Professor Ostrum said sharply. "Somewhat more advanced than knowing bowroot is good for headaches."

"I know." My voice betrayed my impatience and irritation, and I bit my lip before continuing. "That's why I want to be an alchemist. This," I said, clutching the book, "isn't enough. But I've also read some of the alchemy textbooks my father sells. There's not much overlap. For example," I continued, feeling as if I had to prove myself. "I'm sure you've heard of the Wasting Death?"

Professor Ostrum steepled his fingers. "I assume you mean that disease among unhygienic people, where their limbs rot?"

"It's been spreading in the north," I said, biting back my retort that Carso and Dilada's parents were not unhygienic by any means. "It's hard to get alchemists to come to rural areas. But we use tincture of blue ivy . . ." I clutched my great-grandmother's book, but Professor Ostrum's eyes were already dismissing my words.

"Blue ivy is in use throughout the hospitals here," he said derisively.

My stomach sank. "Well," I snapped, "that's why I've come here. So I can learn and find new methods to help. From Yūgen *and* my village."

For the first time since I arrived, Professor Ostrum looked interested. "You're saying you want to study modern alchemy and compare it to more traditional methods?"

I nodded. "There's value here," I said, tapping my great-grandmother's book. "And there's value in alchemy."

"Homeopathic cures in conjunction with alchemy certainly isn't unheard of," he pointed out, "but I like the way you think. We can learn a lot from our ancestors." He contemplated me for several moments. I grew uncomfortable under his gaze, but he didn't look away. "Right. Classes here are not like your village school," Professor Ostrum continued, his voice sharper now. "Grades are reliant upon two essays, one at midterm, one at final. You are assigned a master. You will report to your master in a group class at the start of each day, then it is up to you to attend whatever lectures are being given throughout the day. This will include lab work or on-site training at the hospitals in the area. You are expected to report back at the end of the day to your master, where you will be tested on whether or not you have adequately learned that day." He squared his shoulders, his gaze unwavering. "Your master will decide if you pass or fail, if you stay at this academy or not. Your entire fate is in his hands."

I had a sinking feeling in the pit of my stomach.

"You're a late addition to this semester," Professor Ostrum said. "I'm not making another appointment hour just for you. You'll have to share your end-of-day session with another student."

I closed my eyes and breathed deeply. So. This gruff, grumpy man was my master. The holder of my fate. And I was both an afterthought and an inconvenience to him.

This was going so very well.

"Greggori Astor." Professor Ostrum looked up from his folder. "You know him?"

I shook my head.

"You wouldn't," he said, dropping the papers on his desk again. "Anyway, you'll come to me during his session. Seven chimes sharp. Don't be late."

"And when does the morning session begin?"

"An hour after breakfast."

When I looked at him blankly, unsure of when—or even where—breakfast was, he added, "Nine chimes."

He spoke quickly, rattling off a building and room number for the morning session and then giving me a different building and room number for my dormitory, tossing me a long iron key for my room.

"Don't be late tomorrow," he said, standing—a clear dismissal.

"I won't, Professor Ostrum," I said.

"*Master* Ostrum," he corrected, subtly emphasizing the word.

"Master," I said, bowing my head and leaving as fast as I could.

FOUR

Grey

Damn, I loved sparkling wine.

"Not bad, eh?" Tomus said, topping me off. He'd swiped an entire bottle from a waiter and drank directly from it as soon as he filled my glass to the brim.

"A man could get used to this," I replied, grinning.

"Another year, Astor." Tomus nudged my shoulder.

I clinked my glass against his bottle. "Just one more."

We were so close to graduating that I could taste it. Tomus and I held the highest grades at Yūgen, and we were both advised by Master Ostrum. Ostrum was a bear, but he was also the best medical alchemist on Lunar Island or anywhere else in the Empire. Having Ostrum as a master made getting into a top position at the Governor's Hospital, or even a hospital in one of the larger cities on the mainland, a sure bet.

"Well, off we go," Tomus said, his voice only slightly slurring. He dropped the bottle on a tray held by a passing waiter, then turned to me, tapping his nose. "We'll get a bit of brown on here, and it'll be a night well done."

"You don't have to be so crass about it," I muttered, but I still followed him as he strode toward a group of medical alchemists in the back of the ballroom.

Outside of the hospital, alchemists didn't bother with their deep blue robes, but many still wore the color on their persons: a blue cravat, a lace-edged pocket square, a sapphire brooch.

"She's a good choice," one of the men was saying as Tomus and I edged closer.

"Mm." His companion nodded. "Surprised the youngling chose her."

My eyes darted to the raised dais at the end of the room. Emperor Auguste *was* young—younger than me even, albeit only by a few months. Tomus and I were still students, and the Emperor was already leading the largest naval fleet in history—and leading it well. Every day, it seemed like new lands were being acquired into our sprawling empire.

Emperor Auguste lounged on his throne as if it were covered in cushions, not gilded ebony hand-carved by the first settlers of Lunar Island a century and a half ago. In contrast, the middle-aged woman to his left sat with her back ramrod straight, her eyes alight, gazing out at the crowd in the ballroom with genuine interest. As I watched her, she leaned over and said something to the Emperor, who shrugged, then she got up and stepped off the dais, intermingling with the crowd while Emperor Auguste snapped his fingers at a waiter for another glass of wine.

"Adelaide *is* the right choice for Lunar Island," the first alchemist said, as if trying to convince himself.

Tomus sidled up to the group. "We agree," he interrupted, even though I knew he didn't really care who was governor. He just wanted an excuse to break into the conversation. The alchemists glared at us, seemingly surprised we were there.

"I'm glad to see children are interested in today's politics," the second alchemist said, a mocking smirk on his lips.

Tomus stuck out his hand. "Tomus Abertallin," he said. "Top of my class at Yūgen."

The smirk faded.

I swallowed and stepped closer. "I'm Greggori Astor," I said. "And despite what Tomus says, I'm actually ranked highest."

The man chuckled. "Astor? You Linden's boy?"

I nodded but didn't elaborate. Father wanted me in politics, like he was. According to him, medicinal alchemy was a trade, not a profession. Mother didn't care what I did, as long as I married well. I resisted the urge to turn around and look for them. They were both here, somewhere. Father had probably slipped off to a parlor for cards and cigars, and Mother had probably had more to drink than Tomus, although she held it better. It was doubtful they'd seen each other since they arrived, and neither had bothered to check on me.

"So, what do you think of our new governor?" another alchemist in the group asked. I recognized him as Alyx Markhim, a friend of my father's and the chief alchemical director of the Governor's Hospital. He'd supported the former governor's policies rather heavily, lauding the tax cuts that directly benefitted him while ignoring how they hurt the poor who needed his hospital.

I cut in before Tomus could start babbling. "Adelaide has yet to prove herself in terms of law," I said. "Certainly her father, before he passed, was rather liberal, but we have seen no indication that Adelaide herself will follow in her father's footsteps."

I had their attention. Tomus scowled as I continued. "She may be the moderate balance our island needs, with the perspective of her father but the ability to move beyond his mistakes into decisions that are beneficial to the structure of our city."

"So you disagree with Lord Anton?" the chief director said.

"Lord Anton?" Tomus asked, trying to inject himself into the conversation.

"Perhaps the biggest opposition to the new governor," I said, my brain racing to keep up with my mouth as I tried to recall every boring detail from Father. Lord Anton had been voted into the office, but the Emperor had vetoed the choice and selected Governor Adelaide instead. "He is a legacy, certainly, and felt entitled to the position." Out of the corner of my eye, I saw the chief director frown. I remembered too late that he had supported Anton's bid for the governorship. "Clearly he would have been the better choice, but Adelaide had a stronger plan for more lenient taxation of factory owners, which should benefit everyone in the city. And if not, the term is only ten years, and a conservative will certainly succeed her."

"If the Emperor allows it," one of the other men muttered darkly. I couldn't remember his name, but I knew he worked with my father often.

The chief director's lips curved up on one side. "You're graduating next year, right, son?"

I nodded.

Tomus narrowed his eyes as I sipped my glass of wine. The alchemists politely nodded to us before turning away. The chief director's eyes lingered on me an extra moment, and I knew he would recall me when I applied to the Governor's Hospital next year.

"Nice," Tomus said once the men were out of earshot, drawing the word out.

I laughed. "Jealous?"

Tomus's expression went from playful to serious. "I think I'll need to start paying better attention to politics."

A couple of ladies walked by, absorbed in their own conversation. "Did you hear about Henrick's factory?" one of the women said. "All those workers . . ."

"More will move down from the north," her friend replied, peering over the top of her fan.

"I'll host a charity drive," the first said. She looked at the other woman, eyes hungry for approval in a way that reminded me sharply of my mother.

The head steward rang the announcement bell, and the music and chatter around the ballroom faded. The Emperor straightened in his throne, finally caring that all eyes were on him.

"Thank you, guests and citizens of the Empire!" the steward called. "Today we gather in celebration of the inauguration of our thirteenth governor of Lunar Island, Adelaide Amarie Strangmore of Greenhaven Manor."

Adelaide left the ballroom floor and stepped lithely up to the dais. By the time the Emperor bothered to stand from his seat, the grand bishop had already positioned herself on a little kneeling stool between the throne and the governor's chair and bent her head, beginning the prayers for governing. Her voice became a low-pitched undercurrent to the rest of the proceedings, droning on in a way that made it easy to ignore.

Adelaide knelt in front of the Emperor. She was not allowed a cushion. Her head was bent so low that she seemed almost to be kissing Emperor Auguste's feet. It was odd to see a woman at least thirty years his senior genuflect at the teenage ruler's feet.

"Chosen by your people and graced by the Emperor," he said in a bored monotone voice that barely rose above the bishop's murmured prayers. "I, by the rights of my birth and the grace of Oryous, Emperor Auguste, third of his name, rightful ruler of the Great Allyrian Empire, king of all lands, name you, Adelaide of Greenhaven, governor of Lunar Island."

Adelaide's voice was strong and clear. "I accept. May Oryous bless my rule and the Emperor guide my hand."

The Emperor draped an embroidered pallium adorned with three large beads—one copper, one silver, and one gold—over Governor Adelaide's head. She stood, looking out with gleaming eyes as the crowd in the ballroom clapped politely.

"Want to go out?" Tomus asked me as the party wound down. Salis, Amala, and a few other girls stood in the corner, casting eyes at both of us. An evening spent with them would be the perfect accompaniment to the nice buzz I was feeling thanks to the sparkling wine, but before I could agree, I noticed my father standing against the wall, his gaze on me.

"Go without me," I replied, already making my way toward Father. Tomus offered no argument—he knew that our fathers were men not to be crossed.

"Greggori," my father said by way of greeting when I drew closer.

"Sir."

"Have you seen your mother?" he asked.

"Did you check the gaming room?"

Father frowned. "I saw you speaking to Markhim." There was something like approval in his eyes, but it was such a rare emotion from him that I almost didn't recognize it. "He was a prominent bene-factor to Lord Anton's campaign." His gaze grew distant as he lost focus on me. "In a few years, he may step into the political ring. He would be a powerful ally."

"Yes," I said. "Well." Father had long wanted me to follow him into the governor's court. Apparently if he couldn't turn me into a politician, he would politicize alchemy.

"There's talk of Markhim becoming the Lord Commander," Father continued. Now that the governor had been chosen by the Emperor, the next highest government official would be whomever Governor Adelaide selected to be her second-in-command. The posi-tion was highly coveted—it came with a steep paycheck, residence in the palace, and the knowledge that, should anything happen to Governor Adelaide, the Lord Commander would take control of the island for the remainder of her term. "Anyway," Father said, turning. "Come with me." He led me toward the door.

Outside, the air was slightly muggy, the croques buzzing in the leafy green bushes that trimmed a meandering path. Father's feet crunched over the yellow pebbles, his head bent in seeming concentration.

At a gazebo near the base of the stairs, we met my father's political allies. I recognized some, but the most noticeable was Lord Anton. A few of the men glanced at me, curious, but most of them recognized me as my father's son.

"Well," Lord Anton said, his voice as gruff as the salt-and-pepper beard on his chin. "It's done."

He said the words with such finality that at first I wondered if I was somehow unwittingly a part of a crime, but I soon realized he meant Governor Adelaide's inauguration. It was final, approved by the church and the Empire.

"Ten years," one of the younger men said. "We'll have to amp up our campaign procedures. The lesser offices can block her if we shift the polls."

"She's just so *weak*." Lord Anton spit the words out. "How can we expect someone like *her* to lead us in these dangerous times?"

I tried to hide my confusion. *Dangerous times?*

My father shook his head. "As long as she's governor, we cannot proceed," he said.

The men looked bitter. "A decade, though," one muttered.

I wanted desperately to ask questions, but I knew drawing any kind of attention to myself would lead to my father's rebuke and a dismissal from the group. I kept my mouth shut.

"She's no better fit to lead than he is," another man said, his voice low. He cast his eyes behind them, almost nervous.

He's speaking about the Emperor, I realized. *This is dangerously close to treason.*

Lunar Island had a long and unsettling history with the Empire. We were one of the Emperor's most troublesome colonies—at least historically. But the closest we'd ever come to revolution was an uprising that had been squashed a hundred and fifty years ago. Since then, we'd comfortably settled into our role as a province of the Empire.

Aside from ceremonial duties and taxes, the Emperor mostly left us alone, and our governor led the people.

"Well," the youngest man said, "it's over now. She won. We wait."

"It wasn't a true win," my father pointed out. The others agreed darkly. The council had chosen Lord Anton; the Emperor had chosen Adelaide.

I stared at the men around me, including my father. Their dissatisfaction went beyond their candidate not being elected governor. They spoke of Adelaide and the Emperor as if they were enemies to be fought, undermined, and even overthrown.

Father's eyes drifted to me, and he flicked his fingers, a clear dismissal. He had wanted me to see what lay under the politics of the land, but he didn't care about my participation—at least not yet. I followed his silent order, retreating up the stairs and heading to the exit.

I was moving so briskly, I almost missed her. Governor Adelaide leaned against the corner of the white-stoned plaza at the top of the steps, her dress blending with the pale rock.

She had heard everything.

The campaign against her had been messy, sometimes even cruel. Like steel hardened in a forge, though, it had only strengthened the new governor. She didn't look hurt by my father's words. Her spine straightened. Her chin tilted up. Her eyes narrowed with resolve.

Governor Adelaide touched a red poppy-bud pinned to her bodice. That flower was a part of her insignia, often illustrated over her family's motto: *To help those lesser.* She'd used those words in her campaign, and I knew she was thinking them now. While my father plotted with men against her, Governor Adelaide's thoughts were on serving the citizens of Lunar Island.

One eyebrow raised when she turned her attention to me, waiting to see what I would do or say.

Just as I had been in the garden, I remained silent.

Her lips pursed, and she turned, her skirt swirling around her as she marched inside the castle, firmly shutting the door behind her.

I don't really care about politics. I was just . . . there. I'm not like them, I wanted to say. My father would always want a son who sank into the dirty world of politics, rooting through the mud for a string to pull. And I wanted nothing more than to be the opposite of him.

But now I wondered if it were possible to remove myself from politics, or if my silence had been its own choice.

FIVE

Nedra

SOMETIME PAST MIDNIGHT, I heard the sounds of other students re-entering the building. Master Ostrum had told me no boys were allowed in the female dormitory after curfew, but I could hear deeper voices accompanying feminine giggles.

My room was spacious—twice the size of the bedroom I'd shared with Ernesta back home. It was furnished as well—a bed, a small couch against the wall, a desk, and a bookshelf. The attached bathroom had been a surprise; I'd expected to share a lavatory.

My trunk had seemed so heavy and huge as Papa and Carso lugged it onto the boat, and even larger when I wrestled with it on my own at Yūgen's gates. But now, in this enormous room, the box seemed tiny. Unpacking was ridiculously easy. My winter cloak hung in the closet, while my tunics, skirts, and wide-legged trousers fit neatly in a single drawer. My great-grandmother's book and a few old texts on alchemy that Papa had found for me were the lone occupants on a bookshelf taller than I was. I had unpacked everything I owned, and the room still felt empty. The school did not provide linens, though, and I'd not thought to bring my own, so I dried off with a shirt, then lined my bed with the quilt Mama had packed in my trunk. A couch cushion served as my pillow.

The room was mostly dark, but the thin curtains hanging in front of the windows let in the light reflecting from the gas lamps outside.

What must the other girls' rooms look like? Nearly every student at Yūgen started attending the academy after years of being privately tutored, after parents and brothers and sisters attended, with the knowledge of what to expect and the preparations not just for studies but for life here. I pulled my quilt over my head as a group of students outside my room started joking loudly. Something slammed violently against my wooden door, and I jumped.

I had never felt more alone. On the other side of that door were people who knew one another, who were already friends. And they didn't even know I existed, hiding under this blanket, too stupid to have even brought sheets with me.

I'd spent the last few years reading every book Papa had on alchemy, experimenting in Mama's kitchen, begging any traveling alchemist who came through our village to let me see his crucible. When I'd left this morning, I'd envisioned a thrilling new adventure.

I swallowed down my nerves. I could step into that hallway, introduce myself, try to be one of them.

But before I could unravel the quilt from around my legs, doors slammed up and down the halls. The students had already dispersed, each going into their separate rooms, together or alone, but without me.

I woke at dawn the next morning, my thin curtains no match for the rising sun. I dressed quickly, throwing on clean clothes but rewrapping my old braid to save time. Before I left, though, my eyes fell on the gift Papa had given me. With trembling fingers, I pulled the top off the tube, letting it dangle from the leather thong attached to the side. A rolled-up piece of parchment lay in the center, and I shook it out, spreading it across the surface of my empty desk, my hands smoothing down the inked-in shapes of the continents.

The map showed most of the explored world. The Allyrian Empire dominated the left side of the parchment. Long and wide, like an egg on its side, the continent was crisscrossed with rivers and mountain ranges. Mostly straight lines marked where the new rail system had been added across the mainland, and major cities were indicated with stars.

Lunar Island was a tiny fingernail near the middle of the map, the pointed ends of the crescent facing the Allyrian continent, like a moon orbiting the Empire. Small circles of other islands trailed back to the mainland on one side and across the ocean on the other. The Stellar Chain created a convenient series of stops for ships traveling across the Azure Sea, but the Empire's reach stopped at Lunar Island. I traced along the rest of the Stellar Chain to the other continents: Dormia and Euris and Choade. Even the smaller countries, like the southern island nation of Doisha, were marked.

Most maps showed only the Empire, but this one reminded me that the world was larger than the land within our borders.

A small note card was clipped to the top corner of the map, over the compass rose. I unfolded it carefully, revealing Papa's writing—so measured, as if he feared its meaning would evaporate if the letters were sloppy. *The world is vast, and it is all yours.*

Last night, I'd felt like nothing. I wished I'd thought to look at Papa's gift then.

My stomach ached with hunger so much that I felt as if I'd be sick, but fortunately, the cafeteria was easier to find in the light of day—it connected the male and female dormitories.

Unfortunately, it was closed.

"Don't get many students up this early," one of the cafeteria workers said as he hefted a large coffee urn onto a table.

My stomach roared in protest. "Is there *anything* I can eat?"

"Bread," he said, pointing to a table against the wall. "And apples."

I hurried toward the loaf. It was a bit stale, obviously intended to be turned into toast, but I didn't care. I grabbed a few slices and an apple.

"Can't eat here," the worker added, a note of sympathy in his voice. "We have to set up for the rest of the students."

I headed outside wordlessly. It seemed as good a time as any to explore campus.

The square courtyard was empty. As I swallowed the dry bread, my stomach twisted. I came to campus too late; I arrived at the cafeteria too early. Everything I'd done since arriving in Northface Harbor had been just a little off. I longed to fit seamlessly into a world with no openings.

I shook my head, biting back an unbidden smile. Nessie would call me ridiculous and laugh at my doubts. I always did wrap myself up too tightly in my own thoughts.

The dormitories occupied most of the buildings behind me. The clock tower and the administration building lined the south end of the quad, and across from me were most of the lecture halls. And in the center was . . .

I wandered closer. I'd thought it was an odd statue last night, and in the daylight, it was odder still. The base was clearly stone, but it had been covered in iron, black streaked with red rust, towering above me as I approached.

I noticed a small sign at the bottom. It said only one word, but it told me all I needed to know.

WELLEBOURNE

My grandmother had taught me the story of Bennum Wellebourne. He was one of the founding fathers of Lunar Island, part of the first colony that left the mainland and struck out for the crescent-shaped rock in the middle of the Azure Sea. He faced harsh weather, sickness, and near annihilation of the original colony before using alchemy to save a few survivors, who eventually grew to take control of the land.

He was, at one point, the greatest hero of our history. They built a statue in his honor—*this* statue—using a stone that jutted straight up from the land.

But then Bennum Wellebourne turned traitor, choosing to rebel against the very Empire that had supported him in a bid for the island's independence. He'd resorted to the dark arts, twisting alchemy to raise an army of the undead. After he was captured and hung for his crimes, the citizens of Lunar Island tried to remove the stone statue, but it was wedged too deep in the earth. So they melted down iron and dumped it over the top, leaving nothing but a lumpy black monstrosity behind.

According to my grandmother, every single woman in the colony contributed her frying pan to the cause of covering up Bennum Wellebourne's stony face. But Grammy always laughed when she told the story, and cracked another egg in the sizzling cast-iron pan on the stove.

SIX

Grey

THERE WAS A new girl in class, and she was sitting in Tomus's seat.

Master Ostrum's morning lecture was small, just twenty students, and exactly enough desks for each one. Those who had arrived before Tomus and me had either claimed their own desks or hung back, watching. Waiting.

I glanced at Tomus. The girl in his seat had rattled him, an unexpected addition to his morning. His face was passive, but his eyes were narrowed in a way I knew meant trouble.

The girl was about our age. Her long skirt was made of homespun fabric; her hair was wrapped in braids, and she wore no makeup. She sat ramrod straight, staring at the worn blackboard caked in chalk dust as if she were trying to read the words that had long since been erased. Her hands—nails bitten short, skin cracked from labor—were folded neatly atop a short stack of books on alchemy, each so worn that threads leaked from the corners of the clothbound covers.

Tomus strode across the lecture hall, his hard-heeled boots thudding against the wooden floor. She didn't turn to him until he was almost on top of her.

"You're in my seat," he said. He had clearly decided she wasn't worth his veneer of politeness.

"Oh," she said, surprised. "I'm sorry." She gathered her inkwell, pen, and books and stood, shifting her belongings one desk over.

"That's his desk," Tomus said, his voice almost a snarl as he jerked his head toward me.

"It's—" I started, intending to tell her that she could sit there, but Tomus silenced me with a look.

The girl gathered her belongings quietly, then got up, surveying the desks, all of which had now been claimed. No one met her gaze.

"You're *in the way*," Tomus said as he sat down, as if he were speaking to a particularly dense child. The girl's eyes flashed, but she spun on her heel and sat down on the floor, directly in front of Tomus. Tomus's jaw clenched. His foot slid out from under the desk, but she had—by cleverness or accident—sat just out of his reach.

Master Ostrum finally entered the lecture hall and surveyed the room, raising an eyebrow at the girl on the floor, but saying nothing. "By this point," he said, going directly into his opening lesson, "you have learned everything the books can teach you. It's time for hands-on instruction." He hefted a large box onto his hip and slammed three metal vases on the desk in front of the class. One gold, one silver, and one copper.

Every student sat up straighter. *Crucibles*. We knew what this meant. We were *finally* going to perform alchemy.

Tomus's eyes darted to the girl on the floor. He—along with everyone else in the room—was clearly wondering when Master Ostrum would address the new addition to our class. But no one was willing to speak up. Master Ostrum did not like interruptions.

"Alchemy is all about trades," Master Ostrum said, adjusting the three crucibles on the desk so they were evenly spaced. "Copper is for transactions."

We knew this; it had been the first lesson in every textbook we'd studied, every lecture we'd sat through. I glanced over at the girl; her eyes were wide, her attention rapt, and her lips moved silently, repeating Master Ostrum's words.

Master Ostrum picked up the copper crucible, tilting it so we could see it was empty. He plucked a hair from his head and dropped it into the center of the crucible, muttering as runes lit up along the metal. After a moment, he turned the crucible upside down, and a fist-sized granite rock fell into his palm.

The new girl gasped, and though she wasn't the only one to do so, she was the loudest. Master Ostrum cut her a glance so severe that she silenced immediately.

Master Ostrum held the rock up for the class to see. "Silver is for transformations," he said, dropping the granite lump into the large silver crucible. He held his palms around the vessel and spoke the runes for transformation. Symbols engraved into the metal illuminated.

Master Ostrum reached inside the crucible, groping around for a bit before pulling out out a large gray rat. We had all known what was coming; Master Ostrum's demonstration was infamous on campus. But still—to see a rock turned into a rat—the entire class craned forward to watch the delicate, almost transparent whiskers twitching as the rat's little pink nose sniffed the air curiously.

"And finally, gold." As Master Ostrum dropped the rat into the golden crucible, it hissed in protest, then squeaked and scratched at the sides.

I recalled my theoretical alchemical textbooks from our previous semester. Silver crucibles could temporarily transform any object into another object, but if the exchange wasn't equal—like, say, that of a rock into a living creature—then the transformation wasn't "true." Master Ostrum's rat would turn back to stone soon enough.

"Can I have a volunteer?" Master Ostrum wore a smirk on his face—a clue to every single student to keep their hands firmly on their desks or in their laps. We knew better than to knock at a demon's door.

But the new girl didn't.

She lifted her hand. Several of the students behind her snickered, and Tomus bit back a laugh. I wanted to reach over and pull her arm back down, but I knew I couldn't, and besides, Master Ostrum had already seen her.

He motioned for her to join him at the front of the class, and she made her way to the podium. "This," he said, turning her around by the shoulders so she was facing the class, "is Nedra Brysstain. Nedra is a new student at Yūgen, here on a scholarship." The room erupted in whispers, but they were short-lived as Master Ostrum cocked his head and raised his eyebrow. His eyes rested on me. "Greggori Astor, she'll be sharing your evening session time slot."

He waited for me to protest. Tomus turned to me, his eyes bulging. He wanted me to refuse—to make a scene. As one of Yūgen's top students, it was well within my rights to demand the time owed me by my master.

I didn't look at Master Ostrum, though. My eyes were on the girl. Nedra. She was like a jeweled dagger—beautiful but perfectly poised to cut. I couldn't help but notice the determined and defiant look in her eyes. She was clearly from a country village in the north—a scholarship girl in unfashionable clothes, probably handmade. Her sun-kissed skin spoke of laboring outdoors, and I could see an outline of muscle beneath her sleeves that supported that theory. But the way her chin was set, her back straight—she looked ready to take on the entire world by any means necessary.

"Yes, sir," I told Master Ostrum.

Tomus made a noise deep in his throat, disdain meant only for me.

"So, where were we?" Master Ostrum indicated the third crucible. "Gold is for transferal, and it's primarily used for medical purposes. It can transfer pain or even healing properties from one body to another. My dear?" He motioned for Nedra to give him her hand. She did.

And he sliced her palm open with a knife.

Nedra hissed in pain and slapped her other hand over the wound as blood leaked between her fingers.

I leaned forward, feeling rage on her behalf, even though I had suspected what was coming. The students behind me muttered in anticipation. They didn't care about Nedra; they were just excited to witness medicinal alchemy at work. I couldn't take my eyes off Nedra, though. After her one shocked outburst, her lips had clamped shut, and she didn't say another word. Her eyes, however, contained all of the fury she didn't dare speak.

"Here, my dear," Master Ostrum said, his tone light. He pried Nedra's fingers away and covered the cut with his own hand, keeping one palm on the gold crucible with the rat inside it. He muttered another incantation, and again the runes lit up on the golden vessel. Inside, the rat feverishly scratched the metal, trying to escape as Nedra's pain slid from her cut into its body. The rat's squeaking intensified, getting desperate and higher pitched.

And then, a clatter—the sound of stone hitting metal. Master Ostrum sighed, picking up the crucible and turning it upside down. The rock—now rat-shaped—fell onto the desk. "Using a silver crucible to transform an inanimate object into a living one never lasts," he said sadly. "The pain was too great for the creature. But you feel fine, yes, dear?" he asked Nedra.

Nedra held her hand out in front of her, staring at the long cut. "I feel fine," she repeated, a hint of wonder in her voice. But when she squeezed her hand into a fist, blood still leaked from between her fingers. "But I'm not healed," she added.

"Let that be your first lesson," Master Ostrum said. "Pain can transfer, but not the wound."

SEVEN

Nedra

NO ONE GAVE a damn that I was on the floor and bleeding.

I ripped a page from my notebook and clenched it, hoping the porous paper would at least help stanch the cut on my palm. I used my fist to hold my notebook down on the floor and bent over it, determined to continue taking notes.

Master Ostrum carried on with his lecture, concluding with a summary of available lectures for the day and their locations.

I quickly scribbled the names, topics, and locations of the day's classes: *geography, humanities, history, poetry, potions, algebra, physics, philosophy, theoretical alchemy, runes*. It would be impossible to attend them all, but Master Ostrum clearly had no interest in advising us on which lessons we should bother with—he left the room as soon as he finished rattling off the list.

My classmates gathered their belongings, and the rude boy whose seat I'd accidentally taken made a point to step on my notebook as he rushed for the door, skidding it across the floor with his foot.

"Need help?" Greggori, the boy Master Ostrum said I'd be sharing evening sessions with, bent down and picked up my notebook, returning it to me. He looked like he belonged in a painting contained in a gilded frame, and I was the girl who couldn't afford admission into the museum. His jaw was narrow and his cheekbones were high; "elegant features," Grammy would have said. But his eyes were kind.

"Thanks." I took my notebook from him, then stood, my hand leaving a smear of blood on the floor.

"We should get that looked at," Greggori said, nodding to the cut.

"It's fine." My mind raced, trying to figure out which lecture I should go to first. Some started immediately—I didn't want to be late.

"There's only geography first," he said, as if reading my mind. "And it's a *bore*. Just long-winded ramblings about the utter *vastness* of our mighty Empire. If you know your maps, the class is fairly pointless."

"Oh, thanks," I said, not sure whether or not to heed his advice.

"I mean, you can obviously choose whichever lectures you want to attend," he continued. "But I'm going to humanities first—it starts in half an hour—and then probably history, poetry, and runes."

I nodded, grateful for the suggestions, although I wasn't sure what the point of poetry would be for someone who wanted to study medicinal alchemy.

"Thank you, Greggori." I lifted my bag onto my shoulder, turning to the door before I noticed the goofy half smile spreading on his face.

"What?" I asked, unsure of what was so funny.

"I like the way you say my name. Like it's two words. Gray-gory."

"Are you making fun of my accent?"

"Not at all!" he protested. He started to lead me to the door. "I like it."

I bit back a grin as I followed him across the quad to the infirmary to clean and bandage my hand. We walked together to the humanities lecture, which was located in a tall brick building overlooking the quad. Its large glass windows twinkled in the sunlight.

I quickly realized just how in over my head I was. While none of the other students took notes, my pen flew across my paper. The following lecture, history, was even worse. As soon as it was over, I picked up my notebook, now riddled with a list of everything I hadn't understood from the professors. "I think I'll go to the library," I said, tension rising within me.

"Independent study." Greggori nodded as if this was a good idea. "Master Ostrum would probably appreciate that."

I adjusted my bag over my shoulder, grateful he didn't follow me. I didn't want him to know how behind I was.

"Hey!" a voice called from the quad. I turned to see a girl about my age but far taller than me heading in my direction. "You're the new girl, yeah?" she said.

I nodded. I vaguely recognized her from Master Ostrum's opening lecture. "I'm Nedra," I said as I held the library door open for her.

"My name's Salis Omella," she said.

I followed her inside, breathing in the smell of old books. *Home.*

Salis dumped her books on a table and held her arm out, offering me a seat with her. "Sorry about Tomus this morning," she said, gesturing to my notebook that now had a prominent shoeprint across the front. "He's an ass."

I was surprised at her kindness, but grateful for it.

"What lectures did you go to this morning?" she asked, dropping her voice after the librarian glared at her.

"Humanities and history," I said. My notebook felt heavy in my hand, a guilty confessional of all I didn't know.

Salis pulled a face. "You had Newmas for history, yeah?" she asked. When I stared blankly at her, she dropped her chin to her chest and muttered, "Talks like this?"

"Yeah, him," I said.

Salis rolled her eyes. "He's brilliant, and he *knows* it. Such a show-off. None of us needs to know what Merry Twindle the Third thought of the eighth regiment of the Who Cares Battalion in the War of Unimportance." Her voice was rising with her passion, and the librarian shushed her again.

Suddenly, my feelings of inadequacy felt foolish. I pulled out my notebook, showing Salis the list of names and books I'd felt the need to look up after the lectures. Salis snorted. "Yeah, that's classic Newmas," she said. "None of that is important. But, look, if you like history, you should come to the focused study hall my friends and I do. It can count toward your report to Ostrum."

That sounded perfect—there was no way I'd be able to create a reasonable report from the scattered, disconnected, and jumbled notes I'd taken so far.

"A study hall sounds brilliant. More like school back home."

"You're from the north, right?" Salis asked. When I nodded, she smiled. "Your accent gives you away. Well, you're welcome to join us. First meeting's tomorrow at six chimes. We're studying Wellebourne now."

My eyes went involuntarily to the library door and, beyond that, the ruined statue of Bennum Wellebourne in the courtyard.

"We like to focus on *relevant* history," Salis continued.

I wasn't sure how relevant Wellebourne would be; his rebellion was almost two centuries old. But he would certainly be a more exciting subject than whatever Professor Newmas had planned. Wellebourne was reviled—and with good cause—but his use of dark, forbidden alchemy in his battles would make him an infinitely more interesting subject.

The library closed at seven chimes—lucky for me, as I'd forgotten about my nightly meeting with my master. The bell behind the massive clock in the administration building started tolling minutes after the librarian kicked me out of the stacks. I took off at a run and threw myself into Master Ostrum's office just as the last bell silenced.

"Nedra," Master Ostrum said by way of greeting, motioning toward an empty chair across from his desk. Beside it, Greggori had already taken a seat.

"Where were you?" Greggori asked under his breath as Master Ostrum turned to close the small door behind his desk. I craned forward, trying to see beyond our master. It wasn't a closet, as I'd assumed before—it seemed to be some sort of laboratory.

When Master Ostrum noticed me watching him, he turned the lock on the door with an audible click.

"Greggori was about to tell me of the lectures he sat through today," Master Ostrum said. "We will conduct our interview first, so that you can know what to expect." He turned to Greggori. "What have you learned today?"

Greggori squared his shoulders, looking directly at Master Ostrum even though the professor kept his attention on the paper where he was, presumably, assessing Greggori. Greggori rattled off the facts and figures he'd learned in history, linking it to some of the things our first lecturer taught during humanities. He finished his monologue by reciting a sonnet about love and time.

With every word, I felt my heart rate climb. This was so beyond what I was used to in the village school.

Master Ostrum turned to me. "And you, Nedra? What did you learn today?"

My mouth was too dry. I could feel Greggori's eyes on me, waiting. "I—" I started. I dropped my voice. "Can I give my report alone?" I asked. If I had to prove how much a fool I was, it would be better if I didn't have an audience.

Greggori shifted to pick up his bag, but Master Ostrum stopped him with a look. "No," he said simply. "Give your report, Brysstain."

I took a deep breath. I described the humanities and history lecture, but I had nothing really to add beyond what Greggori had already said. I hesitated.

"That's all?" Master Ostrum said. His tone was neutral, but I could tell he was disappointed in me. "You went to two lectures and then simply quit?"

"No!" I said, straightening my shoulders. "I—went to the library."

"The library," he repeated, his voice flat.

I nodded. "I wanted to . . ." I kept my focus on my master and tried to block out Greggori's presence from my mind. "I was aware that I was behind the other students. I wanted to try to catch up."

Master Ostrum leaned back in his chair. "And what did you learn?"

I stared at my hands, twisting in my lap. "I'm not here for poetry," I said in a small voice.

"What?" Master Ostrum asked.

My eyes flicked to Greggori, then to the master. "I'm not here for poetry," I said, louder. "I took the list of all the lecture topics you gave us this morning, and looked up a bit of each. And—" I swallowed down the lump in my throat. "And I didn't see the point," I mumbled. Greggori sucked in a breath at my audacity.

"You didn't see the point." Master Ostrum stated the words bluntly.

I shook my head, my gaze dropping again. "No, sir."

"So that's what you did in the library?" he asked. "Used books to determine the curriculum at Yūgen isn't good enough for you?"

"No," I said again, careful to keep my tone even. "I came here to study medicinal alchemy. So that's what I did."

"Really?" Master Ostrum drew the word out, his doubt dripping off of each syllable like honey.

"Yes," I insisted. "Specifically the Wasting Death. Even though yesterday you said that the Wasting Death only infected people who were unhygienic, you're wrong."

Unhygienic. The word tasted sour in my mouth. I hadn't realized how much it had bothered me until now, but I didn't regret speaking. Master Ostrum *had* been wrong.

Out of the corner of my eye, I saw Greggori's mouth drop open. I scrambled to make my words politer, more acceptable. "You don't know what it's like to be in a northern village. We may be poor, but we're clean," I said. This wasn't enough to sway him, I could tell. I added quickly, "And I found records of similar diseases in other nations, from the more remote areas of the Empire."

"What other diseases?"

I opened my notebook and slid the pages over to him. He bent over my words, reading them slowly. I glanced at Greggori, who stared at me with wide eyes. He shrugged, the barest lift of his shoulders, as if to say, *Who knows how the master will react to this?*

"This isn't the Wasting Death," Master Ostrum started, tapping my notes on a plague that had infected one of the colonies in the east fifty years ago. "A disease isn't the same just because symptoms are similar."

"But diseases evolve," I said quickly.

Master Ostrum shook his head. "Not like this. Diseases don't flare up and then reappear half a century later. If they're going to evolve, they have to spread, change over generations—not just disappear. This was likely some poisoning in this colony's water or crops."

"But—"

Master Ostrum raised his hand, silencing me. "You're dismissed," he told Greggori. I shifted in my seat, but Master Ostrum shook his head. "Not you."

The awkward tension was as thick as wool as Greggori gathered his things. I'd thought I wanted to speak by myself, but now I deeply regretted the desire.

"You have much experience with the Wasting Death?" Master Ostrum asked when Greggori closed the door behind him.

I hadn't been present when Carso and Dilada's parents had died, but the butcher's husband in our village hadn't survived the sickness.

One of Ernesta's girlfriends had lost part of her leg and walked with a cane now. Every time Papa went out in his book cart, Mama would pray he wouldn't come home sick. And when he did return, he told us of black bunting cast over houses in other villages, warning of the disease's presence.

"I live in the north," I said by way of answer.

"So you do," Master Ostrum said, his voice contemplative. The clock chimed eight. "You're right," he added.

I waited for him to continue, afraid to say the wrong thing. Again.

"You don't need to be in a poetry class. I'd like to see you focused more on the Wasting Death and your medical training. The gods know that too few alchemists have even bothered to consider the consequences of such a disease running rampant within the borders of their own city, much less the rest of Lunar Island."

My breath caught in my throat. "I can go to the library more," I said. "Maybe when you give out lecture times, you could give me a list of what books to study and—"

"No," Master Ostrum said. "I'll teach you myself. After the morning session, you'll come back here."

My hands clenched, and pain shot through my palm from the cut Master Ostrum had given me this morning. I suddenly wasn't so sure I could survive private lessons with this man.

EIGHT

Grey

Nedra left the administration building with her head down, lost in thought, and seemed startled when I called her name.

"Hi," she said, veering over to me.

"How did it go?" I asked tentatively.

"He's going to give me extra lessons," she replied.

"Oh," I said, slowly. "Well, that's good, isn't it?"

She peeped up at me, and I saw all the fear swirling inside her. "I thought so, at first. But maybe it's just because I'm so far behind everyone else and—"

I cut her off. "No way. If you were too far behind, Master Ostrum would drop you as his student. The fact that he's giving you private lessons—he must really see something special in you."

"Well," Nedra said after thinking about it, "I *do* want to focus more on medical studies. Poetry isn't for me." She glanced at me quickly. "Sorry," she added.

I laughed. "Poetry's not bad, but it's not my deepest love," I said. "I only went to the class so I could be more well rounded. It looks good on applications."

She shrugged as if none of that mattered to her. I remembered what she'd said in the session, about the Wasting Death. I was ashamed to admit I didn't know much about the disease—all I had heard was that it was an issue specific to the factories at Blackdocks. The solution seemed simple to me: improve working conditions in the factories, and the disease would likely fade away. But that was easy to say from a distance. I didn't know anyone personally who had encountered it.

Until now, I realized. "That's why you're studying medical alchemy. Because of the Wasting Death."

"Of course," she said, passion rising in her voice. "We *have* to figure out a way to stop it." Suddenly, she tilted her head and met my eyes. "Were you waiting for me?"

I smiled. "I figured you hadn't eaten yet," I said. "I thought we might get some dinner."

Nedra looked at me gratefully. "I haven't." She cast her eyes toward the cafeteria across the quad.

"It's closed," I said. "But we can go into the city." I steered us gently toward the gatehouse on the other side of the quad.

"Isn't there a curfew?" Nedra asked.

I jingled my coin purse. "Not a problem." When we reached the guard, I slipped him a silver, and he assured us he'd await our return. I took Nedra to a small pub a few blocks harbor-side of the school. It was located in an old building, the wooden floors covered with rugs to hide the knocked-out knots in the planks. Booths were narrow and built into the walls, something that at least allowed privacy if not comfort.

Nedra's eyes skimmed over the menu. "I can't," she started, one leg already sliding out of the booth.

"Please, get something. I'm paying."

Nedra hesitated for a moment, but her hunger seemed to win out. When the pubmate approached, she ordered soup. I added a loaf of bread for us to share, two pints, and a sandwich, telling the pubmate to put it all on my father's account.

"That was kind of you," Nedra said. "Not just the meal, but waiting for me as well. Thank you." She smiled, and it lit up her whole body. She was the kind of girl who did everything by full measure.

I'd seen that in the way she'd taken notes in the lecture, her single-minded focus on her studies. But now, with her smile, I could tell she treated joy the same way. What she felt, she felt with all her heart; what she did, she did with all her focus. She was *true*. And that made her beautiful.

The pubmate placed a loaf of warm brown bread and a small dish of whipped honey butter on the table. Nedra eagerly grabbed the piece I offered her. "I will never forget cafeteria hours again," she swore.

I laughed. "It must not be easy, coming to a school like Yūgen. Almost everyone's a legacy student."

Nedra fingered a little arrow that had been carved onto the worn wooden table. "Why are you being so nice to me?" she asked, so abruptly that it caught me off guard.

I pulled off another hunk of bread and smeared it with honey butter. "Do I need a reason?"

"It's just—you're friends with Tomus, right? He wasn't exactly welcoming." She didn't say anything else. She didn't have to.

"Tomus wants nothing more than to be his father," I explained. "And I want nothing less than to be mine."

Nedra's eyes shot to mine. "That doesn't really answer my question."

I put my bread down. "We're something like fourth cousins. I've known him forever. You have to understand, he's just very..." I searched for the right words but couldn't find them. "He's not a bad sort, once you get to know him."

"You shouldn't have to know someone in order to be decent to them."

"It's not that," I protested. The pubmate arrived with the rest of our food.

Nedra lifted her spoon to the soup. "I hope Tomus deserves your loyalty," she said. "But I somehow doubt it."

I leaned back in my seat. I'd grown up with Tomus. We likely wouldn't be friends forever, but it was fine for now. "I guess sometimes it's just easier to keep things the way they are."

"I think that depends on what your now looks like."

I wanted to ask her what that meant. What were her friends like in her village? Her family? Even among a group of farmers, there must be something political in the way they lived.

Before I could speak, Nedra changed the subject. "What about you?" she asked. "Why do you want to study medicinal alchemy, Greggori?" I grinned again at the way she said my name, slowly, as if tasting the three syllables.

We slipped into an easy conversation. I had never felt so familiar with someone in such a short time before. There were no awkward pauses, no careful weighing of words. I knew instinctively that when Nedra asked a question, it was because she cared for my answer. And when she listened, it wasn't to try to find ways to twist my words against me later. Maybe she was right about Tomus, and familiarity wasn't enough to make him worth the bother.

As the pubmate cleared our dishes, I said, "Let's go somewhere."

"We should get back." Nedra's voice trailed off, and I could tell she wanted the evening to end no more than I did.

"Or we could take a shortcut through the Gardens."

"But the school is only a few blocks away," she said. "And the Gardens are . . ."

"In the exact opposite direction, yes," I answered. "I'm very bad at shortcuts."

Nedra grinned at me. "Lead the way."

The Imperial Gardens were the only public space in Northface Harbor. They took up six city blocks, all sloping, grassy lawns, with a pond in the center. Cobblestone streets—as old as the city itself—lined the perimeter, with graveled, meandering paths scattered throughout the grounds. The main entrance was located at the northern side of the Gardens and was framed by a giant stone archway, on top of which stood a life-size statue of the Emperor. Whenever a new Emperor rose to power, statues were created en masse and sent to all of the colonies.

Nedra and I used the east entrance—there was little fanfare at that gate, just an iron archway with the date of the Gardens' creation curling over the top.

"I've heard about this place," Nedra said, strolling beside me. "It's smaller than I imagined, not quite the escape from the city I thought it would be."

We reached a high point in the path, and Nedra paused, looking out over the city. In the distance, the bay glittered with lights from boats docked at the harbor, and just beyond them, the quarantine hospital's clockface glowed like a second moon.

Nedra pointed north, to the governor's palace. "All that house for one person?" she asked.

I laughed. "It's not just a house. It's the political center of Lunar Island, where laws are made and court is held. There *is*, of course, a wing for the governor to live in, and there's also a tower for the Emperor when he's on the island." I pointed to a flag mounted atop a large turret. "That means he's in residence now," I said, "which is actually kind of surprising. I would have thought he'd leave right after the governor's inauguration."

Nedra's eyes glittered as she stared at the shining building. The glass windows were cut to reflect light, giving the castle a soft, ethereal glow.

"My nanny used to tell me stories about that place," I said, leaning in closer. "It's *haunted*."

"Is that so, Grey?" Nedra arched an eyebrow at me.

My lips burst into a spontaneous grin, and it wasn't until Nedra noticed that she realized she'd shortened my name.

"Sorry, Greggori," she amended quickly. Her cheeks blushed furiously.

"No, I like it. You can call me Grey." I could tell it embarrassed her, so I dropped my voice to a conspiratorial whisper. "It's haunted," I said. "The castle."

"Oh, obviously," Nedra said, arching an eyebrow at me.

I nodded with authority. "Mm," I said. "Well, Bennum Wellebourne *was* the first resident."

"Really?" The playfulness in her voice was gone.

"Yeah. The old part, where the Emperor is now." I pointed again. "Wellebourne built that for himself when he played at being king. After the battle, Emperor Aurellious turned his home into a prison. He was there for months before his execution."

"No wonder people think it's haunted," Nedra said. I followed her gaze to the Emperor's tower, imagining what it must have been like for Bennum Wellebourne to rot away in the dank cell. He had once been the greatest hero of our colony, helping those around him survive the first year Lunar Island was settled. He'd been elected the first governor; he had been the most revered man on all of Lunar Island.

But that, of course, was before the rebellion. Before Bennum Wellebourne raised the dead and turned the corpses into an army— one that he used to attack his own people.

Nedra shivered, but she refused my coat when I offered it to her. As we continued up the path, changing our conversation to more pleasant topics, I kept looking back to the castle, its windows like eyes watching our every move.

NINE

Nedra

MASTER OSTRUM'S PRIVATE laboratory smelled of earth and rats.

I had wondered what the door behind his desk hid, but when Master Ostrum showed me the small room, I had not been expecting a full lab carved directly into the earth, the walls exposing natural rock. If not for the raised hardwood floor and the shelving units displaying medical equipment, it would have felt like entering a cave.

I had to step up to get into the laboratory, making the roof feel even lower. I jumped at a scratching noise nearby, turning to find cages holding half a dozen rats.

Master Ostrum gestured to a chair, and I sat down, unable to rip my gaze away from the jar in the center of the table between us.

"Is that an—" I started.

"An eye, yes." When I didn't answer, he added, "It's not that unusual for a medical alchemist to study specimens."

"Human," I said.

It hadn't been a question, but Master Ostrum answered me regardless. "Yes."

"Infected."

He didn't answer me this time. I reached for the jar, picking it up and holding it to the dim light of the oil lamp overhead. The eye inside bobbed and floated in the preservation fluid. The liquid was pale yellowish-green, casting the red-veined eye in a sickly hue, but there was an acid-green film over the colored iris that I knew wasn't a side effect of the preservation fluid. I turned the jar in my hand, coaxing the eye around. The film wrapped around the entire ball, adding delicate green tentacles that mingled with the extruding veins dangling at the end.

"You have experience with this disease," Master Ostrum said.

"Yes." I set the jar on the table, watching as the eyeball bobbed in the preservation fluid.

"I wish I'd had you in my class last year," Master Ostrum said with surprising fervor.

"I did apply," I pointed out.

Master Ostrum stared at me; the eyeball stared at me. I shifted uncomfortably.

"You were right," he said finally.

I waited for an explanation.

"I called the Wasting Death 'unhygienic,' and you were right to tell me I was wrong." Master Ostrum leaned back in his chair. "That's the narrative of the news sheets. People in Northface Harbor don't like to look at a truth that makes them uncomfortable. Saying that only the poor and dirty get sick makes them feel safe." He straightened up again. "But you can't pretend a thing is true just because you want to feel safe. I let myself forget what I know because a lack of hygiene in the sick is an easy answer." He shook his head. "Doesn't make it right."

I wasn't sure how to respond to this; it felt odd for someone of Master Ostrum's experience and demeanor to apologize to me.

"And my experience with the Wasting Death has been limited to the docks. The disease is contained in the city within the factories, but it's spreading."

"It's a plague," I said in a small voice. It had become almost a fact of life in the north; everyone knew someone who'd been infected.

Master Ostrum reached into a basket at his feet and pulled out a small stack of news sheets. He tossed them on the table, the flimsy paper fluttering around the jarred eyeball.

Master Ostrum had underlined or circled a handful of passages.

MYSTERIOUS ILLNESS DELAYS SHIPMENT OF CLOTH, one article proclaimed. Another said, FACTORY HOUSING DESTROYED AND REPLACED AFTER INFESTATION AND ILLNESS.

"What is this?" I asked.

"The earliest clues I've found."

I noticed the dates of the articles—all from three months ago, at the height of the governor's race. One of the headlines read EMPEROR AUGUSTE ARRIVES IN NORTHFACE HARBOR—WILL HE OVER-THROW THE COUNCIL'S VOTE? An illness affecting the poor was minor news compared to the election.

"I've been trying to pinpoint the original cases of the illness," Master Ostrum continued. "I hoped it would give me a clue as to how it spreads or what causes it."

"The first time I heard of it was Burial Day, last fall," I said. That had been almost a year ago. "My father told me about a sickness in a village near Hart, where people's hands and fingers turned black."

Master Ostrum sucked in a breath. "I've been too myopic," he muttered.

"It moves slowly."

"It used to," Master Ostrum said. "It's spreading more quickly now. This isn't public knowledge, but a few people on the governor's council have been sent to the quarantine hospital. Rich, powerful men."

"What can we do?" I asked.

The corners of Master Ostrum's mouth tilted up into a smile, though he didn't appear amused. "We? We can't do anything until you're better trained. I have been tasked by the governor herself to help find a cure. While I work, you work."

He turned and grabbed an empty golden crucible from the shelf behind him, then plunked it on the table in front of me, the metal reverberating.

I stared at it, unsure of what to do.

Master Ostrum raised his eyebrow. "Your application stated that you knew the runes."

I *did*. But I'd never actually used them.

"Start with the first form," he said. I could hear the impatience in his voice. He was giving me a chance to prove myself, and I was failing. My mind raced to remember the basic forms of alchemy I'd read about in Papa's books. I knew it all by heart; for years I practiced the forms using a chipped porcelain vase my mother sometimes used to hold wildflowers.

But I'd never actually *practiced* alchemy. I'd never had a real, working crucible, or . . .

I glanced behind me as the first form of alchemy slammed into my head. Shifting life forces. The rats in the cages that lined one wall of the laboratory stared at me with their beady black eyes.

"Don't be timid, girl," Master Ostrum growled.

I crossed the room to the cages. My hand shook as I opened a door, the rat inside hissing at me.

At least this was a smaller rat, bred for science, not one of the snarling, spitting things that lurked in barns, stealing grain from Jojo's stall. I thought of the little kitten Ernesta had when we were younger, and the way a rat had attacked him so brutally his face never fully healed. Taking a deep breath, I threw my hand into the cage, grabbing the rat by its torso, yanking it out, and throwing it into the golden crucible before I could talk myself out of it.

Master Ostrum grunted his approval.

The first form of alchemy required that I connect with a living creature, the crucible acting as a tether. The textbooks I'd read suggested that new alchemists start with a frog or a worm, but Master Ostrum didn't offer me anything but the rat. Most of the texts I read also warned that first efforts usually failed. I bit my lip. Master Ostrum didn't seem the type to forgive failure.

I held the base of the crucible with both hands, whispering the runes I'd memorized from Papa's books. They lit up with bright white light as they activated, and the rat inside the vessel squeaked in fear.

Master Ostrum leaned down, watching me.

I closed my eyes. Through my connection with the golden crucible, I felt for the rat's life. Alchemy might be a science, but it seemed like magic as I sensed the rat's heartbeat through my own veins. I breathed out, and when I breathed in again, I *pulled*. The rat's life flowed into me, and I felt sparking, crackling energy within my body, a jolt of power. I breathed out and *pushed*. The rat scampered at the base of the crucible, its claws tinny against the metal as it tried to escape.

I pulled again. The rat flopped down, passive, its energy filling me. It wasn't dead, just empty, its black eyes dull and its body lax. I let its life force return, and the rat scrambled up, terror sparking its movements.

"You have a natural talent," Master Ostrum said, a flare of new interest in his solemn eyes.

I suddenly felt exposed and vulnerable, like I was the rat in the crucible, trapped under the gaze of a predator. I nodded in acquiescence I didn't quite feel.

"Progress to Form Two," Master Ostrum commanded, turning back to his own experiments.

The dead eyeball that still floated in the jar on the table watched me as I silently reached for another rat.

TEN

Grey

IT DIDN'T TAKE long for the others to notice Nedra hadn't attended any lectures since the first day of class. In only a few weeks, it became the biggest topic of speculation, whispers floating around her before Master Ostrum's morning session began.

"What do *you* think our little gutter rat does all day?" Tomus drawled, loud enough for Nedra to hear. She kept her head down and flicked up the hood of her cloak. It was barely fall; I was surprised she was even wearing such a heavy garment.

I sat my bag down on the floor beside my desk. "Drop it," I muttered.

"Does she even meet with Master Ostrum for her evening report?" Tomus was very aware that every student was listening to him.

"Of course," I said, not mentioning that she often simply sat in while I gave my report, then was dismissed. Occasionally, she mentioned what she learned in a history study hall or a book she read outside of her private lessons.

"Of *course*." Tomus emphasized the last word in a mocking tone. There was a tittering of laughter in the rows behind me.

The door at the front of the room swung open, and Master Ostrum stomped inside. "Pack up," he growled at the class. Nedra was the first to move, standing and slinging her unopened bag over her shoulder. When most of the other students didn't move, Master Ostrum glared at us. "I said, let's go! We have a ferry to catch."

Excitement washed over us, and we all hurried to follow his command. Master Ostrum's class was the most advanced medicinal alchemy course at Yūgen, and his surgical laboratories were so renowned that sometimes even other professors would join the students to observe.

Master Ostrum led the way, not pausing to explain anything as he stomped down the quad and through the gate. No carriage awaited us, and Master Ostrum didn't hesitate as he headed down the main road to Blackdocks.

Tomus fell into step beside me. "I hope there's a carriage to carry us back up," I said.

"A ferry means the quarantine hospital," he answered, glowering at Master Ostrum's back. "That place is for poor people. We should be going to the Governor's Hospital, where there's a chance we'll meet the alchemists we'll actually work for. None of us wants to dirty our hands at a slum like that." His voice carried down the street, and I knew Master Ostrum heard him, but the old man didn't even turn his head.

Nedra, however, had stopped so abruptly that the girl behind her almost ran into her. "You're disgusting," she snarled at Tomus.

Tomus laughed. The sound was not amused, but bitter, spiteful. Nedra strode away, a sense of pride in her step. I thought first of what Nedra had told me, about loyalty. But then I remembered the way Tomus had gotten his governess fired when he was seven because she'd dared to give him a subpar grade for his subpar work.

Master Ostrum had reserved a ferry just for our class. It cut across the water, a cool morning wind whipping up the girls' hair. Nedra pushed through the crowd of students to the front of the boat, her cloak wrapped tightly around her.

She knew, I thought. Master Ostrum had told her that we would go on a ferry today; she knew to bring a cloak with her.

I thought for a moment that Nedra was watching me, but I realized her gaze was focused above my head. I turned, scanning the shoreline of the city behind us as the boat set off. A tall building stood out among the others, black curtains draped over every long window. A little down the street, another one, the same heavy black cloth. More factories closing. The news sheets didn't call the sickness spreading in the poor district an epidemic, but it was only a matter of time. My eyes slipped back to Nedra. *She knew about that, too,* I thought. At the start of the semester, the sickness was a mild inconvenience in the factories, but it was spreading now.

The ferry rocked over a wave, and I stumbled.

"I don't know how you stand it," Tomus said. I hadn't realized he was so close to me until he spoke. His gaze was on Nedra as well.

"She's not so bad," I said. "Actually, she's really interesting. If you got to know her—"

"She's a dumb hick who obviously can't handle the course load. She's not been to any of the decent lectures, and she never shows up to labs."

"She does labs."

Tomus raised his eyebrow.

"With Master Ostrum," I said.

"Master Ostrum is giving her *private* labs?"

I shrugged, my gaze slipping to the waves. I hadn't meant to say anything.

"I doubt they're doing alchemy in those labs," Tomus muttered. Behind us, I heard a girl giggle.

"Drop it," I growled.

Tomus rolled his eyes. "She's not smart enough to be here, Greggori, and you know it. Her scholarship must have been payment for services rendered, if you catch my drift."

"Don't be such a bastard," I snapped.

I immediately regretted the words. "Bastard" was the insult Tomus's father used when he wanted to humiliate both his wife and son, and he did it often enough in public to be a sore point for Tomus. It was a low blow, and I knew it.

"Sorry," I said quickly, but it was too late.

Tomus moved toward the aft of the boat, and most of the students in the class followed him. I was left alone, the cold wind biting at me.

The ferry bumped against the stone steps at the base of the island. The skipper stabilized the boat, and we all disembarked, climbing up the steps toward the hospital. I turned back to look at Northface Harbor.

"Funny how a little bit of water makes the city seem so distant," Nedra said, stepping beside me. We headed up the stairs, a little behind the others. "Thanks," she muttered to me in a low voice. "I don't know what Tomus said to you, but I saw the way he reacted when you replied. So thank you for whatever it was you told him."

I bit my lip. I had tried to stand up for Nedra, but my efforts had potentially been more damaging than my silence could have been. I didn't have the heart to tell her that, though.

"It really is like a castle," Nedra said, staring up at the hospital's brick façade as we reached a large plaza in front of the doors.

"Well, it was built from leftover materials from the actual castle," I said. "Just like the administration building at Yūgen."

"Really?"

I nudged her shoulder. "You'd know that if you attended an architecture lecture."

"I have more important things to do than attend lectures," Nedra said, her tone suddenly grave.

Like attend private lab sessions. I shook the thought away, disgusted at myself for lingering on Tomus's insinuation.

"Wait until you go to the *actual* castle." I grabbed Nedra's hand, pulling her around and pointing to the governor's residence back across the harbor, sparkling under the sunlight. The Emperor was still in residence, having extended his stay after the inauguration.

Nedra turned her back on the city. "I prefer this," she said.

"Move it along," Master Ostrum bellowed from the large mahogany doors that led into the hospital. We rushed to join the other students filing in.

The hospital's foyer was just as beautiful as the outside, with marble floors, ornately trimmed windows, and an iron spiral staircase leading up into the clock tower. Against one wall hung an enormous painting of a man, his wife and son at his side. The woman's hand was amputated at the left wrist, and the man held the residual limb reverently.

Bennum Wellebourne.

His statue at Yūgen had been destroyed, but Lunar Island could never truly escape his legacy. He had funded the building of the quarantine hospital himself, and despite his treason, the hospital still presented his family portrait proudly. People had to pay for better care at the Governor's Hospital, and Whitesides was only available to factory workers who paid fees, so Wellebourne built this hospital and mandated that it be available to all, free of charge.

Master Ostrum led the class to Amphitheater C. Chairs with small desks attached to the armrests waited for us, all empty. Nedra and I sat in the front row, our feet on the surgery stage floor. A giant mirror hung from the ceiling over an operating table. Nedra leaned back in her chair, but she was still close to me, closer than she needed to be. I let my knee touch hers, and she didn't pull away.

An air of excitement settled over the room as the rest of the students claimed their seats and waited for whatever operation Master Ostrum would be demonstrating for us. The clock struck the hour, the sound resonating throughout the hospital, and two aides wheeled in a gurney, positioning the patient beneath the mirror and in front of Master Ostrum.

I felt Nedra tense. Her eyes were glued to the body of the young girl on the metal gurney.

Master Ostrum picked up a scalpel, the silver gleaming under the bright lights.

ELEVEN

Nedra

"WHEN DEALING WITH a patient, first assess the symptoms." Master Ostrum's voice cut across the room.

I took a deep breath and let it out slowly. I couldn't let emotions cloud my judgment. The patient was a girl a few years my junior, maybe thirteen or fourteen. Her skin was the same olive tone as mine, but it looked oddly grayed and shiny, as if someone had poured a thin layer of wax over her face. Her sleek black hair had been hastily cut. Her eyes were closed, and she gave no indication of waking anytime soon. Before anyone could attempt to give a diagnosis, Master Ostrum lifted away the white cloth covering the girl's body.

Master Ostrum wheeled the gurney around, showing us the girl's left leg. Her skin was inky black from the base of her heel to just above her ankle, with dark lines snaking up her leg like rivulets, and they didn't fade until just above the knee. Her foot was withered, the toes twisting oddly, as if they'd spasmed and then frozen.

"Can anyone tell me what this girl's illness is?" Master Ostrum asked, his eyes skimming the students in the amphitheater seats.

No one answered.

"It's the Wasting Death." My voice rang out across the silent room, and I felt all eyes turn to me. "And it's a plague."

"It's not a *plague*." Tomus sat several seats behind me, but I knew his voice without turning.

"She's right." Master Ostrum spoke calmly but with authority. "It is. As we speak, the governor is composing an address on the topic. By the time we're back at Yūgen, it should be in all the news sheets."

The rest of the students seemed shocked, but I felt relief. *Finally.* The official designation would help others see the threat we already knew in the north.

Master Ostrum looked down at the patient dispassionately. "Scientifically, it's a disease that's possibly both pneumonic and septicemic, and we've been unable to identify the specific strain of pathogen." He turned to the rest of the class. "We've not been able to determine how the disease is transferred, but it spreads most often in tightly quartered areas, like the factories in Blackdocks, and it spreads quickly among the poor."

"Maybe it has something to do with hygiene," a girl near the back said.

"Or just bad blood." Tomus's voice was a sneer. I could feel his eyes watching me.

"We have ruled out both those causes," Master Ostrum said. His voice was neutral, but my blood boiled. "It is neither a result of unclean conditions—although such conditions certainly don't help—nor something inherited through bloodlines."

"Maybe it came from the mainland," Salis, the girl who led the history study group, said. "There were a lot of visitors for the governor's inauguration, to say nothing of the mercantile ships."

I shook my head. "The disease was here before the inauguration."

"No one asked *you*," a voice behind me sneered in a whisper. I turned to see who'd spoken, but all the students behind me stared blandly at Master Ostrum.

Master Ostrum continued his lecture. "This illness has proven difficult to study. It's not easy to catch it when it first strikes. Patients feel achy, often with a fever and a headache. Common enough symptoms; everything from spotted fever to a regular cold starts this way. Soon, however, digits exhibit signs of necrosis." Master Ostrum indicated the girl's toes. "The disease seems to spread out from a certain point. No patient has lived long when the blackness starts in the torso, but some have survived when the disease starts in a hand or foot."

I felt tension coiling in my stomach, like a snake weaving through my intestines.

"This is Cyntha. She's from the Simmina factory in Blackdocks, one of the few who worked there and is still alive. We've not yet traced a source or a way to combat the symptoms, but I think you, our brightest students, can surmise what experimental surgery we're going to perform today."

I stared at the sick girl, my eyes roving over her body. Her foot was blackened. Necrosis, Master Ostrum had said. The flesh was dead.

"Amputation." The word felt like poison.

Master Ostrum nodded. "I think here," he said, indicating a spot on Cyntha's leg above the knee, where there was no blackness creeping under her skin.

The two aides returned to the surgical stage, wheeling a cart of tools toward Master Ostrum. The professor ignored us, using ink to mark where the girl's leg was going to be amputated mid-thigh. We all watched silently. No one expected this on the first day of surgical observation. This was far more intense than any of our other hands-on training.

Master Ostrum positioned his scalpel.

"Sir?" I asked, hoping no one else heard the quiver.

Master Ostrum paused.

"Sir, where is the alchemist?"

In surgeries, alchemists used the gold crucibles to cipher pain from the patient into a lesser creature, such as a rat. But there was no alchemist here to help with Master Ostrum's surgery, no golden crucible. No pain relief for the girl's amputation.

"As you have learned from your books," Master Ostrum said, "the alchemist must filter the pain between the patient and the crucible. An amputation is obviously a very difficult process, and the pain is immense."

"But you also taught us that the alchemist feels the pain only temporarily as they push it into the crucible," I protested. I shoved aside my notebook, my hands trembling. Grey reached out for me, but I shook him off as I stood.

Master Ostrum waved his hand dismissively. "The patient has entered a sleeplike state; I've seen it with other late-stage victims of this disease," he said. "This won't wake her." He pressed the blade against the girl's leg, and red burst through her skin.

"Sir!" I shouted.

Master Ostrum didn't look up from his work as he sliced the girl's skin. "If you cannot restrain yourself, you can leave." He paused. "Unless you'd like to be acting alchemist on this surgery?"

"Nedra, don't," Grey whispered, but I ignored him. I had only used rats in my experiments with Master Ostrum, but I knew that I had a high tolerance for pain. This, however, would be excruciating.

But brief.

I marched to the stage, stopping in front of Master Ostrum, bloody scalpel still in his hand. "Where is your crucible?" I asked.

"A medicinal alchemist is never without her own crucible," Master Ostrum said, his voice low, just for me, as one of the aides fetched a generic golden crucible and pressed it into my hands.

"I won't make that mistake again," I promised my master.

There was a scrabbling, squeaking noise inside the vessel; a rat already curled up at the bottom of the vase, awaiting the pain that would be pushed into it.

I sat down on the floor beside the patient, one hand wrapped around the sleeping girl's palm, the other clutching the golden crucible. The vase lit up with runes as the power connection was established.

Master Ostrum ignored me for the rest of the surgery. He sliced away at the sleeping girl's flesh as if he were bored and wanted to be done with the task. Her body didn't move—the sleep stage was deathlike—but the aides held her leg steady when Master Ostrum reached for the bone saw.

The girl on the gurney slept through it all, and she didn't feel a thing.

I felt it for her.

After a long, long time, Master Ostrum touched my shoulder, removing the blood-soaked apron he'd donned before the surgery.

"It's done," he said.

I shook my head, not understanding. Part of the girl's leg was still attached; the amputation was incomplete. Master Ostrum bent down, prying my fingers from the girl's and helping me to stand. I dropped the golden crucible on the floor, and the rat that had been inside it thudded lifeless onto the tiles. Master Ostrum held my arm politely, leading me to my seat and making sure I was settled there. Then he turned back to the girl on the gurney.

The amputation had become an autopsy.

TWELVE

Nedra

THE FERRY WAS quieter on the return to Blackdocks than it had been this morning when we left. The wind had died down, too, and the waves were more like gentle hills than choppy cliffs. I let the boat rock away all my dark thoughts. *This must be what wealth is like*, I thought, *being able to slip away from the bad things others can't escape.*

As we drew farther and farther away from the quarantine hospital, I could see the worry sliding from my fellow students' faces. Their shoulders straightened. They looked toward Northface Harbor, not the hospital.

They talked about what they were going to get for lunch.

Grey and I were among the last to disembark from the ferry. He held his hand out for me to steady myself as I stepped onto the dock. His face turned toward the street winding up to Yūgen Academy. But I looked back.

I wanted to go home.

The longing of it hit me like a punch in the stomach. I missed my family, my friends. I missed being in a place and knowing that I was a part of it. I missed the church hall, I missed singing. I missed *belonging.*

"Ned?" Grey asked when I didn't move.

I turned around, my eyes searching past the small island where the quarantine hospital was, farther, across the bay, to the northern shore. The coastline curved in a crescent, and I imagined picking out the spot where my village was.

Grey tugged at my arm, and I reluctantly turned to follow him. But another boat a few slips down caught my eye, and I pulled free and raced over to it.

Carso had told me when he dropped me off at Blackdocks that I could go back home on his boat at any time. I knew I couldn't really leave—there was too much work to be done at Yūgen, but it would still be nice to see Carso. Maybe he had news from home.

Only Carso wasn't there. "Hello?" I called. I was certain it was his boat.

"Interested?" a girl's voice asked. I turned as Carso's sister, Dilada, approached. "Oh," she said, surprised. "Nedra. I didn't recognize you."

"Where's Carso?" I asked. I'd thought Dilada was going back to her family's farm after her job in the forest.

Grey moved beside me. I knew I should introduce him, but I was more focused on Carso's absence.

Dilada nodded toward the bay. "Remember when I went to the forest?" she asked. "I helped clear the trees. D'you know what it was for?"

I shook my head.

"Pauper's grave." Her eyes grew distant. "The whole field."

"Dilada," I said, sorrow sinking in my belly like a stone thrown in the water. "Where is Carso?"

She stared in the direction of the forest. "Sold the farm. Selling the boat."

For the first time, I noticed which dock we were standing on. A small section specifically for people to line up their boats in the hope of a quick sale.

"I've got another job lined up," she added. "Berrywine's factory. Furniture making."

I tasted bitterness on my tongue. This was exactly the fate Carso hadn't wanted for his sister. But what were her other options? She was about my age. What would I do if my entire family died and I had nothing left but my wits? Factory jobs were hard, but they came with a bed to sleep in and two meals a day. It was something, at least.

"How did he . . . ?" I started.

Dilada looked at the ground. "Blackness in his feet first," she said. "He hid it from me for a while, till he couldn't walk. We paid an alchemist to take away some of his pain." A corner of her mouth lifted up. "There was that at least."

The Wasting Death. The same disease that had taken Dilada's parents.

Worry twisted up inside me. Dilada's village wasn't that far from my family's. And Papa traveled through it, selling his books.

"Are you looking to go back to your village?" Dilada asked me. "I can take you, if you need to go now."

Grey stiffened beside me, but didn't speak. I wondered—if I decided to leave, would he ask me to stay?

"No," I said. "I can't. I have work to do here."

The words gave me courage I didn't know I had. This was why I'd come to Northface Harbor, to Yūgen. This was why I spent my days in the library and the labs, my nights working with Master Ostrum. I wanted to go home—I wanted it so much that it hurt—but I was useless in the north. Here, maybe I could help find a cure.

"Go away." Master Ostrum didn't even look up at me as he pointed to the door.

"There's still work to do," I protested.

"Not today."

I ignored him and tried to maneuver around the desk to the small door behind it. But Master Ostrum shifted his chair, blocking the entry to the laboratory.

"Nedra," he said, his voice kinder this time. "You just did some excellent alchemical work. I'd debate on whether or not it was needed, given the girl's condition, but nevertheless, you transferred her pain away. Not many fully trained alchemists could handle that."

"Are you saying the amputations in the quarantine hospital are done without any kind of pain reduction for the patient?" I asked, horrified.

Master Ostrum shook his head. "I'm saying that most alchemists would have taken shifts on a procedure like that. You more than proved you're ready for this work today."

"Good. Let's continue," I said, trying to go into the lab again.

"Take a break. I don't want you to push your body and your mind to the limits. I need you sharp. Tomorrow we go deeper."

"Today," I insisted, but the fight was leaving me.

The giant bell in the clock tower chimed.

"Don't you have a study group now?" Master Ostrum said, deflecting me.

I hesitated. I'd attended a handful of Salis's history study group meetings, and quite enjoyed the debates and new perspectives I'd learned. But as active as I'd been in the meetings for the first half of the month, in the last few weeks, I'd dropped them. There was too much work to do in the present to dwell on history. But Master Ostrum was right. I was bone-weary after the morning's alchemical work.

"Go," Master Ostrum said, sensing my doubt.

"Tomorrow," I said, making the word a promise.

He bowed his head. "We resume tomorrow."

Because the study group was in the same building as Master Ostrum's office, I was only a few minutes late when I reached the meeting room.

"Oh," Salis said, appraising me with her eyes. "We didn't know you were attending today. Take a seat."

I felt the admonishment in her voice, and my cheeks burned. I hadn't meant to hurt the other girls' feelings by ignoring the group; I'd just grown increasingly focused on my private labs with Master Ostrum.

"For those who've been absent," Salis continued, shooting me a pointed look, "we've already discussed Wellebourne's motivations and major battles leading up to the desecration."

This was all subject matter I knew, although I did regret not getting the girls' take on it. Wellebourne had started off as loyal to the Empire, striking out for an unknown and unpopulated island to lead a colony and expand the Emperor's territories. After a rough winter with little aid, he decided he'd be better off leading his own independent nation and tried to rebel.

One of the other girls in the group plopped a book on the table and started rifling through the pages. Her name was Flora, and she was originally from the mainland. "One thing we have to consider is the abundance of dead people easily accessible to Wellebourne at the time."

She slid the book around to show us an illustration with vivid details of a snowbound village in the early colony. Many of the houses weren't fully constructed; the colony had arrived later than anticipated on the shores of Lunar Island and hadn't been prepared. Forefront in the illustration was a row of dead bodies enshrouded with snow. The ground had been so hard that it had been impossible to bury those who starved and froze to death.

My fingers brushed one of the illustrated corpses. The hands and feet of the man were black—frostbite—but it reminded me of the girl in surgery today. A flare of pain washed over me, an echo of what I'd felt when I aided her, and I was left breathless.

Flora slid the book to the other side of the table so more could see. "We have to wonder, if the bodies were not present, would Wellebourne have . . ." She seemed reluctant to finish the statement.

Salis took the book from another girl's hand, flipped past a few pages, then held it up for everyone to see. The illustration now showed a man, his head tilted at an abnormal angle, his eyes blackened, his shoulders slumped asymmetrically.

"I don't think a man sees a dead body and thinks to raise it," Salis said. "I think a man wants to raise the dead and acts on it when the opportunity arises. You're trying to humanize him, Flora, and make excuses for what he did. But can you look at this and really think he was just responding to the environment?"

"I'm not trying to say it was okay!" Flora protested. She shook her head so violently that the little golden daffodils hanging from her ears smacked against her cheek. "But it's worth considering. Would a man commit a crime if he never had access to a weapon? Would Wellebourne have raised the dead if there weren't so many that winter?"

"I think," I started, then paused as every girl turned to look at me. I began again. "I think that it depends on when Wellebourne started contemplating rebelling against the Empire. If he wanted to rebel before the winter wiped out so many colonists, then he was always a necromancer, just awaiting an opportunity, as Salis said. But if the death of so many colonists was the reason why he wanted to rebel, then he became a necromancer in response to the tragedy around him."

Salis shrugged. "It doesn't matter. Either way, he crossed a line when he used alchemy to raise corpses to fight his battles."

I frowned. It *did* matter, though. Before I could argue further, Salis dropped the book on the table with a loud thunk. "We all know nec-romancy is wrong," she said, and the others all nodded. "Instead, let's talk about the revolution. Because whether or not *that* was wrong . . ." Her eyes shifted to me. "I want to know what Nedra thinks."

"About . . . revolution?"

Flora nodded eagerly. "Surely someone from the north would have a different perspective."

"Why does my background matter?"

"The northern villages have a different attitude about Wellebourne than the south. And that shapes everything, even the way our govern-ment is today." Salis spoke with authority, although I doubted she'd ever been in a village like mine.

I couldn't keep the doubt from my face, but as I looked at the serious faces of the girls before me, I gave her words some thought. Wellebourne's revolt had started—and ended—in the north. The capital shifted from Hart to Northface Harbor, and the former rebels were left to farm their way out of poverty. "It was a century and a half ago, though," I said, still musing over her words.

"Not that long, considering the Allyrian Empire has been around for nine hundred years," Flora said. "Lunar Island has only been set-tled for one hundred and forty-two years."

"One event in history," Salis said, her voice rising with passion, "ripples down and affects an entire nation."

Lunar Island is a colony, not a nation, I thought.

"Because Wellebourne started his rebellion in the north," Salis continued, "the north lost the capital. Because the capital moved here, this city rose in power. The harbor shifted—boats came here, and with the boats came trade."

"The north didn't advance as quickly as the south," Flora said, picking up the conversation. "They stayed farmers—they stayed poor."

My cheeks burned. I knew the girls weren't mocking me or trying to say I was poor, but it stung. I looked out at the group of eager girls. "I promise you, we're not all sitting in our huts plotting a revolution." I laughed, but I was the only one who found this humorous. Flora sat back in her seat, disappointment etched on her face.

"What do you think it would take?" Salis asked finally.

"For what?"

"To mobilize the north."

I gaped at her. "In a rebellion? Against the Emperor?"

She inclined her head, the barest tilt, waiting for me to answer.

"I . . . I don't know?" I said. "Why are we even discussing this? I thought we were studying history." When no one answered, I continued, "If you want to talk about what's happening now, speculating about a revolt against the most powerful man in the world is a waste of time compared to the *actual* problem of the plague."

Salis didn't refute me, she just arched an eyebrow in my direction.

"Aren't you mad he's not doing more?" Flora asked. "It's a bit like Wellebourne's problem all over again, isn't it? Emperor Aurellious let the people of Lunar Island freeze to death, and so Wellebourne rebelled. Emperor Auguste has done nothing to help stop the plague, and so . . ."

She let her voice trail off, the implication heavy in the room.

"One change leads to another," Salis said as the clock tower's bell started tolling.

THIRTEEN

Nedra

As soon as Master Ostrum arrived for the morning session the next day, Tomus's hand shot in the air, his chin tilted up. Master Ostrum didn't acknowledge him, but Tomus spoke anyway. "When are we going to have our internship at the Governor's Hospital?" he demanded.

"There will be no internship at the Governor's Hospital," Master Ostrum said. Everyone in class started talking at once, but Master Ostrum's voice rose above them. "Instead, I would like you all to volunteer at the quarantine hospital." He picked up a sheaf of papers. "Here are timetables of shifts. The alchemists there need help—you saw yesterday how serious this is. Cases of the Wasting Death are piling up."

From behind me, Salis's voice piped up. "But sir, isn't there a chance *we* would get the Wasting Death if we volunteered there?"

Master Ostrum leveled her with a glare. "There is," he said. "Which is why every volunteer will take the proper precautions." He went over the herbal supplements that would be provided for us— wortroot and gold flower to boost the immune system—as well as the heavy screenings, including an inspection of our crucibles, to identify early infection and hopefully treat the illness before it grew.

We all knew, however, that there was still a risk involved.

"I'm not going there," Tomus said, and I could tell he was putting words to thoughts most of the other students had. "It's not worth it. Just get us internships at the Governor's Hospital."

The Governor's Hospital treated the sick just like any other hospital. But the difference was in the types of patients. The Governor's Hospital catered to the rich: old women with colds who decided they needed round-the-clock care; children of wealthy families who were overprotective and needed assurances that the sniffles weren't the plague; men who attempted gardening as a gentleman's pursuit and needed blisters lanced.

"Here're the schedules for the quarantine hospital," Master Ostrum said, ignoring Tomus. "Anyone who works a shift need not attend any lectures that day."

Then he left.

For a moment, everyone waited. We were used to lessons with Master Ostrum in the morning, directives on what to focus our studies on. Not this abruptness. Master Ostrum hadn't even given the class information on the day's lectures.

Tomus was the first to stand. He made a show of loudly picking up his bag, clomping over the hardwood floors to Master Ostrum's desk, selecting a timetable, and crushing it in his fist. He let the wadded paper fall into the wastebasket by Master Ostrum's chair and left the room. The others started moving as if they awoke from a trance, but while they didn't make a show of rejecting the quarantine hospital's schedule as much as Tomus had, none of them picked up a paper for themselves either.

Grey stood, and I found that my breath had caught as I waited to see what would happen next.

He went to Master Ostrum's desk and picked up a timetable.

I let out a sigh of relief before I crossed the room and did the same.

Grey was waiting for me outside the classroom. "If we hurry," I said, "we can catch the first ferry."

His eyes were on the paper. "I . . ." His voice trailed off. "I think I'll go after midterms. I have to finish my essay."

I couldn't hide my disappointment.

"I will," Grey insisted. "I promise."

"Yeah." I shouldered my bag and headed toward the gate. "Okay."

When I arrived at the hospital, a potion maker gave me a quick tour of the different wings.

"You can start with elderly care," he said, pausing in the corridor that led to the east wing.

"I'm only here for the Wasting Death," I said. "I'm not volunteering for anything else."

The potion maker looked down his nose at me.

"I was sent by Master Ostrum," I added, "and I came prepared." I showed the potion maker my golden crucible in my bag, the one I'd made myself, etching in the runes with my own hands under Master's Ostrum's guidance.

"Your funeral," the potion maker said, dumping me in the west wing.

The alchemists and potion makers of the communicable disease wing were more harried than anywhere else. New patients arrived with every ferry, and already they were pulling beds from other parts of the hospital to double and triple occupy the rooms. There was talk of evacuating the mental illness ward to make room, and anyone who didn't have the Wasting Death upon arrival was sent away to one of the other hospitals.

I approached the check-in desk. Two potion makers were talking with the receptionist, their heads bent over a news sheet.

"Hi," I said.

"Be with you in a minute," the receptionist replied, not taking his eyes off the paper.

"'In an unprecedented move, the governor has declared a state of emergency,'" one of the potion makers read aloud. "'The Emperor has made no comment, yet continues his residency in the palace.'"

"Bit odd, that," the other potion maker said. "If I were him, I'd hightail it back to the mainland."

"This is going to be trouble for us," the first one said. "The more people hear about this sickness, the more they'll come here when they have nothing but a cold."

"I can help with that," I said.

They finally looked at me.

I held up my golden crucible. "I'm a volunteer."

"You're an alchemist?" The first potion maker looked me up and down, her eyes taking in my plain tunic and lack of sapphire-colored robes.

"Soon to be," I said. "I'm in Master Ostrum's class, at Yū—"

The potion maker breathed a huge sigh of relief, drowning out my voice. "One of Ostrum's, thank goodness. If you said you were from Pushnil, I'd send you back. But Ostrum can actually teach. Any more of you volunteering?" Her eyes skimmed past me, looking down the hall crowded with patients.

"Just me," I said.

If it weren't for Master Ostrum's evening sessions and living at the dormitory every night, I wouldn't have felt like a student at all. I'd long since given up lectures, and I'd stopped bothering with Salis's study hall as well. In any other school, I would be at risk of losing my scholarship, but at Yūgen, my fate rested in Master Ostrum's hands. And even if he hadn't approved of my work, it wouldn't matter— sacrificing a chance at a second year of school was worth it if it meant I could spend this crucial time studying the Wasting Death.

I spent every morning, lunch, and afternoon at the quarantine hospital. I got to know every potion maker in the wing, and if Alchemist Frue was on shift, many of them came to me before they got him.

"Nedra?" Mrs. Rodham stood in the door of the potion room,

where I'd been taking inventory. Alchemist Frue had a reputation for being stingy with potions, but we were so close to running out of tincture of blue ivy, I could almost forgive him.

Mrs. Rodham was a volunteer like me, but she was neither an alchemist nor a potion maker, just someone who wanted to help the patients. She had come to the quarantine hospital with her entire family, all suffering from the Wasting Death. Her husband and eldest daughter had already passed, but her younger son was still alive, although in the sleeplike state that heralded death. No one had the heart to tell Mrs. Rodham that there was no point in her staying at the hospital; her son was already gone even if he was still breathing. So while he slept, she helped, as best she could with her recently amputated leg, the only thing that had spared her from dying as well.

"Yes?" I asked her.

"There's a family . . ." Mrs. Rodham's voice trailed off.

"I'll be right there." I pocketed a small bottle of tincture of blue ivy; it was running low, but Frugal Frue wouldn't notice one more gone, at least not before our next shipment came.

Mrs. Rodham led me to one of the rooms at the end of the hall, her steps uneven, the cane she now used clacking against the tiles.

"How is it?" I asked. She had adapted well to her amputation, better than many who were younger than her. I suspected all her grief—both over the deaths in her family and at the loss of her limb—were being held at bay by the little rises and falls of her young son's chest, regardless of whether his eyes opened or not.

"I'm adjusting," she said. "There are worse things to lose than a leg."

Mrs. Rodham stopped outside of a door just as one of the potion makers exited a room. "You the alchemist?" the potion maker said.

"Nedra." I held out my hand. "Student, but I can do alchemy."

"Good." He ran his fingers through his hair. "I'm Fadow. They're . . . they need someone. They had a rough trip."

"Trip?"

"Came from one of the villages to the north. We're getting more of them lately."

"That's why I thought to get you, dear," Mrs. Rodham said. We'd talked often of our homes over lunch or quick breaks; most of the potion makers and alchemists were from the city, but we were both from the north.

I walked into the room, my stomach twisting in knots.

"See, someone's here," a man said. He had a low, soothing voice that was cracked through the middle with panic.

Two of the beds were occupied, one with a woman, one with a school-age boy. Along with the man was another boy, maybe a few years older than the first.

"Has Alchemist Frue been here?" I asked, scanning the patient.

The man rushed forward, his hat twisting in his hand. "No," he said, and I could almost feel his frustration. "They shoved us in a room, and they've just given us water and told us to wait, and wait, and *wait.*" He spat the last word out. "Can you help us?"

"The hospital is overcrowded," I said, "and we're short on alchemists. But I can help."

"*Thank you,*" the man said. "My name's Dannix. My wife and son are sick." He gestured to them, then moved to the wall with his other son, giving me room to work.

I checked the child first, at the mother's insistence. Both legs were covered in blackness, his feet so twisted he could no longer keep shoes on them. The inky stain of the disease was well past his knees, and the analytical medical student in me knew that if he survived, it would be a miracle.

The woman seemed better off—at first.

"It's here," she said, pulling her shirt down. Darkness bled over her heart. I kept my face schooled, but I was close enough to the woman that I was certain she saw her own doom written in my eyes. There was nothing I could do to help her; she would either live or not, and only one in a hundred survived the Wasting Death when it infected the heart. Her fate fell to the gods and whether or not her body was strong enough to push the infected blood to a disposable limb.

I forced a cheerful smile on my face. "At least you don't have any film over your eyes," I said, lifting her eyelids to check. "If you did, that would mean the disease was in your brain. No cure then."

The man sagged with relief. "See, you'll be fine!" he told his wife, running to her side and clutching her hand.

Her eyes didn't leave mine. I saw the question there, unasked as her husband knelt, his head over their clasped fingers, muttering a quick prayer. She wanted—needed—honesty. She would hold on if there was hope. But I didn't know what to tell her.

The boy in the other bed moaned, and his mother flicked her fingers toward him. "Take care of my son," she said.

I nodded, swallowing down the lump in my throat. The older boy, the patient's brother, moved closer. "Are you going to do the magic?" he asked.

I smiled at him, and somehow I was able to pretend like this was a normal smile, a normal conversation. "It's not magic," I said. "It's science. But it *does* feel like magic." In the hospital, I carried my crucible on a leather strap, looped to hold the golden vase. I also had a shoulder bag made of cloth-covered metal with a latched wooden door on the front. I set the bag down, opening the door and withdrawing a rat. The brother leaned over, fascinated, as I dropped the creature into my golden crucible.

"What's your name?" I asked my patient.

"Jax." His voice was barely audible. "Are you going to cut my legs off?"

There was no point in lying. The flesh had long since withered and died, the skin black and crackling, dark blood oozing in spots.

"Not me personally," I said. "But amputation is likely."

The boy breathed as if this news was a relief. His brother looked more upset by the possibility of it than him. Behind us, I heard their father start to cry.

"And who are you?" I asked his brother as I adjusted the crucible on a nearby table.

"Ronan," the boy said in a small voice.

"Mrs. Rodham told me that you were all from a village to the north. I am, too. Which one are you from?"

"The daffodil gate."

Mentally, I said a quick prayer of thanks. The villages behind the daffodil gate were on the other side of Hart, in the cliffs, about as far away from my village as it was possible to be.

"Jax," I said, turning to my patient, "this isn't going to hurt a bit. In fact, it's going to make everything better."

I chanted the runes quickly, watching them light up, shining through the golden crucible. The rat sitting in the base of the vessel clawed more frantically along the edges.

"What happens to the rat inside?" Ronan asked, peering into the crucible.

I thought about lying to the child to make the truth easier, but there was no point in that. Someone like Ronan was too surrounded by death to feel the balm of a lie. "The pain has to go somewhere. The rat will take it for your brother."

"That's mean," Jax said, but his voice was already less tightly wound as I connected with his body, forming the bridge between him and the rat.

"I know," I said.

"I don't care," Ronan said, his voice more forceful than before.

I concentrated on the task at hand. Alchemist Frue would likely pull this boy into surgery before the end of the day, but before that, at least, I could help ease the pain. I closed my eyes, focusing on the buzzing sensation of his life force. I tugged the pain from the boy's body, and it passed through me, like a river rushing through reeds, and then I pushed the pain down, down, into the rat. The rodent screamed, but I blocked the noise out.

When I released my grip on both Jax and the crucible, the rat was alive, but barely. The creature's tongue hung out, and it panted against the metal base of the vessel, its ragged breath casting little clouds against the gold. I tipped the crucible over, putting the rat back into the shoulder bag that served as its cage.

"Thank you," Ronan said. Jax had slipped into a blissful, pain-free sleep, his body exhausted.

"And my wife?" the older man said, drawing my attention back to him. "Can you use the magic on her?"

I swallowed. Alchemy wouldn't help her. Taking her pain away might take away her life, stilling her heart so much it quit pumping blood. It would be risky.

"It would be best if you bore the pain," I told her, seeking her eyes. I reached into my pocket and withdrew the bottle of blue ivy tincture. "If it gets to be too much," I said, carefully choosing my words, "take this."

"What will it do?" the husband asked.

I didn't take my gaze away from the woman's. "It will make you sleep." I stressed the final word. "But take no more than three drops every six chimes." Her eyes widened a little with understanding, and her chin dipped, nodding, letting me know she understood. She took the bottle from me and held it in the palm of her hand.

"Thank you," her husband said. He moved around the bed to shake my hand. His grip was painful; he clutched my fingers as if they were a lifeline. "Thank you so much. You're the first person who helped. Thank you." His voice cracked. "Ronan, come here, thank the alchemist."

"I'm not a—" I started. The boy held his hand out to me. His grip was far weaker. For the first time, I really focused on him, not the patients in the beds. Ronan's skin was sallow, dark shadows under his eyes.

Dark shadows on his fingertips.

My grip on his hand tightened reflexively. He saw where I was looking and snatched his hand away, cramming it into his pocket.

His father hadn't noticed. His brother and mother were too ill to have seen.

But I saw it.

He shook his head, just barely. *Don't tell*, his eyes pleaded with me.

His father couldn't take another loss.

FOURTEEN

Grey

NEDRA LOOKED LIKE a ghost, and Master Ostrum didn't care.

I gave my daily report to the professor first, as usual, but when Master Ostrum flicked his hand to dismiss me before listening to Nedra's report of her day working at the hospital, I didn't move.

"It's not right," I muttered.

"Excuse me?" Master Ostrum said, his tone pitching lower.

"You're exhausting her," I said, flinging a hand toward Nedra. Her eyes widened at my outburst. "You're treating her like a slave, as if she'd already taken the robes, but she's still a student. It's been more than a week since you asked for volunteers, and since then Nedra practically lives at the quarantine hospital."

"Grey—" Nedra started.

"It's not fair, and it's not right," I insisted.

"Grey." Her voice was firmer now.

"If Ms. Brysstain would like to forgo her appointments at the hospital, she is free to. She's a volunteer, not, as you say, a slave." Master Ostrum's voice held finality, but I didn't move.

Nedra dropped a hand on my arm. "Grey, I can make my own choices," she said. "Thank you for your concern, but I'm doing what I want to do."

I growled in frustration and stood to leave. I waited at the steps outside the administration building. I wasn't sure what I wanted to tell Nedra, but when she pushed open the doors and descended the steps toward me, all words dried up in my mouth.

"I appreciate your concern," Nedra said, biting off the words, "but don't ever do that again. I can speak for myself."

I opened my mouth, then snapped it shut again. "Sorry," I muttered. We started walking across the quad to the dormitories. "But I'm right."

"Excuse me?"

"I'm right," I said, stopping and turning to her. "You're always at the hospital. You need a break."

"They need *help*, Grey." She sounded defeated. "But apparently Master Ostrum agrees with you. He told me to take tomorrow off for Burial Day."

"Good!" I said, but then I groaned aloud.

"What's wrong?" Nedra asked.

"Burial Day means no school tomorrow."

"I fail to see how that's a bad thing."

"It also means I'll have to go home in the morning to see my family for the holiday."

Nedra snorted. "And that's the most horrific possible fate for you to bear?" she guessed.

"You have no idea," I said emphatically. She laughed.

We reached the steps to the dormitories where the paths split between the male and female housing. "Well," Nedra said, "if you survive, I suppose you could come with me to church hall."

My brows scrunched in thought. "Church hall?" Oryon was the official religion of the Empire, but few actually practiced it. I barely knew where the chapel was on campus.

"You've never been to a Burial Day celebration?" Nedra asked. I shook my head. "Meet me here at four chimes," she ordered. Her eyes were alight, and for one moment, I considered leaning down and stealing a kiss before we went our separate ways. But before I could work up the courage, she said good night and left me under the glittering stars alone.

Mother had outdone herself with the spread, thanks to help, of course, from the servants. The long mahogany table in our dining room held more food than a dozen people could reasonably eat, even though only three chairs would be filled and Mother would insist on eating only half an orange and a soft-boiled egg. Spilling over the lace-lined brocade runner in the center of the table were three different loaves of bread, at least eight sparkling jars of jams in different jewel tones, a pot of herbed honey, a plate of cheeses already sliced and chilling on cold marble, four different bowls of fruit that each had a different fake bird preening in the center, two silver tureens with steam drifting up, a dozen soft-boiled eggs in bowls beside cups and a dozen more deviled and sprinkled with paprika on a platter. One whole cold chicken garnished with lemon peel and rosemary had been placed in the center of the spread.

"Greggori!" Mother cried, jumping up from the chair. Her hair was pulled back so tight it lifted the fine lines near her eyes. She held a steaming mug of tea, black with lots of sugar. Then her eyes narrowed. "Your father should be here."

"It's fine, Mother," I said, pulling out a seat at the long table and plopping into it.

Mother scratched the back of my neck until I straightened my shoulders and sat up in the chair. "I'll be right back," she said in a singsong voice, but I could detect the tension underlying her tone.

I ate three deviled eggs before the door opened again. Mother entered, her arm through Father's, her grip so tight her fingertips were white. "Your son is back from school," she said, her voice crackling like lightning. "We are having breakfast together."

"Hello, Greggori," Father said. Mother pushed him into the chair opposite me, the cold chicken on the table between us. "How is Yūgen?"

My mouth was full of egg, and by the time I swallowed, Father's eyes grew distant and uninterested. He stood and fetched himself a cup of coffee.

Mother chattered away about having the whole family back together again, but I didn't know why she clung to the idea so vehemently. Even when I hadn't been at Yūgen, we rarely ate together. Father had a standing table at the gentleman's club near the castle, and Mother never let something as simple as a meal get in the way of a party that had a good gambling room.

"What I want to know," Father said, his voice silencing Mother's, "is what you kids think about the new governor. And the Emperor." He narrowed his eyes over the cold chicken, and I remembered the whispers in the garden the night of Governor Adelaide's inauguration.

"I haven't really kept up with politics," I said. "I've been more focused on learning medicinal alchemy."

Father grunted.

"You know," I added, "there *is* a plague sweeping through Lunar Island. Didn't you see the governor's declaration?"

Mother tried to steer us to a different topic, but Father interjected. "A plague. It's just those dirty farmers and factory workers. Not a single person uphill of Castleborough has gotten so much as a sniffle. *Plague*," he said again, his voice mocking. "They don't need alchemists; they need soap."

Mother's clear voice cut across the table. "Greggori, have you met any nice girls at Yūgen?"

"Mother, it's the same girls I've been at preparatory school with since I was three," I said.

That wasn't true. But sitting at this glittering table with my parents made me want to keep Nedra a secret, protecting her from their elitism and judgment.

"And none of you kids has even noticed the Emperor's still holed up at the castle like a coward? That the governor's distracting everyone from her policies by blowing this plague out of proportion?" Father continued. His hand gripped a dull knife, jam leaking down one side.

"We're not completely ignorant, Father," I said. I'd heard Salis and Tomus talking. Salis had always been a history nut, but she was taking her studies of Bennum Wellebourne to new heights, recasting his rebellion as something heroic, not horrific. Treason was treason, even if it was dressed up as righteous rebellion. "Tomus said—"

Father grunted in approval. "I like that Tomus boy."

"You should bring him with you during winter holiday," Mother added.

"But I don't care what he thinks. What do *you* think?" Father demanded. There was an eager light in his eyes, a hunger I didn't recognize. The meeting at the governor's inauguration had been a test; this was an offer.

"Do you really believe we're on the brink of revolution? Lunar Island is not 'suffering under the chains of oppression,'" I said, rolling my eyes as I repeated Tomus's argument.

"Taxes have increased exponentially—" Father started.

"Good," I snapped back. "Maybe they could go toward helping alleviate the overcrowded quarantine hospital. Or," I added, my eyes narrowing, "the taxes could buy some soap, as you so eloquently put it."

"They can buy their own damn soap!" Father said, slamming the jam jar on the table so hard that the chicken quivered.

"Oh, what does it matter?" I shot back, my own voice rising. Mother groaned, but I ignored her. "What will it take for you to realize there are more important things than politics?"

Without another word, Father pushed away from the table and left the room. He ignored Mother's pleas to stay.

"Well, this is simply wonderful," Mother said sarcastically, throwing her napkin on the table. Her shoulders hunched in defeat.

No one deserves such aggressive indifference, I thought. I stood and wrapped my arms around my mother's shoulders. She leaned into me, her body relaxing. Then she patted my hand. "Go on," she said. "Go back to school."

I didn't look back as I left the house where I had been raised. It had never been my home anyway.

FIFTEEN

Nedra

ERNESTA HAD SENT me several quick notes throughout the semester. They were little things, dashed off in her barely legible scrawl, the ink smudged as if she wrote them only moments before giving them to the postmaster. *Mama burned all the bread because she couldn't quit reading—I see where you get it from,* she'd write, or, *Papa just got back and brought me jelly candies. I ate them all and left you none; that's what you get for leaving me.* She followed the last one with a quick doodle of herself, cheeks stuffed with sweets, and me, clutching my stomach as if I were starving.

But the letter I'd received for Burial Day was thick, pages and pages not just from her, but from Mama and Papa as well.

Reading their words made me homesick. This would be my first holiday without them. I had never wanted to spend my entire life in my little village beyond the carmellina gate, but I also wished I could slip my family into my pocket and take them with me. I folded the pages and placed them back in the envelope, then tucked it safely into my hip bag. That would have to do.

Grey was already waiting for me, sitting on a bench outside the dormitories. His head was bent, his hands clasped over his knees, almost like he was praying, but there was a hollow expression in his eyes belying that idea. When he looked up at me, his smile cracked across every dark thought that had been etched on his face.

I wove my arm through his and led him to the gate. "How was breakfast with your parents?" I asked.

Grey groaned.

I couldn't help but laugh. "They can't be that bad."

"They really can."

My fingers clenched in the crook of his arm.

"Sorry," he said, looking down at me. "I know you miss your parents."

I offered him a grateful smile, touched that he noticed what had remained unspoken.

"So, what does a village celebration of Burial Day entail?" Grey asked.

"You'll see," I chirped. "I asked around at the hospital—this city isn't completely devoid of celebrations."

We veered downhill, following the same street that I had traveled when I first arrived in Northface Harbor. We heard the revelry before we saw it. The street was overrun with people. Everyone who could play an instrument did, the sound of joy made audible. The warm scent of honey bread wove through the streets. It didn't take us long to find a cart selling buns for a copper. Grey bought us each one, then went back and bought five more.

"Told you they were good," I said, smirking.

"How have I never had this before?" Crumbs flew from his mouth, his cheeks puffed like a chipmunk's.

I laughed, drawing him deeper into the festivities. We passed a mob of dancers and had to weave our arms through theirs, kicking our legs up high in the traditional skeleton dance as we moved through the crowd, winding past a group of children who tried to encircle us, chanting the nursery rhyme "Crows and Bones." Their faces were painted in black feathers and silvery skulls. I knew to break their hands and duck out of the circle before they finished singing, but Grey was trapped and had to pay the children a toll of another copper before they let him go.

"This is so much fun!" Grey shouted above the cacophony.

I grinned at him. A part of me was still sad to be without my parents, but this street festival was far larger than anything my village had ever put on, and it was a good distraction.

Old men and women walked through the crowd, handing anyone unadorned a bright red poppy-bud flower. Grey tried to offer the woman who gave him a flower another copper, but she spit at the ground, shaking her head.

"You don't pay for that," I told him, taking the bud from his hands and pinning it to his jacket.

Grey looked confused, but it was too loud to explain. How did he not know the traditions? The crimson flowers represented the blood of the war; you cannot pay for blood with coins.

"How do you celebrate Burial Day?" I asked. We were close to the dock now, and the intoxicating smell of a fish fry was drowning out the sweet, warm honey from the carts uphill. I pulled Grey to a bench that faced an empty wooden platform that had been built in the street from used pallets. The pubs along the docks had flung open their doors, serving pints on the street, but they started calling for last orders.

"It's just a day out of school," Grey said. "A break before midterms."

I gave him a dubious look.

"I *know* what Burial Day is for, obviously," he said. "It's just that no one celebrates it."

The chimes rang six times. The music died down, the dancing stopped. The loud celebrations faded away to nothing in mere moments.

"What's happening?" Grey asked me in a whisper I wouldn't have been able to hear a minute ago.

"Today's not about the party." Holidays were also holy days.

The crowd in the street parted, everyone moving to the sidewalks, leaving the cobblestone bare. A moment later, the doors of all the church halls up and down the street opened, and the Elders of each one formed a small parade, walking solemnly down the center of the lane. They mounted the wooden platform and dropped to their knees, the soft thuds echoing as loudly as bells tolling.

I slipped from the bench, letting my knees hit the paving stones. Everyone in the crowd did the same, including, after a moment of looking around, Grey.

The church halls in this part of the city comprised people from the north who'd moved south to work in the factories. They kept the old ways. The Elders chanted the prayer of Peace in Death, and my lips formed the words, murmuring them along with the hundreds of others who had gathered for the celebration. Beside me, Grey kept his head bent respectfully, but he stumbled over the words until he finally gave up. Even though the Empire's official religion was Oryon, it was clear the north was more reverent than the south.

The words were the same that my family spoke every year on Burial Day. I shut my eyes. I pretended that I was home, my knees in the dirt instead of on paving stones. I imagined that it was Nessie beside me, not Grey.

As the prayer ended, I touched Grey's elbow, letting him know we could stand again. "That was lovely," he whispered into my ear. His warm breath sent chills down my spine.

In my village, now would be the time the blacksmith passed out iron rings, and we'd all go to the burial ground and place a circle on a different grave. Burial Day was about remembering the history of Lunar Island and promising to never make the same mistakes again. Maybe that's why the north remembered it more than the south;

during Bennum Wellebourne's revolution, he took the bodies of the northerners, raising them from their graves.

There was a story about it in my great-grandmother's journal. When she was alive, there were still people who remembered seeing the dead claw their way up through the earth, their fingers bloody and broken, their eyes rotting from their heads, their jaws slack. Bennum Wellebourne needed an army to lead against the Emperor, and necromancy provided one.

Before he was captured, Wellebourne had been sailing across the Azure Sea with his undead soldiers, intending to take over the whole Empire. Because his army was dead, he let them drag along the boat behind him. They would not drown. When Wellebourne hung for his crimes, his revenants died again—the necromancer's power died with him. The bloated corpses floated to the shore, and the tides brought them to the center of the island, the place where Dilada had gotten a job to clear the forest. Villagers had gone down, identifying which of the corpses had been their brothers and sisters and mothers and fathers. They returned them to the graves they'd left and placed iron circles over the raw earth in the hopes that the old superstition would keep the dead where they had been planted.

But there were no graves in Northface Harbor; the city was too cramped to waste space on empty earth, aside from the Gardens. Cremation was more common here. As I wondered what would happen next, the Elders and acolytes of the church halls started to pass out small iron rings. A teenage boy handed Grey and me one each. A single nail, bent and hammered into a curved circle.

"What do we do with this?" Grey asked, looking at the ring in his hand. He stuck two fingers through the metal and wiggled them.

My attention, however, was on the wooden platform up the street. While the Elders were still passing out the rings, someone else had arrived at the stage. "That's the governor," I said in awe, recognizing her from the news sheets. A ripple of murmurs spread throughout the crowd; everyone shared my shock that the governor would come to the Burial Day celebration at the docks herself.

Governor Adelaide was maybe a decade older than my mother. Slender and tall, she carried herself with assurance and grace. She wore the embroidered pallium that marked her position as governor. Her hair was done up in a crown of braids; a more traditional style, one favored by farmers and factory workers—and me.

"Friends," she said, spreading her hands wide. "I am honored to be a guest of the Elders today, and to take part in the remembrance of one of the most important days in Lunar Island history."

A smattering of applause interrupted her, but most people didn't clap, either because the solemnity of the prayer still weighed on them or, like me, they were still surprised to see Governor Adelaide here.

"I know that today's celebrations are more bittersweet than they usually are. I know that times are not easy now. The plague that has swept through our community has weighed heavily on my shoulders."

I did not miss that she called it "our" community, and neither did anyone else. We were used to being ignored by the government. Even at the hospital, which was funded by the governor and had been for a century and a half, there was constant concern that the doors wouldn't remain open. Frugal Frue was stingy with potions for a reason.

"Please know that I am doing all I can," Governor Adelaide continued. Her voice choked with real emotion. "My own alchemists have been working on the plague and nothing else since I first became aware of the problem. And today, I would like to offer everyone a chance both to continue the traditions of Burial Day and to remember those we've lost more recently."

Governor Adelaide swept her hands toward the dock. Grey and I turned with the rest of the crowd and saw three barges pulling up.

Murmurs rose from the crowd again. My fingers curled around the iron ring.

"'These boats will run until sundown, or until everyone has had a chance to mourn and remember," the governor said, her voice respectful. "Those who wish to visit the city grave may. I also invite you all to join me in the church halls for prayers."

I turned back around to stare up at the governor. Her chin was tilted up, her spine straight, but it was clear that she was on the brink of crying. "It is no easy thing to lead a city faced with an enemy that cannot be fought," she said, her voice lower. "But I will fight with you all."

Cheers erupted throughout the crowd, the sound ringing out so loudly that I thought perhaps even my parents across the bay could hear it.

Grey and I were close to the docks, so we were able to board one of the barges in the first voyage across the bay. He stood at my side, his arm wrapped around me for warmth as the crowded boat plowed through the gentle waves.

Lunar Island was shaped like a crescent, the ends high above sea level and capped with cliffs, the center low with rolling hills and forests. Or, it had once held forests. Now there was a large clearing, black marks in the red soil the only remnant of the trees that had once stood there. Rather than individual graves, long trenches had been dug, filled, and covered again. Dark reddish-brown lines scarred the field in more or less straight lines. The first lines, the ones closest to the road, were only fifteen meters or so long. The mounds grew longer and longer as they neared the forest.

The barge bumped against the dock, and my stomach roiled with the movement. "It's so big," I said in a low voice, but Grey didn't hear me. I clutched my iron circle, the sharp end of the nail pricking my skin.

Working at the hospital, I had seen plenty of death, but not like this, not all at once, with the very earth etched in long tally marks to record just how much had already been lost.

Grey reached for my hand, and I wove my fingers through his, clutching him, letting his warmth root me to this moment.

As we drew closer to the graves, I tried to count the long trenches, to guess how many bodies slept under the earth, but my eyes blurred.

I thought of Jax and Ronan, who had come so desperately to the quarantine hospital from a village in the north. Was their mother in one of these unmarked trenches?

All around me, people knelt, kissing their iron nails and then pressing them into the red earth, their lips mumbling the last phrases of the Prayer for the Dead. They touched the three knots tied into the cords around their necks before they stood and headed back to the barge.

I dropped to my knees, dragging Grey down beside me. I squeezed the iron ring in my hand so hard that it hurt, but I didn't care.

I didn't say the Prayer for the Dead.

I prayed—with all my heart and soul—that my family would be safe from graves like these. It was a sin, and I knew it. I should pray for the peace of those already gone. But the other prayers spoken today would have to serve; there was no other plea in my heart.

SIXTEEN

Grey

THE BARGE WAS silent as it returned to Northface Harbor. I wrapped my arm around Nedra, holding her close as the boat pushed through a cold fog. I had never been a deeply religious person, but the murmured prayers over the mass grave weighed on me in a way I had not expected.

We climbed the hill back up to Yūgen without talking, Nedra and I both lost in our thoughts. Before we reached the gates, a group of students rushed out, Tomus at the head.

"Greggori!" he shouted, waving. Even with one word, I could tell he was well on his way to drunk. "Come with us! It's time to properly celebrate our day off!"

My fingers tightened around Nedra's hand. Tomus's gaze dropped to our clasped palms, and his eyes narrowed with disdain.

Nedra slipped free of my grasp.

"Ned—" I started.

"Go," she said in a low voice. "I want to be alone anyway."

I hesitated, but she used my uncertainty to slip through the gates of Yūgen without me.

I turned to Tomus with flashing eyes. "Now that she's gone, come with us," he said, indicating the girls behind him. "We're going to the pubs."

"We should talk," I said, my voice low.

"We should *drink*," Tomus countered, slurring the last word. "Come on. You're so boring these days."

The group of students with him were growing restless; many had already started down to the Eagle's Nest for pints. I grabbed Tomus by the arm and jerked him closer to me. "Let's talk here," I growled. A few of the lads looked back at us, but Tomus waved his hand, dismissing them.

"Fine," he said, his tone cold. "Let's talk. Let's talk about the way you've been ignoring us all for some country girl who got into Yūgen on charity. Let's talk about how she gets special treatment all the time and no one says anything."

"This isn't about Nedra," I said.

Tomus laughed bitterly. "Is it not? Because before she came along, you used to be my friend."

I bit back my retort. Friend? I supposed that was what Tomus and I had been. I felt revulsion churning in my stomach—not for him, but for myself. I hadn't known what a real friend was until I met Nedra; I had not realized how low I'd let myself sink for companionship.

"We've known each other since we were born," Tomus continued. "She's only been here a few months." He spit the words out. "I didn't know your loyalty was so weak."

Nedra's words echoed in my mind. "I *have* been loyal," I said. "I've defended you while you've been nothing but a jerk." I stared at him as if I were seeing him for the first time. "And trust me, it hasn't been easy."

"Defended me?" He rolled his eyes. "To her? Oh, thank you so much."

"People aren't worthless just because you can't use them," I said.

"Gods, you're *boring*," Tomus said again, an insult that used to make me do whatever it took to impress him.

My hands closed to fists, but I forced myself to take deep breaths. Tomus would never be my enemy, I knew that. My father was too important to his father's work.

If I acted now, it would be Nedra whom Tomus would punish. His power was limited, but she didn't deserve his attention. No one did.

"So this is how it is," Tomus said, his eyes on my fists. I made my hands relax.

"Let's go drinking," I said, taking a step down the sidewalk in the direction the other students had gone.

"No." Tomus's voice was clear, no sign of slurring. I wondered if he'd sobered up while talking to me, or if the drunkenness had been faked. So much about Tomus was just a show to manipulate the way people saw him. I had known that for almost as long as I'd known him, but I never realized before that I had only ever seen him behind a mask as well.

"You want to get serious?" he continued. "Let's get serious. You're spending all your time with your slummer girlfriend, and you have yet to see what's really important these days."

"The plague?" I asked. "Because it seems to me that you are the one who's ignoring that."

"Plague." Tomus rolled his eyes. "The docks needed purging anyway. This is Oryous's version of rat poison. I'm not talking about that, Greggori," he continued, speaking over me when I tried to interrupt. "I want to know when you'll be ready to *rise up*." He spoke the last words as if they were significant, as if I should know what they meant.

The pieces clicked in my head too slowly. "Are you talking about rebellion?" I asked, my voice dropping to a whisper.

"Of course I am!" Tomus said, shouting at me and throwing his hands up. "Are you that blind? Has your little girlfriend made you *that* oblivious?"

"Has the alcohol made you that dense?" I shot back. "You *are* drunk."

Tomus looked more disappointed in me now than he had been when talking about Nedra. "Just wait, Astor," he said, shaking his head at me. "Just you wait."

"What do you know?"

"I know enough to keep clean." Tomus tapped his nose. "I know enough to only talk to those who are *really* loyal."

"Keep your secrets," I said, exasperated. "Just leave me out of it. And Nedra."

"All right, Astor." Tomus leaned against the wall. I ducked my head, turning, and made my way back to the school. I could feel his eyes on me the whole time.

This wasn't over.

SEVENTEEN

Nedra

I HAD INTENDED to seek out the school's chapel for a moment of prayer to myself, but as soon as I passed through the gates into Yūgen, I veered to the administration building. I wasn't sure what I would do if he wasn't there, but Master Ostrum was definitely in his office—along with someone else. My eyes darted between the door and the stairs, unsure if I should stay.

There was a bang from inside the room, and I jumped.

"—Now!" a deep voice from within said.

Heavy thuds, like books slamming on a table, reverberated through the glass-and-wood door. This sounded more like a fight than a scholarly debate.

The door swung open before I could make a run for the steps, and Master Ostrum stood in the entryway. He seemed surprised to see me at first, but then his arm swung out, gesturing to me. "As you can see," he said to the other man inside, "I have a student waiting."

The man grabbed his hat—a fancy affair, with a gold crest on the band—and stormed from the room.

"Inside," Master Ostrum ordered me. Once the door was shut, he sat down at his desk. "That was Lord Anton," he said, as if the name meant something to me. I shrugged. "He ran against Governor Adelaide."

"I saw Governor Adelaide today," I said.

"Yes." Master Ostrum's voice dripped with derision. "I heard about her little stunt."

I frowned; I didn't think the governor had pulled any stunt with her speech or by providing the barges. It had been a kindness, one that was needed after the plague had hurt so many.

"You know," Master Ostrum mused, "the Lord's Council voted in Lord Anton as the next governor."

"But then why—?"

"The child Emperor appointed Adelaide instead," Master Ostrum said.

I hadn't known it was legal to overrule a vote, but I supposed anything was legal for the one who made the laws.

"You don't like them very much, do you?" I said. "The Emperor or the governor."

"No," Master Ostrum said without inflection. "He's too young and inexperienced, and he thinks only of himself. And she's a pawn."

Emperor Auguste was my age, but I could see Master Ostrum's point. *I* certainly didn't feel adequate to rule a vast empire.

"But there's nothing you can do about it," I said with a shrug.

Master Ostrum leveled me with an intense gaze. "That's your poverty speaking," he said bluntly.

I felt my cheeks heat with embarrassment. I didn't like to be reminded of just how out of place I was at Yūgen. My eyes dropped to my lap.

"Don't be ashamed, girl," Master Ostrum said. "That's just the way it is. Someone is raised poor, they don't see the system, because the system doesn't work for them. A man tells you that you have to pay a tax, you pay it because to you, the only other option is jail. Men like Greggori," he continued, raising his eyebrow when my gaze shot up at Grey's name, "taxman goes to his parents, his parents look at the law.

Find a loophole. Don't pay. Get wealthier. Then *your* family's taxes go up again.

"When you're an alchemist," Master Ostrum continued, as if he weren't slicing me up with his words, "you'll be richer than your parents. You'll start to see the system. See how it's unfair, and how it's made to be unfair. And then you'll have to decide if you want to change it or if you want to take advantage of it."

He leaned back in his chair, the wood squeaking in protest. "I thought I told you to take a holiday, Nedra," he said, his tone much gentler. "What are you doing here?"

"I can do more," I said. "To help with the plague."

Master Ostrum's lips curved up, but I wouldn't call it a smile, exactly. He stood and opened the door to his private laboratory for me, following me inside.

Instead of the experiments we'd set up, there was only a book in the center of the metal table.

Master Ostrum's fingers trailed along the open pages as he took his seat. I sat opposite him, curious. It was a slim volume, bound in deep tan leather almost the exact same hue as my skin, and while there had once been a title gilded on the cover, it had long ago faded to nothing but golden flakes in vaguely letter-shaped outlines.

As if making a decision, Master Ostrum picked the book up and thrust it in my hands.

"What is this?" I asked, gently opening the cover and turning the first few pages. They were stiff and crumbly with age, the paper beige, the ink faded to a russet color.

My fingers found the title page. *The Fourth Alchemy.*

I read the words several times before I understood what they meant. Transformative alchemy was sometimes called the "first" alchemy. Those alchemists used silver crucibles and dealt with chemistry and physics. The second alchemy was medical, with gold crucibles. The third alchemy was for transactions, a simple alchemy most merchants and bankers knew, using copper.

My eyes raised to Master Ostrum's. He looked grim. "The fourth alchemy is necromancy."

The book dropped from my hands, landing with a thud on the metal table. A tiny cloud of dust rose from the pages.

"That's illegal." I choked the words out, but they seemed long and heavy. Bennum Wellebourne's legacy had dogged me all day, from the iron rings on the graves to now.

"It's not illegal to study necromancy, just to practice it," Master Ostrum said. He closed the book and again held it out for me to take. After a moment, I did.

"We've been researching this plague a long time," Master Ostrum said. "But I don't think the answer lies in science."

"You think it lies in necromancy?" I couldn't hide the disgust in my voice.

Master Ostrum shook his head. "No," he said. "In history."

I didn't know what to say.

"You were the one who made me start seriously considering this, Nedra, although I must confess I'd worried it was the case before."

"Me?"

"Some of the phrases used in your great-grandmother's journal piqued my interest," he said. "And when you mentioned your history study group in your report, I was reminded of some old books students don't have access to."

He stood, disappearing into his office again, leaving me with the book on necromancy. I put it on the table. I didn't want to touch it.

When he returned, Master Ostrum laid a heavy tome in front of me, opening to a page that he had marked. I gasped at what I saw.

Illustrated on one side was the figure of a bare-chested man. Blackness spread out over his heart. It was definitely not somthire like in the drawing in Flora's book.

"This," Master Ostrum said, "is an illustration made by one of the first colonists. Rayburn Alfinn, Lord Commander to Bennum Wellebourne when he was governor of Lunar Island. Alfinn fought beside Wellebourne until he crossed the line into necromancy, then became one of his greatest opponents. It's hard to find primary sources from that time period; much has been lost, and the few remaining works are locked up in the governor's treasury, inaccessible even to scholars."

He frowned again, and I remembered his disdain for Governor Adelaide. After seeing her this evening, it was hard to share the sentiment.

"I was able to dig this up thanks to a few friends," he added.

I stared at the illustration. It *looked* like the plague, but I wasn't certain. My eyes skimmed the old text. The writing was out of date and particularly florid, but the crux of what was written was clear.

"And you think maybe the plague was . . ." I paused, thinking, remembering my history lessons. Wellebourne's treason had very nearly been successful—but only *after* he had raised his army of the dead. Prior to that, the conflict had remained grounded on Lunar Island, split between the north, which sided with him, and the south, which was against. He was only able to unify the island with his reign of terror, and it was only with the reanimated corpses that he had the strength to be a threat to the Empire.

"When he needed a larger army of revenants," Master Ostrum said, "he simply created more dead people."

My stomach churned, thinking of the long graves in the field at the center of the island. There were hundreds—thousands—dead now. "But there is no war," I pointed out. "No need for an army of revenants. We're all Imperial."

But even as I said the words, Salis's history study group rose in my mind. Not everyone wanted to stay Imperial.

"It's just a theory now," Master Ostrum said. "But an angle worth exploring. Read this." He handed me *The Fourth Alchemy* again, pressing it into my hands. "Please."

A few months ago, I would have thrown this book down in disgust and walked away—maybe even returned home, where the only books I knew reminded me of my father. But now . . .

My fingers wrapped around the spine of the book.

Now I was willing to try anything.

EIGHTEEN

Grey

Two weeks passed, the days turning into a blur as we all focused on writing our midterm essays. There was no more precious real estate than a table at the library.

Every night, I gave my reports to Master Ostrum, detailing what I had read about and how I intended to shape my essay. Nedra talked about the plague. She brought news sheets to our sessions, reading aloud accounts of Governor Adelaide speaking on the steps of the castle, calling upon all alchemists in the city and beyond to aid in developing a cure or a way to prevent the disease from spreading further. The Emperor had barricaded himself in his private quarters. The news sheets claimed that he sent constant advice and aid to the governor and stayed in order to help, but the rumor mill eviscerated him for not doing more in the island's time of need, mocking his cowardice at quarantining himself.

A few factory owners and merchants had grown ill. The Governor's Hospital started inspecting people before admittance. Any signs of blackness on the skin meant the patient was rejected and sent directly to the quarantine hospital, no matter their social standing. The quarantine hospital, meanwhile, was relocating any patients who didn't have the Wasting Death. The mentally infirm would be sent to a sanitarium on the mainland in the coming weeks, and other illnesses were being treated by apothecaries directly.

A few professors quit giving lectures at Yūgen—dedicating their attention to the illness—which came at a fortuitous time for those of us who were so focused on writing our midterm reports that we had stopped attending lectures.

Everyone was on edge the day our midterm grades were due. The nervous chatter died down as soon as Master Ostrum opened the door and walked to his desk, a box full of folders in his hands. Inside each one was a student essay—mine was twenty-two pages long—detailing all we'd learned so far in the semester and how we intended to continue to focus our studies.

Master Ostrum handed Nedra's folder back to her first. It was considerably smaller than the rest, including mine, which Master Ostrum dropped on my desk unceremoniously. I flipped it open and saw one word scratched across the top: *Acceptable.*

My hands curled into fists. Acceptable? *Acceptable?* I had uncovered books the librarians hadn't even known existed in my research. I'd translated ancient alchemical runes myself. I'd even reached out to some of Father's connections for interviews. My essay was far, far more than *acceptable.* I flipped through the pages, hoping to see some other note, a check mark, a smudge in the ink to indicate he'd read past the first page.

Nothing.

"What's the meaning of this?" Tomus asked loudly as he looked inside his own folder.

"Silence!" Master Ostrum barked. Tomus—for once—bit his tongue and shriveled into his desk, although his cheeks were flushed and his eyes bright with anger.

Once the folders had all been distributed, Master Ostrum turned to the class. "For many of you," he said, "this is the last time we will interact."

I straightened in my desk.

"I have asked for reassignments for the students I will no longer be advising. Your new masters are listed in your folders."

Tomus glowered. "My parents didn't donate a hall of laboratories to Yūgen for me to be advised by Professor Pushnil!" he said, his voice loud.

Master Ostrum leveled a cool look at Tomus. "That," he said with a shrug, "isn't my problem." And with that, he left the lecture hall.

The class erupted into chaos. Tomus stood and shoved his desk away, kicking at it when it fell over. Then he noticed Nedra, sitting on the edge of her chair, stuffing her folder into her bag.

"You're still with Ostrum, aren't you?" Tomus's voice was low and cold, but it drew every eye to him.

Nedra stood and swung her bag onto her shoulder. She very distinctly tried not to meet his gaze. Nedra only made it a few steps before Tomus maneuvered around his desk and stood in front of her. "He didn't drop you, did he?" he asked, leaning in close to her face.

Everyone was still. Watching.

Nedra shook her head no.

Tomus made a noise deep in the back of his throat, more snarl than laugh. "Of course not!" he said, sweeping his arm toward the rest of the class. "When Ostrum said 'many of us' were being dropped, what he really meant was everyone but you, right? Anyone else not being reassigned?"

I looked behind me—every other person in the lecture hall glared at Nedra. I was tempted to lift up the cover of my folder and see if I'd somehow missed a reassignment slip there, but I knew I hadn't missed it. Master Ostrum had not only kept Nedra—he'd kept me as well.

"What I want to know," Tomus snarled, pushing his fingertips into Nedra's shoulders, "is just what you do with Ostrum to make him want to keep you and no one else."

At those last three words—*no one else*—Nedra's eyes flicked to me. *She knows I'm still with Master Ostrum, too,* I thought. But how? How would she know who else Master Ostrum kept unless . . . ?

Unless she knew he was cutting the other students, and she asked him to keep me.

Tomus was an ass but a clever one. He watched me with narrowed eyes, and I was certain he'd guessed what Nedra's glance meant.

Nedra ducked her head and tried to move away from Tomus, but he stepped in front of her.

"Please move," she said, her eyes on the open door at the other end of the lecture hall.

"*Please move,*" Tomus mocked.

"Look, I don't know why Master Ostrum reassigned everyone," Nedra said, throwing up her hands. "Maybe he kept me because I actually give a damn about the work we're doing."

Tomus's eyes were on me when he said, "Maybe."

But he didn't move out of Nedra's way.

She hefted her bag. I could see the determination turning her bones to steel. She shouldered past Tomus, making a point to knock into his shoulder. His face purpled with rage, and he spun around to stop her again, but I lunged forward, grabbing his shoulder and holding him back.

"You too, Astor?" Tomus said in a low, angry voice. He shook his shoulder free from my grasp and stepped away from me.

As Nedra escaped through the door, the rest of the class dissipated. Without an object for their anger, there was little point staying in the lecture hall.

I stepped away from Tomus, but I hesitated before turning my back on him in order to pick up my bag. When I straightened, we were alone in the lecture hall. He hadn't moved from his spot where Nedra shoved him.

"It's not right," Tomus said, a grim set to his jaw. "She comes in a year behind us, is bumped to the bear class, and then steals the professor from us. From the rest of us, I mean."

"It's not her fault," I said. "Nedra doesn't make Master Ostrum's decisions for him."

He watched me for a moment, not speaking, but so intent that I felt too awkward to leave.

"My father hates your father," he said finally.

"I'm . . . sorry?" I said, confused by the change in conversation.

"He always said Linden Astor was useful because of his connections and power, but that he would use anyone and anything to get ahead. You're not like him." He paused. "But you're still going to get ahead."

"That's not what this is about."

"That's what everything is about."

I started for the door.

"Are you coming to my party tonight?" Tomus said, holding me back.

"I don't know," I said warily. I'd been planning on it, but after this morning . . .

"Come." Tomus sounded sincere. "Bring your little girlfriend."

"She's not my—"

Tomus tensed, as if my denial was a personal insult.

"Come," he said again, his voice brooking no argument.

I found Nedra in the library. She was in the restricted section, where the oldest records were kept.

"Whew," I said, sitting down beside her.

"What's wrong?"

"I thought you might be at the hospital and that I'd missed you." I spoke in a whisper not because we were in the library, but because the books were so ancient looking I worried they would fall apart if I breathed too hard.

Nedra wore white cotton gloves as she carefully turned the page of a book bound in cracked and flaking leather. "I'm going there after lunch," she said.

I should go with her. I knew I should. I couldn't recognize the twisting reluctance in my gut to stay on campus. Was it fear? My father's prejudice rang in my ears: *They need soap.* I shook my head. Dirt was not a virus.

"What are you doing?" I asked.

"Research." Nedra did not look up from her book, but I couldn't see how there were any answers for a new disease in a book as old as that.

"So," Nedra said, leaning back from the tome. "Are you going to ask me to Tomus's party?"

I blinked several times. "I—you know about that?"

"I heard the others talking. Although I doubt Tomus wants me there, not after this morning."

"He does," I said slowly. "He said he does."

"Then he's either planning something horrible for me, or he wants to suck up to me as he thinks I may be useful to him in the future."

She seemed to have summed him up rather succinctly. "The latter, I think," I said. "I'm not sure, but . . ."

Nedra nodded. "It's more his style." She paused. "I think I'll go."

"Are you sure?"

"I want to show him that he can't intimidate me."

I sat down beside her, and she read in silence for a few moments before turning the page.

"Why did you ask for me to stay with Master Ostrum?" I blurted out.

She didn't try to deny it. "You have to ask?"

I looked down at my hands. I wanted to hear her say it.

"Tonight," I said slowly. "Would you like to come with me? Together, I mean?"

Her eyes met mine, alight with hope. "Yes," she said simply.

NINETEEN

Nedra

GREY'S INVITATION KEPT me warm as the ferry drew me across the bay—at least until the winds picked up. The days were getting colder; fall was almost as harsh as winter on Lunar Island, with all the wind and cold but none of the snow. I wrapped my cloak tighter around my frame, breathing into the cloth, my breath warming my face. My smile was hidden by my collar as I remembered the way Grey had said *together.*

My boat docked, and everyone disembarked. I was halfway up the stone steps when I heard the sounds of another boat arriving. I turned, surprised; the ferry couldn't have returned that soon.

It wasn't the ferry to Blackdocks. This ferry had come from the north.

I rushed back down the steps. I didn't recognize the skipper, but she was grateful for the help as I secured the mooring and then helped the people inside the ferry disembark. The ones who could walk got off first, then I called for stretchers for the dozen or so people whose legs were black and twisted. Potion makers and aides rushed down the steps toward me.

"Thank goodness you're here," one of the potion makers—Lufti—told me as I helped him load a middle-aged woman onto the stretcher. "We're so backed up today."

"Where did this ferry come from?" I asked, looking to the skipper.

"Hart," she said.

"I'm from the village beyond the ivy gate," the woman on the stretcher said,

"'The ones that can, come to Hart. I take them here." The skipper started pulling up the moorings now that her boat was empty of passengers.

I helped Lufti carry the woman from the village beyond the ivy gate up the stone steps. It was a perilous climb, and even thought she was strapped to the stretcher, the bindings pulled against her diseased leg. She moaned.

"It will be okay," I promised her, trying not to jostle the stretcher too much.

Her laugh was bitter. "No, it won't," she said, and I didn't have the heart to lie to her again.

When we reached the heavy mahogany doors, another aide took over for me. I was left in the foyer, my arms aching, trying to catch my breath. My mind swirled. The ivy gate was just a half day's ride from my own village. Papa went there often.

I shook myself. There was no time to worry.

I had work to do.

I checked in with the front desk and was sent immediately to help process the new patients. They were sick and scared and overwhelmed and far from home, and at least my accent matched theirs. Mentally, I tracked the villages. None closer to home than the village beyond the ivy gate. I tried to tell them that they were safe now, that the best alchemists in the land were here.

The first person to die that day was a baby.

The mother had fallen sick when she was close to giving birth. She'd hoped it was late enough in the pregnancy to save her child, but the little girl had been born with black swirls over her heart. The mother had given birth just the day before, rushing straight from her labor bed to the boat in Hart. She was still bleeding from the pregnancy, her skin ashen, her eyes sunken. She held her baby with one arm—her other was dead and black and twisted, the fingers useless.

Her scream ripped through the hospital, long and loud and filled with such pure anguish that everyone turned to witness the manifested sorrow.

I rushed over with the other potion makers and Alchemist Addrina. Addrina tried to get the mother to let go of the little bundle in her arms, but she finally had to pry the child from the woman's hands. The alchemist passed the baby to me. Her flesh was cold to the touch. She had been dead for some time, probably since the ferry ride, and the mother had somehow been able to deceive herself until that moment in the crowded hospital hallway.

"She's mine!" the woman screamed, snatching the baby from me, clutching the tiny body to her chest, choking back dry sobs. The woman dropped to the floor, cradling her child against her.

Addrina injected something into the woman's neck, and in a few minutes her body grew slack. It looked as if she were sleeping. As if they both were.

Monkswort, I thought, looking at the syringe. A mild sedative. It allowed the aides to come and take the baby away, put the woman on a gurney, and find her a room.

But she will still wake up eventually, I thought, tears pricking my eyes.

"Nedra!" Alchemist Addrina barked at me. I'd only worked with her a handful of times before, but she was always kind, respectful of my work with Master Ostrum. She'd trained under him, too. "There's work to do," she said, her shoulders stiff. Addrina had never been so abrupt before.

This life was wearing on us all.

I nodded tightly, clutching my golden crucible. "Bring me a cart," I told the nearest potion maker. "I'll make surgical relief rounds."

The potion maker went running, meeting me in the hall with a cart full of rats. I went from bed to bed, siphoning off pain from those recovering from recent amputation, pouring the pain into the rats. The work was hard, and I began seeing spots in the edges of my vision, but I forced myself to continue.

"It's you."

I looked into the face of the boy on the bed. His arm was gone just above his elbow. I knew him. My mind struggled to find his name, the connection of who he was.

And then a man roared at me. He lunged over the boy's bed, his hands grappling for my throat. "You!" he screamed, his voice raw and ragged.

I scrambled back, dropping my crucible with an audible crash on the tile floor. There was nowhere to run—the room was crowded with beds. I fell against the bed of a sleeping girl whose leg had been amputated, jostling her so roughly that she woke up screaming. The man's eyes were wild as he pushed aside the nearest bed. His fingers wrapped around my arm, digging into my flesh. "You, *you*!" he raged at me.

Others had realized something was wrong, and two large boys who worked as aides were trying to get through the maze of beds to come help me.

The man still held on to my arm, so when he raised his other hand and slammed it, open, against my jaw, I couldn't pull away, and I took the full force of the teeth-clacking blow. My vision blackened, and I tasted the sharp metallic sting of blood on my lips.

"Hey!" one of the aides shouted. "Let her go!"

The man did—but so abruptly that I fell. He dropped on top of me, one of his knees pinning my arm. I tried to scoot away, but he leaned over, pressing his weight against me. "Your fault," he snarled. "It's *all* your fault." He punctuated each word with snapping teeth, drawing closer to me until he was just millimeters from my face.

Finally—*finally*—the aides arrived. One knocked the man away. I rolled under the nearest bed, my body trembling, as the other aide held down the man's arm. He kicked and thrashed, bucking his body, his head smacking the tile floor so loudly that it sounded like pottery cracking.

"Get help!" one of the aides shouted.

A potion maker arrived as if from thin air, holding a bottle of tincture of blue ivy.

"Not that," I croaked. That medicine was too expensive, too hard to come by. The patients needed it.

The man's body stilled. He wasn't knocked out, but his pupils grew large, and his twisted rage melted into a placid expression.

"He didn't mean it!" the boy on the bed called as the aides dragged him away. "He's just—" His father was already gone from the room. The boy's eyes fell on me. "Angry. He's just angry."

I stood, trembling. The potion maker helped me up. "Are you okay?" she asked.

"I'm fine."

"I can give you some to help calm you—" She held the bottle to me.

"I'm fine, Gella," I said again, shaking her hands off me. My nerves were shot, but I wouldn't take blue ivy from the patients.

She looked concerned, but finally shrugged and walked away.

My hands trembled as I reached down and picked up the golden crucible. I put it back on the table. I could feel the other patients' eyes on me.

"I'm sorry," the boy said.

And I recognized him, finally. "Ronan."

The boy smiled weakly. When I had met him and his family, he'd had his other arm. And he'd had a mother and a brother.

"They didn't—?" I asked.

He shook his head.

I had known the mother wouldn't live, but I'd hoped the younger brother might . . . but now they both were gone, and Ronan's father, Dannix, blamed me.

"It's okay," Ronan told me as I dropped a rat into the crucible. "It's not too bad. You don't have to help me; go to one of the others . . ."

I placed one hand on his residual limb and held the golden crucible with the other. I chanted the runes, focusing on them as they burned white. I took as much of the boy's pain as I could, but I knew it wasn't enough.

It was never enough.

Alchemist Addrina came in to relieve me of duty soon after. No doubt, from her worried gaze, someone had told her about the man who'd attacked me.

"Go home," she told me in a low voice.

"I can do more," I started.

She shook her head. "Go home," she said again. "That's an order."

I swallowed. The inside of my cheek was still raw from where my teeth had smashed into it, but I'd siphoned some of my own pain into the rat while I'd worked on Ronan. I hoped my jaw wouldn't bruise. All around me, people were coming to terms with amputated limbs, lost loved ones, or a doomed foretelling of their own death, and here I was worried about looking pretty for my party.

"I can—" I started, but Addrina whirled around on me.

"I'm not saying it again."

I ducked my head and muttered my thanks to her. I trudged down the hall, trying to block the sounds of the patients—crying, bargaining to keep their dead limbs, praying for a salvation that wouldn't come. I couldn't bear to look at the silent patients, the ones who had already given up.

Before I left, I paused at the desk. I needed a friendly face.

"Where is Mrs. Rodham?" I asked the receptionist. She had been the one who'd brought me to Ronan and his family; she would understand.

The receptionist's eyes watered with pity. "Oh, Nedra," she said. "Didn't anyone tell you? Last night. It—her eyes turned green, and—" A green film over the eyes meant the plague was in the brain. There was no cure. It was certain death.

I walked away, unwilling to hear anything else.

TWENTY

Grey

"GREGGORI ASTOR," TOMUS called as soon as I pushed open the door and stepped onto the administration building's flat roof. Tiny oil lamps decorated the rooftop, and someone had brought a gramophone to play music until enough musicians arrived to put together a band.

"Tomus," I said, by way of greeting.

Tomus snorted. His breath stank of ale, and there was a pale brown stain of liquid on the front of his shirt. He'd started celebrating early, it seemed, but I knew him well enough to know when his drinking was for fun and when he used it to drown his anger.

"It's not that big of a deal," I said. "Professor Pushnil is every bit as respected as Master Ostrum, and—"

"Easy for you to say," Tomus growled, but then his face cleared. "It's fine. I'm fine. I may be an ass, but I'm an honest ass. Your father is in politics. You're moving up the ranks. I'm not going to toss you out." He leaned in closer, his eyes struggling to focus on mine. "Truce. For you and the slummer. But just you remember this," he said. "I've done you a favor."

A favor? Him? I owed him nothing just because he decided I was too valuable to pick a fight with.

"And there she is!" Tomus shouted, tipping his mug as Nedra stepped onto the roof. I rushed to her, ignoring Tomus.

"Don't let them see any fear," I whispered, taking her elbow and steering her near the gramophone, where people wouldn't be able to overhear us.

She shot me a look I couldn't quite place. "I never do," she said. Then she shook me off her arm and moved to the edge of the party. Her body was stiff, her face too schooled. Something was wrong—something more than Tomus being an ass.

"Wounded puppy, you are." I hadn't realized Tomus had approached me again; the gramophone was louder than I'd thought.

Soon, the band started up, and the real party began. It was a whirl of ale and noise and furious motion as we all spun atop the roof. The entire world was at our feet, or so it felt, and we were a storm about to be unleashed upon it.

Except Nedra. Nedra sat on the edge of the roof, her feet dangling over dangerously. The bright glow of Yūgen's clock tower illuminated the rooftop dance floor, but Nedra's eyes were on a different clock, one halfway across the bay.

"Come dance," I said, holding out my hand to her.

She shook her head. "This isn't the kind of dancing I'm used to," she said.

"Not much dancing in your village?"

She smiled. "Not this kind, anyway."

"What kind of dancing did you do?" I asked.

If she noticed my flirting, she ignored it, turning back to look out toward the bay, to the clock tower in the distance and the quarantine hospital beneath it.

"Dance with me?" I asked again, more urgency in my voice.

I could feel the others watching us. I was starting to get used to the way people looked at us, the way their eyes slid from me to Nedra, a question never spoken but always present about why we were together. But we *weren't* together, not like that, not yet, even if . . .

Finally, after what felt like ages, Nedra stood. She placed her hand in mine. My whole body relaxed, and she laughed at me.

"I'll tell you a secret," Nedra said, standing up on her tiptoes to whisper in my ear. Her breath made the tiny hairs on the back of my neck stand up, made my heart race, made my body forget that anyone was watching us. "I learned a long time ago that as long as you don't care what others think of you, you're much, much happier. And besides, no one ever really cares about anyone but himself."

Well, that just wasn't true. I whirled Nedra around, relishing the feel of her body pressed against mine, then tilted her so she could see the crowd dancing on the roof, and the eyes that watched us.

"That girl's staring," I said in a low voice, nodding subtly to a girl standing by the clockface.

"Not at us," Nedra said, her voice much louder. "She's looking in our direction, sure, but she's not really thinking about us. She's wondering if she should dance, too. Her feet are tired and she wants a break, but she's not sure what others will think if she leaves. And that guy?" She nodded to Ervin, who leaned down to whisper something to his partner as he stared at us. "He's asking his boyfriend when he thinks they can leave and no one will notice. And her? She's upset that she didn't eat more before coming up; her stomach hurts. And he's worried people will notice the mustard stain on his shirt. No one cares about you, about us, not really. They may use us as words to fill the silence because they can't think of anything else to say, but we are not their true focus."

She wrapped her arm around my neck. "So quit worrying about what others think, Grey," she said in a soft voice. "Worry about what *you* want."

I'd gotten used to the hard glint in her eyes, her stiff spine, the way she never let herself betray an ounce of emotion in front of others.

But she had emotion now. There was fire in her eyes.

A fire for me.

My body stilled. The whole damn world stilled. Because she had said my name like it meant something to her.

She looked at me, and it was as if she had only just then realized that she'd let her walls come down for a moment. She stopped dancing, and she glanced around, and she saw that I was right.

Everyone was watching us.

She took one step back, and then another. And then she turned around and fled, away from the party, away from the prying eyes of our classmates.

Away from me.

TWENTY-ONE

Nedra

THE LETTER IN my pocket weighed a million pounds. It clattered against my leg, it bruised my skin, it threatened to crush me under its weight.

I hadn't been expecting the slim little envelope. The letter from home that came in time for Burial Day had been large enough to sustain me for weeks. But when I'd finally gotten home after such a disastrous day at the hospital, I'd seen my sister's handwriting, and my heart had surged with hope. I needed her cheerful voice in my head. I needed it to drown out the screams of the mother whose baby had died, the rage of Ronan's father, the taste of my own blood on my teeth.

I opened it again now.

Dearest Nedra, it started, in Ernesta's almost illegible script. For a page, she talked about small things. How she hoped I was happy, how Mama burned the bread and she and Papa ate it anyway to spare Mama's feelings, how a new kitten had taken residence in Jojo's stall.

Then she said that Kava had died. The shoemaker's apprentice, the one she planned to flirt with when I left for Yūgen.

Her fingers turned black, Neddie, she wrote. *Withered up like dead sticks. She said it hurt so much, but then she didn't feel it at all anymore. And then she died.*

She scratched something out after that. Heavy black ink, gouged into the page so hard that it had started to rip.

Maybe it's best you're not here now. Her words bit at me, a wolf nipping at my heels. *I worry about Papa all the time. He won't quit going out with his book cart, even though so many villages are draped in black bunting, warning people not to enter.*

She had crossed through something else then, a little less violently, but not more legible.

I worry, she wrote instead.

Nessie *never* worried. It wasn't her style. *I* was supposed to be the twin who worried for the both of us.

It was too easy here in the city. Too easy to forget about the bustling world beyond the walls of Yūgen. Too easy to believe that I had done enough, that the plague existed in the hospital but not out there. Not where they were.

Too easy to put an iron circle on the graves, and promise myself it would never be *them.*

You! Dannix had roared. *It's all your fault!*

After I read the letter the first time, there had still been about an hour before I needed to go to the party. I washed my skin and imagined the soap could seep into my soul. And then I read the book Master Ostrum had given to me. I read the whole thing, cover to cover, and I was almost late to the party. Every time I heard Dannix's voice again, I forced more words from *The Fourth Alchemy* into my head.

I had tried to pretend the letter didn't exist, at least for the night. But it had been there the whole time, in my pocket, blacker and heavier than coal. It dragged me down like an anchor, pulling me under the waves until I couldn't breathe.

One night, I had promised myself. I would give myself one night to forget.

Just the one.

But even that had proven too much.

TWENTY-TWO

Grey

I CHASED AFTER her. I didn't care what the others thought, the whispers that tried to follow me as I ran down the steps of the clock tower. I chased after her, and the only thing in my head was the hope I could find her before whatever magic had made her open up to me disappeared.

By the time my feet hit the grass, she was gone. I thought I saw her near the statue of Bennum Wellebourne, so I ran down the quad, but she wasn't there.

The clock on top of the administration building tolled the time—midnight. Echoing across the bay, the clock in the quarantine hospital rang.

And suddenly, I knew where Nedra had gone.

It was late, but not too late for the ferries.

The hospital at this hour was a different creature than when I had visited during Master Ostrum's morning lectures. With each new day, there was hope. But a hospital at night was a desolate place. Families gathered in small clusters in the foyer, praying for the dark to last forever because they knew this would be the last night with the person they loved still in this world. Mini tragedies played out on the edges of the hospital—a couple holding each other near the door, a family with three small, tired children, pulling chairs into a row to make a

bed for the young ones to sleep on while the adults whispered among
themselves.

I approached the receptionist. "Who are you here to see?" she
asked, pulling the patient registry closer to her.

I opened my mouth, unsure of how to answer. "Er—" I started. "Not
a patient. Someone who volunteers here? Her name is Nedra Bryss—"

"Oh, she went up the clock tower," the receptionist said, pointing
to the spiral staircase. Her eyes narrowed at me.

"Nedra's here?" a potion maker asked, leaning over. "That girl is
so sweet."

The receptionist still seemed skeptical of me. "She looked upset,"
she said.

The potion maker bristled.

"We're friends," I promised, holding my hands up defensively.

The receptionist jerked her thumb to the stairs, dismissing me.
My legs ached by the time I reached the top. While the clock tower
at the administration building opened onto the roof, the stairs at the
hospital brought me to a small platform behind the large clockface.
Time was shown in reverse through milky glass, and the giant gears
and hanging pendulums churned behind the steps. Two small doors
stood on either side, enabling people to step out onto a small observation platform and walk across, like the little mechanical dolls on
clocks from Doisha that marched out every hour on the hour.

I half expected Nedra to be outside, on the platform, watching
the city illuminated by oil lamps and starlight. But she wasn't. She sat
under the clockface, her head leaning back against the large number
six, her eyes watching the gears whirl, tick-tick-ticking away the time.

The easy openness from the party was gone. Whatever whimsy
had infected her had now melted into pensiveness. She stared at the
clock mechanics with morose sadness.

"Hello," I said.

Her eyes remained fixed on the clock's gears, whirring, ticking, moving inexorably forward, one second at a time.

I didn't know what else to say, so I sat down beside her. She leaned her head down onto my shoulder, and a wave of warmth washed over me.

"I don't have time for this," she said in a whisper.

"For what?" I asked.

She didn't look at me when she answered. "For you."

Her head pressed gently against my shoulder. Her whole body leaned into me; if I moved, she'd fall.

I wanted to wrap my arms around her, to pull her close, but this moment was so fragile that I was afraid moving would break it.

Just thinking it, though, must have been too much, because Nedra pulled away. She wrapped her arms around her legs and rested her chin on her knees, and still she watched the gears tick away. "I *don't* have time for this," she repeated, a little louder now, with a little more conviction.

I couldn't rip my eyes away from her. "The plague isn't your fault, and it's not your responsibility."

Nedra didn't answer for a long time. "I wanted to escape my village," she said finally. "I wanted to see what else was out there. I knew there was a sickness spreading, and I wanted to help with that, I did, but I also wanted to escape." She watched the gears tick by. "But I always thought I would go back."

My heart sank at that. It was impossible for me to envision Nedra in some obscure, nameless village.

Her head dropped onto her knees. "My father is a bookseller," she said, her voice so low I could barely hear her. "He has a wagon and he goes from village to village, selling books. Some written by us, some written by people on the mainland, some even from differ-ent nations in the Empire. Everyone knows him." She sighed. "The very best books—the oldest, rarest books—he keeps those in the house. And my sister and I, we'd read them every night when he was on the road. She always liked the fairy tales. I always read the textbooks."

"No wonder you like the library so much," I said, half joking, but she didn't smile.

"He told me about the plague first—not that he called it that. Papa saw the sick. Some of the villages in the far north hung black flags, warning people not to come. Papa started carrying around news and potions, along with his books." She dared a glance at me. "It's only a matter of time before he falls ill. He's trying to help; he won't quit. 'If I don't bring them books, they won't have books,'" she said, lower-ing her voice to sound like her father. "He's distributing potions, too, and whatever else he can get from Hart to help the sick. But he thinks books are the most important thing in the world."

"He's not wrong," I said gently. "It was his books that brought you to me."

She bit her lip but didn't say anything for a long moment.

"I have one year," she finally said. "One year to learn as much as I can. That's all the scholarship I was given allows for. Maybe I'll get another one, maybe not—I'm not sure. But I have to make this one year count. I have to learn all I can, so I can do . . . something. Help. Somehow."

I studied medicinal alchemy because I wasn't good enough at math to study transactional alchemy, and government work bored me, and I wanted to avoid politics in an effort to purge any remnant of my father from my future. I liked the idea of being a top alchemist at the Governor's Hospital. I liked the prestige and the gold that came from it. I'd chosen my area of studies for myself.

I lowered my head. I couldn't be more different from Nedra.

"It's not on you," I said finally. "Maybe we were slow to recognize the problem, but the top alchemists in the city are working on the Wasting Death now. You don't have to do it all yourself."

Nedra just shook her head, her chin bumping along her knees. "They don't really care," she muttered. "The only sick people are those this city doesn't mind disposing of anyway."

I took a deep breath. "I'll help," I said. "You've been volunteering here during almost all of your free time, and I haven't pulled my weight. Let's work together. I'll come with you. I'll volunteer, too."

"I'm going with Master Ostrum to the factories tomorrow," she said.

"I'll be there."

Nedra turned to me. I tried to read her eyes. Did I see hope? Or defeat? Or . . . or something else? I could feel the tension coiling between us, the questions unasked.

I leaned forward, giving her time to pull away.

She didn't.

My lips pressed against hers, hesitant, wary. She reached up, her body turning toward mine, her hand snaking up my arm, around my shoulder, to my neck, pulling me closer. Our kiss deepened. My fingers tangled in her braids; hers grappled at my back.

And then she broke away, turning her face, struggling to stand up and move away from me. She wrapped her arms around her body, facing the wall.

I stood, too. When I touched her shoulder, she jerked away from me. "I can't," she whispered.

"You said before that the people of your village don't dance like we do," I said, trying to sound casual, as if her words hadn't just sliced me open. "Show me."

She looked back at me, a hint of a smile on her face.

"It's just a dance," I added, but we both knew this was the moment where everything would change.

She held out her hand to me, and I took it. We had no music, just the ticking of the clock, moonlight streaming through the milky glass. She showed me the careful, rhythmic steps, guiding my body so it was perfectly timed with hers. She spun away, then back again, my arms encircling her.

TWENTY-THREE

Nedra

"ARE YOU WAITING for someone?" Master Ostrum asked as I lingered by the iron-clad statue of Bennum Wellebourne the next morning. The sun had barely risen, and everything seemed cast in gold.

I looked back at the boys' dormitory, but the door didn't open. "No," I said. "Let's go."

Master Ostrum was not one to talk in the morning. Instead, he chewed on coffee beans and walked too fast. I thought about asking for some, but I knew I wouldn't be able to handle the bitter taste.

Last night had been long.

The anger of the other students, the ones Master Ostrum had dropped, felt a million years away. So did my day at the hospital, where everything had gone wrong and everyone I touched seemed only to hurt more. And the party. And the letter. It all felt blurred, pushed aside by something else. *Grey*. Dancing under the illuminated clock-face, dancing along the edge of a choice I wasn't prepared to make.

I pushed it all out of my mind. I had work to do today.

Almost all of the workers at Berrywine's furniture factory had fallen ill, so it made more sense for a handful of potion makers, aides, and an alchemist to go to them rather than find another ferry to cart all the workers to the hospital.

"Have you had a chance to read the book I gave you?" Master Ostrum asked when we were several blocks downhill from Yūgen.

I noticed he didn't speak the title aloud.

"Yes," I said simply.

For a few paces, he left it at that. But then he said, "And?"

I thought about what I'd read. "It is . . . dangerous," I finally said.

"Mm," Master Ostrum grunted. But I didn't think he understood what I meant. The book wasn't dangerous just because it was about necromancy—it was dangerous because it was giving me ideas.

Master Ostrum didn't speak again, and soon we arrived at the factory.

The smell hit me first. A foul, sour stench mixed with the mustiness of sawdust and a sickly sweet odor too close to rot. I recognized potion makers from the quarantine hospital, rushing from cot to cot to distribute painkillers or offer comfort, but there were no alchemists other than Master Ostrum and me.

Berrywine's factory was mercifully small. Only one level, with about thirty or thirty-five workers. A dozen or so were partitioned off to one side—they showed only moderate signs of illness, the early stages of the plague. Fatigue, headaches, sore muscles. They huddled on the floor, their eyes wide and scared.

More than twenty other workers were laid out on cots and makeshift beds. Curtains had been raised in some sections to give a semblance of privacy, but it was plain to see that these people were in pain. Pant legs and shirts had been cut to expose infected limbs, and I counted fifteen with black on their hands or legs. Three had inky stains on their chests, over their hearts—there was little I could do for them.

A handful of workers were already dead, a green film covering their unblinking eyes.

"All this in less than twenty-four hours?" I muttered to Master Ostrum.

"The disease is spreading faster. It's getting more aggressive," he said.

He paused. "I'm going to investigate the grounds and question the workers who are still able to speak to me. If there's any common link, I'll find it."

I was struck by how much studying diseases was like being a detective of a crime. The murderer was a plague, but the deaths were just as sure as a blade across the neck.

"I will do what I can," I said, but Master Ostrum was already disappearing deeper into the factory. I liked that we could work as a team. I doubted other masters would treat their students like partners, but Master Ostrum trusted me.

I withdrew my golden crucible. It was worn now, but familiar, comfortable. I grabbed the nearest potion maker. "Take me to your supplies," I said. She glanced at the golden crucible in my hands, then touched the three beads at her neck.

"Thank Oryous you're here," she said. "We have no tincture of blue ivy. Just poppy oil. It's not doing much."

"Do you have rats?" I asked.

She nodded. "Oh, there's plenty of those."

Before she could lead me away, the door opened, spilling in a blast of cool air. A surgeon strode forward, his kit in his hand, and he cast his eyes over the patients.

"Oh, Blye, thank you," the potion maker said, waving him over. "This is Blye. He's a butcher by trade, but he offered to help at the factories for a morning."

"Thank you," I said, offering him my hand. "Nedra Brysstain."

"Alchemist?" he asked, eyeing my crucible.

"In training."

"Don't worry, she's very good," the potion maker said. I gave her another look and realized I knew her from the quarantine hospital. Her name was Marrow; she usually worked night shifts. From the dark circles under her eyes, I suspected she'd been here since early evening yesterday. She probably started treating patients about the same time I was dancing with Grey, pretending that there was nothing wrong with the world.

I swallowed down the bile rising in my throat.

Blye nodded without speaking as Marrow started to tell him about the patients he'd be seeing. I could tell Blye wasn't the kind for small talk, and as he laid out his tools on a small tray, I recognized some of them from the butcher shop in our village. Tools meant for cows and pigs and sheep.

He'd come from one slaughterhouse to another.

TWENTY-FOUR

Nedra

"FIVE THIS MORNING," Marrow said. "Are you up for it, Nedra dear?"

I nodded grimly.

"Legs or arms first?" Marrow asked, turning to Blye. Another potion maker scurried forward, presenting me with a wheeled cart holding four rats in small wire cages.

"Arms," Blye said.

I pulled back the curtain for us to enter the surgery room. Room. A room would indicate walls, not heavy cloth partitions.

"Nedra?" a weak voice said.

My eyes snapped to the girl who'd spoken. My heart lurched as I recognized the patient.

No.

"Dilada." My voice was a strained whisper, a plea, begging for this not to be real.

She held up her left arm, exposing withered black fingers, the shadows creeping like ink through her veins, all the way past her elbow.

"Carso would laugh," Dilada said as Blye pulled his cart closer and took a seat above her shoulder. "He always said we had the worst luck of anyone on the island."

"I thought—" I shook my head, my words dissipating on my tongue. Dilada wasn't supposed to be here. She was supposed to be on her farm, with her parents and brother, safe and sound. But her parents had died, and so had Carso, and the job in the forest—the one clearing land for graves—had ended, and she'd come here. And caught the plague.

"I'm so scared," Dilada confessed, her voice almost silent.

I crouched closer to her. "It'll be okay," I said. "I've been working with my master since I started here. People live, when we catch it early enough." *Sometimes,* I thought to myself.

She shook her head. "No, I mean—I felt ill two days ago. But I came to work anyway. If I missed a day, they would have fired me . . ."

"Oh," I breathed. She was scared that the illness spreading through Berrywine's was her fault. That she had brought the death here. Maybe she had; we had no way of knowing.

Blye moved his cart, rattling his instruments, his eyes on me. He was waiting.

Dilada swallowed. "I know what has to be done, Nedra," she said.

Of course she did. She'd seen the millworkers who survived the plague but couldn't go back to work. She'd seen the beggars on the streets.

"Will it hurt?" she asked, her voice wavering.

"I can make it hurt less," I promised. "At least for a while."

I set my crucible on the table. It was tall and narrow, about six inches in diameter. Although it was made of solid gold, it was scratched and dull. I ran my fingers along the runes. Master Ostrum had given me the chunk of gold, but I had been the one to pour the molten metal into its mold, and it had been my fingers that scored the runes onto the surface.

I turned to the tray Marrow had given me. The rats inside were not clean like the ones we used at Yūgen. These rats had been caught on the street, and they stank of garbage and piss. I did not flinch as the nearest one snapped at me when I opened its cage. I grabbed it by the scruff of its neck and dropped it into the golden crucible. It snarled in protest, clawing against the smooth metal interior, but it couldn't escape.

"Do you know how alchemy works?" I asked Dilada, attempting to distract her as Blye marked her arm with a butcher's pen.

Dilada lifted her eyes from her deadened fingers and shook her head at me.

"It's science," I said.

"My father always said it was magic."

"So did mine," I said.

"And mine." Blye's deep voice startled Dilada. She'd almost forgotten he was there, but now her gaze drank in the shining scalpel to slice away her skin, the pins to hold the flesh back, the rags to mop up blood. The bone saw.

I shifted, drawing Dilada's eyes back to me and not the tray of tools.

"But it's not—not really, anyway. Alchemy exists on the principles of balance." I was careful to keep my tone even and light. I put one hand on the crucible and quickly muttered the awakening incantation. The runes glowed white on the golden surface.

Dilada gasped.

"Ready," Blye said in his gruff voice.

I squeezed Dilada's shoulder, then touched the crucible on the table. The rat inside screamed in protest as the feeling from Dilada's arm left me and entered its much smaller body. Just existing caused the rat pain now, but when Blye sliced into Dilada's skin and flesh, she would feel nothing at all. When Blye sawed through Dilada's humerus, she would only be aware of the motion, the tugging and pulling, but not the pain.

The rat carried her pain for her.

"Thank you," Dilada whispered.

"Don't look," I advised, and Blye turned his scalpel to her skin. All the fear she'd kept tamped down burst through her eyes for just a moment, then she squeezed them shut and turned her face away.

Dilada's pulse thrummed violently in her throat. I could make her body numb, but I could do nothing for the agonizing anticipation. My grip on her arm tightened. I had to maintain the connection between her and the rat.

"I wish—" Dilada started, but she didn't finish. Blye made the first cuts, and although Dilada's arm was numb, she was still cognizant of what was happening.

Blye worked quickly. Marrow jumped in to help, siphoning off the blood even as it splattered over the floor, soaking into the sawdust. I clenched my teeth, past the point of being able to do anything but provide a link between Dilada and the rat. I felt her pain in waves, washing through me and into the dirty gray body writhing inside the crucible.

From inside the golden vase, the rat screeched sharp and high, then was suddenly silent. Its body couldn't take any more.

"Marrow," I grunted through gritted teeth. With nowhere else to go, Dilada's pain whirled inside me. I could feel myself growing dizzy with it, my grip loosening.

Marrow didn't hesitate to reach inside the cage and dump another rat into the crucible. The connection was remade almost instantaneously, and Dilada only whimpered once as Blye picked up the bone saw. I breathed in relief, letting the pain flood through me into the rat.

After Blye was done, after the hand and part of the arm had fallen with a wet thud against the floor, after Dilada had slipped into a poppy oil–induced sleep and Blye had sewed up her skin to cover the shorn bone—after all that, Blye stood and moved to the next patient, a young boy who was losing his entire left leg. Blye didn't talk; he let me distract this patient, too.

It must be easier that way. To see only the dead limbs that must be sawn away, not the people attached to them. To have never held the hand before it was severed.

TWENTY-FIVE

Nedra

BY THE FOURTH patient, my body ached, my flesh burned, my bones shattered. No one could see it. Even though I transferred as much of the pain as I could into the rats, there was always a little that lingered inside me. I stumbled, my body forgetting that my feet were still attached to my legs. My fingers bent slowly, as if I had to remind the tendons in my arms and hands that they'd not been severed, too.

When we got to the last rat—and the last amputation—I forced some of my own feelings into the creature before it died. It was easier to do this job wide awake and a little numb. It was easier to get through the day that way, too.

"Are you okay?" Marrow asked, wide-eyed, as I fumbled with the crucible, dumping the last furry, stinking body onto the metal tray piled with the rodent victims.

I shrugged.

Marrow shoved the cart of dead rats and severed limbs at Blye. He wheeled them away without a word. When Marrow saw my face, she added, "There's a crematorium on his way back to the butcher's."

I was glad the amputees were all sleeping, and I was glad I'd be gone before they woke. I didn't want to be here when Dilada opened her eyes. I didn't want to watch her look at the place where her hand had been.

I stepped outside to catch my breath, to not think about death and blood. Weaving in and out of my thoughts were the events of yesterday morning: the still body of the baby, the way Ronan's father had blamed me. I slid down the rough brick wall, landing on the bare cobblestones and letting my head rest on my knees. Blackdocks was coming alive, loud and bustling. I wondered if Dilada had ever been able to sell her boat.

The clocks started chiming. The one in the bay, at the top of the quarantine hospital, was a second behind its twin at Yūgen. The day would be starting there soon. Students waking up, eating breakfast, going to lectures.

The thought of it exhausted me.

Master Ostrum appeared at the door. "Nedra," he said.

I looked up, too tired to stand.

"One of your patients needs you."

"I'm . . ." I heaved a sigh. "Can't someone else . . . ?"

But I knew. It was my responsibility.

I pushed against the wall and stood, following him back inside. The black curtains on the windows that marked this place as plague-ridden made the light dim and bleak. The surgical patients were still sleeping from the poppy oil, so at first I didn't understand why Master Ostrum had led me to Dilada's bedside. But then I noticed the way her breathing had slowed, faint and stuttering.

I lifted her wrist, feeling for a pulse. It was barely there.

Master Ostrum watched me as I peeled up Dilada's eyelid and saw the thin film of green covering her rich brown irises.

I cursed.

"We could remove the eyes," Master Ostrum said in a matter-of-fact voice. "Professor Pushnil has a theory that it would be about as effective as amputating diseased limbs."

"Professor Pushnil is an idiot," I snapped. "The green film indicates that the plague is in the brain, not the eyes."

Master Ostrum nodded once, agreeing with me.

I dropped Dilada's hand. "Why did you bring me back here?" I asked, not bothering to hide the hurt in my voice. "We could have gone back to the academy without my knowing. You could have spared me."

"Sometimes, being an alchemist means accepting the limitations of alchemy. It is a hard lesson, but one we must all learn."

The limitations of alchemy. The book Master Ostrum had given me, the one about necromancy . . . it talked about there being no limitations.

I bit my lip.

"I want to try something," I said.

"There's nothing—"

"Please."

Master Ostrum stepped back as I pulled out my crucible. *The Fourth Alchemy* spoke of life and death as if they were both temporary, and it offered incantations that touched on the space between the two. Though necromancers used iron crucibles—the metal forged in a series of dark arts—it didn't mean I couldn't try to implement those incantations with my golden crucible. It wasn't quite necromancy, what I planned to try.

But it was close.

Master Ostrum snapped his fingers for someone to bring us a rat, but I shook my head. My crucible was empty, and that was fine. A rat wouldn't do anything to help Dilada. Alchemy relied on fair trades of equal value. A rat's life was nothing compared to hers. If I wanted to give Dilada any chance at survival, she required a human life force.

Mine.

TWENTY-SIX

Nedra

IN ALL THE other alchemical trades at Berrywine's, I was the gate through which pain flowed from the patient into the crucible. But that was reversed now. Now, the crucible was the gate, allowing the plague to flow from Dilada and into me.

I felt the sickness inside her, swirling around the center of the crucible and flowing into me, greedy, wanting to devour her and me both.

Dilada had already slipped into the coma-like sleep of the plague's final stages, but while she couldn't feel pain, I was still very much awake and aware of the agony as I attempted to pull the disease from her body into my own. The crucible grounded me, enabling me to tug the strands of the plague into my palm, wrap them around the bones of my fingers, and contain them in one area. Vaguely, I was conscious of the fact that if I let myself go too far, I'd lose my hand or even my whole arm.

But it might save Dilada's life.

Connecting to her through the crucible felt like trying to force hot black tar into my veins. The disease moved slowly from her to me, boiling my blood and searing my flesh, but when I forced my eyes open, I could see no signs of damage on me, let alone the disease. But I could *feel* it. I could feel it pooling inside of me. I could feel it clawing under my skin, trying to reach up into my brain, to kill me like it wanted to kill Dilada.

She was just a child, really. She had just been trying to survive. She didn't deserve this

"Nedra?" Master Ostrum's voice was deep, hesitant, unsure of whether he should interrupt me. But he knew better than to pull me away. Interrupting an alchemical transfer could prove disastrous for Dilada, for me, for anyone nearby. This was powerful science, volatile and dangerous.

Why am I doing this? The words flitted through my mind, severing the haze of pain, and I almost pulled away from Dilada at the thought. I liked her well enough, but I barely knew her. I had nothing to prove and everything to lose. But it didn't take love to sacrifice something of yourself for someone else. It just took desperation.

"Come on, come on," I whispered.

The plague slipped through my fingers like water in a sieve. I was losing ground. As much as it was against everything I wanted to do, I forced myself to pull harder, straining to entice the sickness back to me, away from Dilada.

"Nedra," Master Ostrum said again, his voice stronger this time. My senses were sharper now. They should have been dulled by the plague; I shouldn't be able to hear. I cracked my bleary eyes open, and I saw Dilada, still and motionless on the bed. I saw the potion makers gathered around me, their looks a combination of awe and fear.

"You must know when to give up," Master Ostrum said. He touched my arm, and I could feel his warm grip, the sensation overriding the pain that was already fleeing my body.

"No!" I shouted, finally understanding why I could think and feel and hear so much despite the connection.

Because it hadn't worked.

Dilada was already dead.

"No," I said again, although perhaps not aloud. I knocked Master

Ostrum's arm aside and slammed the crucible back into the table, repositioning it and refocusing my energy.

"Brysstain!" Master Ostrum ordered, calling me by my last name, something he only did when I'd angered him. I kicked at him blindly, connecting with one of his legs and forcing him away from me as the alchemical runes lit up again.

Not this time. Just this once, just this one time, I needed a win. I needed to know that what I'd been doing at the hospital wasn't futile. That leaving my family behind had been worth it. I needed to know that I could make a difference.

I needed Dilada to live.

Power surged from me and into the rim of the crucible, flowing into my body like a wave, filling me up and draining back into the crucible's well, over and over again.

I could still feel Dilada. Not her life force—no, that was gone. Cold. But there was something, some small spark of Dilada still there. I reached for it blindly.

I saw into the black behind my eyelids. I saw past the veil between life and death. I saw past myself and into the depleting shell of Dilada's body.

I saw Death itself.

It was a feral thing, made of smoke and shadow. It was hollow and empty.

And hungry.

Starving.

It turned on me as my soul seeped past my own body and into the connection between Dilada and me. Death swam and slid and crept and glided, its black formless being splattering darkness over my essence. It licked at my life force, and I shuddered involuntarily, feeling Death crawl inside me, slithering into the depths of my being.

"Nedra!" Master Ostrum's voice was concerned now, pitched high with worry, and he forced me to break the bond, shoving me away from the body and the crucible, severing the connection I'd had with both Dilada and Death. The crucible clattered to the ground, and I followed behind it, crashing against the floor. For a moment, all I could do was stare straight up at the flickering lights of the oil lamps hanging from the ceiling. My entire being was repulsed by the feeling of Death taking up residence in my body, gnawing at me.

And yet . . . I craved it. It had infected me with its insatiable hunger. I wanted more.

"Are you all right?" Master Ostrum asked, dropping to his knees beside me. He reached for my arm, feeling my pulse. It seemed like it should be strong; my heart wanted to race and rollick out of my body, but I could tell by Master Ostrum's frown that he could barely find its beat.

I pushed him away and sat up on my own. Dilada's body still lay on the table, but her normally olive skin looked bleached, abnormally pale, like a layer of ash had been rubbed all over her.

"What have you done?" Master Ostrum said in a low voice, meant only for my ears. He did not try to hide the morbid fascination welling in his eyes.

TWENTY-SEVEN

Nedra

MASTER OSTRUM TRIED a couple of times to get me to tell him what I had experienced in that last alchemical transfer with Dilada, but I wasn't ready to speak about it.

"Tonight," he said as we passed through the gates to Yūgen, "we will discuss what transpired." His tone brooked no argument, but he allowed me to head off on my own.

I started for the library, but it wasn't books I wanted. Instead, I veered in the other direction, toward the small chapel.

I had discovered the chapel on my first weekend at Yūgen when I heard its bells ringing in the morning. I'd thought it would be filled to the brim with students, but instead, I was one of the few people who visited it. There was no Elder. I hadn't quite expected one, as the chapel wasn't a full church hall, but I'd thought perhaps someone would lead the prayers or give a sermon. For all of this school's famous lecturers, none of the professors came to teach religion.

But there were prayer candles. And it was quiet. And I needed both of those things now.

I stepped into the small chapel with my head down, not inviting any engagement, but there was no one else there this early on a weekday. I supposed most of the people on campus were in the cafeteria, eating breakfast, chatting, completely ignorant that another factory by the docks had closed to plague, that these endless mini tragedies unfolded around them just outside the academy's gates.

In the center of the chapel was the eternal flame, a candle as tall as me and as thick as my arm, set into the floor. The round glass inset in the roof was supposed to symbolize the eye of Oryous watching us at all times, never blinking. I took my small prayer candle from the basket by the door and lit it on the eternal flame.

As I stared at the flickering light, I was overwhelmed with nostalgia and then fear as I remembered Ernesta's letter. In a way, I was glad that this chapel was different from the church hall back home, smaller, neater, less used. It would have been too much like saying goodbye all over again if it had the warm familiarity of my village but didn't have the people I loved inside.

The walls were painted with various holy scenes, but I was drawn to the mural opposite the door. In it, Oryous stood before an image of Death, ghostly white and draped in black, the cloth billowing from an unearthly wind that did not bend the blades of painted grass or shake the trees in the background. The lesser gods stood behind Oryous, all of them rebuking Death, who stood alone. Oryous held his hand out, his palm in front of Death, stopping him. It was supposed to symbolize how we do not truly die when we believe in the gods.

The prayer candle shook in my hand as I approached the mural, the small flame dancing. Cushions were laid on the floor in front of each mural, but I did not kneel. We never knelt or sat at the church hall in the village. We were supposed to stand before our gods, not crouch.

I stepped over the cushions to get closer to the mural. My eyes were not on Oryous, but instead on Death itself. This was not the Death I had seen when I reached into Dilada, trying to pull her back to life. That Death had no shape, nothing as clear as this.

I blew my candle out. I did not need it to pray.

I was not sure who I wanted to pray to.

Instead, I turned to Oryous's painting. But when I mimicked his stance, when I reached my arm out in front of me, I did not raise it in objection. I reached for Death like a friend.

"Nedra?"

The voice startled me, and I dropped my unlit candle, the hot wax spilling on my hand.

Grey stepped into the chapel, his eyes seeking me. He smiled when he saw me, and I was grateful that he hadn't seen me a moment before, and that he couldn't read my blasphemous thoughts.

"What are you doing here?" he asked.

I held out the prayer candle as answer. "How did you know to find me here?"

"I checked the library first," he said. "Then I went to Master Ostrum's office. He suggested the chapel." He looked around, drinking in the paintings. I realized this must be his first time here.

I stepped back over the kneeling pads and past the eternal flame, dropping my candle into the basket to be reused by other worshippers. It wasn't until Grey had followed me out of the chapel that I turned to him. "I thought you were going to come with me this morning," I said, not meeting his eyes.

"Are we not still going?" Grey asked.

I gaped at him. "Where have you been?"

"You've already gone down to the factory?" Grey asked.

"I told you last night," I said. "Sunrise."

Grey laughed, but cut himself short when he saw my look. "But the cafeteria doesn't open until . . ." his voice trailed off. "I'm sorry," he said. "You *did* say sunrise, but I just assumed . . ."

"The gods forbid you miss breakfast," I said, not bothering to bite back my tone.

"It's not like that," Grey said.

I raised an eyebrow at him. He did not deserve my rage, but all I had within me now was anger boiling, steeping in sorrow.

"I messed up," Grey confessed. "I'll be ready tomorrow. I'll meet you at sunrise, like you said."

"Sure," I said as if it didn't matter.

I wondered what he would have thought of me if he'd seen me today, reaching past the limits of medicinal alchemy. Would he have tried to stop me?

And then I wondered: If he had been there, would I have even attempted it in the first place?

TWENTY-EIGHT

Nedra

I LOOKED ASKANCE at Master Ostrum's cluttered laboratory, not willing to meet his intense gaze. We both knew what needed to be said.

"So," Master Ostrum said. "Today."

"Today," I replied.

"Today you . . . crossed a line."

I looked down at my hands in my lap. "I just . . . I wanted to help."

"You realize," Master Ostrum said slowly, considering each word, "that you were toying with necromancy."

Something inside me ached with a hunger that mirrored the greedy maw of Death. And then I remembered the statue of Bennum Wellebourne in the center of the quad, and how people hated him so much they poured molten iron over his image.

"It wasn't necromancy, though," I said. "I used my golden crucible."

Master Ostrum's eyes were furrowed in concern. "If you had an iron crucible, would you have used it?"

I swallowed, hard. "I just wanted to help."

He nodded grimly.

"It is good that there was no alchemist there but me," he said. "Any other, and you might have been faced with an inquiry."

The punishment for practicing—or even attempting to practice—necromancy was death.

"I'm sorry," I stuttered. "I didn't think—"

"That's the problem," Master Ostrum said. "You didn't think."

"But I'm *not* a necromancer—"

"And yet, you seem to have a natural inclination."

I stood up so suddenly that my chair clattered to the floor, protests already bubbling on my lips.

"Peace, Nedra," Master Ostrum said. "I meant that as a compliment."

His words surprised me, and I reached behind me for the chair, setting it upright again.

"Necromancy itself is forbidden," Master Ostrum said, "but *studying* it, knowledge of it, is not."

His eyes were intent on mine, and I felt the weight of his words settling on my shoulders. This was a test.

"Nedra," Master Ostrum said, "how long have you been helping me research this plague?"

It felt like all my life.

"And yet," he continued, "you know as well as I that we are no closer to a cure. What causes it?"

"We don't know."

"How is it spread?"

"We don't know."

"Is it pneumonic or septicemic?"

"We don't know."

"Why does it affect some in the extremities, and others directly in the heart or brain?"

"We don't know." With every admittance of our limitations, my voice became more and more desperate until it broke.

Master Ostrum leaned over the table. "Doesn't it strike you as odd that this much time has passed, and we don't even know how the disease is transferred?" he said. "It is a simple test. If nothing else, a control group could determine if the disease is airborne or blood-borne. And yet, the answer is elusive."

I frowned, still not understanding.

"Today, Nedra," Master Ostrum continued, "you came very close to a form of alchemy few know anything about. And yet I cannot help but think you came closer to understanding this plague than anyone else has to date."

"What are you saying?" My voice sounded distant, as if someone else were asking the question.

"I am saying that, at least within the confines of this laboratory, we must consider that perhaps the plague is caused not by a disease, but by a necromantic curse."

He waited for the words to settle on me, a truth I couldn't dispute. We had been dancing around this idea ever since he had given me *The Fourth Alchemy*.

"But if that is true," I said slowly, "how can we fight it?"

He leaned back in his chair. "How indeed," he said slowly, his eyes glittering as they appraised me. Then he frowned. "You disagree with me? Even after today, after reading the book, you doubt this is necromancy?"

He made this conclusion a long time ago, I realized. *He just didn't trust me with it until now.*

"No, what you're saying makes sense," I replied. "But who could be the necromancer? It's nearly impossible to make an iron crucible."

Master Ostrum barked with bitter laughter. "Oh, it certainly is."

Something about the way he said it made me feel uneasy. He noticed my change and shook his head. "No," he said gently. "I don't have one. I am no necromancer. I am just a scholar."

"Of necromancy."

"Of all forms of alchemy." He did not break his gaze.

"But no one has practiced necromancy in almost two hundred years."

Master Ostrum's eyes widened. "Two hundred—you think Bennum Wellebourne was the last necromancer? No. There have been others, although none so advanced or well-known. Anyone who has come even close to creating an iron crucible has been put to death. It *is* rare, though," Master Ostrum allowed. "It requires a specific type of individual. Not everyone can be a necromancer. In Bennum Wellebourne's private journals, he called it 'death in the blood.'"

"You mean, you have to be born with something inside of you?" I asked, frowning.

Master Ostrum shook his head. "That part is unclear. It could be an inherent trait. Or it could be merely a willingness to allow oneself to be infected by death . . ."

My eyes shot down. I thought of how Death had felt in my hands as I tried to save Dilada. How I had invited it inside me.

How I wanted more.

"*The Fourth Alchemy* wasn't clear," I said, keeping my tone even, "but to make an iron crucible . . . it seemed extraordinarily difficult."

"It's not a matter of difficulty," Master Ostrum said. "It is a matter of sacrifice."

"Sacrifice?" I repeated, the word barely audible.

Master Ostrum nodded. "There are other books than the one I gave you. Most of them focus on the sacrifice the necromancer must make himself. The more sensational volumes say that the necromancer's soul is traded for the power." He dismissed this. "But they all mention that the necromancer does have to give up something. Health. Blood. Something."

I thought of the painting of Bennum Wellebourne hanging in the quarantine hospital. I wondered what he had given up.

"The older books are clear," Master Ostrum continued. "Truth gets watered down over time. The more I go back to the earlier texts on necromancy, the more I see that the necromancer must sacrifice more than himself."

"What do you mean?" I asked.

"Runes, for one." Master Ostrum didn't look at me; he looked at a book on his shelf, but I couldn't tell which one. "Carved into the flesh of someone you love, or who loved you. The books differ."

"Carved into the *flesh*?"

"Dead flesh. You start with the death of a loved one. And then a knife." He picked up a scalpel from the table. "The runes mark the body for sacrifice."

"But if the person is already dead, that doesn't seem like much of a sacrifice."

"You're treating the desecration of a corpse rather lightly, Nedra," Master Ostrum said, but he didn't sound as if he were chastising me, merely commenting. "Could you so easily carve into the flesh of someone you loved?"

I thought of Ernesta. I caught my reflection in the glass covering Master Ostrum's potions cabinet, and I imagined that it was her, not me, looking back. I imagined her eyes empty, the scalpel slicing into her skin, a trickle of blood between her eyes.

I looked away. "No," I said slowly. "No, I don't think I could do that."

TWENTY-NINE

Nedra

BY THE TIME I left Master Ostrum's office, the sun had long since set. There was no moon on the horizon, just the glow of the quarantine hospital's clock.

I made my way slowly back to the dorm, thinking of what Master Ostrum had revealed to me. I didn't notice the boy sitting on the stairs until I almost stepped on him.

"What are you doing, leaving a professor's office so late at night?" Tomus sneered. I could smell the ale on him from several steps away, but his words were not slurred, and his eyes glittered in the darkness.

"Research," I said without pausing. I kept my head down, one foot in front of the other.

Tomus grabbed my arm, jerking me around. "Research," he repeated, sneering.

I tried to pull away. His grip was viselike, his fingers digging into my forearm, purposefully twisting my flesh.

"What are you going to do?" I said in a low voice.

"Anything I want," he snarled.

He thought he could scare me, but I had seen Death today. Nothing could scare me. He thought his leer would make me cower. I could see it in his eyes. He *believed* in himself, in his ability to intimidate others. It was almost laughable, the idea that he had any power at all.

"Hey!" Grey came from the other side of the building. "What's going on?" His voice was unusually aggressive.

Tomus threw his hands up. "Nothing, nothing," he said in a mocking tone. "Your girlfriend's out late, that's all."

"I can stay out as late as I want," I snapped, moving down the steps and away from them both.

"Have you thought about our last conversation?" Tomus asked Grey, holding him back from joining me.

Grey jerked away, jogging to catch up with me. "Mind if I walk you to your dormitory?" he asked, somewhat breathlessly.

I shook my head. My fingers ran along the long, narrow scar across my palm.

Grey pulled my hand away and wove his fingers through mine. "He's just jealous," he said.

"He's not." Our steps didn't slow; we both wanted to leave the quad. Tomus wasn't following us, but he was still there, watching. I knew it without turning. "He isn't jealous of you, and you have the top alchemical marks."

"He is," Grey said. "He just thinks he can use me later, so he hides his anger from me."

"What did he mean?" I asked as we reached the door to the dormitory. "About your last conversation?"

Grey's face flashed with exasperation. "There's a group of students who think now is the perfect time to start protesting the government." His fingers ran up and down a little arrow that had been carved into the doorframe.

"The governor?" I asked.

"And the Emperor," Grey said. He stepped ahead of me, opening the door to the girls' dormitory. "Don't worry about it. They can't really do anything but shout."

Rather than step through the door, I reached for him. "Come up with me?" I asked. "We could study."

I could see the hesitation in his eyes, but he nodded and followed me to my room. Once inside, Grey looked around my bare room. It was a little homier since I moved in, but not by much. He casually opened the scroll of parchment on my desk, revealing the map my father had given me.

"Why don't you have this framed?" he asked. "It would look nice on the wall."

I raised my eyebrows at him. Did he think I put up with paper-thin curtains over my window and couch cushions as pillows for my bed because I was so focused on work? I hadn't framed Papa's map because I *couldn't* frame it. It cost too much.

"I understand," he said, letting go. The large paper curled slowly, like a cat preparing for a nap.

"What do you understand?" I asked.

"This isn't permanent for you." Grey turned in a slow circle, taking my room in. "None of Yūgen is."

I picked up a book from the bed, fiddling with it. In a way, he was right. I hadn't come to this school expecting it to be my home. School was merely a doorway for me to pass through in order to enter the rest of my life, not a place to make attachments or friends.

But when I looked at Grey, at the hope that somehow still flared within him, the hope for *us*—none of my plans mattered.

"What is this to you?" Grey asked me. "I know you are dedicated to your work. I respect that. But what about us? Do I have a chance, or should I—"

I crossed the distance, wrapping my arms around him and pulling him closer to me. It was still so new, this easy way we touched each other, but it came from instinct. A week ago, I would never have dreamed of touching him like this, of feeling the length of his body against mine, but now it was as natural as breathing.

He lowered his head as I looked up at him. My eyes fluttered shut as he kissed me. The book dropped to the floor, the sound echoing in the small room, and I reached up to slide my arms around Grey's neck, pressing my lips hard against his. His hand cupped the back of my head, and shivers raced up and down my spine.

Grey whirled me around, my feet skimming the floor, and he dropped me on the edge of my bed. I held on to him, pulling him down with me. My hands slid under his shirt, trailing up his back. He growled, the sound low and deep and needy, and he pushed me back against the mattress.

I wasn't sure how I felt—I wasn't indecisive, I just couldn't name this deep longing inside of me. I could see the same thing reflected in Grey's eyes. Something primal. Something needy.

Something *hungry.*

As soon as the thought flitted through my mind, I shivered, repulsed that what I felt now reminded me of that moment in the factory. Dilada's pain shot through my hands, up my arms, into the center of me.

I pushed Grey aside. He sat on the edge of the bed for a moment, catching his breath. When he looked at me, there was concern in his eyes.

"It's . . ." I took a deep, shaky breath. "There is work to do," I said.

His worry was replaced with disappointment.

"There's more to life than work," he said.

I got up and moved to the couch. "I know," I said, but I didn't think he heard me.

I stared down at my book, not comprehending any of the words on the page. After a few moments, Grey got up from the bed. He strode across the room and knelt in front of me, one hand on my cheek. "I understand," he said.

And I knew he didn't. He couldn't.

But I loved him for trying.

Before I could say anything, I heard a voice outside my window. My room faced the street, but the gatekeeper must have been lax about letting Tomus outside the campus grounds after curfew. He was clearly even drunker than he had been before, and he was singing a bawdy song at the top of his lungs.

"He doesn't know this is your room," Grey said, frowning at the thin curtains over the glass.

I nodded. Tomus wasn't being overtly threatening. He was just *there*, closer than I'd like him to be.

My mind flashed with the anger Tomus wore beneath his mask. He was used to getting what he wanted, and he seemed intent on finding someone to blame.

"I can make him leave," Grey started, standing. I wasn't sure if he intended to shout at Tomus out the window or go down there and physically remove him, but I caught his arm, holding him back.

"No," I said. "Just . . . stay?"

He looked at me for a long moment, a flicker of desire still in his gaze. "Of course," he said.

We spent the night reading, pretending like everything was normal. And then I curled up in the center of my bed, and Grey stretched out on my couch. I turned down the wick of the oil lamp. It was dark. Tomus was long gone. The city was asleep.

I stared into the blackness and tried not to think about how Grey was just over there, lying on the couch. I could hear his breathing, and I knew he was awake, too. I tried to force myself to fall asleep, but I heard every tiny motion Grey made.

Before sleep could overtake me, I threw my quilt back, swung my legs over the side of the bed, and padded across the room to him.

"Grey," I whispered.

He sat up immediately.

I didn't speak again. I didn't trust myself to. I took his hand, and he followed me back to the bed, under the blanket. My heart was oddly calm, but I could feel his pulse thrumming chaotically in his chest as we settled onto the mattress. Questions hung around him, but when I curled up next him, resting my head on the space where his shoulder met his chest, one arm flung across his body, his breath softened. A long, low sigh escaped his lips, and he held me closer, tight, like he was afraid I would slip away. And then I felt his entire body sink into the bed, relaxing. Within moments, he was asleep.

And for the first time since I danced too close to Death, I felt safe.

THIRTY

Grey

WHEN I WOKE the next morning, it took me a moment to remember where I was.

I sat up, rubbing my bleary eyes. Nedra was already dressed for the day, her long skirt flowing under a tunic, with a cloak over her shoulders, the big square pockets bulging. Her alchemical bag sat by the door, and I could see her crucible peeking out from inside it.

I stretched, yawning hugely. Nedra turned, watching as the blanket fell away from my bare chest, and a surge of heat filled me—I liked the way she looked at me. "We could stay for a little," I said, lifting an eyebrow at her suggestively.

Nedra smirked at me, but she said, "I need to go."

"Then I'm coming with you."

"You don't have to. It's not like I'm getting extra credit or anything. Master Ostrum won't even be there."

"I'm not going for him," I said. "I'm going for you."

Nedra glanced at the window and the red light of the rising sun creeping through the curtains, then she turned to me, still mustering the energy to get out of bed. "You better hurry, then," she said, mockingly. I faked a yawn that turned real, my jaw cracking. She laughed and dropped a kiss on the top of my head.

I liked that kiss just as much as the passionate one last night. This kiss was casual, easy, the kind of kiss people share when they're certain of each other.

174

I dressed hurriedly in the same clothes I'd worn last night. As we left, Nedra made a point to check the lock on her door. "Thank you," she said in such a small voice I almost didn't hear.

"For what?" I asked.

"For being on that side of the door last night."

Blackdocks was already busy by the time we arrived. I could sense Nedra's impatience with me; I was slowing her down from her usual schedule. Transport boats crossed the bay from the north carrying produce or tools and crafts—these were subjected to a new waiting period while one of the governor's inspectors checked for signs of the Wasting Death among the crew. But there were ships from the mainland as well, and even some from Doisha and a grand caravel from Euris. Lunar Island was a safe port and restocking area for the surrounding island colonies and the countries to the east that traded with the Allyrian Empire.

The hospital had its own ferry that ran back and forth between the island and the dock, and there was already a large crowd waiting.

"Please," a woman pleaded, making her way along the line of flat-bottomed boats that knocked against the stone steps of the dock. "Please take us now! I can pay!"

One of the boat drivers spit at the woman's feet. "You couldn't pay me enough to take a sickie."

The woman begged some more, but a man pulled her away by the arm, saying something to her in a low voice. He led her to a group of people waiting for the hospital ferry to arrive. They huddled around a small boy with glassy eyes and blackened fingers, and my heart sank.

"There won't be room on the next ferry for all of the sick," Nedra said, her eyes scanning the crowd by the dock, her fingers moving as she took a silent headcount.

"We can leave room for two more seats," I said. I went down the stone steps to the flat-bottomed boats used for local rides. "Take us to the hospital," I said, tossing my coin at one of the closest ones.

The skipper caught it, but she looked at me questioningly. "You sick?"

"Do I look sick?" I said. Nedra held up her hands, turning them backward and forward to show that there were no inky stains on her fingers.

The skipper jerked her head for us to board her boat. The ride was quick and mostly silent. The skipper was so eager for us to disembark that she pushed her boat away from the hospital's steps before I was even fully on the island. I slipped, almost falling into the water.

A large sign hung on a post on the steps leading up to the grand front doors of the hospital: NO VISITORS.

It was chaos inside. Aides directed people where to go, shouting down the usually peaceful corridors.

"No visitors," an aide said when I stepped forward.

"I'm not a—"

She started to snap at me again, but then saw Nedra. "Oh, thank Oryous," she said, rushing to her. "Can you help with the east wing?"

Nedra nodded. "We both can."

The aide gave me an appraising look, but she didn't ask me to leave. "Half of our alchemists didn't show up today."

"Why not?" I asked.

"They're quitting."

Behind us, the large mahogany doors opened, and a stream of people poured inside. The ferry had arrived.

"We can't handle this many new people," the aide said, a hint of panic in her voice as the mob of new patients streamed in. "There aren't enough rooms, the next shift of workers hasn't even shown up yet, and we're almost out of tincture. We can't do this." She spun around to Nedra, as if she would have the answers.

Someone in the crowd from the ferry started shouting. Potion makers and alchemists rushed forward, hastily sorting patients.

Nedra grabbed the frantic aide by the shoulders. "Focus on one thing at a time," she said. "You can't do everything. So do what you can."

"But—" the aide started doubtfully.

"It'll be enough," Nedra said, with such conviction that even I believed her.

THIRTY-ONE

Nedra

WHEN I FIRST arrived at Yūgen, I was flummoxed by the iron gates surrounding the campus. I didn't understand why the students were caged like animals, a zoo of teenagers and books.

Now I finally understood: It wasn't a matter of keeping the students in. The gates kept the rest of the world out.

As Grey and I made our way through the east wing of the hospital, helping where we could, praying when we couldn't, I realized that despite the fact that Grey had been at Yūgen longer than I had, he was overwhelmed. Yūgen had kept him safe. It kept him ignorant. Patients in textbooks were made of ink and paper, their illnesses detailed on a chart.

I could see the weariness etched on his face. I wondered if Master Ostrum started out this way, and he only looked old now because he had seen too much of the darkness in the world.

"You there!" an authoritative voice cut across the hallway. Silence fell immediately. A broad man with white hair and pallid skin pointed at Grey and me. "Fetch your masters."

I crossed the corridor to the man. "Our master isn't here."

The man glanced at the golden crucible in my hands. "You any good?" He was dressed stylishly and spoke with the quick, clipped tones of someone from the city.

"She's the best," Grey said, his voice icy. I wondered if he knew the man standing in front of us. He *did* look familiar, but I couldn't quite place him.

The man jerked his head toward a nearby suite of rooms that had clearly already been prepared for him. A potion maker stood to the side, a large bottle of tincture of blue ivy in his hands.

The man got into the bed in the center of the room. I blinked away my surprise—he spoke with such authority that I'd assumed he worked at the hospital, not that he was a patient. But then I noticed the black stain on the fingertips of his left hand.

"Do you have plague anywhere else?" I asked. "There are many more people outside who need immediate attention—"

"It is *not* that gods-forsaken disease!" the man roared, clutching his hand to his chest.

Grey moved protectively behind me. "Lord Anton," he started.

The man barked with bitter laughter. "So, you recognize me."

And I did, too—the man Master Ostrum had argued with in his office, who had a large gold crest on his hat.

"This is *not* the plague," Lord Anton said, extending his hand past me and to Grey. "I do not interact with the filth of this city."

My jaw set, and I stepped back. So. It was like that.

"Excuse me," I said as Grey attempted to examine a man whose diagnosis was as visible as the nose on his face. "I have filth to attend to." I left the room before Grey could protest.

And I bumped directly into the governor, almost knocking her down in the hallway.

"Your, um . . ." I started. She was the governor, ruling in regency for the Emperor, so she wasn't technically a "highness."

"Hello," she said kindly. "I'm Adelaide."

"Yes, ma'am, I know, ma'am," I stuttered foolishly.

She was one of the most beautiful people I'd ever met. She wore a dress of embroidered silk that cinched in at the waist with a silver girdle, and her hair was chestnut brown, shot through with strands of white that looked almost decorative. A silver diadem was woven through her locks. Even though the hospital was muggy and oppressively hot, she was cool and collected, and made it seem as if we were the only two people in the entire building.

Her smile was kind and genuine. "Are you an alchemist here?" she asked.

"Studying to be one," I said.

"At Yūgen?"

"Yes, ma'am."

"Good," Governor Adelaide said. "We need all the people we can get to help with this plague—both in treating patients and in finding a cure. Who is your master at the academy?"

"Master Ostrum," I said.

I had become accustomed to people being impressed when I mentioned my master's name; his reputation was well established. Instead, Governor Adelaide frowned slightly. "I'm afraid he doesn't like me very much," she said when she noticed my look of concern. "But he's one of the best, that's for certain."

"If it helps," I said, "I don't think Master Ostrum likes much of anybody."

Governor Adelaide laughed.

"Get that infernal woman out of here!" Lord Anton bellowed from his suite.

"Well, off to work," Governor Adelaide said, and although I knew she was trying to be cheerful in the face of Lord Anton's rudeness, her smile was strained. She entered the suite. I hesitated a moment, but then followed her inside.

"Lord Anton," Governor Adelaide said.

Grey's eyes widened as the governor swept into the room. He looked past her shoulder, probably expecting an entourage of lords and ladies, and seemed a little surprised when it was only me.

"Get out," Lord Anton growled.

"I came to wish you well," Governor Adelaide said. "I heard you were ill, and—"

"*Your* hospital sent me here," Lord Anton said. "Despite the fact that I do *not* have the plague."

Governor Adelaide looked down at his hand, but did not say what we were all thinking.

"It's a filthy, disgusting poor man's disease," Lord Anton muttered. "This is just another attempt to malign my good name."

"We're no longer campaigning for the governorship," Governor Adelaide said gently.

Lord Anton wouldn't meet her eyes. "Get out," he grumbled. And then, after no one moved, he added, "Please."

"Young lady," the governor said, turning to me, "would you be so kind as to show me how I may help out here?"

"Nedra, ma'am," Grey said. "Her name is Nedra Brysstain, and she's the brightest alchemist at Yūgen." Pride radiated from him as I escorted the governor from the suite, leaving him with a grumpy Lord Anton.

"Nedra," the governor said, musing. "I've heard your name here before. The potion makers speak highly of you."

"Thank you," I said.

The governor maneuvered her dress through the crowd of people in the corridors waiting for a room. "I must confess," she said, "that I am ashamed of myself for not coming to the hospital sooner."

"It's best for your health to stay away—" I started, but she cut me off with a wave of her hand.

"The Emperor is still at the castle; did you know?" she said. "He came for my inauguration, but since the plague hit . . ."

She didn't want to say he was too cowardly to leave the protection of the castle, but she didn't have to.

"My time has been occupied entertaining His Imperial Majesty, but . . ," The governor lifted both her palms as if in defeat. "I feel my presence could be better used here or in the factories at Blackdocks."

I smelled sawdust and blood, and resisted the urge to gag. "Have you been to one of the factories infected by the plague?" I asked.

"No," the governor said. She paused, evaluating me. "But you have?" She spoke the words as if they were a question, but her look suggested she knew the answer already.

I nodded.

"I am aware of the horrible conditions at Blackdocks," the governor said, leading me down the corridor. "When I ran for this position, I had to play the political game, but my intent was to lead with compassion, especially for those less fortunate than us."

Us. Had I been so long in Northface Harbor that I was so easily mistaken for a city girl, born into a life of wealth and education?

"Prior to being elected governor, I worked in the treasury," Governor Adelaide continued. "There are items there of immeasurable value—some items from the days of the colony, from before." She paused, looking down the hallway, her eyes lingering on the families waiting to be treated, the children with black on their fingers or toes, over their hearts. "This hospital is funded from the treasury. But it's supposed to be supplemented by the factory owners. The factory owners are supposed to send all workers here straightaway at the first sign of sickness."

Her shoulders sagged. "But they don't. Because they're supposed to send a bit of money with their workers to help support the quarantine hospital. Instead, they let them die."

My stomach churned, but I was too horrified to speak.

"It's cheaper, you see," the governor said. "Cheaper to just replace sick workers after they've died rather than pay for treatment."

"Can't you do something?" I asked.

She smiled at me, but it was sad. "I'm trying," she promised.

As Grey and I walked back to Yūgen from Blackdocks, I paused outside of Berrywine's furniture factory. The black cloth was being pulled from the windows. A line of new workers stood outside the door, waiting for the dead bodies to be carted to the pauper's grave before they began their new jobs.

THIRTY-TWO

Nedra

"THE GOVERNOR WAS at the hospital today," I told Master Ostrum.

"Oh?" His voice was monotone, indifferent.

"She came to see Lord Anton in the quarantine hospital, but stayed to visit many of the sick."

Master Ostrum snorted. "She should have selected him as Lord Commander. Instead, she has yet to choose a second, and that weakens her position."

"Still," I said. "It's more than what the Emperor's doing."

Master Ostrum conceded the point. "The Emperor is a child. We treat him almost like a god, but he's a child."

"He's my age," I pointed out. "Like it or not, he *is* our Emperor."

Master Ostrum leveled me with a stare. "He's been locked up in the castle since the plague got worse. He's too afraid to peek outside the silk curtains of his own bed, too trembling to make his way from the governor's castle to his own on the mainland. He's not of stout enough blood to be Emperor, that's for certain."

His voice had risen with each word, and the resounding silence after he ceased talking hung between us. My mouth gaped. It seemed wrong to speak against the Emperor, and yet, I couldn't disagree. I could tell he was waiting for me to do just that, to protest that this Emperor was best not just for our island, but for the whole of the Empire, the whole of the world, including the unclaimed lands. But Master Ostrum had a point. The Emperor had proven himself a coward. He had not been the one to walk the halls of the hospital. It had been Governor Adelaide, her kind heart and gracious words making the patients smile through their pain, giving them more hope than even my crucible could.

"But perhaps," I said, "it is best not to speak such thoughts of the Emperor aloud."

Master Ostrum raised an eyebrow. "Perhaps it is also best not to work along the edges of necromancy, yet here we are."

I felt my cheeks grow hot. My efforts to save Dilada felt long ago, but the desire to do more still bubbled under my skin. All day at the hospital, I'd had to limit myself. I knew Grey thought I pushed too hard, helped too many people, but each time was like slaking my thirst after walking through the desert. The victims of the plague who weren't going to make it, the ones closest to Death . . .

I touched the three knots on the necklace I wore around my neck, reminiscent of Oryous's stars in the sky, symbolic of our greatest god's three eyes watching over the past, the present, and the future. *Death is not a god to worship,* I reminded myself.

Master Ostrum watched me, seeming to follow my unspoken train of thought. "Let us forget what we should and should not say and instead speak the truth simply." He stood and walked to the center of the lab. "This building is the oldest one on campus. Bennum Wellebourne himself walked the halls. But as time goes by, people forget about the foibles of old buildings."

Master Ostrum knelt on the wooden floor, feeling along the edges of the boards and then prying his fingers in a crack. I gasped as the entire panel of the floor opened up. I ran over to where Master Ostrum peered into the dark.

I had known the floor of the lab was slightly higher than the floor of Master Ostrum's office, but I hadn't realized that it covered the cool, packed earth of the foundation of the building. A small ladder descended into the shadows, and Master Ostrum eased himself over the side of the floor and down into the subbasement. When he reached the bottom, he lit an oil lamp, illuminating the area. Leaning over the edge, I could see that the hidden room was smaller than I'd expected, but still large enough for Master Ostrum to comfortably stand and stretch his arms out without touching the sides.

Shelves had been dug into the packed earth walls, little burrows that looked like ancient catacombs. Master Ostrum grabbed a box from one of the shelves, then lifted it up for me to take.

It was heavier than I'd expected, and I had to leverage it against the floorboards to pull it into the lab. Master Ostrum climbed back up the ladder, first moving the panel to hide the secret entrance and then taking the box from me. He had to beat on the sides of the crate to get the lip to come undone, and when he lifted the lid, I found myself holding my breath as I peered inside.

Straw covered three crucibles—one gold, one silver, and one copper.

Master Ostrum lifted each of the crucibles, holding them out for me to take after he swept the straw aside. I had never used a silver crucible—transformations were difficult to master—but the golden crucible felt comfortable in my hands. I turned it over, examining the runes etched into it. I turned it upside down and saw two initials scratched into the bottom: *B.W.*

My eyes shot to Master Ostrum's, and he nodded gravely. "Bennum Wellebourne's personal crucibles."

"How did . . . ?" I started, my awe at holding such ancient artifacts in my hands silencing my question.

Master Ostrum ignored me. "Wellebourne was one of the few who mastered *all* forms of alchemy. Transfer, transform, transact." He touched the golden, silver, and copper crucibles as he said each word, but then pulled the copper one closer to him. "Transcend."

Master Ostrum pointed to a knife on the table, and after a curious look, I fetched it for him. I recognized the blade. It was the same one he'd used to slice open my palm on my first day at Yūgen. This time, he turned the blade on himself, piercing the pad of his index finger and squeezing a drop of blood into the copper crucible. The bright red splattered on the empty base, but in a blink, the crucible was no longer hollow.

"What is that?" I asked as Master Ostrum withdrew the object.

"A crucible cage," he said.

I felt the smooth, black thing. "It looks like . . . bones," I said. "This could be the metacarpals and carpals." I touched each of the three sections on the longer pieces that pointed up. "Proximal, middle, distal . . ." As I named the bones, I suddenly realized what I was holding.

A hand.

"This is a replica . . . ?" I started, but Master Ostrum shook his head.

"It's real."

"And it's made of—"

"Human bones, yes," he said.

I should have been disgusted by the idea of holding hands with a dead person, but I wasn't. I was simply curious. "Why do the fingers point up like this?" I used my other hand to mimic the position of the bones. I scrunched my fingers together, keeping them flat and pointed.

"All crucibles must be made of pure metals. A necromancer's crucible is made of blood iron." He held his hand out to me, and I saw the red smeared on the finger he'd cut with the knife. "Our blood is the color of rust for a reason. We have iron in our veins, Nedra."

"Yes, but not enough to make a whole crucible," I started.

Master Ostrum shook his head. "This is dark alchemy," he said. "I tell you about it now only so that you know what we're up against with the plague."

The plague Master Ostrum believed was no true illness, but a nec-romantic curse.

"It's not enough for a necromancer to have inherent power, he must have an iron crucible as well. And that can only be made with a crucible cage—a cage built of sacrifice, the hand of a loved one, the bones burnt in a sulfuric inferno."

I thought of all the hands that had been amputated since the plague. And then I recalled the portrait of Bennum Wellebourne that hung in the quarantine hospital, and the woman who stood beside him with her hand missing.

"His wife," I said. "He cut off her hand . . ."

"And created the crucible he used to raise the dead. This is the sec-ond crucible cage he made—and it's still very powerful. Especially if . . ."

The implication was clear. This hand—this cage—could be used to make a crucible.

"I told you, to be a necromancer, sacrifices must be made. Not just of yourself, but of those you love and who love you." Master Ostrum stared down at the bony cage. "Perhaps that is one reason why nec-romancers are so hated, because their sacrifices extend beyond them-selves. Wellebourne took his wife's hand first and used it to create the crucible that raised the dead. That relic is in the treasury—broken, but a reminder of all that happened."

Master Ostrum's face was grim. "That crucible was taken when he was captured. Wellebourne was locked in the castle while he awaited trial."

I remembered what Grey had told me, about how the castle was haunted.

"He was so desperate to escape," Master Ostrum continued, "that he actually sawed his own hand off in an attempt to make a second crucible. He got that far." He nodded to the hand I still held, and revulsion filled me. *This* was Bennum Wellebourne's hand, burned and cursed?

"He called his son to him, the day before he was going to be hung." Master Ostrum spat the words out bitterly. "He intended to burn the boy to ash and complete the crucible. His son was about twelve at the time. Of course, the guards in the tower stopped Wellebourne. The boy stole the crucible cage and escaped. And Wellebourne was hung."

"How do you know all this?"

"These are Wellebourne's own crucibles," he said, looking me in the eye. "The copper one will only reveal its contents with Wellebourne's blood."

My gaze dropped down to the bright red on Master Ostrum's finger and the blood he shared with the island's greatest traitor.

THIRTY-THREE

Nedra

"You're—?"

"His descendant, yes," Master Ostrum said. "The son who stole the crucible was my great-great-grandfather. I'm the last of the line."

"I didn't know," I said.

Master Ostrum snorted. "It's not something I publicize. My family has changed its name several times over the years." He looked around at the office, at the floorboards covering the subbasement. "Ironically, quite a few of the professors who have resided in this office have been ancestors of mine. Wellebournes do have an affinity for alchemy, and we seem drawn back to this school."

I put the crucible cage down on the floor. It didn't disturb me to hold it while I knew it was made of human bones, but once I learned that human was Bennum Wellebourne, I was disgusted.

Master Ostrum picked it up. "My family has kept this hidden for nearly two centuries."

"Why not just destroy it?"

"You think it would be that easy?" he asked in a low voice.

After a long moment, I asked, "Why are you telling me these secrets?"

"Because someone else has done all of this," Master Ostrum said. "Someone has severed a hand, burned flesh to ash, spilled his own blood. Someone has followed all of the steps—and they've started the plague."

Outside, we heard a noise—a thump of some kind, perhaps a door closing. Master Ostrum stood, returning the bones to the copper crucible and then packing it and the others back into their crate. He opened the hidden passage to the subbasement and motioned for me to follow.

The area beneath the floor was cool and slightly damp. My father would have been shocked to see books stored on the earthen shelves, but they showed no sign of damage or mold.

"My family has gathered what they could through the generations," Master Ostrum said. "Guilt is hereditary."

"You had nothing to do with—" I started, but he waved his hand, cutting me off.

"What's important now is that so much time has passed, people have forgotten what necromancy really is and what it can do."

I felt sick to my stomach.

"Nedra, you can see it, too, can't you?" There was desperation in his voice. "You've studied this plague as much as any of the professors have. You *know* it's not biological. It's alchemical."

"And targeted against the poor?" I asked. "Who would do that?"

"Someone rich." There was bitterness in his voice. "Or merely one who doesn't value human life. But you see it's necromantic, don't you? Now that you see the evidence, now that you see . . ." His voice trailed off, his eyes wide, searching mine.

And I realized: He wasn't certain.

But he was *eager.*

Master Ostrum had spent his entire life with the secret of his family's dark past. Now there was a hint of it rising up again, and his reaction was . . . excitement.

I tasted bile in the back of my throat. Master Ostrum and I had been studying the plague since my earliest days at Yūgen, but he'd never been as passionate for the cure as he seemed fascinated now with the curse.

"You can't be sure," I said. "People are afraid of necromancy. And this knowledge—" I swept my arm to the tiny collection of books and items hidden in the subbasement. "Who else would know all this?"

"I don't know, I don't know," Master Ostrum said, shaking his head. "But someone else must . . . There are books. Necromancy is illegal, but learning about it . . . There are books. Rare tomes. Hidden in corners of libraries, forgotten, old books with old knowledge."

The back of my heel touched the ladder leading back up to the lab. How long had Master Ostrum suspected necromancy? How much of our shared laboratory time had been wasted with him already knowing the answer?

Dilada flashed through my mind. Had he sent me to the factories, to the hospital, hoping I would eventually push myself that far, that deep into the arms of Death?

My stomach twisted.

"I have to go," I said, one foot on the first rung.

"Nedra, wait," Master Ostrum said. "I know this is a lot, but—"

I shook my head, climbing a few more steps up. "I have to go," I repeated. "I have to . . . I have to think about this. I have to . . ." But I didn't finish. I was already back up in the lab. I crossed the small room quickly, throwing open the door, running out of the building. I didn't slow down until I reached the center of the quad, until Bennum Wellebourne's iron-encased statue loomed over me.

THIRTY-FOUR

Grey

WHEN NEDRA STOPPED going to the hospital as often, my initial reaction was relief and hope that she would finally start taking care of herself. Instead, she went from treating patients to working day and night in the laboratory hall.

I joined her, helping where I could. "Did you and Master Ostrum have a breakthrough?" I asked, hoping this nightmare of a plague would soon be over.

"Maybe," Nedra said slowly. "But I have to be absolutely, entirely sure."

"Why aren't you working in his lab?" I asked.

She opened her mouth to answer, then her brow furrowed into a frown. "It's better this way," she said finally.

Master Ostrum had blocked off a lab in the main hall just for Nedra. One wall held a row of cabinets that were all closed, many of them with locks. The other wall held a locker full of rats, each in its own cage.

"So what is this big theory of Master Ostrum's?" I asked as Nedra pulled slides of samples from a box and lined them up with the microscope.

She bent over the microscope, analyzing the contents of the slide. But her eye wasn't focused through the lens; her gaze kept drifting. She leaned back and pulled her bag closer to her. Through the open top, I could see a book. Not a textbook—something old, the title worn away.

She sighed as if she were making a decision, one she wasn't sure about in the least. Then she turned her full attention to me, staring at me intently. "Grey," she said, "there's been no cure for the plague. Nothing has worked."

"But you have a theory?"

"We . . . we do." She said the words like they were a confession, a sin to be absolved of. She opened the book in front of her.

"What's that?"

"My papa says . . ." She paused. "'A good book will give you answers to questions you didn't know you had.'" She opened the book, the thin pages brown and dull under the bright light of the lab. "'A great book will give you questions to answers you thought you knew.'"

Even the rats in the cages seemed to be listening to her.

"I don't think I understand," I said. My throat was tight; the way she was looking at me and speaking made this feel more momentous than a simple conversation. I felt like she was testing me.

I leaned over her to look at the text, but it was written in a florid font, difficult to discern.

Nedra slowly turned the pages, her mouth silently forming the words within. It felt like a dismissal, so I moved to the back of the lab and opened one of the cages, selecting a rat and dropping it into my golden crucible. I had my own experiments to try.

My eyes drifted to the paper pasted on the back of the door, a map of Lunar Island that had been reprinted in a news sheet. Marks indicated where the plague had struck, along with numbers—the death toll. The northern villages were mostly a collection of question marks; it was harder to collect information from there. The factories and poor district of Northface Harbor were so heavily inked that it was nearly impossible to discern any of the writing. I couldn't help but wonder why anyone would still agree to take a factory job.

I turned back to the work table, the rat inside my crucible peering up at me. It scratched at the gold as I activated the runes.

"What're you doing?" Nedra asked.

"Did you read Professor Xhamee's brief?"

She shrugged. Nedra had no intention of following any of the professors' experiments; she was using the lab for her own theories. The only professor whose opinion she cared about was Master Ostrum.

"His theory is that he can draw out infection with the pain transference," I said. "He's come up with a different rune combination—"

Nedra's head jerked up. "Really? Let me see."

I shifted my crucible, showing her the sequence of runes lit up along the side. She squinted in thought as she read them, but then she shook her head.

"It won't work."

It was true that, although the theory was promising, Professor Xhamee had not yet been able to get the right rune sequence to create a working alchemical exchange. But a theory couldn't be proven until the experiment worked, and I wasn't going to dismiss it just because we'd run into some obstacles.

Nedra continued reading her book, but she watched me out of the corner of her eye. I set up the experiment, focusing on the alchemy. The rat inside the crucible clawed at the edges, its squeaks turning frantic as the crucible's energy boiled around it. Rats couldn't carry the plague, but if I could draw out a minor wound infection already festering on this rodent, it would be one step closer to proving Professor Xhamee's theory.

"You're hurting it," Nedra pointed out, still pretending to read.

Hurting rats was part and parcel of being an alchemist, but the rat inside my crucible seemed to be in agony that far outweighed anything

I'd seen before. I was concentrating too hard, struggling to maintain the alchemical connection, but even though I didn't answer Nedra, my focus was shot. The rat died.

Nedra pulled my crucible closer to her when I leaned up, peering inside it with a strange look on her face.

"It's not fair, what we do to rats," she said.

"We should leave our patients in pain when we could relieve them of that much at least?"

I pulled the crucible away from her and tilted it to its side. The rat flopped onto the table, its claws seized into sharp angles from the pain I had put it through before it died. A twinge of sympathy shot through me. Maybe Nedra had a point.

She reached over me and picked the rat up as if it were a dear pet.

"Nedra," I said. "It's not ideal. It's not fair. But the basic principle of alchemy is equivalent exchange. You can't just make the pain of our patients disappear. It has to go somewhere. And better it goes to a worthless rodent than a human."

"You're just saying that because rats are ugly," she said, her eyes still on the rodent. "If we had to sacrifice fluffy bunnies or kittens or something, more people would protest. It doesn't have to be this way," she told the dead creature in her arms.

"Alchemy is about equivalent exchange," I said again, gentler this time.

Nedra ignored me. She carefully placed the rat's dead body on the table, as if it were in a casket being laid into the ground. She held her hand out for a scalpel, and, thinking she was going to perform a dissection, I handed it to her. Instead, she carved a rune through the fur and into the skin of the dead animal. Nedra consulted the book she'd been reading and muttered some runes I didn't recognize.

"Nedra, is that . . . ?" My stomach dropped.

"It's not necromancy," she said quickly, in a hushed voice.

"But—"

"Grey." She said so much in that one syllable.

And the rat squeaked back to life. Just a moment, just a tiny little sound, but it was deafening.

"That's—" I started, horror growing inside me. She might not have a necromancer's crucible, she might not be a true necromancer, but using her golden crucible to go past healing into resurrection was absolutely forbidden and the first thing all alchemists were taught not to do. Such twisted use of her golden crucible wouldn't last, much like animation with a silver crucible failed after moments, but it was still *wrong*.

The rat's snuffling squeaks pitched higher, into a squeal, a pained sound. Its eyes bulged; its body spasmed. In seconds, it was dead again, but this death seemed much more excruciating. The rat's lips were curled into a snarl, its sharp yellow teeth gouging the table. In moments, its fur started to sizzle, melting away in a grayish-whitish-pinkish blur, filling the room with an acrid stench. Soon there was nothing but sizzling bones.

"It wasn't supposed to happen like that," Nedra said, shock on her face.

"It wasn't supposed to happen at all!" I roared, throwing back my chair.

"Don't tell anyone," she said immediately. "I'm still learning—"

"Learning? *Learning?*" I snarled. "Nedra, that's *necromancy*. You can't be *learning* necromancy! This isn't just against the rules. This is illegal. And . . . wrong." Wrong on such a deep, fundamental level. That rat had been *dead*. And then it wasn't. And now it was again, but much, much worse.

I stared blindly around the room, at a loss for words. I saw Master Ostrum's name scribbled on the sign-in sheet at the door. "Is *this* what Master Ostrum had been teaching you?" I asked.

"No, no, Grey—it's not what it looks like."

"Really? Because it looks like necromancy."

"Not to practice it," Nedra insisted. "To *study* it. I think maybe . . . maybe it could help us figure out the plague."

"Don't *ever* do it again." My voice was vicious, but I didn't care. Nedra never thought about the consequences. She could be imprisoned for a dead *rat*. "Promise me," I ordered.

"I—" she started, but then gasped, her hand reaching for her head as if it suddenly pained her. Through her fingers, six long strands of her black tresses turned solid white.

"This kind of stuff—it's bad, Nedra. You understand?"

She nodded, her eyes on her hair.

"Even if it has something to do with the plague, don't *you* get caught up in it."

Nedra wound the white strands around her finger and yanked them from her head. She scooped up the bones of the rat, cradling them as if they still had life, and moved toward the rubbish bin.

"Someone will see it there," I said. "Here." I thrust out my copper crucible to her. She dropped the remains and her hair inside, and I sealed the crucible, hiding the evidence of Nedra's first necromancy experiment gone wrong.

We didn't speak again as we left the lab. The other rats watched us, their beady eyes focused on Nedra as I turned off the lights and darkness swept over us.

THIRTY-FIVE

Nedra

I WAS WAITING at the iron gates before the sun rose the next morning.

"You're up early," the gatekeeper said. He was friendlier than he had been when I first met him, so many months ago with my trunk and my ideals and my ignorance.

He moved in aching slowness. I knew Grey would be waiting for me at my dormitory, expecting another day at the hospital. But I couldn't see him, not today.

I slipped through the door before it was fully open. Heading downhill, I chased the sunrise. Behind me, long streams of sunlight spilled onto the street, but in front of me it was still dark, the oil lamps flickering. I ran to the shadows.

Blackdocks was not quite awake yet, but a few ferries cut through the hazy water. I found a bench overlooking the main dock. My eyes went north, to home, where my family waited for me to finish an education I was no longer sure I wanted.

The sun finally caught up with me.

Light spilled over the water first, twinkling up through the caps of the small waves in the bay before turning the air golden, burning away the fog.

The housing units uphill seemed to wake all at once, people pouring from the buildings and heading to the factories along the waterfront. It was particularly cruel, I thought, that the workers resided uphill, giving them an easy walk to work, but a harder climb to get back home after they were tired and broken.

Younger boys and girls started walking up and down the streets, shouting the headlines of the news sheets they sold for a copper coin. "Wasting Death claims life of government officials! Epidemic growing!" a girl said, her voice pitched low but loud. She stood on the top of a stack of news sheets and waved one around emphatically. "Governor Adelaide shows signs of illness after recent hospital visits!"

I couldn't afford to spend a copper, but I did it anyway, tossing the girl a coin and taking the news sheet from her hand. I scanned the top stories. Lord Anton's infection was worsening, and he wasn't expected to make it. Other politicians—notably a handful that were close to Anton—were also infected or dead.

Governor Adelaide's photograph from her coronation with the Emperor dominated the front page, along with a story detailing all the work she'd done for the sick since the plague first hit Lunar Island. She'd spent her own personal funds supporting the hospital, pled in the council for stricter governing of the factory owners, and often visited the sick.

The Emperor was distinctly left out of the article, save for a single line that read only, "His Imperial Majesty currently resides in the castle but has distanced himself from Governor Adelaide after her personal alchemist declared her too ill to continue with her charitable works."

I turned to the back of the news sheet and saw a map of Lunar Island. It was larger than the one Master Ostrum and I had hung in the school lab, and it had more details on the northern villages. A list of names ran down the side, and I scanned for my parents, for my sister, for anyone from my village, but my eyes blurred. There were too many names to keep count.

"Make way!" A large cart parted an ocean of people walking toward the factories. Two draft horses pulled the wagon, and a driver sat on a raised seat. "Make way, make way," he shouted impatiently. He finally broke through the crowd of people, and the empty wagon rattled on the cobblestones toward one of the factories.

It stopped at a three-story-tall warehouse with black draped over the windows. The man bellowed for someone to hurry up, and the doors opened.

I watched as people dragged bodies from the factory. They were thrown haphazardly onto the back of the cart, arms and legs spread wide, ashen faces staring in all directions with unblinking eyes. As soon as the wagon was full, the driver turned the cart around, driving it straight to a large ferry that had no seats or benches.

I watched from the road as the skipper and the driver dumped the bodies from the wagon and onto the boat. They were nearly done by the time I reached the dock. The skipper pushed off from the dock, his boat cutting through the water like a knife. I watched until I couldn't see it anymore, even though I knew where it was going: the field Dilada had helped clear, the new grave where victims would be out of sight and out of mind. I wondered how many hundreds were there already, how many had been so swiftly forgotten.

Grey sat down beside me.

"Nedra?" he asked, leaning over to brush my hair from my face. "I thought you were going to wait for me at Yūgen, that we would walk down here together."

"Sorry," I said hollowly. "I needed some time to think."

He saw the news sheet in my hand. "I read about that this morning. Everyone's talking about how the governor is sick. Tomus was going on and on about how the Emperor will take over if she dies."

This is why citizens accused Governor Adelaide of being negligent for not appointing a Lord Commander, a second-in-command to run the government if she was incapacitated. I wondered what *would* happen if the Emperor took control. The girls in the history study group probably would say this would be the tipping point toward revolution.

What did it matter, though?

"Is everything okay?" Grey asked.

I looked him in the eyes. "No," I said.

He frowned, but I could see he didn't want to talk about what had happened at the lab. He leaned down, bumping his forehead against mine, and we stayed there for several long moments, willing the world to not exist outside our touch.

"What do we do when everything falls apart?" I asked, still not opening my eyes.

Grey wrapped his hands around my face, drawing my gaze. "We do what we can," he said. "I learned that from you."

I nodded and took a deep breath. *My blood is made of iron*, I reminded myself, and the thought did not disgust me.

I was surprised to discover that Master Ostrum was at the quarantine hospital when Grey and I arrived. The receptionist directed us to a suite where he was working, assuming he was waiting for us. He did not seem pleased by our interruption, blocking the door and the patient inside when we knocked. He stepped into the hall.

"I thought you were focusing on research, not patients," I muttered to him.

Master Ostrum ignored me. "Greggori," he said, "go find the head potion maker and see how much tincture of blue ivy is left."

Grey shot me a worried look, but he turned back down the hall, toward the foyer. I hesitated, but my curiosity overcame me; I followed Master Ostrum into the suite.

Lord Anton lay in the same bed as before, but his skin was sallow, his breathing slow. The blackness of the disease had spread to both legs. His right arm had already been amputated, bloody gauze covering the wound.

Master Ostrum greeted Lord Anton like a friend, but all I could do was stand and stare. When I had last seen Lord Anton, he had barely a shadow of the illness. It had spread enormously through his body since then.

"She'll be happy I can't vote against her anymore," Lord Anton said weakly, lifting up his residual limb.

"You'll have to vote with your other arm," Master Ostrum said. He busied himself inspecting his patient, tilting Lord Anton's head to the light, lifting his eyelids. My attention focused on the hazy green film, barely visible, over Lord Anton's dark brown eyes. Master Ostrum looked at me. We both knew what that meant.

Rather than move on to other patients, patients that could actually survive, Master Ostrum sat down on the edge of Lord Anton's bed.

"You have to continue," Lord Anton said in a weak voice. He glanced at me.

"Nedra is safe," Master Ostrum said. "You can speak freely in front of her."

"What's to say?" Lord Anton's voice was bitter. "Everyone knows I would have torn Lunar Island from the Empire if given half a chance. Lucky for the child Emperor that Adelaide took the castle, not me." His lips snarled bitterly. "Not luck. He controls everything, doesn't he, in the end?"

I blinked several times but knew enough to keep my mouth shut. Lord Anton might have politically opposed Governor Adelaide, but I for one hadn't known he was so against the Emperor himself.

"This land should be free and independent," Lord Anton continued, turning to Master Ostrum. "Don't let the movement die with me."

"I won't," he promised.

The clock chimed noon, the sound reverberating throughout the hospital. In between the bells, I thought of what Lord Anton's words meant, of how large the movement must be, and how hidden. I thought of Governor Adelaide, kind and good—but loyal to the Emperor.

Master Ostrum disappeared soon after Lord Anton died, returning to his lab. I was bone weary by the time Grey and I got off the ferry at Blackdocks. The temperature had unexpectedly dropped. Before, I'd chased the shadows going down the hill to the docks; now the sun sank at our ankles, oil lamps sputtering on in our wake.

The gates were already closed, but the gatekeeper stood in front of the iron bars. His eyes looked anxiously behind us. "You're the last of the lot," he said, opening the gate. "Hurry, hurry." As soon as we stepped through, the gate locked, despite the fact that curfew wasn't for another hour.

"What's going on?" I tried to ask, but he was already walking away from us.

"Come on," Grey said. "Master Ostrum will know what's happening."

We rushed toward the administration building. In the center of the quad, a group of students huddled near the statue of Bennum Wellebourne. They held nails and files, and they made no attempt to hide what they were doing—scratching tiny arrows pointing to the sky into the iron that covered the statue.

"We will rise up!" they called out after us, their empty revolutionary chant echoing ominously across campus as the darkness grew.

THIRTY-SIX

Grey

MASTER OSTRUM LOOKED, for lack of a better word, frazzled. It didn't suit him. He was typically grave, his hair smooth and tied at his neck, his suit immaculate. But now his skin was haggard and his clothes were wrinkled and limp. Despite the fact that we'd seen him just this morning, it appeared as if a sleepless week had passed for him.

"The school is closing," he said. "Temporarily."

"What?" Nedra's voice raised. "Why?"

"Parents want their children home," Master Ostrum said. "They're concerned about the plague. With the governor ill and the Emperor hiding, the administration thinks it best—"

"Let the others go," Nedra insisted. "We have work to do!"

"Nedra." Master Ostrum steepled his fingers. "The entire campus is closing. You'll have nowhere to stay. You have to go home. The school will send for you—*I* will send for you—when Yūgen reopens."

I leaned in closer to her, gently rubbing my thumb on her hand. "Besides," I added, "you could see your family."

"Just because you leave campus doesn't mean you stop working." Master Ostrum gave her a single book, slender and worn. Then he pulled out a parchment envelope and handed it to me. "You're dismissed," he said as I took the paper.

I frowned but left anyway. "I'll be waiting outside," I told Nedra.

In the corridor, I opened the envelope. My parents informed me that I was to meet the family carriage at the school gates by eight chimes. Word traveled fast.

Nedra opened Master Ostrum's office door a moment later, her head down, her bag slung over her shoulder, the book in her hand.

"What did he want?" I asked.

"He gave me some money," she said, as if still surprised by it.

"What for?" I led the way up the stairs to the door of the administration building.

"So I could pay a skipper to take me to my village."

I was ashamed that I'd not thought of it myself. I had plenty of coin to pay for her travels. It would mean nothing to me and everything to her. But I'd not even considered it. "Nedra, I—"

"I'm going to stop at the quarantine hospital on the way," Nedra said. "Then take another ferry up to the north shore."

She paused, as if waiting to see if I would accompany her. "My parents are sending a carriage . . ." I said lamely.

The air outside was crisp. Nedra leaned up on her toes and kissed my nose. "I'm horrid at goodbyes," she said. "It's better this way."

We walked slowly across the quad, then lingered in front of our separate dormitories. "Well," Nedra finally said.

I tried to hold her tighter, but I could already feel her pulling away. "It won't be long," I said.

She kissed me again, lightly on the lips, but when she pulled away, the look in her eyes was distant. She was still right in front of me, but she was already gone.

THIRTY-SEVEN

Nedra

I AWOKE WITH parchment stuck to my face and my nose pressed into the open spine of a medical tome.

Maybe Grey was right. Maybe I did need a break.

I peeled myself out of my desk chair and stood, my muscles aching and my spine popping. Grey had left the evening before, and I was glad that we didn't have to linger over farewells today.

I packed quickly, but my satchel was heavier now than when I'd first come to Northface Harbor. I carried with me not just my golden crucible, but also books—including the one Master Ostrum had given me last night. I'd skimmed through it, but even though the volume was thin, the text was handwritten and difficult to read.

"This was Wellebourne's," Master Ostrum had said. "It's been passed down through my family over the generations. Ancestors have added a few notes here and there. But it was his."

It felt odd, knowing that I would be reading Wellebourne's own words, written in his hand—the same hand that I had held after it had been cut off and turned into a crucible cage. I'd read some of his work before—his poetry as a young man, his treatises as the first governor of Lunar Island. But nothing from after his descent into necromancy—they didn't cover those writings in textbooks. A quick scan of the journal last night indicated that this was far more personal than an instructional manual.

The last chapter had been written by Wellebourne's son. The first part was a description of Wellebourne's last days, particularly the hope his son had when he'd been called to his father's prison, followed by the horror when he saw the bloody wound where his father's hand should be. The rest of the chapter was a warning—not just to hide the crucible cage so no one could use it to become a necromancer, but also to avoid necromancy at all costs. *It is a madness,* the chapter concluded, *one I hope is not in our blood.*

I was the last person to leave the dormitories. The cafeteria was already closed, nothing but a basket of apples on the doorstep for anyone who remained. Most of the students—even the ones whose families lived just a few miles away—left the school in fancy carriages, fine horses throwing their heads back, their hooves clattering on the street.

I kept my head down, lost in thought, as I made my way downhill to Blackdocks. I was so distracted that I almost collided with the wagon being pulled up the street, bumping on the cobblestones.

"Watch'er!" the driver shouted, yanking on the reins and pulling his cart up sharply.

The scent of blood and death hit me as violently as a punch. My eyes drifted down the side of the cart, to the grimy cloth covering lumpy contents. Behind him, the sun crept over the bay, glittering red on the water. The death cart was early, out even before the first shift of workers left for the factory.

"You all right?" the driver asked.

"Yes, sorry," I said. "I wasn't paying attention."

He tipped his head back. "I've seen you around. Where's your city boy?"

The corner of my mouth twitched in a smile. *Mine.* "He's visiting his family."

The driver took in the pack strapped to my back. "That where you heading?"

I nodded.

"You're from the north, yeah?"

I nodded again. Our accents gave us away.

"I can take you halfway there, if you want to save some coin." When I hesitated, he added, "I mean, if you don't mind . . ." He glanced over his shoulder, at the bodies on the cart.

I hefted myself up to sit beside him. I'd intended to stop by the quarantine hospital on the way, but if I could save some silver, I could bring the money home to my parents.

The driver clucked at his draft horses, leading them down to the docks. "So what's your story?"

"A student at Yūgen, going home," I said.

He looked impressed. "I wondered as much. Good to see a local girl not in a factory."

That was the way of the north; everyone there was local.

"Scholarship," I said, unable to hide the pride in my voice. I never spoke about the scholarship from the mysterious benefactor at school; it was too close to bragging, too likely to draw the kind of attention I didn't want. But this man reminded me of Papa.

"Good on you!" he said. "You taking alchemical robes and all?"

"Maybe," I said. Who knew if only one year at Yūgen would be deemed worthy enough.

"Always a string, nah?"

We hit a bump in the street, and the bodies behind us thumped heavily. "Always a string," I said.

The cart clopped onto the dock, the horses' hooves landing with a hollow thud. The driver had me get down while he unhitched the horses in front of a flat-bottomed boat, larger than any of the others out there. When we were ready to go, we pushed off from the dock.

We stopped at the quarantine hospital. I thought again of getting off there, but before I had the chance to volunteer, workers emerged with more bodies. The driver tied up the ferry, then jumped down to help put the dead into the boat. I climbed down after him and moved to help.

"Nah, you're a lady; you wait up there," the driver said, nodding to the boat.

"I am *not* a lady," I replied, reaching to help bear the burden.

I am not one of them. My heart belonged to the north, my soul to the church, my hands to the hospital.

The driver nodded appreciatively, and together we loaded new bodies onto the cart on the boat. The workers thanked us—one of them calling me by name—and the driver pushed off away from the stone steps.

"So what's your story?" I asked him as we crossed the open water, heading to the forest in the center of the island and the field Dilada had helped clear.

"Parents worked in the mills."

"Which one?"

"Grindhouse. Dust killed 'em."

"I'm sorry."

The driver focused on the boat, but we were gliding smoothly through the water. "Didn't want that life. Tried to cut it as a farmer. Couldn't. So here I am."

Bearing the dead to their graves.

I looked behind us, past the quarantine hospital on its little island and toward the rocky cliffs upon which Northface Harbor sat. The southerners saw features in the dark spots—a face looking out at the bay—but the northerners saw features in the light parts. My grandmother used to say the cliffs held an image of a rabbit. I liked that story much better.

As the sun rose higher into the sky, the bodies began to smell. I turned my face away, but there was no escaping the strange, sweetly rotting humid stench.

"Yeah, it's bad," the driver said when he noticed my expression. "You get used to it, though."

I thought about the quarantine hospital.

"I guess you can get used to anything," I said.

At the clearing, I could still see the small iron rings that Governor Adelaide had given us, spread intermittently along the rows of graves. More graves had been added since then, and more rings, too—it was good to know that someone was memorializing the dead. The smell of earth, fresh and damp, filled the air—a welcome relief from the stench that clung to the death cart.

"Avoid any villages with black marks," the skipper warned me when I disembarked.

I knew this from Papa, but I nodded anyway and thanked him.

Cutting through the forest and approaching my home village from the south was a different route than I was used to, but it was easy enough to stick to the coast and then veer up at the first village. I got lucky; I walked only about five miles before I ran into another cart that carried me for the next ten. I walked another three or so when that cart stopped at a village with sassoon blooms carved into its gate, and then joined a caravan that dropped me less than a mile from my own village. The sun had set by the time I passed under the gates with carved carmellina flowers. I breathed a silent prayer to Oryous; there was no black bunting on the tall wooden planks.

In the spring, people from villages miles away would come here to celebrate the solstice, and carmellina flowers would pop up in the trees, huge and red and fragrant. In the winter, my sister and I would slide across the icy pond until fishermen cracked it open, dropping their lines below the surface. People knew our village because it was home to the flowers, and to the fish, and to my father, the only book seller in the area.

The main road gave way to the heart of the village. Stone houses and stores with thatched roofs, shared walls, and a covered walkway lined each side of the street. I peered into the dark windows, my heart singing. I spotted the dry goods store where we bought feed for the mule, the bakery where Mama sent Nessie and me to fetch bread when she was too busy to bake it, the church hall creating a dark outline against the stars.

Home.

I broke into a smile as I left the main road and veered toward my parents' house. Every window was dark, but not theirs.

I ran the last few steps, and the front door swung open. My sister stood in the light from the door, and even though I couldn't see her face, I heard her laugh. "You're home!" she called, running down to greet me. "What are you doing home?" She wrapped her arms around me, laughing, saying that Mother was already asleep, and I closed my eyes.

I wanted to be nowhere else in the entire world other than here.

THIRTY-EIGHT

Nedra

ERNESTA AND I crept through the house, careful not to wake my mother. Papa was still out on his latest book run. My bed was all made up, as if I'd never left, my sheets crisp with sprigs of dried lavender tucked inside. "This is heaven," I said, throwing off my clothes, slipping into a camisole, and falling into bed.

"Those fancy beds in the city no good?" Nessie said, grinning at me.

"*Nothing* is as good as this bed," I said, sighing heavily as I rubbed my face against the sheets.

"Not even that boy you wrote me about?" Nessie's eyes twinkled mischievously. I considered throwing my pillow at her, but decided it wasn't worth the loss.

We talked late into the night, just like when we were little kids. Our beds were so close that we could reach across the distance and touch each other's fingertips. When I woke the next morning, I was curled up to the very edge, one hand slung across the valley between our beds, resting on the corner of her pillow.

Ernesta was gone. But at the foot of my bed was a simple brown dress, the hem embroidered with red flowers. I threw back the covers and tossed the dress over my shoulders as quickly as possible, then snuck out of my room. I crept down the hallway, toward the sound of voices—my sister and my mother, eating breakfast in the kitchen.

Bookshelves lined both walls of the hallway, and I breathed deeply. Nothing was as intoxicating as the smell of old books.

I caught Nessie's eye through the doorway, and she winked. She was wearing the exact same brown dress with red flowers on the hem. Her black hair was braided in a crown, just like mine.

"Excuse me, Mama," Ernesta said politely. "I forgot something in my room." She got up and left the table, heading down the hall to me. She paused, grinning, and I couldn't help but mirror her smile. That's what we were—mirror twins, identical in almost every way.

Ernesta stayed in the hall while I walked to the kitchen, sitting down at the table.

"I'm going to have to tell the boy to bring more milk next time," Mama said, her back to me.

I bit back a grin. Ernesta and I hadn't tried this trick in years.

"I want to make a cake for when your father gets back," Mama continued. "But for tonight, I'd like to make that stew Papa likes, the one with lamb. Can you go to the butcher for me?"

"Of course, Mama," I said, careful to keep my voice light like Ernesta's.

Mama whipped around, squinting at me.

"Is something wrong?" I asked innocently.

Her eyes narrowed a fraction more.

Just then, Father's cart rumbled outside the kitchen window. Mama rushed to the door, slinging it open as Papa unhitched Jojo. I followed Mama outside.

"Bardon!" Mama called. "You're home early!"

Papa beamed at her. "I missed my girls!" he said. And then his eyes fell on me. "Nedra! What are you doing here?"

"Nedra?" Mama glared as I burst into laughter. Ernesta ran from the kitchen, cackling. "Nedra!" Mama screeched. "I *knew* it was you, but you—oh!" She growled in frustration, but Papa whirled her around, spinning her in the air and kissing the anger out of her.

Ernesta punched my shoulder. "She fell for it!" she said, laughing. That was no small accomplishment; Mama almost never mistook us.

"Honestly, Mother, how can you not tell the difference between your only two children?" I asked in a superior tone. Ernesta wove her arm through mine, and we pressed our cheeks together, smiling up at our parents innocently.

"You demon-children!" Mama shouted, but she was laughing. She took a book from Papa's cart and threw it at us.

"Not the books!" Papa said, snatching for it, but it was already out of his reach. I easily caught the tome—a history of the Oryon religion—and placed it back on the cart.

Mama grabbed me, wrapping me in a hug. "Nedra," she whispered. "My Nedra." She squeezed me tightly. "But what are you doing back now?"

Joy slipped from my face. "The plague—" I started.

Mama smoothed my hair and pulled me back into her hug.

"We worried about that," Papa said. "Here and in the city, if reports from Hart are to be believed."

"They are," I said.

Mama squeezed tighter. "And to think," she said, pulling back. "I was worried I wouldn't recognize you when you came back from the city."

"Technically, you didn't," I pointed out.

"Inside!" Mama announced. "Food!"

After we helped Papa put Jojo into her stable, we gathered in the kitchen and Mama started cracking eggs into a hot pan. Ernesta had drilled me yesterday about the city, and I had to repeat almost all of it, describing everything from the food to the clothing to the people.

"And I met the governor," I said.

"You didn't!" Mama gasped.

"You didn't tell me that," Ernesta grumbled.

"She's *really* nice," I said. "She came to the hospital to visit the sick."

"She's not bothered coming north," Papa muttered.

In the flurry of catching up and eating breakfast, we'd not noticed how little Papa had spoken.

"Papa?" Ernesta asked.

He held his head up with one hand, and he tilted his face toward her without really looking up. "Sorry, little flower," he said. "I'm just tired. Long day on the road to get here by morning." He leaned back in his chair. "And it was worth it for the surprise when I got home," he said, beaming at me.

I grinned at Papa. His eyes were red-rimmed, and the alchemist in me started analyzing him. Sallow skin, hunched shoulders, slightly glazed eyes.

"Are you feeling okay?" I asked.

"I pushed Jojo too hard," Papa said. "Two more villages were closed," he added, looking up at Mama.

Ernesta and I exchanged a worried look.

Papa pushed his chair from the table. "Sorry, loves," he said. "I think I need to take a nap."

He leaned down to hug me in my chair, but all I could think about was how hot his skin was against mine.

THIRTY-NINE

Nedra

"YOU'RE BEING PARANOID," Ernesta said as we walked into town together.

"He took a nap," I pointed out. "Papa *never* naps."

Ernesta paused to peer into the window of the general store. "He was tired. He'd just come back from a long trip." She turned to me. "He's doing that more. Going farther and farther out to sell books. Past Hart, even."

"It's not just books, is it?" I asked.

Nessie shook her head. "Potions, too. Messages between healers. He helps keep a ledger, recording who lived and what treatments were given to them." She caught my look and added, "Nothing seems to work."

"That just worries me more," I said. "So many villages are closed because of the plague, and Papa is exposing himself with these travels."

Ernesta held the door open for me. "Who's going to stop him? You?"

I sighed as I followed her into the butcher's shop. Papa was stubborn.

"Ah!" Lorrina, the butcher, said, grinning at us. "My two favorite girls. Nedra's back again! For good?" Her eyes darted from my sister to me and back again; she wasn't sure which of us was which.

"For a bit," I said.

Lorrina harrumphed, and I ducked my head down, pretending to look at a beef brisket as Ernesta ordered lamb for Mama's stew. My parents and sister were proud of me for finally getting into Yūgen, but many in the village weren't as happy. Lorrina was on the Elder council; I knew there was gossip that I would leave and never come back home, ignoring the people I'd vowed to help with alchemy.

Lorrina slapped the wrapped lamb on her counter, but before Ernesta could pay, I slipped a silver coin from my purse.

"Ned!" Ernesta said, but both Lorrina and I ignored her.

"We've been praying," Lorrina said in her deep voice, "everyone on the council. I don't care if the cure for the plague comes from the city or from the healers here; I just want a cure."

"Me too," I said.

"We're proud of you, Nedra," Lorrina said. "We all are."

Ernesta and I left the shop, the little bell clanking against the door as we stepped out onto the sidewalk. "Look at you," Ernesta said, bumping into my shoulder and grinning at me with pride.

My cheeks warmed, and I looked away.

Ernesta stopped to stare at the big cake on display in the baker's window, then turned to me with excited eyes. "So, tell me more about this boy," she said. "The fancy one."

"Grey's nice."

"'Nice,'" Ernesta mocked me. "Handsome?"

I shrugged dismissively. "I don't want to stab my eyes out when I look at him."

"Oh, be still my heart!" Ernesta shoved against my shoulder. "So you really like him?"

I smiled. "I really do."

But my sister caught the hesitation in my voice. "You really like him, but . . . ?"

"But I should be working on a cure for the plague. He's a distraction."

Ernesta stopped in her tracks and turned around to face me. "Nedra Brysstain, I know you. And you always default to guilt. This plague does not rest on your shoulders alone. Your life is for *living.*"

"You didn't see it," I said. "The pain, the suffering—the families torn apart. It's awful, Nessie, and no one is paying attention. The poor are just . . . forgotten. The wealthy don't care."

"They can stay locked up in their houses until the threat is gone, just like that useless Emperor." Ernesta rolled her eyes. "But you're just one person. It's not your job to save everyone. Besides, didn't you say that the governor was helping out? And that there were others from Yūgen working at the hospitals?"

"Yes, but—"

"So take a break. Just for a little while, give yourself some time to breathe. And if you're not going to tell me more about Grey, then I'm going to tell you about Kyln." Ernesta strode down the street, not looking back to see if I was following.

"Kyln?" I asked. "The fisherman's boy?"

A group of children raced past us, shouting to each other.

"The fisherman's *man,*" Ernesta said. "Pulling up nets all day does wonderful things to biceps."

I laughed at her enthusiasm. Kyln was only the flavor of the month; Ernesta was as easily distracted by beautiful men and women alike. But I was glad to see she was over Kava, the shoemaker's apprentice who'd died of the plague soon after I left for Yūgen.

I wondered what Nessie would do if she ever met Grey, with his narrow chin and broad chest and that perfect spot on his shoulder that seemed as if it were made for me to place my head. And his eyes, brown with gold flecks. Whenever he looked at me, it felt as if I were the center of the universe.

I didn't notice that Ernesta had stopped until I almost bumped into her. Her eyes were wide, staring at the heavy black curtains being strung up over the windows of the house four doors away from our own.

"The Longshires," I said, thinking of the family who lived inside. When I left for Yūgen, Sarai Longshire was pregnant with her first child, and Benn Longshire was ecstatically telling everyone he knew.

The group of children who'd rushed past us threw rocks at the little house.

"Have some respect!" Ernesta said, rushing forward and snatching a stone from the closest boy's hand.

"Elder Gryff said we could," the boy said in a snotty voice.

"You're Levin, aren't you?" I asked.

He glared up at me. "You're the girl who went to live down south." He picked up another stone and threw it at the window. It plinked on the glass.

"Let them throw rocks," I told Ernesta as I pretended to walk away. "When they break a window, they'll be the first to be infected by the plague."

I smiled as a half dozen stones clattered to the ground. "Really?" Levin asked.

"What's the point of sealing someone who's sick in their house if you break a window and let the sickness escape?" I said.

Levin considered me for a moment, then turned to the other children. "Come on," he said, and they ran off.

Ernesta bowed her head and turned toward home. I grabbed her arm, stopping her. "Is a healer coming?" I asked. "For the Longshires?"

"I don't know," Ernesta said. "None came last time."

My stomach twisted. "Last time?" I gasped.

"Mama didn't want me to tell you," she said, looking away. "But there've been two other families infected this month. The Xandies and the Redavs."

"The Redavs?"

"They all . . ." She couldn't bring herself to say it. There were seventeen members of the Redav family, all living in the big farmhouse half a mile outside of the main village. All of them . . . gone.

"I didn't know," I said. "There's no black bunting on our gates."

Ernesta laughed, but the sound wasn't joyous. "They don't do that when there are only a few cases," she said. "Kava was one of the first."

"I'm sorry," I said softly.

"But she lived farther out. Not really in town, you know." Ernesta kept talking as if I'd not spoken. "And just two—three families in town. It's not so bad." She saw my face. "It's *not*," she insisted.

She started back toward the road home, but I didn't. I stared at the Longshires' door for several more moments, and then I turned on my heel, racing down the hill toward my house, rushing past Ernesta, still carrying the meat for dinner. I burst through the front door, bounded down the hall to the room I shared with my twin, and rooted around in my bag until I had my golden crucible in my hand. Then I dashed back out the house and toward the Longshires'. Ernesta called something to me as I raced past her, but I didn't catch it.

I couldn't cure them. I knew that. But I could help ease their pain. I had to do something.

I pushed open the Longshires' yard gate and marched toward the front door.

"Nedra Brysstain!" a voice bellowed so loudly that I jumped in surprise.

Elder Gryff strode toward me, his old face turned down in a deep frown. "What do you think you're doing?" he asked.

"I'm going to help," I said. "I've been working at the hospital in Northface Harbor; I've treated dozens—hundreds of plague patients. I can help."

"There is no cure."

"No," I confessed, "but I could alleviate their pain until a surgeon arrives." I turned back to the door, but Elder Gryff grabbed my wrist and dragged me forcefully back through the yard gate and onto the street.

"Let me go!" I shouted, trying to pull away.

"I've heard what you do in the hospitals, Nedra," Elder Gryff said, and there was some emotion in his voice . . . was it sympathy? "But we cannot allow that here. When someone falls sick, their home is closed. That's the way."

If this was a normal illness, quarantine would be effective. But it hadn't helped anyone at the hospital.

"I can help," I said again, brandishing the golden crucible in front of him.

"No," he said, pushing me toward my own home. "No, you can't. Go home. We know how to deal with this."

I tried twice more to go to the Longshires' house, but Elder Gryff had set a watch. Friends, neighbors—they patrolled the house, ensuring that no one went in and no one left. I could see the fear on their faces, the most powerful motivator to drive them into action.

That night, I snuck out. The guard was sleeping; it was easy to slip by him and creep to the front door, my golden crucible in hand.

But when I knocked, no one answered. And I knew.

I was already too late.

FORTY

Nedra

WHEN I AWOKE the next morning, Ernesta's eyes were already open and staring at me. She knew I'd snuck out last night.

"I had to try," I said.

"You always do."

It was strange, how easily I fell back into the old familiar habits of home. I'd been away for months, becoming someone new. A girl who defied traditions and attended a school that didn't want her. A girl who worked tirelessly to make a difference in a world wracked with plague.

A girl who knew what to do with love.

But now, being home, lying in bed across from my twin, it felt like the mask I wore at Yūgen had cracked away.

"I've missed you," I told Ernesta.

She grinned. If we were solemn, we were identical, but it was our smiles that always gave us away. Mine was never quite as bright as hers.

"You have *Grey* now," she said, rolling onto her back and saying his name in a singsong voice.

I threw my pillow at her, then snatched it back so I could rest my head on it.

"Things have to change, though, don't they?" Ernesta said, her tone more serious as she continued to stare at the ceiling. "We have to figure out what we want to do with ourselves. We can't stay here forever."

"Growing up is overrated," I said, waiting for her to turn to me so we could share a smile. "Let's just stay here forever."

"Says the girl who's leaving as soon as that school opens again."

"*If* it opens again."

Nessie groaned. "Quit being so pessimistic. There will be a cure. The plague will pass. And you'll be gone again."

"But not forever."

"You know," Ernesta said, "if we stay here forever, we won't get any bacon."

Once she said it, I smelled the bacon Mama was frying in the kitchen. Before Nessie could protest, I threw my quilt on her and dashed out of our room. She shouted in frustration as she got tangled up in the heavy cloth but soon chased after me.

"Shh," Mama said as we sat down at the table. "Your father's still sleeping."

Ernesta and I exchanged a dark look. Papa had gone to bed early last night after barely eating any of Mama's stew. He must have slept ten hours, and he still wasn't up?

"I'm going to check on him," I said, pushing back my chair.

"Eat breakfast first," Mama said. "Let him sleep."

I shook my head, already heading back down the hall. Dread rose in my throat.

You're being paranoid, I told myself. *You've been around the plague too much, and now you're seeing it everywhere.*

"Papa?" I said softly, pushing open the door to my parents' bedroom.

He didn't stir. He lay flat on his back, his eyes shut, and for one horrible, horrible moment, I thought it was already too late.

I rushed to his bed, picking up his left hand and feeling for a pulse. *There.* Relief flooded through me as I felt his heartbeat thudding through his veins.

"Papa?" I asked gently. Behind us, Ernesta and Mama crowded into the doorway, blocking some of the light.

"Nedra." Papa's voice was weak, dry.

"I'll get him some water," Mama said, darting back down the hall.

"What's wrong?" I asked. "Where does it hurt?"

Ernesta moved forward, reaching for Papa's other hand. And in the light from the hallway, I saw the thing I dreaded most in the world.

The tips of Papa's fingers were black.

Cold terror washed through my blood.

"What do we do?" Ernesta asked in a whisper.

Mama came back with a glass of water. She saw the way I held Papa's hand, the light illuminating the blackness in his fingers. The cup slipped from her grasp, crashing to the floor. The glass shattered, and water spilled everywhere.

I stood up.

"Clean that," I said, pointing to Mama. "Get my bag, the new one I brought from school," I told Ernesta.

My words spurred a flurry of motion as Ernesta leapt over the mess, and Mama went to fetch a towel. I ripped Papa's blankets away, pulling up the legs of his trousers. There was blackness on both of his feet, creeping up from beneath his toenails, over the tops of his feet, swirling into his calves.

I covered him with the blanket again.

Mama didn't look at Papa as she knelt in the doorway, clearing away the glass and water. Ernesta called my name and handed me my bag, leaning over Mama.

"We need rats. Or some other small animal that will fit in here," I said, lifting out my golden crucible.

My mother gasped. She had never seen that much gold before.

"We don't have any traps," Ernesta said. "The Sens had a litter of kittens, and they've been in our stable . . ."

"A kitten then," I said, not thinking about how horrible it would be. "Go. Now."

Ernesta turned on her heel and ran outside.

"What can I do?" Mama asked, her voice empty, small, tired. Weak. She stood up, the broken glass wrapped in the wet dish towel.

I crossed the room and wrapped her in a hug.

"It's too late, isn't it?" she whispered into my hair.

I held her tighter.

Ernesta was gone for so long that I had time to set up the crucible, mix a tonic, and feed it to Papa before she returned. I could hear her and Mama whispering outside Papa's room, but I couldn't make out their words.

"Finally," I said.

"I couldn't find any."

I looked up at my sister. "I even went into town. No rats. No kittens. I couldn't find anything."

I growled in frustration. Papa hadn't slipped into the coma-like sleep of a late-stage victim. He didn't moan, but I could tell he was in pain.

"Fine," I said, nodding my head, my decision made. I held Papa's hand in one of mine and gripped the edge of the empty crucible. I muttered the runes, and they glowed dimly in the dark room.

Ernesta watched in silence. She didn't know how alchemy worked; she was never interested in the old textbooks I'd get from Papa's stacks of books. She didn't know what I was about to do.

Pain flowed from my father's body, through me, and swirled into the base of the crucible. I frowned, concentrating. With no vessel to take the pain, there was only one other place for it to go.

Into me.

I gritted my teeth, tugging at the pain. Its presence in the crucible felt like rain falling gently, but when I directed it back into myself, it burned like acid, white-hot heat spreading through my veins, seeping into my bones. Agony soaked into me, lingering on my skin, tearing through my joints.

I gagged, choking for air, and Ernesta made a move toward me, but I shook my head. I couldn't let her touch me; I couldn't risk breaking contact. I had to take all the pain, and I had to do it now before I lost my nerve.

My breath came out in rattling gasps, and I forced my mind to focus, my body to accept. Pulling the pain from Papa's body was like pulling water from a river by pinching it between my fingers.

Black spots dotted my vision, and I collapsed.

I woke up in the chair I'd placed beside Papa's bed, the crucible in my lap.

"I couldn't move you," Ernesta said. She'd pulled up another chair beside me.

"Papa?" I asked.

"He's sleeping." Her voice was low.

I tried to stand, and my back seized with pain. I collapsed back into the chair. Pins and needles prickled through my flesh, burning in agony.

"You pushed too hard," Ernesta said.

"I had to do something."

She helped me stand up, and we walked gingerly down the hall. She tried to take my crucible from me as she helped me into bed, but I couldn't relax my grip; my fingers were frozen like claws. I curled up around the warm metal and fell asleep.

When I woke, it was dark, but according to the clock on my wall, only a few hours had passed. I let go of the crucible. The pain was fading from me, which meant it must be re-emerging for Papa.

It was so dark in the hallway I almost couldn't see. Mama had a fire going in the hearth in the front room. It was stifling hot, the orange glow of the flames casting eerie shadows around the room.

"Has he woken?" I asked.

Mama shook her head. "How are you?"

I tried to shrug, but even that movement hurt, so I sat down in a chair by the door. "Why'd you light a fire? It's too hot." Even though it was winter, the weather was mild and warm, unusually so.

Ernesta started to answer, but Mama caught her eye and she fell silent.

"We should open a window," I said. I started to move, but Ernesta jumped up, pushing me gently back into the seat.

"No point," she said.

I turned to the window, and realization hit me as forcibly as the stench from the death cart: It wasn't dark outside—the windows were covered in heavy black cloth.

We'd been quarantined.

FORTY-ONE

Nedra

"THEY CAN'T KEEP us here," I said, jumping up despite the pain and moving to the door.

The second I opened it, a rock slammed into the doorframe. Another soared past my shoulder, smashing into a vase on the table behind me, and a third rock hit me in the chest so hard that I took a step back into the room. Ernesta got up and slammed the door shut.

"They can't do this to us!" I said.

"Elder Gryff saw me calling for the kittens," Ernesta said. "When I went out. He caught me. I tried to lie, but he guessed the truth. They came while you were asleep."

I looked at my mother and sister. "We have to get you out," I said. "I've been around this sickness before, I'll be fine, but you could catch it—" I knew I wasn't immune just because I'd been lucky before, but I was desperate to ensure my family's safety.

Mama was already shaking her head. "It's for the best. We can't risk spreading the plague to the rest of the village."

I thought about the Longshires. I could still hear the empty, hollow knocks on their door when no one answered.

"I have friends. We'll take Jojo and the wagon and go into the city. The hospital will help us."

Mama shut her eyes. "Your father wouldn't survive the trip."

"You two, then," I insisted.

"You can barely stand," Ernesta said. She held my arm, supporting me. The aftereffects of taking Papa's pain still burned in my blood.

"There has to be something . . ." I muttered as she led me to our room.

My crucible still lay in the center of the bed. I clutched it to me, and Ernesta pulled the quilt over my shoulders. I fell asleep again, exhaustion overwhelming my body.

"Nedra."

My eyes creaked open, crusty and dry. My mouth was dry, too. My throat. It felt like I'd walked through a fire.

"Nedra."

I sat up in bed. "Nessie?"

Ernesta grabbed my hand. "Are you okay?" she asked.

I could smell bread baking. "Yes," I said.

"You've slept for hours."

I stood up straighter and realized that my body felt like my own again. "I've never tried to take away someone's pain without a creature to funnel it into."

Ernesta's face was sunken, her eyes red-rimmed and dark.

"What happened?" I asked.

"Papa."

She didn't have to say anything else.

He was gone.

I took his pain, but he died anyway.

"Come on," Ernesta said, and it wasn't until she spoke that I realized I had sort of sunk into myself, my body collapsing to mimic the way my soul felt.

I turned to the sheet on my bed. I grabbed a pair of scissors and cut the cloth quickly, fashioning masks for myself, Ernesta, and Mama.

"First things first," I said, showing Ernesta how to put the mask on, then tying one for myself. I didn't meet her eyes when I added, "For the smell."

"I'll take this to Mama," Ernesta said, picking up the third cloth. "She put some bread in the oven before going to take a nap. It's probably done now."

I suddenly realized I was starving. I headed to the kitchen, opening the oven door and pulling out the loaf of crusty bread baking in the center. I rapped my knuckles on the top of the loaf, listening for the hollow sound inside to tell me it was done.

No one baked bread like Mama. It was perfect. I sank my teeth into the first steaming slice, and for just one moment, I let myself believe the lie that being home meant being safe.

Ernesta entered the kitchen and sat down at the table. The cloth mask for Mama was still in her hands. She didn't meet my eyes. Tears fell from her cheeks and plopped onto the cloth.

"No," I whispered, my head shaking, my body shaking.

I dropped the slice of bread onto the floor and ran to the front room.

She was sleeping. She was just sleeping.

"Mama," I said.

Just sleeping.

I dropped to my knees beside the couch, feeling her wrist for a pulse. There wasn't one. I leaned over her body, reaching for her neck, and Mama's loose shirt fell open a little. And I saw the shadow. I ripped the cloth more, exposing her chest. A black stain swirled over her heart, creeping through her veins up and down her torso. How long had she been infected? Since Papa? When she kneaded the bread, when she sprinkled salt across the top of the loaf? Was she dying as she baked for her daughters? Did she know?

I gagged, still tasting the warm, buttery goodness. My stomach heaved in protest, and I choked down the vomit burning up my throat.

I stumbled up. I had to get out. Get away. I couldn't stand it. The fire, still blazing, stifling, making it hard to breathe. Mama, there on the couch. I couldn't be here. I couldn't be in this house. This wasn't my home. My home couldn't exist without them. It wasn't right. Everything was wrong, bad, off. I had to get out. My heart was thudding, pounding. I couldn't breathe. I couldn't feel my feet, my hands. Maybe the plague was in me, too, blackness creeping through my blood, sucking away my life. I kicked my shoes off and stared at my toes, then looked down at my fingertips. Nothing but the shadows from the fire.

But my heart wouldn't stop racing.

We had to get out of here. As far away as possible.

I stumbled to the door, ripping it open. Something hit me in the shoulder, knocking me back. I didn't stop. Another rock, hitting me in the head. I kept moving. Blood leaked down my face. I touched it. Red. Not black. *Red.*

Dimly, I was aware of the gathering crowd of children holding stones. Of Ernesta, calling for me to return.

A shot rang through the air, the sound cutting through my panicked thoughts, ricocheting through my ears, silencing the chaotic pulsing in my brain.

I stopped.

"Not one step further." Elder Gryff stood in front of our yard gate, a gun leveled at my chest. He wore a heavy cloth mask over his face, and his eyes were wide with terror. Behind him, people clutched stones. Not just children—neighbors. Friends. Kyln, the boy Ernesta thought was handsome. The Petrasens, whose son I had cared for when the mother was laid up in bed with her second child. There was

Lorrina, the butcher. Tears streamed down her face, but she gripped her heavy rock

"They're *dead*," I said, my voice pleading. I turned to the house and saw Nessie in the door, afraid to step out onto the porch. "Please, let me and my sister leave. We're not infected. My parents . . . they're already gone."

"Go back inside."

"*They're dead!*" I screamed. "We can't stay in there with them!"

Elder Gryff tilted his head, looking down the barrel of the gun. His finger was tight on the trigger.

"Please," I begged.

"We can't risk it," he said.

Up and down the street, more than a half dozen homes had black cloth over the windows. Our village was dying, and the council was trying its best to save who was left. A part of me understood it. Agreed with it. But my parents were dead inside that house, and this mob wanted to trap me with their corpses.

"Please," I said again. "We'll take the mule cart and go. I have friends in the city."

"You could infect every village you pass on the way out." Elder Gryff's voice was choked.

I bowed my head, turned, and went back inside. Ernesta shut the door behind me, the sound of the metal latch echoing throughout the house.

FORTY-TWO

Nedra

I sent Ernesta to the kitchen as I gathered Papa's stiffening body onto a quilt and dragged it down the hall lined with the books he loved so much. I put him on the floor beside Mama, and then I doused the fire. My sister and I did what we could to pay respect to our dead parents. We said the Oryon prayers. Nessie lit candles near their eyes, so that the light could guide their souls to the afterlife. I took off their shoes and rubbed dirt into the soles of their feet so that it would be easier for their spirits to leave the bodies. We carried out the traditions, we mourned as we were able, and we slept that night in each other's arms, huddled in the corner opposite my parents' corpses.

The next morning, I blinked away the fear and panic and sorrow and forced myself to become Nedra the student, not Nedra the daughter. I took Ernesta by the hand, and we left the room where my parents were laid to rest, shutting the door firmly behind us.

"How long will we have to wait?" I asked my sister.

"A week," she said. "When the Sens fell sick, Elder Gryff made us all wait a week, then he shouted to see if there were any survivors."

"Were there?"

Ernesta didn't look at me. She was staring at the loaf of bread Mama had made, still sitting on the counter. "The middle child, Ivynna. She came outside."

I hadn't realized I'd been holding my breath. "I'm glad one of them lived."

"Her hand . . ." Ernesta looked down at her own hand, extending her fingers in a way I knew Ivynna must not have been able to. "They sent her back inside and waited another week. When she didn't come to the door a second time, they burned the house."

We busied ourselves with emptying out the cabinets, laying all the food on the kitchen table. We left Mama's bread on the counter. We weren't going to eat that.

"This will last us the week," I said. "We just need to be careful."

"I'm not hungry," Ernesta said.

We sat down at the table, and we tried not to think about what was behind the closed door of the front room.

That night, Ernesta and I slept in our beds, our hands bridging the distance between our mattresses.

"Tell me about the school." Ernesta whispered. "And the people you met, and the city. Tell me about Grey."

I pretended to be asleep.

Ernesta and I went through the motions of being alive, but we moved carefully, as if we'd planned these slow dance steps, picking our way through the house, our eyes sliding over the closed doors. We lit a fire in the kitchen for light—the black curtains blocked the sun, and the oil in the lamps would run out quickly. In the stifling heat, I spread open the book Master Ostrum had given me.

I read every word Bennum Wellebourne had written on those pages. I studied it closer than I'd studied any book before. But there was nothing about the plague.

Ernesta opened the trunk at the end of the hall, the one that held Mama's crafts—gifts she had been making for us for when we married or moved away from home. Mama had started working on it when I first received my acceptance letter from Yūgen, but already there were two quilts inside, one for me and one for Ernesta. Nessie took hers and lay in bed, clutching the cloth against her chest as if it were a doll.

My eyes blurred as I struggled to read. I didn't want Wellebourne's words. I wanted Papa's. I felt guilty to put aside the text Master Ostrum had given me, but maybe there was something else on Papa's shelves, something like my great-grandmother's journal.

I sprawled on the hallway floor, pulling book after book from Papa's shelves. His organization system was chaotic, and some books had handwritten notes on scraps of paper inside. *Reserved for Rocwyn*, or *A gift from Aunt Gaitha; don't sell*.

The ones closest to the kitchen—and the back door—were those he intended to load onto his cart for his next trip out. The books nearer his bedroom were more valuable tomes, some of them wrapped in leather or protected by specially sized wooden boxes with bronze latches. Some he intended to sell for the right price; some were priceless.

There was a slender book of poetry in cheap cloth binding nearest to the bedroom. I slid it off the shelf, turning it over in my hands. It didn't look particularly special, a cheap volume of mass-produced saccharine drivel made popular by the Emperor or some other important mainlander. Not at all the kind of thing Papa would usually cherish.

I flipped it open.

To my darling love, it said in my mother's handwriting.

The days ticked by.

I wondered if Yūgen was open again, if they would let me know when I could come back.

I'd take Ernesta with me. They wouldn't let her in the dormitory, but we could sell Papa's cart and find a small apartment in Whitesides.

I hoped someone was feeding Jojo.

Once I returned to the city, I could get a job as a medical alchemist even without officially taking the robes, and eventually we could afford a better place to live. And if not, we could travel the outer regions together, working to help stop the plague.

Or we could leave. Sail the world.

Go anywhere but here.

I clawed at the edges of the house, trapped like a rat in a crucible. It was strange how death turned a home into a prison. I couldn't stand the walls, the heavy black cloths that blocked out the light. *Keep me here, fine, but let me see the sun.*

Ernesta stayed in bed, wrapped in our mother's quilt and her own sorrow.

The food on the table dwindled.

We didn't touch the bread.

I read.

I stuffed tablecloths into the cracks around the door of the front room.

It was starting to smell.

After poring over the books on the hallway shelves, I ventured into my parents' room. The bed was unmade; unusual for them. A sharp pang sliced through my stomach. My mother cared so much about things being neat. I shook out the crumpled quilt and straightened the sheets. I fluffed the pillows and arranged them just right.

I tried not to think about the long dark hair on my mother's pillow, or the way my father's side smelled of his shaving soap. I tried not to think of the lies that whispered up to me from the bed, promising that my parents weren't gone, that I'd see them again. After all, here was their bed, their room, their life—right here, waiting for them.

Papa had books lined up on a shelf in his room, too. These were his treasures, his personal library. Some I recognized from my grandparents' house before they passed away, some he simply kept for sentimental reasons. They were Papa's "finds" in his travels, the books he'd picked up on the road that were so valuable he kept them out of reach, even from us.

I sat on the floor, my back resting against Papa's side of the bed, his worn slippers by my knees, and I pulled the books from his shelf.

I opened an old leather-bound Oryon-illuminated manuscript, each page decorated with gold and silver paint, the words handwritten in fading brownish-red ink. There was no title, just three faded stars on the cover representing Oryous, the three-in-one god, past, present, and future. He has seen me grow up, he is with me now, he knows what I will do in the future. He knew, he knows, he will know forever.

I leaned over the book, squinting through the embellished letters. The old tongue wasn't an easy language to learn, but I sounded out the opening passages, partly from memory. They were about faith and love and forgiveness and acceptance, but my parents were still dead and gone, and none of these words would ever make that okay. I knew it, I know it, I will know it forever.

I closed the giant book and leaned down, resting my forehead against the cover. Hundreds of years ago, someone pressed heavy stamps into the leather to decorate the book, and someone else bound the pages that had been toiled over by someone else, and every single someone from so long ago had done that for this moment, to reach out to another they'd never know and hope the words meant something.

They didn't.

But when I leaned back up, I saw not the words, but the love and work and hope that led to their creation, and maybe *that* meant something. Maybe.

I pulled down the next volume. An old atlas, with lines marking the Empire's reach, the maps now incorrect. The mainland and capital city hadn't moved, but the Emperor's rule now stretched deep into Siber to the east, Enja to the south, and into the sea, into islands like this one. Pockets of colonies scattered across countries, each one with a new regent ruler like Governor Adelaide, each one serving under the Emperor. I wondered if the governors in Siber or Enja had ever experienced a civil war like we had so many years ago. I wondered if they still felt the repercussions, a century later. I wondered if some people scratched arrows on old buildings and whispered about another rebellion; I wondered if the Emperor knew or cared.

I shut the book with more force than I'd intended. What did I care about the rest of the world when my own was crumbling down around me?

I reached for the next book.

The cover was so worn I couldn't read the title embossed into the tan leather. I opened it carefully; the paper was thin as onionskin.

It was an alchemical text, but handwritten in an older style, not Standard Imperial. Hope surged within me as I recognized some of the runes. Finally, finally, here was a book that may help me.

"Neddie?"

I was so startled that I dropped the book, losing my place. "Ernesta!" I snapped, impatient.

She shrank against the doorframe as if I'd hit her.

"What?" I said in a softer tone.

"Nothing." She slipped back into the hallway, silent as a petal falling.

I rolled my eyes and carefully picked the book back up, my fingers peeling the thin pages apart. She had spent almost the whole week huddled on her bed and had chosen now to interrupt me.

The ink was faded and the light was failing, but I read anyway. My head ached. The book was mostly full of warnings about the evils of necromancy, but then I found what I was looking for.

"A skilled necromancer manipulates both death and life," the book said near the middle. "Death comes in many forms. Perhaps the easiest to manufacture is by means of a plague. The necromancer's hand can be seen by the black stain of the victim's blood."

"This is it," I whispered to the dark. Proof, finally, that the plague really was caused by necromancy. My hands trembled as I turned the page.

But there was nothing else. No hint of how the plague was made, exactly, or how to stop it, short of killing the necromancer. "No," I whispered, turning the thin paper so frantically that several pages ripped.

What good was knowing the cause if I still didn't have a cure?

"Nessie?" I said gently on the seventh day. She didn't lift her head, but she opened her eyes.

Dehydration, my student brain thought, taking in her symptoms— sunken eyes, sallow skin, ashen look. *Lack of vitamins and sunlight. Depression.* I had spent so much time trying to ignore reality that I hadn't taken a proper look at my sister since this nightmare started.

"It's time," I said.

"Time?"

"We can go."

From outside, we could hear a bell. "Brysstain family!" a male voice called from outside. "Do any of you still live?"

Ernesta wouldn't put the quilt down. She carried it wrapped around her shoulders, the end dragging on the floor behind her, as we staggered down the hall together. I went to the front room door but stopped. We could go out the back. We went through the kitchen. Only dry goods left on the table—some beans, flour, salt.

I opened the door.

We blinked in the sunlight, our eyes stinging from the brightness. The bell that had been ringing silenced.

A dozen or so people stood at the gate. They all had masks covering their faces. I did not recognize any of them, and I didn't care to.

"Just the two of you?" the man called.

I nodded.

"Any sickness on you?" In one hand, he held the bell. In the other, he clutched a gun. I looked past the fence, to the other houses on my street.

Every single one was draped in black cloth.

I held up my bare hands, then lifted my skirt to show my unblemished feet. When no one did anything, I pulled down my shirt, showing that my chest was uninfected.

"And her," the man said, waving his gun to indicate Ernesta.

She tugged down the front of her tunic, then lifted her feet, first left, then right. She shifted the quilt from hand to hand, turning her wrists to show all sides. She kept her eyes straight ahead, staring at the man.

The man let his bell drop the ground. He aimed his pistol with both hands.

"Back inside," he said.

I started to scream at him in protest, but then Ernesta held up her hand to stop me.

And I saw the blackness leaking from her fingertips into her right palm.

FORTY-THREE

Nedra

BACK INSIDE THE house, I paced up and down the hallway.

"Why didn't you tell me?" I demanded, not stopping.

Ernesta sat in a chair by the door, her shoulders slouched. "I didn't notice."

"You didn't notice!"

But I hadn't noticed either. I'd let Nessie lie in bed, clutching the quilt, while I read and read and read. I had believed I might find answers to the plague in either Master Ostrum's old book or my father's, but they had proven woefully inadequate.

I snatched up her hand and squinted in the dim light at the darkness leaking through her skin. "It's not that bad," I said. "I've seen worse."

"You can stop it?"

I froze for a moment.

Yes.

I knew how to stop it from spreading.

"We have to get you to the city," I said. "To real medical alchemists. To a . . . to a surgeon."

"A surgeon?" she asked.

Then her fingers curled over her palm. She understood. She wasn't naïve. She'd heard Papa's stories about the plague; she knew what I did at the quarantine hospital in the city.

Amputation.

"It'll save your life," I said. "It's the only thing that's worked to contain the disease."

She set her jaw and nodded.

"We'll go tonight. With that many houses fallen from the plague, there aren't enough people left to stop us from leaving. We'll take Jojo, and we'll go."

"Do you really believe I have a chance to—" Nessie's voice was soft, and she didn't finish her thought.

I gripped her hand—the uninfected one. "Yes," I said, pouring every ounce of hope I had left into that one word.

We packed. And we waited. Darkness fell.

Ernesta held the quilt around her shoulders. I slid boots over her feet, using the action to confirm that they weren't infected as well.

"I can carry something," she said as I slung the knapsack over my shoulder. At the bottom rested Master Ostrum's book and the old book I'd found in Papa's room, the alchemy text. And I packed a few knick-knacks to remind us of home. Because we were never coming back.

And my crucible. Nessie wouldn't let me take any of the pain from her hand. "You need your wits about you," she said, and she was right.

"I have this," I said, adjusting the pack on my shoulder. "Ready?"

Ernesta nodded.

I gripped a rope in one hand. Trying to take the cart would draw attention, but we could take the mule. Nessie could ride, and I'd lead.

Ernesta opened the back door. Quietly, we crept out onto the smooth stone step, the one my grandfather had found one day while plowing. We moved onto the path, my eyes fixed on our stable.

Nessie gripped my arm at the same time a shot cracked out across the night. I shifted my gaze. A stream of gray smoke rose from a man's gun. I didn't know him; he just vaguely looked like someone from our village, or perhaps the next one over.

"If you take one more step closer, I will kill you," he said.

I had hoped that there wouldn't be a night watch. That darkness would protect us, hide us for our escape.

"If you try to leave your house again until we call for you," he said, "we *will* kill you."

Under the starlight, I saw more people emerge from the darkness, lining up around our fence. They were all armed, their faces set in grim lines. There were no more children throwing rocks. The plague was spreading, and so was the fear.

"You won't get another warning," the man said.

Beside me, I felt Ernesta slouch, defeat radiating from her body.

"You understand," the man said.

"We're just trying to survive," he said.

"Six more houses have fallen ill," he said.

"We can't risk it," he said.

We said nothing. We turned and went back inside. I locked the door.

Ernesta sat down at the kitchen table. She put her head into her arms, her right hand sprawled out in front of her.

The windows were dark with night and the black cloth that covered them, but I could still feel the villagers watching us, their eyes like wolves'.

I lit the oil lamps and every candle I could find and set them around us. The flickering light bounced off the walls. I lit the fire in the oven and stoked it.

"There's no food left to cook," Nessie said.

I sat down across from her. I held her infected hand. I looked into her dark eyes, the same shade of amber honey as mine.

"We have to do it," I said.

Her fingers curled into a fist, hiding the stain of black.

"We can't wait until morning." Mama and Papa had gone so *fast*, "No one has lived with their blood stained black. No one but those who cut it from their bodies."

Nessie was my baby sister by only twenty-three minutes. But she seemed so small in that moment, so helpless, like we were years apart.

Papa kept grain liquor under the sink in a glass jar. I poured Nessie a shot and watched as she drank it, and then I poured her another one, and another. She kept clenching her hand into a fist, as if memorizing the way it felt for her fingers to fold over her palm, for the muscles to tighten and the skin to stretch and the bones to obey her will.

I pulled out Papa's toolbox. The hacksaw, the teeth still stained with sawdust. The sharpest knife from Mama's drawer. A needle, thread. Towels. Every towel I could find. Papa's leather belt.

I stretched the belt out on the table and hacked off a piece, then used a punch to make more holes. I handed Ernesta the smaller piece of leather.

"What am I supposed to do with . . . ?" Her voice trailed off. She lifted the leather to her mouth and bit down on it. It was as much pain relief as I could give her.

I put the cast-iron skillet on the stove, letting it heat up. My grandmother had cooked on that skillet, my mother.

Silent tears leaked down Nessie's face. Her fingers clenched, relaxed, clenched again.

"More," I said, pushing the jar of liquor at her. She downed the rest of it, choking on the burning liquid, then took up the bit of leather again.

My heart raced, thudding against my ribs as if I'd just run for miles.

"Are you sure we can't wait?" she asked in a small voice.

If I could give her anything, it would be time. I wanted so much to give her *time*.

"No," I said.

Papa's jar was empty.

The rope I'd intended to use as a lead for the mule now tied my sister to her chair. "Try not to struggle," I said. "It's instinct, but . . . try."

I took Nessie's hand in mine, turning it palm up, and stretched her arm on the table. Oh, Oryous. How quick could I make this? I couldn't take her pain, not now, not when I needed my strength. I could only be fast. Fast as I could while still getting the job done.

"Neddie," she whispered.

I shook my head. I couldn't be Neddie right now. I had to be Nedra Brysstain, the top alchemical student at Yūgen, the girl who volunteered at the quarantine hospital.

There had been blood on my hands many times before. Just never my sister's.

"Here," I said, running my finger over an invisible line above her elbow, more than three inches from the faintest tint of black under her skin.

Ernesta nodded.

A human thinks of the pain, of the suffering. A human sees a hand and also sees the person attached to it. I couldn't be a human in this moment. I had to be an alchemist. An alchemist sees the skin that must be sliced apart. The arteries that must be tied off. The bone that must be sawed through. An alchemist knows to hold the arm down so it doesn't wiggle too much.

An alchemist folds the flaps of skin and flesh over the raw wound and stitches it. An alchemist moves to the stove quickly, picking up the hot cast-iron skillet and pressing the bottom against the wound to cauterize it.

An alchemist doesn't hear the screams.

FORTY-FOUR

Nedra

WHEN I FINISHED, Ernesta was still awake, staring at her hand on the table. I untied her from the chair, then moved through the scent of blood and burnt flesh to pull the golden crucible from my bag. She watched me with deadened eyes as I clutched her shoulder and pulled the pain out of her and into me. I took it all without a drop of hesitation. It roared over me like an ocean wave, and I fell to the floor, whimpering. Nessie sighed and slumped against the table.

When I woke the next morning, she was gone. The hand was gone, too.

I staggered to my feet. I *ached*, my entire body tense, my bones flowing with fire. The kitchen was stifling hot. The lamps and the candles had long since died; the fire in the hearth smoldered.

I crept down the hall. Nessie lay curled in my bed, her severed arm held carefully out. I inched my way forward, looking at her skin for signs of infection, feeling her forehead for fever. Her skin was clammy, but she was going to be okay.

She might never forgive me, but she was going to be okay.

I lay down in the bed beside her. Without thinking, I reached my hand toward hers, but I stopped before my fingers brushed her wound.

When I woke the next morning, I went to my parents' room.

I opened the book I'd found earlier—the old alchemy text—and laid it beside the one Master Ostrum had given me. Wellebourne's journal was, at its heart, instructional. Step by step, in clear, simple terms, it outlined the journey to become a necromancer. The first step I already knew: *Create an iron crucible, formed of blood and bone and ash, melded together through sacrifice.*

Sacrifice was described in Papa's book as well. In fact, it seemed to be a central theme. "Should the alchemist determine to cross the god-placed boundaries twixt life and death," the book warned, "his very soul may prove to be the price paid." But just in case the reader was willing to be such a heathen, the book suggested a chant, one that mentioned both the power needed and the willing trade for it. There was no chant in Wellebourne's book, just runes that had to be drawn prior to developing the iron crucible.

Papa's book warned of how addictive necromancy could be. "Once a crucible is made," it said, "the necromancer's voracious need for death will be all-consuming." I shuddered, remembering the strange hunger that awoke within me the first time I danced too close to Death. "Should the necromancer grow powerful enough to form a reliquary and become a lich, he will be invincible in the mortal realms."

I forced myself to analyze both texts, trying to find some connection, some knowledge I'd not been aware of, something. Anything. The most I found was in Wellebourne's book, but while it spoke of necromancer curses, it wasn't specific to the plague. My heart sank as I read, "There are ways to free the undead, should the necromancer be weak. But even if the necromancer's crucible is destroyed, a curse will linger as long as the necromancer lives."

Master Ostrum's book also included detailed charts and diagrams. I opened to one of a crucible cage, but immediately closed the book in disgust. I'd held Bennum Wellebourne's crucible cage in Master Ostrum's office, but now the image reminded me too sharply of my sister and what she had lost. I thought of her severed hand resting on the dining room table my mother used to roll biscuits on.

"Ned?"

I shoved the books under Papa's bed and turned around. Nessie stood in the doorway, her silhouette blacked out against the light in the hall.

"What are you doing up?" I said.

"I missed you."

She had the quilt wrapped around her.

"Go back to bed." I tried to make my voice kind, but it was strained with worry. And guilt. Reading that book made me feel as if she'd caught me doing something deeply wrong.

Instead of going back to her room, Nessie sat down on Mama and Papa's bed. "Tell me about the city," she said.

"I told you everything in my letters."

She smiled at me, a weak little thing that barely curved her lips. "I want to know more. How did it *feel* to be there?"

I shrugged. My fingers inched near the books under the bed. I needed to read more. Even if it was necromancy, even if it was forbidden . . .

"Nessie, I need to work," I said.

Her body seemed to shrink. "I want to hear about your life there," she said, her voice soft. "About the school and Grey and alchemy and . . ."

Her voice trailed off. She could tell she didn't have my attention. I looked up at her, guilt swimming inside me. "I want to help *you*," I said. "I need to read more . . . Maybe there's a way I can help you feel better. It . . . it must hurt." My eyes dropped to her arm, hidden beneath the quilt.

"I understand," she said, and she left the room. I watched her go. Guilt crept through me, but I knew there would be time enough to tell Ernesta my stories later. When she was fully recovered and our parents were buried and we were freed from this house. I'd take her to

Northface Harbor with me. She wouldn't need my stories; she'd make her own.

I retrieved the books from under the bed, skimming the pages for anything, anything at all that I could use.

I fell asleep on the floor, my body curled around the books like a pillow.

The next morning, I woke, my back stiff. I went to the room I shared with my sister.

She wasn't there.

I went to the kitchen. Empty.

There was only one other room in the house.

When I pushed open the door to the front room, I was hit with the rotting smell of my parents. I gagged, but I turned my focus to Ernesta, who sat in the chair by the door, cradling her severed arm in her lap.

"Nessie?" I whispered.

She rocked in the chair. Her eyes were on my parents. The doors were barred and the windows covered, but flies had come anyway, buzzing around my parents' corpses. My mother's face was slack and shiny, a thin film of wax building on the surface. Papa's body was bloated, pale on top, stained purple on the bottom. We'd weighed their eyelids down with buttons when we placed their bodies in the room, but one had slid away from Papa's face. He had a strange, empty wink.

"We should go," I said.

Nessie held out her arm to me. I'd wrapped the wound in thin bands of ripped cloth, but she had unwound it. And even though the room was dark, I could see the black creeping up her skin, swirling toward her heart.

FORTY-FIVE

Nedra

I DRAGGED ERNESTA from the room and shut the door again.

"We can fix this," I said.

"Are you going to hack more of me away?" Her voice was cold, emotionless. Tired.

I ripped her shirt as I pulled it back, examining her as quickly as I could. My eyes traced the stain under her skin. One thin line reached all the way from her wound up her shoulder, swirling over her chest, sinking into her heart.

"No," I whispered. "No more amputation."

"I'm dead, aren't I?" Her calm voice cut me to the core.

"There's a chance—"

But I knew she didn't believe me.

"Go back to bed," I demanded. "Rest. There *is* a chance. Not everyone dies from the plague."

She turned her glassy eyes to me. "You work with people who are sick every day in the city, don't you?" she said. "And you don't get sick." Her gaze dropped to her arm.

She didn't say it, but we were both thinking it: *It's not fair.*

"Rest," I said again. "I'll find a way to help you."

I led her back to her bed, tucked her in. She was so weak she just shut her eyes, and in moments, her soft huffing breath told me she was truly asleep.

I took a deep breath. I went back to the kitchen and fetched my golden crucible.

I couldn't take all her pain, but I could take some.

My hands trembled, after. My skin felt like it was vibrating, shaking loose from my body. My bones felt too heavy, like they would sink into my muscle, like they would weigh down my bed, crack through the frame, sink into the earth.

As soon as I was able, I stood. I paced.

I knew what I had to do.

I lit the oil lamps and candles we had left and I stared at the alchemy texts, flipping the pages so urgently they tore. I didn't care. The books were only valuable if they could help me save her. Papa's book was of no use. It had confirmed what Master Ostrum and I suspected—the plague was made by necromancy. But it gave no solution.

Wellebourne's journal showed more promise.

There was a picture of a skull, its eye sockets empty, and it reminded me of the way my father's one eye stared.

I couldn't let Nessie die. I needed her to live.

I allowed myself to consider the horrible truth that she might not.

And I opened the books again. Between them, there was enough. *I need a crucible cage.* I could use Master Ostrum's. *The ash of a human who loved me.* Papa and Mama, dead in the front room.

It was Papa's book that revealed the third thing I needed. The words had been written as a warning, but I took them as instruction:

> *All of alchemy operates on a balance. The price must be*
> *paid. For necromancy, the sacrifice is even greater than in*

other alchemies, because the reward is so much higher. Much has been written on the laws of ash and bone, flesh and blood.

But there is a higher cost. A necromantic crucible will never be truly complete if it is not imbued with a soul. And if the necromancer does not supply one, the alchemy will still demand a price.

It will take the necromancer's soul.

My eyes went to the hallway, to the door, to the room where my parents lay.

I stood up. I got a knife.

Before, I had to be Nedra the alchemist to do what needed to be done.

Now I would be Nedra the necromancer.

"Ned?" Ernesta's voice was weak as she sat up in bed, calling after me as I strode down the hall. "Neddie?"

I kicked away the oilcloth that had blocked the stench from the front room and swung open the door. I stared straight ahead, but my nostrils flared with the acrid, sickeningly sweet smell of rotting flesh. I forced my head to tilt down, my eyes to focus on the bodies.

Specimens.

Not bodies.

Not Mama and Papa.

"Neddie?" Ernesta asked, more urgently this time. She'd gotten up and stood outside the front room, propping herself up against the wall for support. Fear filled her eyes.

I ignored her as I knelt down beside my mother's body.

Here, the necromantic texts diverged. Master Ostrum's book spoke of carving the runes directly into the flesh of the dead. Papa's book said they should be sealed with the necromancer's blood. I decided to do both.

"Nedra!" Ernesta cried as I pressed the tip of the blade onto my mother's forehead. She had been dead long enough that her blood was thick and oozing, like syrup. I worked quickly, slicing the skin in the shape of the rune for Death. Then I shifted, pulling off the thin cloth of her chemise and exposing her breast as I carved the rune for Life over her heart. I turned the blade to my own hand, pushing the point into the pad of my fingertip until my skin burst. The bright red was vivid against the almost black blood of my dead mother. I retraced the open lines on her skin with my own blood, smearing the two together.

Ernesta said something else, but she was so quiet I did not hear her.

I stepped over my mother's body and knelt beside Papa.

A sharp pain sliced into my gut, and black stars danced behind my eyes.

Not Papa, not Papa.

The specimen.

My hands shook as I carved more runes into his dead flesh. Mama would provide the blood for the crucible; Papa the soul. The rune for Hope on his head, Love on her heart. I had to pierce my finger again and force the blood out to retrace the symbols.

I stood up, letting the knife lie on the floor between the two bodies.

The iron within a human body is limited, but the runes will enable the trace amounts to be easily discovered amid the ash, Master Ostrum's book had said.

The soul will cling to the ash until it is forged within the crucible cage, Papa's book had said.

Now I needed a fire.

"Nedra!" Ernesta screamed as I moved past her, gathering armfuls of Papa's books. "What are you doing?"

I dumped the books onto Mama and Papa's bodies. I closed my eyes and breathed through my mouth, grateful that the pages shrouded their faces. More. I needed more. I ran back to the hallway, my movements frantic. Books spilled out of my arms. Fairy tales with happily ever afters. Children's stories about rabbits and frogs, the margins filled with doodles drawn by my sister and me. The poetry my mother loved so much. Plays from the mainland, histories of the Empire, maps of the world.

Ernesta shrank away from me, her eyes wide and fearful.

You'll see, I thought. *This will save you.*

Leather-bound books with gilt edging on the pages spilled over my mother's legs. The spine of an ancient text broke as I tossed the book, the pages fluttering like butterflies.

And then a spark, a flame, a fire. I expected the smoke, the heat.

I didn't expect the smell.

But I stood there and watched. I knew what had to be done.

Ernesta watched me watching it all burn.

Neither of us spoke. The only sound was the crackling of our world catching ablaze.

FORTY-SIX

Nedra

TIMBERS CREAKED.

"Nedra? Ned? We have to . . ." Ernesta's fingers on my arm were as light as a butterfly's touch, but I could feel the urgency within them.

My home is on fire, a part of me thought, the part of Nedra that wasn't an alchemist or a necromancer. *What have I done?*

My heart leapt into my throat. "We have to get out of here," I told Ernesta, clutching her shoulders.

She nodded, eyes wide. "I *know*," she gasped. "Come on."

She tugged at me with her remaining arm, but I jerked away, rushing to our bedroom. I could feel the heat through the walls; I choked on the air. Hastily, I grabbed my bag and the golden crucible, Master Ostrum's book and Papa's. Ernesta was already in the kitchen, her hand on the back door.

"What if—" she started, but I barreled past her, throwing open the door.

There were people in our yard—neighbors, villagers—the ones who were left, who hadn't yet died of the spreading plague. No one threw rocks at us to go back inside, but no one moved to stop the fire either. Our house was by itself, no risk of the flames jumping to burn another home.

And it was too late anyway. All the houses were illuminated by the flickering orange of our fire—and all of their windows were covered in black cloth. Beyond, I was sure black bunting hid the carmellinas carved on the gates that led to our town. Almost everyone was gone. Anyone left alive now would leave, drift away like petals scattered by a cold wind.

Ernesta cried. Eventually she turned away from me, curling up amid the books in Papa's wagon after feeding a hungry Jojo some musty oats from the bin.

I stayed. I watched it burn. And even before all of the embers died down, I sifted through the ashy remains of the only home I knew.

There, amid the blackened timbers and soot-stained stones of the hearth, were two red outlines where my parents' bodies had been, the runes of Death and Life and Love and Hope glittering like rubies and glowing with an ethereal light.

I sifted through the ash, picking up every trace of my parents that remained, the tiny bits of blood iron ore imbued already with an alchemy I should never have attempted.

Ernesta was asleep as the sun rose over our village. No one else was around. I wondered how many dead were in each house, rotting as the survivors fled. I wondered if there were people trapped inside, like Nessie and I had been, waiting in a hollow building with the hollow shells of their now-deceased family members in rooms that stank of rot. Would they come out? Would they be driven mad? Would they hope to leave but feel the black stain of the plague creeping over their bodies?

I paused, turning to check on Ernesta. Her skin was clammy, paler now, the black streaks in her blood like ink beneath her skin.

"I'll take care of you," I promised.

Jojo was nervous, her hooves stamping the ground, her nostrils flaring. I clucked at her, and she leapt forward, eager to leave. Ernesta moaned as the cart jostled her. I patted her back once, then turned toward the road.

We had a long way yet to go.

• • •

I stopped the cart twice before we reached Hart. Both times I led Jojo off the main road, hidden behind trees, and I took some of Nessie's pain for myself. Although I had my parents' ashes now—enough, I hoped, to make an iron crucible—a small part of me still believed I might not have to use them. A living Ernesta was better than one raised from the dead.

It took all day to get from my parents' house back to Hart and the main harbor in the north. A crowd gathered near the dock, people jeering and throwing rocks at the large, flat-bottomed ferry. One was already halfway across the bay, and I thought I recognized the driver who had brought me home, taking a boat of dead to the graves. The other boat was painted in black tar, and it would be going to the hospital.

"Get out!" a man in the crowd shouted, hurtling a heavy stone at the boat. "No more sick here! Quit bringing the illness to Hart!"

"We're going!" the skipper bellowed.

I stood up in my cart. "Wait!" I screamed. "Wait!"

The people nearest me turned, rage in their faces. "She's sick!" someone shouted, and a rock thudded against the book cart. More damn stones. I could go the rest of my life without seeing another rock.

Ignoring the crowd, I scrambled to the back of the cart, dragging Ernesta up. A few people stood their ground, screaming obscenities at us, but most backed away at Ernesta's evident illness. Jeers of "Get out!" and "Go!" followed us as we stumbled toward the end of the dock.

The boat was crowded, and people lay or sat as they could. I shoved an old man down the bench and pushed Ernesta into the space he vacated. Before the too-eager skipper could push off from the dock, I leapt into the boat, the angry mob still shouting behind us.

"Is it like this every time?" I gasped as waves beat on the hull.

"Nah," the skipper said, not looking at me. "Just bad now. Won't have to worry about it soon. This is the last boat for a while."

I let those words sink in. Last boat? Was the plague lessening now that it had taken so much from me already? Did that mean Yūgen was reopening?

Ernesta groaned, her body shivering. A pang of remorse shot through me—since the fire, the one thing Ernesta had was the quilt my mother had made for her. In my haste, I'd left it on the book cart. I looked behind us. The people on the dock had already unhitched Jojo, letting her run away. The cart was in flames.

One more piece of home gone.

I clenched my teeth and turned toward the quarantine hospital. I still had Ernesta.

That was enough.

FORTY-SEVEN

Nedra

POTION MAKERS AND aides waited at the stone steps. The skipper hailed them as the boat bumped against the edge. Ernesta groaned.

"They'll help you," I whispered in her ear.

I struggled to stand on the rocking boat, Nessie's limp body and my bag weighing me down. Hands reached out, and someone helped pull Ernesta and me onto the steps.

The aides quickly separated people into groups, sending some immediately onto another boat. I guessed the quarantine hospital was so crowded they had to open another treatment center on the mainland. I kept my head down, following Ernesta as we went up the steps.

I'd been to this hospital dozens of times, but never as a patient, with a patient. Even though I knew the building well, knew where we were being taken and why, I felt scared. In the foyer, we were pulled into a tight circle, and aides dusted us all with cans of berrilias powder to prevent the spread of lice.

A cloud of white dust blew into my face, and I stepped back, choking and wiping it from my skin.

"Nedra?" the aide said.

"Nedra Brysstain?" another said, turning.

I knew these people. One was Fare, a potion maker who often worked in the factories; the other was Alric, a fairly new aide who came to the hospital for his mission work.

"You're sick?" Alric asked as Fare reached forward, wiping white powder from my arms, looking for the stain of the plague on my skin

"No—" I said, still choking from the dust. "My sister." I turned to Ernesta. Powder clung to her, but she made no effort to wipe it away.

Alric and Fare exchanged a look.

"Please," I said. "Can you see to it that she's taken care of?"

Alric started to speak, but Fare gripped his arm, her fingernails digging into his skin. "Alric, you take—"

"Ernesta," I supplied. "Ernesta Brysstain."

"Get her some tincture of blue ivy," Fare said.

Alric looked as if he wanted to say something else, but he nodded and led Ernesta away.

"I'll be back!" I shouted behind her. I turned to Fare. "Thank you." I knew all too well how limited their supply of tincture of blue ivy was.

Fare turned to me. "I'm sorry, Nedra," she said. "But I have to be sure."

She waited for her meaning to sink in, and when I nodded, she followed me to a semiprivate hallway where I unbuttoned my shirt, showing her my bare chest. I kicked off my shoes. Fare sank to her knees, carefully inspecting my feet for signs of the plague.

"Oh, sweetness," she said finally, standing and hugging me. "I'm so glad you're okay."

My bag felt heavy, the ashes of my parents waiting inside.

Chimes rang throughout the hospital. I looked at Fare, confused. These were not the normal bell tolls of the clock tower giving the hour. I realized for the first time that while some patients had been hustled to the mainland on a separate boat, the hospital wasn't as overcrowded as I'd assumed. On the contrary, it was almost empty.

"Fare, what's going on?" I asked.

"Come with me," she said.

The hallway was bustling—but not with patients. Aides and potion makers, as well as a handful of alchemists, headed to the main door. In the foyer, I saw Alric, Ernesta still with him. She moved slower now, and he settled her on a chair before running up to Fare.

"Why did you leave Ernesta like that?" I asked. Fare tugged at my arm, pulling me to the door. The bells kept ringing. "Ernesta?" I shouted, louder, but my sister didn't even look up. I yanked free from Fare. "What's going on?" I demanded.

Fare grabbed for me again. "They're closing the hospital." She tried to pull me forward, but I stood firm as the other hospital workers streamed past us. "Come on, Nedra," Fare said. "We have to get on the boat."

"Closing?" I couldn't wrap my brain around it. "But—there are patients. My sister—"

Fare leaned in close. "We've left a case of tincture of blue ivy," she said. She pulled me a few steps closer to the exit. More people had paused now, watching me. I recognized many of them. I'd worked with almost everyone at the hospital during my volunteer stays.

"Is Nedra sick?" an aide named Cor asked Alric.

He shook his head. "Her sister's here," he said.

"Aw," the man said. "Damn shame."

"Tincture of blue ivy . . . for the pain?" I asked, still not fully understanding. I looked behind me. The crowd of workers was gone now, except for the dozen or so waiting for me to follow. But there were still patients everywhere. Some wandered the halls, peering behind doors. Many just lay or sat where they had been left, too tired to move. These were the worst cases of plague. The hopeless cases.

Ernesta looked up at me. I saw a small bottle in her hand. Looking around, I saw bottles in all of the patients' hands—tincture of blue ivy had been passed out like candy. A few of the patients were already unscrewing the tops.

The tincture would cut the pain. But one needed only a few drops. An entire bottle . . .

"No," I said, horror dawning on me.

Fare and Alric leapt to action, both of them taking me by an arm. I struggled against them, throwing Alric off, but not Fare. "You want them to kill themselves?" I asked, my voice pitching to a scream.

"We have to go," another potion maker said. I forgot her name, but I recognized her face.

"No!" I screamed, breaking free and running toward Nessie. She looked up at me.

"The hospital's too crowded!" another aide said. "We don't have a choice!" His words were ridiculous. The hospital was nearly empty now.

"We can take her to Whitesides," I said. "To the Governor's Hospital!"

Fare yanked me around. "They're not taking plague patients there," she hissed at me. "Not ones this far gone."

"How many?" I choked out.

"There are thirty left, with the new arrivals," Alric said. "Just thirty."

"*Just* thirty?" I spat. "That's thirty people you're leaving to die!"

"Nedra, we have to go," Fare said firmly.

She pulled at my arm again, but I jerked away and made a dive for Ernesta. "Not," I started as one of the larger aides grabbed me around my stomach, "Without. My. Sister!" I kicked at him, screaming in frustrated rage, angry tears springing to my eyes. Alric joined the fray, and Fare, and someone else, a potion maker who flirted with me sometimes during breaks. I bellowed, kicking out, scratching Fare across the face, making the potion maker wheeze when my foot connected with her stomach, but I didn't care, they had to let me go, they couldn't just expect me to leave my sister here to die.

Alone.

I was losing ground.

"Don't drink that!" I shouted as Alric and Farc and the others pulled me to the door of the hospital. I lashed out, grabbing the heavy mahogany, holding on as long as I could, my fingers slipping on the smooth wood. "Nessie! You hear me? Don't you drink that! I'm coming back for you!"

I lost my grip, and the others pulled me to the boat, holding me so tight that my bucking body never touched the stones. The alchemists already on board tutted at me, some sympathetically, but I didn't care. "How could you?" I spat at them as the skipper pushed the boat away. "How could any of you?" I stood up, the boat wobbling. I think they thought I would dive over the side, swim back to the quarantine hospital. A few people even reached for me, aiming to hold me back, but I shook them off.

"The Emperor gave the order," one of the alchemists said. It was Frugal Frue, the alchemist who had been stingy with potions. I wondered if he knew how much tincture of blue ivy had been left behind.

"The hospital is closing," another alchemist said. "And besides"—she turned her head toward the huge castle-like building—"none of them would have made it anyway."

FORTY-EIGHT

Nedra

I REFUSED TO speak to any of the traitors on the boat.

As soon as we disembarked, I tried to board a ferry back.

None would go to the island.

Fine, I thought. *I'll steal a boat tonight. I'll go back on my own.*

But first there was something else I needed to steal.

I barely registered the walk up to Yūgen. Mentally, I stoked my rage, preparing to pry the iron gates apart myself to get to campus—but I didn't need to.

The gates were already open.

School had resumed. Posters littered the gates detailing new methods to protect the students, including strictly enforced potion regimens, no off-campus activities allowed, screening for visitors, and no visitations to any hospital, even for medical students. I wondered how many parents kept their children at home regardless.

I marched onto campus, the feeling surreal. Everything felt so aggressively *normal*—students casually walking from the cafeteria, study groups gathering by the library. I wondered what day it was. How long had classes been back in session?

Didn't they know that everything was different now? That the world had ended already?

I ignored the graveled paths that intersected with the lumpy iron statue of Bennum Wellebourne and went straight to the administration building. I stormed down the stairs to Master Ostrum's office and grabbed the doorknob.

Locked.

I rattled the metal, pulling on it, but it didn't budge. My open palm slammed into the frosted glass window on the door, and it shook so violently it nearly cracked. I kicked at the wood, cursing, and tried the handle again. As I pulled away, the door opened.

"Nedra?" Master Ostrum looked surprised to see me.

I pushed past him. "I need your crucible cage," I said, heading straight to his laboratory. The office door slammed behind me.

He grabbed my shoulder and pulled me around. I spun away from him, but paused. My chest heaved with exertion.

I caught my reflection in one of Master Ostrum's gleaming gold crucibles lined on the bookshelf.

Hair wild and unkempt, body dusted with white lice disinfectant, grimy dirt and soot streaking down my face. My eyes were wild and red-rimmed, my lips cracked with small spots of blood at each corner of my mouth. I looked down at my hands. My nails were jagged, caked in grime, the cuticles ripped. I didn't remember the last time I changed clothes. The last time I bathed.

"I need your crucible cage," I said. The voice reverberating throughout the office didn't sound like my own. It sounded hoarse, cold, broken.

"What happened?" There was nothing but concern in Master Ostrum's eyes, sincere worry at what I had become in the weeks since he'd seen me last.

What would Grey think if he saw me now?

It was with a numb heart that I realized I didn't care. I didn't care what Master Ostrum thought, what Grey would think. None of that mattered. None of it mattered at all.

"You're right," I told Master Ostrum. "The plague is necromantic. It will take a necromancer to stop it."

Master Ostrum frowned, deep lines etched into his forehead. "I've thought that, too. But it will not be you."

Didn't he understand that it was already too late?

Clomping boots echoed throughout the hallway outside Master Ostrum's office. He jerked around like an expectant dog on alert. "Go to the lab," he ordered.

I went around his desk, stepping up into the lab. I closed the door behind me, but not all the way.

"Open up!" a loud voice called. "By order of the Emperor's Guard!"

My hand clenched. I backed away from the door, deeper into the laboratory.

Master Ostrum hesitated.

The Emperor's Guard pounded on the door again, and the glass window shattered, dozens of shards skittering across the floor. Master Ostrum cursed, reaching for the door as the guards stormed in.

I ran to the center of the laboratory, my fingers scrambling along the wooden planks, searching for the hidden panel. I opened it as silently as I could, although the shouting in Master Ostrum's office would hopefully block any sound. I tossed my bag into the cool, earthen hole of the subbasement. It landed with a thud, and I bounded down the ladder, pausing only to slide the floor panel back into place.

"Don't go in there!" Master Ostrum shouted as the laboratory door opened. There was a scuffle, a thud against the wall, books falling from the shelves.

Feet overhead.

The boots of the Emperor's Guard thundered into the laboratory. There was hardly any light in the little subbasement, but I knew what was there. And what I wanted. As the guards searched the lab and Master Ostrum's office, I rifled through the shelves, finding the small wooden box that housed the copper crucible.

Above me, an authoritative voice rang out. "Phillious Ostrum, you are under arrest."

Master Ostrum sounded indignant. "On what charge?"

"On treasonous use of alchemy," the master of the guard said.

The silence that followed felt thick and heavy.

"Say it," Master Ostrum said in a disgusted voice. "Don't be a coward."

"You are under arrest for necromancy," the master of the guard said, his voice cracking on the last word.

There was a scuffle then, and Master Ostrum shouted—far more loudly than was strictly necessary. "Be careful, you oaf!" His voice carried down toward me. "You've cut me. Now my blood is all over this table."

"If you will not go willingly—"

"I'll go, I'll go," Master Ostrum growled. "Try not to destroy any more of my lab."

He's doing this for me, I thought. *Leading away the guard before they find me. Letting me know his blood has spilled.*

"I know why you're doing this." Master Ostrum's voice came from his office now, but was loud enough to carry down to me. "I'm being damned for my blood. But you're fools. I'm the only person who could have helped you."

Not the only *person.*

"My daughter and my wife both died of the plague," the master of the guard said. "And the Emperor says the plague isn't natural, that it's caused by someone like Wellebourne."

"Still scared of the word?" Master Ostrum mocked.

A heavy cracking drowned out whatever else he was going to say as the guards slammed their fists into Master Ostrum's body again and again.

• • •

It was hard to tell how much time had passed. After Master Ostrum was carried away, some of the guards remained behind, shuffling papers, moving books, shaking out boxes. Their footsteps pounded over me. I strained my ears to listen for the big clock in the tower, wondering how long Ernesta had been alone in the quarantine hospital. Wondering if she was still alive.

Have faith in me, I prayed. *I'm coming.* I had all the ingredients now. I could make a necromancer's crucible. I could become a necromancer. If a necromancer had created the plague, surely one could stop it. I would find a way.

I can save you.

After the last guard left, I counted to a thousand. Then I counted a thousand more.

I climbed up the ladder, my bag strapped to my back. The floor panel crept open.

It was dark.

Debris and papers shifted as I slid the floor panel all the way open and crawled out. I readjusted it, then kicked some books with broken spines over the entry. *Father would be so disappointed in my treatment of books lately,* I thought. Then I remembered where my father was.

I moved to the table with a streak of red blood across it. Clever of Master Ostrum to alert me to its presence. I used a glass slide to scrape some of the blood from the table, then let it drip into the bottom of the copper crucible I had retrieved from the subbasement.

The price had been paid. The copper crucible, once empty, now contained a bony, dried-up hand. The crucible cage I needed.

Outside the lab, I heard a sound. Glass crunched. I froze.

Someone was entering the office.

FORTY-NINE

Nedra

"HELLO?" A VOICE said softly in the dark.

"Grey," I breathed.

He didn't hear me. Flickering candlelight flowed into Master Ostrum's office, and I stepped out of the lab.

"Who—" Grey started, cursing. The candle shook in his hand as he let out a relieved sigh. "Nedra," he said. "I've been wondering when you'd return."

"I arrived today," I said, keeping my tone neutral. I stuck to the shadows, remembering my reflection.

"Is everything all right?"

I laughed aloud, perhaps a bit hysterically.

"Nedra?" He stepped closer; I shrank further back. "Are you okay? How is your family?"

A knife to my heart, twisting. I couldn't answer. "What are you doing here?"

"It's my appointment time." Grey looked around him. "But I guess it's true."

"That Master Ostrum was arrested? Yes."

"For treason?" Grey asked. He searched for an oil lamp, finally finding one on Master Ostrum's desk. "That's the rumor anyway. That he was secretly performing necromancy."

Grey turned away from me and lit the lamp behind him, the steady flame providing more light than his feeble candle. His back stiffened. He didn't look up at me as he asked, "That's not what he had you doing, right?"

"No." My tone remained neutral, my face remained in shadow.

"Because the rat—"

"I have not raised the dead," I said. "Nor has Master Ostrum."

He mumbled something.

"What?" I asked.

"I said, you can't know that for sure. About Ostrum, I mean. They say the Emperor himself decreed his arrest."

"Master Ostrum isn't a necromancer," I insisted. "And we couldn't perform necromancy even if we wanted to. We don't have an iron crucible." *Not yet.* "But, Grey," I added, "you know that the plague is necromantic, right? A necromancer started this, and it will take a necromancer to finish it."

"Have you ever wondered," Grey said, looking around the smashed office, "if it could be the same necromancer?"

"What's that supposed to mean?"

"Ostrum is one of the best alchemists on Lunar Island. He could be showing off. Start a plague . . . then end it. Be a hero."

I stared at him for several moments. "That's the stupidest thing you've ever said," I snapped.

"You're too close to him," Grey protested. "He likes the fame. The prestige."

"Yes, that's why he became a teacher. For the lucrative pay and the respect."

"Nedra," Grey said. "While you were gone, Ostrum presented at the court. He talked about his legacy, he rambled on about the importance of preserving history—it was weird, to be honest. The Emperor started an inquiry *because* Ostrum was dancing around the subject of necromancy. In court. In front of everyone. Like it was nothing."

"Master Ostrum."

"What?"

"*Master* Ostrum," I repeated, subtly stressing the word. "Show some respect."

Grey shook his head. "We're going to be reassigned," he said. "Probably Professor Pushnil. Or Professor Xhamee. That would be better. More connections."

"Sure. *Connections*," I said, my voice hollow.

Grey crossed the room and, for the first time, seemed to actually *see* me. "Oryous's stars, Nedra, what happened?" He stroked my ratty hair, his fingers falling to my face. I could feel the dirt and grime that stood between us. "Is this berrilias powder?"

"For lice," I said as he wiped the white dust from his fingers.

"Lice? What happened in your village?"

"I was at the hospital for that bit," I said. "After—"

"But you said—" Grey frowned. I *hadn't* said I was all right, that my family was fine. He'd just heard in the silence what he hoped to be true. "Nedra, what *happened*?" His question was gentler this time, his attention finally focused.

It was too late.

He wrapped his arms around me in a hug I didn't return. "You're safe now," he whispered into my dirty hair. "You're home."

I watched a dust mote falling through the lamplight. Did Grey think that *this* was home? Yūgen? School? *Him?*

I pulled away, ignoring the hurt I could see in his eyes. I adjusted my bag on my shoulder. "I have to go," I said.

"Go? Where?"

"To the quarantine hospital."

"Ned," Grey said, "didn't you hear? They closed the hospital."

"I know that." My eyes bore into his. "Did you know they left thirty patients behind? Left them to die?"

Grey looked surprised enough that I trusted he hadn't known. That made me feel a little better.

I moved past him, toward the door, battered and broken as it was. Grey reached for me. It reminded me of the way the others pulled me from the hospital, the way they carried me, kicking and screaming, from my sister.

I jerked away from Grey with more force than was needed.

He stood there in the light, watching me in the shadows, concern etched across his face. "What happened while you were gone?" he asked. He reached for me again, and I let him hold my hand, pull my wrist to the light, see the bruises and scratches from my struggle.

My bag felt very, very heavy.

He pulled me closer. My head tilted toward his. My lips were dry and cracked, but none of that mattered as he pressed them against his, his body holding me gently but firmly, as if I were a bird he was afraid would fly away. I closed my eyes and sighed, letting myself have this one moment. This one kiss. His body felt strong and warm and safe. When he pulled back, I felt myself drowning in his eyes, not in the same gaspy, hungry way as before, but slipping under, just sliding down into darkness where nothing mattered, nothing at all.

His hand supported the back of my head, and I leaned into his touch, relishing it for a moment before finally letting my feet come back to earth.

"Grey," I whispered. "I have to go."

He silenced me with another kiss, deeper this time, more insistent. More desperate, as if he hoped a kiss would be enough. Maybe it could be. My arms reached up, sliding up his back, his neck, my fingers twining in his hair. I felt the spark again.

The hunger.

I broke away, gasping for air. "Grey," I said, more forcefully this time. "I have to go."

"There's no one left at the quarantine hospital," he said. "You can take a break, Nedra."

I shook my head.

Grey straightened, and I knew he was trying to catch his heart and calm it the same way I was doing with mine. He let his gaze linger on the broken pieces of the room, the shattered glass, the bent pages of books tossed on the floor.

"Just promise me one thing," Grey said. "Promise me you're not going off to finish Ostrum's work for him."

I met his eyes.

I did not speak.

"Nedra," Grey said, his voice a warning. "Ostrum's been arrested. He'll hang for treason."

"Without a fair trial?" I snapped.

"Maybe," Grey said. "Kill the necromancer, kill the necromancy. Worked on Wellebourne." It wasn't until Bennum Wellebourne's body had quit bucking in its noose that the dead army he had raised fell lifeless once more.

Grey's eyes were pleading. "That's why you need to quit. Forget everything he told you. Distance yourself from him. Don't let him drag you under."

"I will do what needs to be done," I said. I started for the door again.

"I love you, Nedra, but . . ." I didn't realize until that moment just how much the "but" canceled out the "love." Love could not exist when it came with conditions.

Whatever he was going to say died on his lips as the weight of his words fell on him. We had said many things to one another since the day we met, but we'd never said *I love you*. "Does it really matter what

I do if it will stop the plague?" I asked, giving him one last chance. "If it will save people from suffering? From dying?"

"Yes," Grey said emphatically. "Necromancy is a line you cannot cross."

I shook my head. "There is no line," I said.

"I won't come with you," he said, taking a step toward me. "If you do this, Nedra, if you choose necromancy . . . I will not follow you into that darkness."

"Oh, Grey," I said, shifting my bag on my shoulder. "What do you know of darkness?"

FIFTY

Grey

I WATCHED HER go.

She was different now. Something had happened. At her village, at the hospital . . . maybe here, in this ransacked office with shattered glass on the floor, crunching beneath my feet.

Something had happened.

And she had emerged on the other side a different person.

There was something wild in her—I could see it in her eyes. Like a monster caged inside her skull, scratching along the edges for escape.

I listened for her footsteps to fade to silence. She was gone. Out of my reach.

Fear welled up inside me, and I wasn't sure if I was more afraid for her, or of her.

FIFTY-ONE

Nedra

STEALING A BOAT was my first crime this night, but it would not be my last.

The water was warmer than the air, and mist rose up like steam, blurring out the waves, the other boats in the bay, and, I hoped, me.

My muscles strained as I maneuvered the oar through the water. The flat-bottomed boat was small—designed to carry two people, maybe three—and the bay was particularly gentle tonight, but it was still rough going. I had not truly slept since the night I turned my parents to ash, and the weight of all that had happened since then made my entire body ache.

The clocks chimed midnight.

The bells rang out, one chime from the tower in the quarantine hospital, one chime from the tower at Yūgen, and then back and forth, twelve each, followed by a resounding silence. I pulled up the oar, resting it on the bottom of the boat. My shoulders sagged.

The emptiness of the world enveloped me.

My hands—calloused and cracked, with blood and ash and dirt caked under my fingernails—rested in my lap, palms up. I was surprised at the first lines of wetness that cut through the grime, my tears gliding between my fingers.

I tilted my face toward the quarantine hospital. The boat bobbed in the water.

I was alone.

I could go back. The thought came to my mind, unbidden and unwelcome.

It's not too late.

I had carved runes into the dead flesh of my parents. I had stolen a crucible cage created by the worst traitor in all of history. I had taken the horrible, soul-crushing first steps.

But I could still turn back.

My eyes dropped to the water. It was black—cold and unforgiving, but there was a hint of sapphire reflected in its depths.

That blue reminded me of the robes of the alchemists who had fled, of the tincture the potion makers left behind before closing the hospital doors, abandoning those who needed them most.

I picked up the oar, sliding it noiselessly into the water. I pointed the boat back toward the hospital.

I had promised my sister.

I'd promised her I would return.

FIFTY-TWO

Nedra

THE BOAT BUMPED up against the stone steps. I had no rope, so I hauled it up a few steps, hoping the tide wouldn't carry it away.

The walk up to the hospital's entrance felt eternal. I pushed open the heavy mahogany door, not bothering to shut it behind me. Starlight chased my heels.

"Ernesta!" I shouted. My voice echoed, long and loud, fading into nothing. "Nessie!"

I tripped over the first body, my knees crashing onto the marble floor, my palms bursting with pain as I caught myself. I scrambled over the sprawled legs of a little boy, his eyes glazed over with green film, looking up at the ornate ceiling of the hospital, the gilded decorations reflected in his pupils.

Breath was expunged from my body as if I'd been hit in the stomach. I knew this boy. His father had blamed me for his brother's and mother's deaths. *Ronan.* The amputation hadn't worked; the plague had traveled to his brain.

A thin dribble of deep blue liquid trickled out of one corner of Ronan's mouth. He was so close to the doors. I wondered if he had tried to get outside, to die under the stars.

"Ernesta!" I screamed. My eyes grew more accustomed to the darkness, and I searched frantically.

No one answered my call.

She couldn't have gone far. She had been weak and tired when I left her, barely able to remain standing. I ran down each of the wings, shouting for my sister.

I found only death.

The victims left behind had been in the worst shape of all. Legs and arms of the bodies I found were withered and black, so brittle they looked as if they would snap off. Some had taken the tincture; many had not. It was easy to tell the difference, quite apart from the tinge of blue on some of the lips. The ones who chose death on their own terms mostly did so in beds or chairs. They arranged themselves so their bodies were decent, and although many of them slid onto the floors after they died, it was evident that they had been thinking of who would find them, of what condition they'd be found in. Several victims were in beds, their hands folded over their chests as if they were hoping death would be like sleep. I found some in the courtyard, earth rubbed on the bottoms of their bare feet, their three-beaded necklaces clutched in one hand and the empty bottle of tincture in the other.

But the ones who had not chosen death, even when it was the only choice, had defied it to the very end. I found their bodies in the hallways, collapsed against walls. Their faces were slack, but I imagined there was still anger in their empty eyes. Three were in a medical supplies closet, obviously looking for something that might help, something not as final as the tincture of blue ivy.

But no Ernesta.

I ran back to the foyer. I was so *tired*. My body longed to fall to the floor like the dead around me.

"Nessie!" I screamed.

A cool breeze from above, a whisper of a chill, floated down in answer. My eyes caught a bit of blue—an unopened bottle of tincture resting on the bottom of the spiral staircase that led to the clock tower. My gaze drifted up and up. To the body draped over the steps.

"Ernesta!" I gasped, racing to the stairs. I took them two at a time, but I was clumsy in my weariness, and I slipped and skidded down several steps, the wrought iron burning against my skin as I struggled to stand again. I gripped the railing in one hand, my bag in the other, leaping toward my sister. She had made it nearly to the top. I dropped to my knees on one of the stairs, feeling for a pulse, praying she was still with me. I peeled back one of her eyelids—no green film.

"Ned," she said, her voice barely there.

"Nessie!" Tears caught in my throat, and the word could hardly escape my lips.

A shadow of a smile passed over her. Her lips moved, but I couldn't hear anything else. It didn't matter. I didn't need her words; I never did. I knew why she had come up here. She had been remembering my stories—she wanted to see the city.

We were closer to the clock tower than to the main floor of the hospital, so I helped Ernesta to stand and carefully pulled her up the remaining steps. Her body was heavy, but my labored breaths sounded so riotously full of life compared to her shallow ones.

"Almost, almost," I said as we crested the final few steps. Ernesta dropped to her knees, but I coaxed her up again, pulling her closer to the reverse clockface, which cast a warm glow over the tower.

Ernesta lay on the floor so still and quiet, her frame more gaunt than thin, her skin sallow, her still-healing amputation so new that it pained me to look at it. I dropped to my knees beside her.

This plague is necromantic.

It will take a necromancer to stop it.

I pulled Bennum Wellebourne's crucible cage out of my bag, setting the severed, shriveled hand on the floor beside Nessie.

Next, I needed the iron forged from the blood of a person who loved me. My parents loved me. They loved my sister. They would want this.

I told myself, *They would want this.*

I carefully held the waterskin of my parents' ashes over the palm of the crucible cage, pouring the blackened flecks in the center and chanting the runes as they landed. There was far more ash than should fit in the open hand, but as I spoke the runes, the ash swirled in the center, condensing, becoming a hardened black lump. I didn't stop until all the ash had been poured.

I finished speaking the runes.

In the center of the mummified hand of Bennum Wellebourne was a small lump of blood iron. I reached for it with trembling fingers.

I turned to show the creation to my sister, to prove to her that it had been worth the wait.

But Ernesta was no longer breathing.

FIFTY-THREE

Nedra

"No, no, no," I said, scrambling over to my sister's body.

I pressed my fingers against her pulse points, but her heart was silent.

Her skin was already cold.

My empty stomach churned. Had I imagined hearing her say my name? Had I imagined her breath, shallow but steady? Had I, in my exhausted state, pretended my twin was alive as I pulled her body up the stairs? Or had she passed as I knelt beside her, playing with a darker magic than she'd ever dreamed existed?

"Nessie, Nessie," I begged, tears blinding me so much that I could almost pretend her chest rose and fell, rose and fell again.

It's not too late.

I turned back to the crucible—not a crucible. Not yet. The iron was made, a hard lump in my hand. But there was still one step left. I dropped the iron bead into the palm of the crucible cage.

A sacrifice.

I grasped for my father's book, flipping through its worn pages. I remembered what Master Ostrum had said about Bennum Wellebourne, how he'd almost been bled dry. How there needed to be death in the blood.

I found it. My eyes lingered over the runes, but when I opened my mouth to read them aloud, no sound came out. I took a deep, shaking breath and forced myself to begin chanting. *Take what you must.*

Leave me the power. Take what you must, leave me the power. An open promise, a blanket offering.

My mouth kept moving as I crouched over my sister's remains.

Take what you must, leave me the power.

Ernesta's body glowed, tiny bits of bright gold flickering over her body, rising like fog on the water.

Take what you must, leave me the power.

I felt the burning in my fingers first, fire traveling up my arm, past my elbow. My nails melted, white hot. I hissed in pain, but kept chanting.

Take what you must, leave me the power.

Anything for her.

My blood boiled. My skin ripped apart as tiny bubbles of red burst through, spilling out over my arm. The veins of my left wrist cracked open, a fountain of crimson spilling over my fingers. I screamed in pain, but through the sound, I did not stop chanting.

Take what you must, leave me the power!

My flesh unwound.

Strings of muscle and ligaments unraveled past my elbow.

My blood, my skin, my flesh was unspooling off my left arm, pulling into the hardened black center in the palm of the crucible cage, wrapping around the iron bead made of my parents' ashes. My flesh wove between the bony fingers of the hand, around and around, forming a tapestry of gore. Blood hovered like red mist, staining everything.

Take what you must, leave me the power.

The chanted words were desperate now, my plea for this to end. The flesh of my arm fell away, leaving only bone.

I flexed my bony fingers, white stained pink with blood. I could identify the carpus, the ulna, the radius.

I had never thought to see the interior of my own hand, exposed and brittle.

Take what you must.

My fleshless hand started to glow with the same golden sheen my sister's body did.

Each bone, at the same time, without warning, *shattered.*

I screamed, blinded by pain. My voice shriveled to nothing. The dust of my bones hung suspended in the air, forming the outline of my elbow and arm and hand, and then slowly, slowly, the bone dust swirled down, down, falling over the crucible like rain.

About four or so inches remained of my left arm, less bone, more flesh hanging limply. The muscle sizzled as if being burnt, the stench so sickening I gagged. The skin knit together, raw and pink and thin.

The words of the runes flashed in my mind.

Leave me the power.

I turned to my sister, prone and motionless beneath the illuminated clock. Her body still glittered with a glowing aura I could never describe with words, as if the particles of air were gilded.

Her right arm, amputated. My left arm, taken. We were still, even in this strange space between life and death, mirror twins.

Take what you must, leave me the power. The words were bitter in my mouth now, but still as true and sincere. I would give anything— my other arm, my legs, my heart, my soul—to just get Nessie back.

The glow lifted over Ernesta's body. The air no longer smelled of blood and burning; it was sweet, but sharp. The bright mist rose higher and higher.

Take what you must, I said in the ancient tongue, *just give me back my sister.*

The golden light swirled into a stream, the end pointed like a pen tip. It flowed into the iron, wrapping around, hardening, shining so brightly that I had to look away. It formed the bead into a small, hollow cup, about the size of the tip of my thumb. I bent to pick it up, almost losing my balance as I reached out with my right hand, forgetting I no longer had a left one. As soon as I touched it, the crucible cage crumbled to dust.

The iron crucible was crudely made, but I could feel its power overtaking me, surging inside my body.

I turned immediately to my sister. "Nessie," I whispered. My voice was raw and cracked, as if I had been breathing smoke.

She did not move.

I ran to the top of the spiral staircase that led into the foyer, hoping the air would clear my head. At its base, the bodies of the other plague victims lay haphazardly. And above and around them all, the same golden glow that had clung to Ernesta before pouring into the crucible.

"No," I whispered.

I cupped the crucible in my palm. The truth settled on my shoulders like rain.

I had thought my arm was the price I paid for the power, but I was wrong. Ernesta's soul had been the sacrifice. These other dead bodies—their souls were still there. Still intact. But Ernesta's had been ripped from her, imbued into the iron, forced into the crucible.

I ran back to her side.

"Nessie," I said, my voice cracking. "Come back to me."

I knew what to do instinctively. I cradled the crucible in the palm of my hand. I saw—now that I knew what to look for, I *saw*. The golden glow of my sister's soul bound to the crucible, not her body.

"*Come back*," I ordered, and there was power resonating in my voice.

Ernesta's body did not move.

"COME. BACK." I ordered again, channeling everything inside of me through the crucible.

Her eyes opened.

FIFTY-FOUR

Nedra

"Nessie!" I cried joyously.

Her flesh was cool, like the iron bead in my hand. She had no heartbeat.

I pulled back.

No life in her eyes.

"Nessie?" I asked, leaning back and looking into her expressionless face.

She blinked.

There was nothing of my sister in this shell of a body. Was this what necromancy was? Raising the bodies but losing the souls? What point was there in that?

Unblinking, she watched me.

I couldn't stand to look at her expressionless eyes. I had to get out. I ran across the metal landing, heading straight to the spiral staircase. But when I reached the top of the steps, I was stopped short by a wave of power, the sheer force of which hit me like a gust of wind in a hurricane.

From my vantage point, I could see almost all of the abandoned bodies in the hospital. But I could also see the golden glow that clung to them, much like the glow that had enveloped Ernesta when I first raised her. *Souls.*

But unlike with Ernesta, I could *hear* these souls. Not with my ears, but in my mind—I could hear every last one of them. And they were crying out.

Help me.

Time. Give me more time.

Bring me back.

Can you hear me?

There's more I want to do.

Each voice was distinct, each imbued with its own sense of long-ing. And each voice was directed at me. Just as I could sense the dead, they could sense *me.*

I remember you, one voice said, and my eyes drifted to the body of the boy on the floor, Ronan.

What do you see? I thought the words, but I knew he understood. *Darkness,* he said. *And light.*

Do you see my sister? My internal voice was urgent, begging. *She looks like me.*

Nothing looks like anything here.

Ernesta? I called loudly in my mind. *Can you hear me?*

But as I tried to reach through the veil that seemed to separate me from the voices, I couldn't get any sense of my sister. I could not find her cries among the others. Now that I'd made my presence known, they called to me even louder, screaming, begging, a long, low moan that sliced through my brain with the finesse of a sledgehammer.

I took a deep, shaking breath, trying to make sense of it all. And in the sound of my exhale, I could feel others, ones I'd not noticed before. Silent ones. They shrank away from me, pulling deeper past the veil.

In the palm of my hand, the crucible pulsed like a heartbeat.

A glimmer of silver caught my eye. I looked to the left, to where my other arm should be. Extending from the remaining bit of my shoulder was a pale, ghostly limb, transparent but bright. I flexed my fingers. Nothing I had read had hinted that my flesh and blood would be taken and replaced with a spirit arm. But I had also never read of someone using a crucible cage they had not made themselves. Perhaps this was payment for not sacrificing enough, or perhaps there was some dark magic Bennum Wellebourne had placed on the burned bones of his own hand. Trembling, I tried to touch this shadow arm with my real right hand. I felt nothing—my fingers slipped through the air—until the ghost arm touched the iron crucible.

That I felt.

I let go of the crucible with my real right hand. It rested in the shadow hand as if that pale mist was solid.

Help us, the voices cried. They were weaker now.

They didn't have much time.

I held my shadow hand out, the crucible in it small and insignificant looking, and in my mind, I called back to the voices that called to me. I saw the golden mists rise up from the bodies—most, but not all. They swarmed to me, to the crucible, and the light poured inside, swirling like a black hole eating a star.

I felt their souls. I knew each of them in a way I had known no other person—bare and true. My ghostly fingers clenched the crucible—it was both hot and cold at the same time, the temperature so extreme it felt as if it would burn me, and yet I couldn't let go, even if the hand that clutched it was not real.

In a brilliant supernova of light, the souls shot out of the crucible and back into the bodies of the people they belonged to. They each took a huge breath of air in, their backs arching, then exhaled, sinking back down. None of them breathed again.

And, one by one, they stood.

FIFTY-FIVE

Nedra

THE FACES OF the dead tipped to me.

I could sense each person—dimmer now than when I'd held their souls—and I knew them. I understood their thoughts. Their feelings. There was sadness within them, but also hope. And I knew that hope came from me.

There were three who remained dead. They were the souls that had shrunk away from me. They had not wanted a second life, so I had not given it to them.

But twenty-seven others watched.

It wasn't a true life.

But it was enough.

Ernesta. I turned on my heel and darted back onto the landing. The shell of my sister stood there. I reached for her unwittingly with my ghost arm, stroking her cheek, and her head tilted into my touch as if she could feel the hand that wasn't there.

"Follow me," I said, intending to drag her to the stairs if I needed to. But she moved at my command without my touch, followed me as I raced down the spiral staircase, the only sound throughout the entire hospital our clattering footsteps.

I reached Ronan first. "Did you see her?" I asked, shoving Ernesta toward him. "Wherever you were . . . ?" My voice trailed off.

He shook his head. "No." And because he could sense my sorrow, he added, "I'm sorry."

Something shifted in my vision. There was a glimmer of gold inside the boy, shining through his eyes.

"It doesn't hurt anymore," he said, standing up on his disease-withered leg. "In fact," he said in a slower voice. "I don't feel . . . anything."

"But you can talk. You can think?"

He nodded.

But Ernesta couldn't. I scrutinized her, trying to figure out why she was different.

Other revenants drew closer. "Did any of you see my sister? In the other place?" I asked desperately.

They all shook their heads, but there was some hesitation within them. "What?" I asked. "What is it?"

A woman stood from the crowd. I had not known her before, but I knew her now—her name, Phee, her three small children, who all died before her, her husband, who killed himself when he saw her blackening hand. She pointed now with her withered fingers. At the crucible I still held.

"She's there," Phee said.

My eyes darted between the revenants, the crucible, and my sister. *The golden glow.* It wasn't in Nessie's eyes. When I'd tried to raise her, the light didn't sink back into her body. It melted into the iron crucible.

I dropped to my knees, the crucible in my hand. Now that I knew what I was looking for, I could feel it, sense it within the metal. I had given my twin her body back, but I had trapped her soul.

Surely I can get it out. I have to get it out.

I concentrated, forcing my eyes to focus on the unnatural light. It wisped around the edge of the metal. Almost . . . almost . . .

The light slipped through my fingers, snapping back to the crucible. At the same time, the revenants around me screamed as if they were experiencing agony no human should ever feel. They dropped to the ground, their bodies writhing

"What's wrong?" I gasped, moving to Ronan.

"I don't know," he choked out. "But please, stop whatever you're doing. It *hurts.*"

"There has to be another way," I mumbled, standing.

But I could sense the answer from them all. Their souls had passed through the iron crucible. They had felt her the way I felt them.

And they knew she was past the point of saving.

The dead did not sleep. But I was not afforded the same luxury. It felt creepy to claim a former hospital room as my own, so I set up a little nest of blankets and pillows in the tower and let the dark, dreamless night engulf me, my heart keeping steady pace with the ticking clock. Ernesta sat in the center of the floor, unmoving.

When my eyes opened the next morning, I was immediately aware of all my revenants.

Someone's coming, they told me.

I walked out onto the balcony in front of the clock. The sun was rising over the bay, the water so bright that it was at first hard to see the boat that drew closer to the stone steps leading to the hospital.

I took the stairs two at a time as I raced down. My revenants were all waiting for me, save Ernesta, who I left in the tower.

"Who is it?" I asked.

"My father." Ronan stepped forward. "And others."

My mind flashed to Dannix's anger when he'd assaulted me after his wife's death. What would he try to do to me when he saw his child turned into a revenant?

As one, my revenants looked to the door. I knew—because they knew—that the boat had arrived. I mentally ordered the others to stay in the foyer as I strode to the door and stepped into the morning light.

Five men and three women were making their way up the stone stairs. They stopped short when they saw me.

"What are you doing here?" I called down to them.

One of the men—Dannix—broke into a run. He stumbled up the last steps. He looked far wearier than when I'd last seen him, his face pulled tight with stress, his eyes rimmed in red. "You," he said, recognition dawning. "Did you come to help—?" He choked over his own words, unable to continue, then turned and shouted to the others, "She's an alchemist!"

Dannix stumbled up, grasping my hands. "You came back," he said, his eyes alight with hope so fierce it was almost painful to see, like looking at the sun. "You came to help treat the ones who stayed."

My heart thudded in my chest. I couldn't tell him that his son was dead, not with him looking at me like that. "What are you doing here?" I asked again.

The group of people reached the top steps, and one of the women stepped forward. For the first time, I noticed her pallium. "You're a priest," I said.

She nodded. "We came to give the proper rites to the dead," she said.

I thought of the plague victims who had not wanted to be raised. "Thank you," I said. "There are three who—"

"Three?" the woman interrupted. "We were told to expect closer to thirty."

My eyes were on Dannix. I couldn't voice what had happened.

So I opened the door.

"Ronan!" Dannix screamed, rushing forward. The others were more hesitant, stepping slowly into the foyer. The priest touched the three beads she wore at her throat, a prayer slipping past her lips.

"What is this?" she said, horrified.

Dannix knelt in front of his boy, holding him tightly, sobbing in relief and joy. He had not seemed to realize that his son was not truly alive.

But the others did.

Some backed away slowly, their eyes wide, as if the sunlight would protect them. A few stepped into the shadows, reaching out for other loved ones. They were all, I realized, related to the dead who had been left behind. They'd pooled together their resources and come here to perform the holy rites.

They did not expect the undead to meet them.

"This is . . ." the priest started, horror filling her face.

A revenant stepped forward. I knew through our connection that it was the priest's mother. The priest's lips moved wordlessly, though in prayer or curse I wasn't sure.

"She's a witch!" one of the people in the group—a heavyset man with dark eyes—shouted, pointing to me. "No better than Wellebourne!"

Dannix leaned back. For the first time, he seemed aware that his son wasn't alive. "Is it you, Ro?" he asked.

Ronan nodded.

Dannix stood and turned. He dropped to his knees in front of me. "Thank you," he said with palpable fervor.

"This isn't right," the priest said in a low voice, unable to rip her eyes away from her mother.

Footsteps echoed down the stone steps. Almost half the group was running away, back to the boat. With a horrified look in my direction, the priest turned around and chased after them.

Dannix, two other men, and a woman stayed behind. We watched as the others fled.

They would not keep this secret.

"You're staying?" I asked Dannix and the others.

"I'd rather stay on this island with him than be anywhere else without him," Ronan's father said. "If you'll have me." He looked down, seeming to remember the way he'd attacked me just after his son's amputation.

"You don't care that it's—"

"Blasphemy?" the woman said. I nodded.

"No," Dannix said. His hand clutched Ronan's as if he were afraid his son would disappear again. If he noticed how cold his son's dead flesh was, he didn't care.

FIFTY-SIX

Grey

THE NEWS SHEETS had been brutal.

TOP PROFESSOR AT YŪGEN ACADEMY ARRESTED FOR TREA-
SON, they said in bold letters. SECRET HERITAGE OF BENNUM
WELLEBOURNE EXPOSED!

What bothered me more were the questions.

"So, did you know?" Tomus asked, putting his breakfast tray on
the table and sitting across from me in the cafeteria.

"You'll have to be more specific," I mumbled, not looking up.
Several more students, emboldened by Tomus's temerity, sat down as
well, not disguising their starvation for gossip.

"Oh, any of it," Tomus said, rolling his hand. "That Ostrum was
a traitor. Or related to Wellebourne." Tomus leaned forward. "Or
maybe you know something about the school's charity case."

"I bet that's why she's not back," Salis said haughtily. "She was an
accomplice."

My head snapped up at that, and Tomus grinned, knowing he'd
struck a nerve. "Nedra's not been in school for ages, Greggori, didn't
you notice?"

"Of course I've noticed," I growled. I tried to ignore their laughter
as I stormed away.

Tomus cornered me before I had a chance to escape the dining hall.
We were both deeply aware of the rapt audience straining to listen.

"Wonder if she's been arrested, too," Tomus mused. "Your little girlfriend, I mean."

"She's not my girlfriend," I said immediately. *Not anymore.*

Tomus raised an eyebrow. "Oh," he said, drawing the word out. "You know, Ostrum was arrested before your meeting time with him. Did you run into him being dragged out in handcuffs?"

"No." I bit the word off.

"I must admit," Tomus said, raising his voice so others could hear, "I'm honestly surprised little Nedra hasn't come sniffing around for Ostrum. I had thought, you know, if *you* two weren't an item . . . well, there were all those *special* sessions . . ."

I knocked Tomus's shoulder as I tried to move past him, heading to the door. Before I could reach it, however, it swung open.

Two men and a woman strode inside, their bright red coats announcing their position as Emperor's guards. My stomach sank. They walked straight toward me. They knew who they were after.

"Greggori Astor?" the woman said in a clear, loud voice.

"Yes," I said, tired. "Do we have to do this here?"

The guard looked surprised, blinking at the rabid attention of every single student in the cafeteria. "If you could come with us," she said in a softer voice that nonetheless carried throughout the silent hall.

"Let's get this over with." I headed to the door, the Emperor's Guard in my wake.

Outside Yūgen's gate, horses stomped and snorted, their breath forming clouds around their heads, obscuring the crimson tassels on their bridles.

"Please get in the carriage," the captain said.

It wasn't a carriage, though, not really, and we all knew it. There were no fancy seats behind elegant doors. This was a wagon atop wheels, the few windows barred and a heavy lock on the door. This was a prisoner transport.

"Am I under arrest?" I asked, hoping some of my father's authority was in my voice.

The captain opened the transport door. "Please get inside," she repeated without looking at me.

For a brief moment, I felt a rush of panic. I focused on the narrow spot between the guards, and I believed if I burst through them, I could escape. But I had no reason to flee—I was guilty of nothing except, perhaps, association.

I stepped into the carriage, the wagon shifting under my weight until I settled on the bench on one side. One of the male guards followed, sitting across from me. The captain shut the door, and she and the other guard clambered to the bench atop the transport, tapping the horses with a whip to get them moving.

Chains I'd not noticed before rattled as the wagon bumped over the cobblestones. I slid over the smooth wooden seat before I steadied myself. We were moving at a fast clip, and I stood despite the uneven motion of the carriage, holding on to the bars at the window so I could watch my neighborhood slip away.

Once the cobblestones gave way to smooth paving stones, the ride got easier. Outside, the buildings were smoother, too—made of sleek, carved stone, not ramshackle wooden planks. I guessed that was what wealth did, wore away all the rough edges of everything it touched. Money was nothing more than sandpaper made of diamond grit.

I knew where we were going before we got there. Still, I couldn't help but gape in awe as the door to the carriage opened.

We were at the palace.

At the beginning of the school year, Yūgen had hired sleek black carriages to carry us up to the grand entrance, the curving marble steps cascading with roses, the flapping banners of silk and gold lamé flapping in the wind as we proudly walked up the stairs as if we belonged nowhere else. Now the prisoner transport carried me to the back.

"This way," the captain said politely as the other officers accompanying her dispersed. Despite my arrival, I was not treated like a prisoner.

The captain led me inside. The hallways were marble, protected by a lush red carpet, and the doors along the plastered walls were made of rich, shining cherry. We walked in silence for several minutes. The farther into the palace we went, the more richly decorated the hallway became. Little niches built into the walls displayed paintings and busts of important, long-dead politicians on short stone columns. The doors grew wider, and they were carved with bas-relief designs that indicated who worked in each office. A battle scene for the governor's general, a scale weighted with gold for the chief tax collector, three stars for the governor's personal Oryon confessor and advisor.

The door we stopped at had a single mark engraved in the wood: a circle with a lopsided *T* spilling out from it. The first rune of alchemy.

These were the chambers of the Lord Commander.

FIFTY-SEVEN

Nedra

THE EMPEROR'S GUARD came in a red lacquered boat. The priest and the others who'd come to my island had been quick to report us. But I had spent the night preparing.

I waited by the door, watching through the crack as the captain pulled out a vocal horn. "By order of Emperor Auguste, you must surrender your person for trial."

I could still hear the boots of the Emperor's Guard when they had come for Master Ostrum. They beat him bloody and dragged him away. I had hidden in the darkness, and even though most of the emotion had been cauterized from me with my parents' death, I still had the capacity to fear.

I was not afraid now.

My revenants stood behind me. They could sense my plan, and they awaited my command. The living who'd come to my island were nervous.

"What are you going to do?" Dannix asked. "The Emperor—"

I shook my head, not bothering to hide my smile. How could Dannix be afraid of a little boy hiding in a tower when I was right in front of him?

"The Emperor sent a whole ship to capture me," I said. I looked back at my revenants. "It will not be enough."

"This is your last chance!" the captain on the boat shouted up to me. I didn't move. I had learned from Tomus that the gravest insult to most men was simply to ignore them.

A plank lowered from the ship to the stone steps, and six men walked onto my island, rifles at the ready. They called up at me again to surrender.

My eyes cut to Dannix. He clutched his son. I refrained from rolling my eyes. He had no reason to fear.

I pushed open the double mahogany doors and stepped into the light.

The Emperor's men cowered beneath me. Behind me was a troop of the undead.

I felt drunk with power.

"We're here to arrest you," the captain called up at me.

I couldn't help but smile.

Come out, I whispered in my mind.

My revenants moved as one, an unstoppable force descending upon the soldiers. I laughed aloud as the men with rifles panicked. They fired their weapons, but it did no good, and soon enough they turned tail and fled.

The captain shouted for the retreat, and the few brave men who'd tried to stand their ground raced behind him, up the plank, and back on the ship. The captain's eyes drifted up to me at the top of the stairs. I relished his terror.

Let's play with them, I told my revenants.

As one, every single revenant turned to the captain. Eyes wide, teeth bared, lips snarled up. Staring at him.

"*Go!*" the captain screamed at his men. They fumbled with the oars, trying to push away from the stone steps.

I want the ship.

The revenants drew closer. It didn't matter that the captain had thrown away the gangplank. The revenants moved with superhuman strength, leaping at the boat, grappling up the smooth lacquered sides, scrambling onto the deck.

"Abandon ship! Abandon ship!" the captain screeched. The crew raced for the lifeboats on the other side. They let the pulleys drop before everyone had gotten inside, and some crew jumped from the ship, landing in the water as the lifeboats crashed into the waves. The men in boats pushed off, rowing as fast as they could, and the men in the water screamed for them to wait, come back, save them.

For a brief moment, I wondered if the captain would try to go down with his ship. He had the look of a noble martyr. But as soon as my revenants boarded the ship, he scrambled portside, tossing himself directly into the bay and swimming frantically to his men waiting for him. Shivering, he huddled on the lifeboat, his head bowed in defeat.

I grinned. I had my castle behind me, my army was growing, and now I had a ship. When I found the other necromancer, the one who had caused so much suffering, I would be ready.

FIFTY-EIGHT

Grey

THE LORD COMMANDER was the governor's right-hand man. Usually a person of extreme importance already, and an adept alchemist. I hadn't known that Governor Adelaide had selected anyone to take the position since her inauguration. The news sheets had reveled in the tragedy of her falling ill, but the boring politics of who had acquired which title hadn't been as popular.

The captain of the guard swung open the door of the Lord Commander's office, and I followed him inside. Rather than a room, we were in another hallway.

The captain stepped back through the door. "Wait here," she said, then shut it, trapping me inside.

I waited for several minutes, but nothing happened. I drifted closer to the door at one end of the hall; it was marked again with the Lord Commander's seal, and I assumed it was his private office. I walked the length of the hallway to the other end and shifted the cloth just enough to see what was on the other side.

The throne stood on a dais overlooking the marble floor. An enormous oil painting of the Emperor hung from velveteen ropes behind the throne—a reminder that Governor Adelaide served the Emperor first and that he was the true ruler of Lunar Island.

I stepped farther out, surprised that no one rushed to stop me. Movement caught my eye, and I noticed a woman sitting on a chair positioned at the bottom of the raised dais, just under the throne.

She was wrapped in black damask, with long dark hair streaked with gray. She turned her head, and I caught a flash of gold—a diadem was braided into her tresses.

I stepped down from the dais. Governor Adelaide looked up at me with milky eyes.

Her image was plastered throughout the city, but I thought of the last few times I'd seen her in person. At the quarantine hospital, walking with Nedra, her body regal, gracious, an easy smile on her lips in the face of tragedy—a mask clearly worn for the benefit of those around her. Before that, standing strong with her people on Burial Day. And before that, at her coronation ball, her face alight with laughter.

She was a shell of who she had been. The woman who sat before me now was faded, her face sunken in, her hair dull and brittle, her skin ashen. I had known she was sick, but I didn't realize just how bad it was.

"We keep her from the public eye for obvious reasons." Master Ostrum swept aside the red velvet curtain and strode into the throne room. "It would be demoralizing."

"Os—Master Ostrum," I said, shocked. "I thought you'd been—"

"Yes, the papers greatly overstated the situation." His voice was dry. "I wasn't arrested. I was promoted." He tapped the bronze badge pinned to his alchemical robes. It was shaped like a hand forming the first rune of alchemy.

"You're—"

"Lord Commander now, yes."

I bowed my head quickly, then looked over at Governor Adelaide.

"I misjudged her," Lord Commander Ostrum said as he walked closer to the governor. "My politics seem silly now, in the face of this plague. Especially since we were more politically aligned than I'd thought."

"I've never seen symptoms like this," I replied. Although I spoke right in front of her, it was as if Governor Adelaide was in a world of her own, not even registering the sound of my voice. The only movement she had was in her fingers, as she rolled a small iron bead in her hand. While all the news sheets reported that she had contracted the Wasting Death, she didn't have blackened appendages or amputations, no green film in the eyes. This was . . . different.

Master Ostrum motioned for me. "Greggori," he said. "Come with me."

We crossed the throne room, heading toward a door on the other side. "Where is everyone?" I asked.

"Staff has been systematically reduced. Plague took many, soon after the governor fell ill. The others . . . were fired," he said, as if that wasn't the right term for it.

"But the governor is too ill to—"

"By the Emperor."

I drew up short. Master Ostrum paused, impatient. "Try to keep up, Greggori," he said, exasperated. "And forget what you've read in the news sheets." He paused. "I assume your father has kept you abreast of the current political situation."

"We rarely talk," I said immediately, but while that was true, I did have some understanding of the unrest in the government.

"The citizens of Lunar Island want freedom. That's what your father's group wanted."

I was reminded of how Master Ostrum had been close to Lord Anton before his death. "But not you?" I asked.

"Oh, I wanted freedom, too. Our island deserves to be its own nation, out from under the thumb of the Emperor. What I didn't know—what none of us knew—was that it was Governor Adelaide's plan as well."

I stopped short.

Master Ostrum nodded, a knowing smirk on his face. "Oh yes. She kept her true intentions well hidden, but Governor Adelaide knew how to play the political game. She intended to find a way to break from the Empire peacefully. Her plan would have worked, too . . ."

"But then she got sick?" I guessed.

Master Ostrum's bark of laughter was bitter. "No. Then the Emperor found out."

FIFTY-NINE

Nedra

DEATH WAS COMING to my island.

I could feel it, the way my grandmother used to feel a storm approaching. The rain made her bones heavy and her joints creak, but the closer Death came to me, the more alive I felt. It buzzed through my blood, electrifying my body.

I consciously pushed my shoulders down and lifted my chin, lengthening my neck and straightening my spine. I could feel their eyes on me, watching as I glided down the hallway. I was always aware of where my revenants were. That was something the necromancy books hadn't told me—when you raise the dead, you become connected to them body and soul. I felt them, each one of my subjects, as if there were an invisible string tethering us.

From throughout the building, they gathered closer to me, pulled to Death just as I was.

Head up. Eyes straight ahead. Do not hesitate.

Do not let them see your fear.

It was animalistic, the way they tilted their faces to me as I drew closer, the silent acceptance as they bent to my will and followed behind me. Most of the time, they could pretend they were alive again—that normalcy had returned. But not when I was around. I called out to the darkest part of their souls. I merely whispered, and their bodies were under my control.

I pushed open the hospital doors and stepped into the crisp night air. A crescent moon curved over the river, sending ripples of its arch dancing across the water. My gaze drifted to the city, sparkling beyond. From here, it looked beautiful.

When everyone in the city dies of the plague, I wondered idly, *will I want to bring them all back?*

Not everyone was worth saving.

The still air was disturbed by the sound of a wooden oar smacking against the water. I glanced down and saw a ferry. The skipper looked grim even from here, his eyes casting back to Blackdocks. But four adult passengers huddled on the boat, and they looked eager, scanning the edges of my island, looking up at my hospital.

By the time my revenants and I arrived at the bottom of the stone steps, the flat-bottomed boat was already pulling away, the skipper slapping the water noisily in his haste to leave. These people would have had to offer the skipper a lot of money to convince him to take them here. The people from the boat stepped forward, their faces slack with fear as they saw me and my revenants. I wasn't sure who they feared more.

One man dressed like a mill worker bent down, touching the mound on the dock. As I drew closer, I saw that he was holding the still hand of a dead child, covered by a knit blanket.

The man nearest him had clothing stained with oil, his fingers black with soot. A mechanic, I thought, or maybe a cleaner in the factories.

"We were told you could help," he said. He didn't look down at the body. When I didn't reply, he added, "To give us back our little girl."

"And our son," the other couple said, the man holding the child out to me.

Children. I closed my eyes, swallowing down the lump in my throat.

"It was the plague," the mill worker said. "It happened so fast. We saw the black in her fingers, and we thought there was a chance . . . but then her eyes paled, and we did what we could, we tried, we never left her side, we both lost our jobs, but it was too late."

I didn't care. How she died didn't matter. The method never mattered. Dead was dead.

Unless I brought them back.

I started with the boy. His father wouldn't put him down, instead holding him as I pulled out his soul, fed it through my crucible, then returned it to the boy. He gasped—a rattling, eerie sound—and the revenants behind me turned to him, watching. His father released him, and the boy walked over to the other revenants, joining their ranks.

I waved my right hand at the boy's parents, and they melted into the crowd, fear evident on their faces. They weren't sure they'd done the right thing tonight.

"Please, please," the mill worker said, drawing my attention to the little girl. His babbling faded to silence as I ripped away the blanket covering his daughter.

I fingered my iron crucible with my right hand, then slipped through her skin with my left one—the ghost one. I dug into her body, lifting out the golden light of her soul. None of the living could see it, but the dead did.

I did.

My eyes grew warm, and the heat spread down and in, washing over my mind and seeping into my bones. It was relaxing, but had an edge of panic and urgency, like slowly realizing I was drowning in a warm bath.

There were only moments now, just a few breaths of time before the warmth was replaced with utter, still cold. Before the little girl's soul slipped forever past my reach. There was no time for formalities or niceties. I could not linger over small talk like the girl's name, or her past, or if she was happy. I had time for just a few questions, asked directly in my mind, answered by her fading soul.

Do you want to come back? I thought the words with no tone or inflection. *I can bring you back, and you can be here again.*

But I won't be there? she responded.

I did not know where *there* was, but it was a place the dead often talked about, quietly, among themselves when they thought the living couldn't hear.

If you are here, you can't be there, I answered.

Are my fathers sad? she asked. Her voice was like a high-pitched bell, the words ringing in my mind.

I was dimly aware of the way the mechanic had choked back a desperate sob, the way the mill worker had stood to be beside him, the way they were clutching each other's hands.

That doesn't matter, I replied. The cold was starting to creep in. *Do you want to come back?*

. . . No.

I let go, because I knew *she* wanted to let go. Her soul slid through my shadowy fingers, and I tucked my iron crucible back under my tunic. The golden mist evaporated into the night air. I tilted my face up for a moment, watching as the glittering light disappeared among the stars far above. Then I stepped back.

"Well?" the mechanic asked gruffly.

"No," I said, giving him the same answer his daughter gave.

The mill worker sputtered in disbelief. The mechanic's face shadowed with rage. I turned my back to them and started walking back to the hospital.

"Wait!" the mill worker roared, his meek sorrow replaced immediately with fury. "You *can't* just say no! You can't! You brought that other boy back. Bring *her* back! Bring her *back*!"

He surged forward. I did not pause as I walked into the crowd of my revenants. They allowed me to pass, but then stood between me and the fathers. The men tried to claw and fight their way to me, but my revenants stood in silent protection, watching as the men finally broke.

"Fetch them a boat to the mainland," I told the closest revenant.

I could still hear the fathers' anguished pleading as I pushed open the doors of the hospital and let them slam shut behind me.

SIXTY

Grey

"THE EMPEROR?" I asked. His portrait stared down at us, and I repressed a shudder.

"He knew," Master Ostrum said simply. When I remained confused, he elaborated. "Emperor Auguste knew about Lord Anton. He knew about the protests from students, the dock workers who wanted to form a union. He knew that Governor Adelaide had been planning to peacefully pull from the Empire. He knew it all, and he came here to remind us who was in power."

It seemed impossible; the Emperor was about my age. I shook my head, unable to absorb what it was my master was saying.

"He started the plague as a show of power. I think he stayed after the inauguration to see if he could use Governor Adelaide to stifle the protests," Master Ostrum said. His eyes were sad as he looked at the shell of a woman. "When she proved unmalleable, he—"

"You're saying the Emperor is a necromancer?" I gaped at him.

"It was Nedra who helped me to see it," Master Ostrum said. "The plague seemed to target certain people—namely, the poor. Worthless fodder to the Emperor. He still has supporters among the upper classes, who benefit the most from his rule. And the few powerful people who opposed him . . ."

He let his voice trail off. Lord Anton, his biggest detractor, dead of plague. Members of the governor's council who might have supported a revolution. The governor herself.

"He's used the plague to terrorize the people," Master Ostrum continued. "I have no doubt he plans to be the hero who stops it." He glanced over to Governor Adelaide. "She's hanging on, somehow. She's stronger than anyone realized. But once she's gone, the Emperor will use the plague to declare a state of emergency and dismantle the governorship. He'll have complete control of our island, and anyone who thought to oppose him will be dead."

Nedra had known. She had tried to tell me. The plague was a necromantic curse. I didn't listen to her.

I let her go.

"We have to do something," I said, but my voice was already weighed down with hopelessness. What could we do against the Emperor? Against a necromancer?

"The Emperor will not be easy to defeat. But it's the only way," Master Ostrum said. "If he dies, the plague will die with him."

"We have to let people know," I said. "If everyone knew he caused the plague, we could storm his rooms, drag him out . . ." I swallowed, unwilling to speak aloud what would have to happen next.

Master Ostrum barked with bitter laughter. "You think I haven't tried that? He's in the old tower, Astor."

I frowned, not understanding the implication. The old tower surely wasn't impenetrable. It had been built a century and a half ago, by . . .

By Bennum Wellebourne.

Realization dawned on me, and Master Ostrum nodded knowingly. "Wellebourne used necromantic runes to protect the tower. The Emperor is safe, as long as he stays in Wellebourne's tower. That's why he hasn't left." He paused. "But if we had a necromancer's crucible, we could break down the door. We could reach him, and stop him."

Governor Adelaide stirred in her seat. The iron bead she'd held in her hand clattered to the floor, rolling over to our feet. Master Ostrum picked it up. The bead was hollow and cracked, nearly split in two.

"When she was inaugurated, Governor Adelaide went to the treasury." Master Ostrum's voice was lower now, as if he were speaking in front of a casket. "She found Bennum Wellebourne's relics. This was his crucible."

I stared down at the rusted, hollow black bead, and I wondered at the souls that had passed through it. An entire army of dead.

"I suspect it's protecting her, somehow," Master Ostrum said, placing the bead back in Governor Adelaide's limp hands. "But it won't last. The crucible is breaking. It's not strong enough to break through the runes protecting the Emperor."

"But—can we make another crucible? Do we have to use Wellebourne's?"

"No and no," Master Ostrum said. "We need any necromancer's crucible, but we can't simply make one. They are . . ." His eyes grew distant. "Almost impossible. The sacrifice too great."

I let out a breath. "But then how . . . ?"

"Astor, there is another necromancer's crucible." He paused. "I tried to send men to bring her here. There was some . . . confusion. She's scared; she doesn't understand the power she's unleashed."

I shook my head. *No.*

"Nedra Brysstain is a necromancer now," Master Ostrum said, "and we need her crucible."

"She's not," I muttered, but I knew even as I spoke that this was not the case. I had seen her just before she left Yūgen for the last time. I had seen the darkness within her.

What happened while she was gone? I asked myself again. I should have asked. I should have *known.*

"You can talk to her. She'll listen to you, Greggori. She'll come with you—or let you have her crucible. And with it, we can get to the Emperor." He looked down. "I won't lie—even when we break down the doors, it won't be easy to stop what he's done. But one thing is for sure: Kill the necromancer, kill the necromancy."

If the Emperor died, the plague would die with him.

We could stop the illness.

We could save lives.

We would be committing treason.

SIXTY-ONE

Nedra

ERNESTA WATCHED ME impassively as I paced around the clock tower. I had read all the books again, quizzed the revenants about their deaths, done everything I could think of to find out more about the plague, but I kept coming up short. I knew it was the creation of a necromancer, but who? And, more to the point, how could I stop it?

I paused in front of Ernesta.

And why could I still not give her the life she deserved?

I stared into her face. Identical to mine. Same gold-flecked eyes. Same high cheekbones. Same large forehead and black hair and big ears and pointy collarbones.

And yet, now we didn't look alike at all.

"I'm sorry," I told her blank face. I said it like a prayer.

I pulled up the crucible from the chain around my neck, and I held it in the palm of my shadow hand. I closed my eyes.

I could still feel her soul. There were whispers of my parents, too, deep in the blood iron. My family was not quite past my reach. Their souls echoed in the crucible, whispers, reminding me of who I was, of love that was true. I couldn't hear words in the echoes, just . . . just feelings. Of calm. Of love. Of peace.

I opened my eyes and my vision filled with the empty stare of the thing that looked like my sister. I had only this pale imitation of Nessie, a soulless, lifeless puppet that shared her name and that stood in the corner of my workroom, watching me, waiting for me to command it.

Her. Waiting for me to command *her*.

She stepped forward.

"Get me a cloak," I told her. "I'm cold."

Ernesta silently moved across the metal floor to the crate I used as storage, rifling through the contents and emerging with my cloak. She walked back to me, holding it out. I took it from her hand, and she lowered her arm. She stood there. Waiting. For my next command.

Rage pricked at my eyes, and I slammed my fist into the face that looked like my twin sister. I felt her nose crunch; her flesh gave way beneath my pummeling. She didn't move to defend herself. She stood there until my force knocked her over, and then she fell to the ground, and still I raged, kicking her viciously in the ribs, stomping her weak body, crouching over her and driving my knuckles straight into her face.

I stopped when I grew exhausted. Her body was bent and broken, bruised and bleeding.

I touched the crucible, spoke the runes. White light encased Ernesta's body, and, in a moment, she was healed and whole again.

She stood up. She looked at me.

She waited for her next command.

SIXTY-TWO

Grey

KILL THE NECROMANCER, *kill the necromancy.* The words moved my feet forward, filling me with determination. It didn't matter that the necromancer was the most powerful person in the world.

He had to be stopped.

I went to Blackdocks. The factories loomed along the bay like hulking giants, blocking out the stars on the horizon.

"Come on." A man's voice carried through the night. "You have to take me."

"Not for just a silver," another man said.

The fog thinned as I reached the water's edge. Usually there was a large cluster of flat-bottomed boats that ferried people up and down the coast. But tonight there was only one.

"Where you going?" the skipper called to me. His accent was thick and heavy, making it all sound like one word: *waryougwan?*

"The quarantine hospital," I said, looking past him. The tall brick building was barely visible in the dark, only identifiable by the illuminated clockface.

The skipper spit a stream of blackleaf juice into the bay. "Told *him*," he said, jerking his head to the other man. "Ain't going there. Not without proper gold."

"Please," the first man begged, his voice cracking. He stank of alcohol, but he seemed sober. My eyes drifted down to the large lump at his feet. I gasped—it was a woman, her body covered by a cloak but clearly dead.

"That place is cursed!" the skipper said. "I ain't gonna—"

"Ten gold," I said.

The skipper gaped at me. "Yeah, all right," he said.

"Him, too." I nodded to the other man and the dead woman.

"For ten gold I'll take whoever can fit."

The other man turned to me and grasped my hands. "Let's go," I said, more abruptly than I meant to, but his effusive thanks made me uncomfortable. That, and the corpse.

None of us talked. With every bump in the water, the dead woman's head lolled. Her mouth was open, her tongue fat and heavy. The man kept adjusting her cloak, as if keeping her warm mattered.

As soon as the boat touched the stone steps leading up to the hospital, the skipper started rushing us off. I got out first, looking toward the hospital. The man grunted, awkwardly trying to get the dead woman from the boat onto the step. The skipper pushed away with his oar, and the woman's feet splashed into the icy water before the man could pull her up to a step.

I watched the boat fade into the darkness.

"Hello?" the man called. "Hello? We need help!"

I turned. The doors to the hospital opened.

A woman stepped out. She carried herself stiffly, her chin tilted up. "Nedra," I whispered.

As if she could hear me, she looked down, her gaze intent. She stumbled on the step, but regained her balance quickly. My heart plunged. She'd thrown her arm out to try to catch herself—but she no longer had her entire left arm. I tried to recall if she had signs of black in her skin when I'd seen her in Master Ostrum's office. How had so much changed in such a short time?

"Hurry, hurry," the man pleaded under his breath, but Nedra's pace was slow.

And then, behind her, more people emerged from the hospital. Dozens—just under fifty or so, I guessed. These people moved as one, flowing like liquid over the steps, a wave of people that surrounded her.

The man started to pray.

The crowd behind Nedra seemed a random assortment of people, male and female, all different ages. Some had blackened limbs, but they didn't show pain.

They didn't show any emotion at all.

I sucked in a breath, my eyes watering. I hadn't wanted to believe it was true. Not my Nedra.

But when she stopped, they stopped. When she looked at the dead woman, they looked.

And when she turned to me, every dead eye focused on my face.

I opened my mouth to speak, but Nedra turned away without a word, crouching down to inspect the body of the woman at the man's feet. The man's hands twitched nervously as Nedra pulled away the cloak, revealing no sign of plague. Instead, she had bruises blossoming on her throat.

My head jerked up to the other man's face. "It was an accident," he said. "I swear. Can you save her?"

Nedra still didn't speak as she reached under the collar of her cloak and pulled out a chain. At the end of the necklace was a small iron bead, dark and whole, unlike the broken bead Governor Adelaide had held. I sucked in a breath. *Would it be enough to take down the Emperor?*

Nedra's eyes cut to me, narrowed and fierce. She raised an eyebrow, as if daring me to comment on her necromancer's crucible.

When I didn't respond, she reached toward the dead woman with her residual arm. Nedra's eyes softened, but her focus intensified.

Behind me, the man's babbling stopped. He stared in horror at the revenants. Whatever they were looking at, it was the same thing Nedra's attention was focused on.

"Can you bring her back to me? I love her," the man said. "She's my wife."

"She's not." Nedra's voice was tight, and I could tell she was angry. "And she doesn't want to come back to you."

She stood.

The man's face purpled. "You *will* bring me back my wife, you—" he started.

Nedra held a hand up. "I only bring back people who want to come back," she said. "And besides, I don't see why you want to bring someone back after you murdered her."

The man sputtered, rage overwhelming him. "I would never murder her!" he snarled. "I *love* her."

Nedra cocked her head. "The dead don't lie," she said simply. "You killed her. I'm not bringing her back against her will just so you can pretend to apologize."

"I'll make you—" he started, lunging for her.

I jumped to protect Nedra, but I needn't have. Her revenants circled the man, and he couldn't break through them. "Come along, Grey," Nedra told me, heading back up the stairs.

"What are . . . what are they going to do to him?" I asked. The revenants were so tightly packed around the shouting man that I could barely see him.

"Whatever they want," Nedra said, shrugging, not slowing her pace back up to the hospital. "They all saw the poor woman's soul, too. They all heard what she had to say about him."

The man's voice went from angry shouting to terrified screams, but all I could hear was what Nedra had told him before: *The dead don't lie.*

I glanced behind me once before I stepped inside the hospital after Nedra. I could not see what the revenants were doing, but the man's screams had stopped.

Nedra didn't pause as she made her way sedately to the spiral staircase leading to the clock tower. I followed, my mind a riotous mess, caught somewhere between panic and fear. Those monsters outside—they had worn the faces of humans. There had been *children*. My dread grew with every step. I could not tell if I feared the monsters inside more than the one I followed.

Nedra is no monster, I told myself firmly, but I could not calm my heart.

Someone waited for us at the top of the stairs. I gasped and stumbled down a step, my eyes unable to comprehend the exact mirror copy of Nedra standing beside her. The real Nedra had an edge to her I'd almost forgotten, something rough like splintering wood. This other girl didn't have that. Behind her eyes, it was as smooth as glass. My Nedra was missing her left arm; the other one's right arm had been amputated above the elbow. But other than that, they were identical.

Identical . . .

My gaze dropped to Nedra's hand, wrapped up in the hand of the creature that seemed to be a mirror copy of her. The monster's fingers were loose, resting in Nedra's grip, but Nedra had white knuckles, she was holding on so hard.

All of Nedra's stories about her family came flooding back to me.

"Nedra," I said slowly. I looked at the empty shell of a person who stood placidly beside her. "You didn't tell me your sister was your *twin.*"

She sniffled. For the first time, I realized Nedra was crying. Nedra, the feared necromancer who raised revenants and clutched their souls in her hand, was silently crying, fat tears slowly leaking from her eyes, one after another.

I acted without thinking. I reached for her, cradling her face with one hand, my skin immediately wet and warm from her tears. "Nedra," I whispered, "why didn't you tell me?"

"Why didn't you ever *ask?*" she growled, jerking her face away. Her hand slipped out of the monster's.

She reached for me with what remained of her left arm, the residual limb twitching. Nedra looked down at her shoulder as if angry at its betrayal, but she didn't try to touch me again.

Instead, she looked at her sister, who, I realized, was not a monster at all.

"I'm sorry," I said. It wasn't enough, it would never, ever be enough, but I had to say it.

"Go," she whispered. I hesitated, but then the reanimated corpse of her sister walked placidly down the stairs. Nedra had sent her away, not me. Nedra sank to the floor, her head resting against the clock, the minute hand ticking by. I sat down beside her, and she didn't object.

For a long while, there was nothing between us but silence.

"I thought you wouldn't follow me into the darkness." She threw my words back at me, but her voice sounded tired and defeated.

"This is wrong, Nedra," I said. "You shouldn't be playing with life and death."

"You know *nothing* of death."

"But why?" I asked. "You can't give them life. Not really." Even if the other revenants hadn't been as hollow as Nedra's sister, it was still obvious they weren't truly alive.

It took her a long moment to answer. "They didn't ask for life. They asked for more time." She paused. "'If love will not stop for death, time should.'"

My lips twitched into a shadow of a smile. That line came from the poem I'd recited on our first day of lessons at Yūgen, in Master Ostrum's office, for our first report of the semester. She had remembered it. I loved her for that, for the way she noticed things no one else would bother with.

The thought came quickly, unbidden, but I knew it was true. The first words lingered within me. I loved her.

I love her.

It was an emotion I no longer recognized. Love wasn't sweet and pure. Love crept slowly, like a river rising, seeping into the earth, saturating it, spilling over the banks, drowning everything in its wake.

Nedra stood and shrugged out of her cloak. I scrambled up and helped her with the fasteners. The cloth fell away, exposing a plain beige chemise underneath. I looked at the snaking scars on what remained of her left arm, unusually long and puckered, as if the arm had been ripped from her, not cut.

I made myself look at the scars, still fresh, raw, and pink. At first to see if there was infection or any pain I could help take away. But then to make myself imagine how it had felt. I wondered, not for the first time, what had happened to her.

When I looked up from her arm, I saw Nedra watching me. Waiting for me to comment.

"You're still beautiful," I said.

She shook her head, disappointed. "Oh, Grey," she replied. "How do you always know to say just the wrong thing?"

I frowned, unsure.

What was this thing between us? It didn't feel like before, at school. It was different, deeper and darker, but perhaps more real. My eyes drifted to the chain that held her iron crucible. We needed to talk about the plague. What Lord Commander Ostrum had told me.

As soon as I spoke, I knew the spell between us would be over. We would not be able to face each other anymore; we would have to face our mutual enemy. Selfishly, I wanted to do nothing but stay here, the heavy ticking of the giant clock wrapping around us, and forget about the world and death and necromancy and everything, everything else forever.

But I couldn't let the plague continue. I opened my mouth to speak.

Nedra sighed and leaned toward me, resting her head on my shoulder.

We had kissed—many times—before. We had come close to doing more than kissing. But that moment, with her hair falling down my back, her skin's warmth seeping through my shirt, her weight leaned against me, was more intimate than anything we'd done before.

SIXTY-THREE

Nedra

GREY PULLED BACK, purpose in his gaze.

I knew it from the moment he had looked at my iron crucible. He had not come back for me. He had another reason.

"Why did you come here, Grey?" I asked, my voice as tired as my body.

He took a deep breath. "Ned, there's another necromancer."

I rolled my eyes. "Yes," I said. "I noticed. What with all the plague victims that keep dying."

He reached for me, to grip my arms, but there was only one for him to touch. "No," he said, letting his other hand drop, "you don't understand. It's the Emperor."

I gaped at him. "The Emperor?"

Grey nodded. "He's hiding in the castle, not because he was afraid of catching the plague, but because that part of the castle was made by Wellebourne. It's protected by necromantic runes."

I held my hands up, pausing Grey, trying to process this information. The *Emperor*? But Grey explained it all—the revolution attempts, the plague, the conspiracies. I couldn't hide my joy when I learned Master Ostrum was still alive—and not just cleared of charges, but vindicated and promoted to Lord Commander.

"We have to stop the Emperor," I said.

"Master Ostrum said we have to kill him."

I could tell Grey was uncomfortable with the idea, but it didn't bother me. Kill the necromancer, kill the necromancy. Once a necromancer died, every necromantic action dissolves. My heart tugged, thinking of Ernesta. She only lived—with what little life she had—while I did. The same was true of all my revenants.

"But how can we reach him?" I asked. "If Wellebourne himself built that part of the castle . . ."

"Ostrum said we needed your crucible."

My hand went unconsciously to the iron bead. Despite the fact that it rested between my breasts, the metal was ice cold. So too, I found, was my heart. The Emperor had done all this to me, to my people? He had let loose a plague that devastated the neediest on my island, simply to prove a point to some restless, spoiled, rich people who thought taxes were too high?

"I'll bring him more than a crucible," I said coolly.

My chin tilted up; my spine straightened. *Come to me*, I thought.

And they came. Twenty-seven I raised when I first came to the hospital. Fourteen more since then. And my sister. Forty-two revenants.

My revenants needed no sleep. The ones who stayed with family members left them in their rooms. I led Grey back down the steps, and as we descended, the revenants spilled into the foyer of the hospital, coming closer, huddling at the base of the stairs.

Awaiting my command.

"Let's go," I said.

They parted before me, allowing me to pass first. Grey raced to keep up. His nerves were apparent; he did not like my revenants.

I did not care.

Without stopping, I turned to the revenants closest to me. "Bring my ship," I ordered. They left wordlessly. I smirked, remembering the silly captain who had been sent to arrest me.

Forty-two revenants and a ship with two cannons. And me and my crucible.

I was ready for war.

Our ship sliced through the water like a knife. As we grew closer to Blackdocks, Grey tugged at my arm. "They'll see," he said.

It was late, the moon high, the stars silent observers. But there would still be people awake, wandering the city. There always were.

"Let them see," I said.

The boat bumped against an empty slip, and I led the way, careful not to lose my balance as I descended the steep gangway. My revenants moved behind me.

I took the main road.

My connection with my revenants meant that I was aware not only of my own thoughts, but also of theirs. It wasn't all-consuming, but it was present. I felt what they felt about the church halls we passed, a mix of joy and sorrow. Their shared hatred of the factories. A memory of a kiss stolen in one pub; a fight in another. This city belonged to each of them, and that did not change just because they were dead.

The only one I couldn't sense was Grey. His skin was pale, his eyes wide with a sort of silent terror. But he walked beside me, and that was enough.

Dimly, I was aware of the commotion we were causing. Forty-two revenants and the girl leading them to the castle. Alarm bells clanged.

But no guards came.

I wondered what had happened to the captain of the warship after I stole his boat. Did the guards not come now because they were cowards, or because they had been instructed to give us clear passage to the castle?

Lights flared in the windows of the houses we passed as we crossed the poor district, and the cobblestones gave way to smooth pavers.

Curtains shifted as people looked down at us. One door opened, and a servant let out a large dog, teeth snarling. But as my little army of revenants drew closer, the dog's growls turned to whimpers. It scratched the bright blue paint of its owner's door, trying to get back inside, before fleeing in terror.

The entire Emperor's Guard stood on the steps of the castle, their red coats stark against the white stone. I knew now why they hadn't stopped us at Blackdocks; they were waiting for us here.

"Halt!" a woman cried from the top of the stairs. Her insignia indicated she was a general; the fact that she was as far away as possible from us indicated she was a coward. She did not look down at us but instead stared straight ahead as she barked her orders. "We have been informed that you intend to harm the Emperor. Stand down."

Beside me, I could feel Grey's fear radiating from him.

I wondered how the Emperor's Guard knew what we were coming for. There were about a hundred guards on the steps to the castle; perhaps a hundred more inside.

Mentally, I reached for my revenants. *Protect me,* I said.

I strode forward, confident. The first row of the Emperor's Guard swung their pikes into a defensive line.

I twitched my fingers. A dozen of my revenants raced forward. It didn't matter if they were pierced, hacked, or sliced.

Nothing could stop them.

I smiled.

Nothing could stop *me.*

SIXTY-FOUR

Grey

BLOOD SPRAYED OVER Nedra's face. It wasn't hers. She wiped it away and mounted another step, her small feet stepping over the bodies of the Emperor's Guard who had not fled.

A man in a red coat screamed, sword raised, running toward Nedra. She didn't pause or even flinch; one of her revenants just shifted in front of her, taking the blow. He plucked the sword out of his shoulder, where it stuck in the bone, and then turned it on the man who'd attacked.

Nedra strolled forward.

A body slammed into me—a revenant or an Emperor's guard, I wasn't sure—but before I could fall, Nedra's sister caught me.

"Thanks," I muttered, trying to find my footing on the stone steps slick with blood. Nedra's sister said nothing. She had not helped me; she had merely been following Nedra's orders to protect me.

Nedra mounted the last step. Through the open doors of the castle, more guards waited, their eyes so wide with fear that I could see the trembling whites. Nedra paused, turning to the steps and the straggling guards who remained.

She lifted her hand.

The fallen bodies of the Emperor's guards rose in the air. Their heads sagged on their shoulders, and their limbs were floppy, as if held by puppet strings. Silence fell, broken only by the soft plops of drying blood falling onto the steps. I stared in horror. This was the kind of thing Bennum Wellebourne had done, commanding the bodies of the dead like marionettes.

Nedra twitched her hand, sending the bodies into a macabre dance.

"Nedra," I said in a low voice, "they didn't choose this."

Her eyes were on the remaining Emperor's Guard. Their fear was palpable; Nedra's threat could not be more obvious.

Run, or become like them. Dead puppets.

They fled.

Nedra let her hand drop. The echoing thuds of bodies crashing onto the stone reverberated throughout the front of the castle.

She turned to the open doors.

"Hold!" a general in the front shouted.

Nedra walked forward as if the castle were her home. Her revenants swarmed around her. Their wounds did not bleed; their blood was not fresh enough for that. Some had limbs dangling; some staggered unevenly. But they showed no signs of pain. Nothing but obedience.

"Hold!" the general called desperately, his voice trembling.

Swords clattered as some of the guards ran in terror.

But others remained.

"Go," Nedra said casually, flicking her fingers.

Her revenants ran to the swords, crashing against the blades without stopping.

Nedra turned to me. Her left eye stood out, bright white against the smear of blood on the side of her face. "They're distracted enough," she said. "Lead the way."

My ears were full of the screams of the dying, the squelching sound of sword meeting flesh.

"To the tower, Grey," Nedra said, an edge of command in her voice.

I nodded. My heart ricocheted around my rib cage. I turned from the battle, leading Nedra into the castle, to the tower where the Emperor hid behind the men he had sent to die.

As we broke from the main hall, there were still guardsmen to fight. Nedra had not brought her army of revenants with her—we could still hear their battle raging, no matter how deep into the palace we went—but she had brought her sister's shell.

Ernesta moved with inhuman strength. She easily took out the straggling guards who cornered us in the ballroom, striking with machine-like precision as she snapped necks and broke arms and snatched eyeballs. Was this a reflection of the necromantic power with which Nedra had imbued her sister's corpse, or did this emotionless killing come from some other, darker source Nedra had accidentally tapped into? I found that I did not want to know.

"This way," I said in a shaking voice as Nedra walked over the bodies of the men her sister's corpse had killed.

Near the throne room, I heard my name being called. I was so numb with shock I almost didn't stop, but then Master Ostrum stepped out. Governor Adelaide trailed behind him, a ghost of her former self, so weak she seemed barely capable of standing.

"Astor?" Master Ostrum said again, his eyes wide with wonder. "And Nedra—oh, thank the gods. You have it?"

Nedra held up her crucible for a moment, then let it slide behind the material of her shirt again.

"We have to be quick," Master Ostrum said, taking over as he led us deeper into the castle. "The Emperor's Guard attacked soon after you left, Greggori. I was able to hide Adelaide, but . . . it's tonight or never. I don't know how he got the word out to his guards. He's stronger than we thought."

"How did he know we were coming?" Nedra asked.

"Does it matter?" Master Ostrum said. He turned a corner, and I picked up my pace, trying to keep up, but when he drew up short, I slammed into his back.

Ten red-coated guards stood in front of the stairs leading to the iron room and the turret.

"Nessie," Nedra said in a low, easy voice.

The shell of her sister flew into action. She ran at the guards, senseless to the pain any attack against her brought. Nedra, meanwhile, looked past the fight, to the stairs and the iron door beyond.

"Can you get through?" Master Ostrum asked. Behind us, Governor Adelaide made a noise; a vocalization that meant nothing. Her hands were clasped together, her body shaking.

Nedra's eyes skimmed the door, moving her head around so she could see past the guards who screamed as Ernesta killed them, one by one. She seemed to be reading something in the wall, but I couldn't see whatever she could. "Yes," she said finally. "I think I can do it."

As more of the Emperor's guards fell, Nedra strode forward. She ran her fingers along the iron door, circling the rings that looked so much like the ones Governor Adelaide had given us for the graves on Burial Day. Nedra withdrew her crucible.

Power crackled around her. Her eyes seemed both focused and unfocused at the same time, as if they were pulling apart the threads of a tapestry I couldn't see. Her voice made a guttural noise, and then I recognized that she was chanting runes. I tried to decipher them, but they were unlike any runes I'd used before in medicinal alchemy.

"*Yes.*" Master Ostrum's voice reached me through the sounds of the dying battle.

A crack echoed through the hall, so loud that the stones rattled in their mortar.

Nedra reached forward, pushing the door open.

SIXTY-FIVE

Nedra

Darkness swarmed around me.

And in the darkness, I heard a voice.

"Hello?" It was weak, pitiful.

My eyes adjusted to the dim light, then an oil lamp flared to life. I blinked away black spots.

A boy about my age crouched against a wall. He was emaciated, his skin pale, his cheeks hollow, his arms wrapped around his middle. "Hello?" he said again, straining to see.

"Emperor Auguste?" I asked.

"You've come to save me?" There was so much *hope* in his voice.

Master Ostrum shoved past me, a knife in his hand, raised over his head.

Kill the necromancer, kill the necromancy.

I felt for Nessie; she still battled against two guards. No—only one now.

Master Ostrum drew closer to the Emperor. He was so young, small and weak. He raised his bony fingers in front of the blade, as if that would stop it from plunging into his heart.

I reached for Grey. He squeezed my fingers as if he thought I was scared of the impending murder of the Emperor, but that wasn't it.

This Emperor . . . he was nothing. He wasn't a necromancer. He had no power, none at all.

This room. My eyes scanned the iron walls. It would provide protection, yes, but it could also be a prison. Wellebourne's incarceration was proof of that.

The Emperor looked like a prisoner. He held his hands up pitifully as Master Ostrum advanced, his blade glimmering in the oil lamp's light.

"Please," the Emperor whimpered. "I've been trapped here for weeks . . . months . . ."

Grey had described a puppet-lord, pulling strings from the protection of this tower.

"I've been hiding from—"

Master Ostrum kicked the Emperor in the jaw, his teeth clattering and blood spraying up. His eyes closed as he blacked out, but he wasn't dead. Not yet.

Hiding from . . .

The Emperor was a coward, but a smart one. He knew the plague was caused by necromancy, and he hid here, in the one place that might protect him, the tower Wellebourne himself had made. He wasn't the necromancer; he'd been hiding from the necromancer.

Master Ostrum's lips curved up in a smile as the blade came rushing down to the Emperor's chest.

No, I thought. Then I said aloud, "No."

Without thinking, I rushed forward. I slammed my left shoulder against Master Ostrum's back, and he stumbled, the blade sliding along the black iron wall instead of into the Emperor's chest.

"Nedra?" Grey asked.

"It's *him*!" I shouted, pointing at Master Ostrum. Master Ostrum had never liked the Emperor; he'd been Lord Anton's friend. They'd plotted treason together.

Ernesta! I shouted in my mind. The last guard was taken care of. Her soft footsteps echoed up the steps. She burst through the door, moving between me and Master Ostrum. Behind Grey, I saw Governor Adelaide, frail and sick.

Master Ostrum had hated her, too.

"Why?" I asked, my voice breaking over the word. "I trusted you."

"And look at what you became." Master Ostrum's voice rang with pride.

I tugged my crucible out, holding it in the palm of the only hand I had left. "You?" I asked again, incredulous. "You started the plague? You were the necromancer all along?"

He had been my mentor, my ally, my partner against the plague. But now he stood there, beaming at me as if everything he'd done had been honorable.

"Where's your crucible?" I asked.

"In your hand," he said.

My eyes widened as I realized what he meant. He'd used Grey to lure me here, corner me against the iron walls.

"You told the Emperor's Guard," I said, my voice catching up with my thoughts. The Emperor was a prisoner used as bait to lure me here. Master Ostrum had taken control of the Guard and used them to occupy my revenants and separate me from them. I had no protection. Just Nessie—who was strong, true, but perhaps not enough against another necromancer.

"I will take that crucible, girl," Master Ostrum said, stepping closer.

Attack, I thought desperately to my sister.

Nessie had just single-handedly defeated more than a dozen guards, but she showed no strain. She moved silently and quickly against Master Ostrum. He countered her initial attack, but Ernesta slammed her arm against his. He dropped the knife from numb fingers, and Nessie swooped down, spinning the blade in her hand and plunging it into his chest.

He looked down at the hilt sticking out over his heart.

Then he looked up, meeting my eyes. He pulled the knife out of his body.

There was no blood.

"You cannot kill what is already dead," he whispered.

SIXTY-SIX

Nedra

"THIS HAS NOT gone according to my plan, but things rarely do." Governor Adelaide's clear, strong voice cut through the room.

I turned slowly—still keeping an eye on Master Ostrum—as the governor straightened, rolling back her shoulders. She was still sick, just not as ill as she had seemed moments before. She rolled Bennum Wellebourne's crucible in the palm of her hand.

Noticing my gaze, Governor Adelaide held the iron bead up, looking at the cracked surface. "It belonged to a master," she said, admiration in her voice, "but its time has passed. I'd hoped for something better when I raided the treasury."

"It was enough to cause the plague, though," I said. My eyes darted to Grey. He was closer to the door, but I knew he couldn't escape.

The governor beamed. "The plague was already in the crucible. I just released it from its slumber."

"Is that what you want?" I asked, spitting out the words. "To follow in Wellebourne's footsteps?"

"To succeed where he failed," Governor Adelaide said, as if it were obvious. "All of this, from the very start." When I looked at her blankly, she added, "There would be no change without rebellion. Even Lord Anton, my opposition, knew that. But he had been a fool. Of *course* the boy Emperor would veto any election that elevated someone like Lord Anton as governor. If we want our island to be free, we have to take it. And we need an army that cannot fall."

I pushed aside what I had believed about the governor—that she was good and kind and generous—and forced myself to instead see her actions as part of a plan.

She had entered politics in order to gain access to Wellebourne's crucible, protected in the treasury.

She had released the plague. Her opponents—like Lord Anton— had died. The poor had been fodder, supplies created in advance for an undead army to lead against the Emperor.

But the plague had been more than that. It had made her into the people's hero. She had been the only government official to serve the sick. She had fed stories to the news sheets about the weak Emperor, and those articles had run beside glowing editorials of her own generosity.

She had already gained the trust of the people, and ensured that even in the remote villages, everyone thought the Emperor was a feeble coward. I glanced at him now, still passed out on the floor from Master Ostrum's blow to his head. Perhaps that part had been true.

"He put himself in the tower," Governor Adelaide said. "After the inauguration. I'd hoped to starve him out, but he had help somehow. And Wellebourne's runes protected him."

"But you have the crucible," I said. "Why didn't you—oh."

Governor Adelaide nodded grimly. She had Wellebourne's crucible, but it was old and cracked. It could call forth the plague it had already developed once, but it would not have been strong enough against the door to the Emperor's room. It could raise some dead— like Master Ostrum—but I doubted the governor would be able to raise and control an entire army.

Master Ostrum . . . My heart ached for him. He had never been my enemy. I felt such bitter sorrow for his fate. He'd been arrested, killed without trial, just so the governor could use him. *I could do that,* I realized. I could control my revenants the way Governor Adelaide

controlled Master Ostrum, stripping him of his personality and forcing him to bend to her will. It had just never occurred to me to be that
cruel.

My eyes roved over Governor Adelaide's body. Her frailty wasn't
an act. Using Wellebourne's crucible drained her.

My hand clutched my own crucible. It was new and strong. That's
why she wanted it.

I wondered why she didn't make her own crucible. Perhaps she
was not strong enough. Perhaps she was a selfish coward—not afraid
to kill her people, but too scared of sacrifice to make her own crucible.
Or perhaps it was simply that she had no one to love or any who loved
her that she *could* sacrifice.

Regardless, she wasn't getting mine.

To me! I called for my revenants.

Through the narrow door, golden light swirled—but it was not
under my command. The bodies of the dead Emperor's Guard stood
and moved to the entrance, blocking us inside the room. I had no
doubt that all the dead guards we'd fought were standing—and fighting my revenants. Neither side could die again, but they could be
hacked to pieces.

Bright light crackled through the crucible in Governor Adelaide's
hands. She was barely able to control the power of this broken crucible. She stumbled as she struggled to maintain a connection—but
maintain it she did.

"The guards won't strike," Governor Adelaide told me. Unspoken
was the threat, *yet.*

My panicked eyes met Grey's. The Emperor could do nothing for
us. Nessie would be able to hold off Master Ostrum, but the raised
guards would eviscerate my revenants. We were far too outnumbered.

"What do you want?" I asked. My knuckles were white as I
clutched my crucible. *That* I could not give her.

But her answer surprised me. "Freedom," she said. "It's what our people want—*need*. We've struggled as a colony for nearly two centuries. Look at him," she added, her lips sneering in disgust at the Emperor. "He's a pathetic child. Why should he take our trade routes and pocket our profits? Why should we bend to his laws rather than make our own?"

Growing up in the north, I had never cared about politics. Who took what throne . . . none of that had mattered in my village. We would still pay taxes; what did we care who they went to?

"You killed your citizens to free them?" I asked. I almost didn't recognize my cold voice.

"No," the governor said. "I will immortalize them. They will be the greatest heroes in the legends that will come."

I thought of the grave in the forest. Governor Adelaide had paid for barges to take us from the city so that we could pay our respects. While we mourned and prayed, she had planned a revolution with the soldiers that would claw their way up through the packed red earth.

"You understand, don't you?" Governor Adelaide said. There was sincere pleading in her voice, but when I glanced behind her, I could still see the dead guards, trapping us within the cell. "This was worth it. Our nation, free at last. It will all be worth it."

I looked down at the crucible in my hand. Made from the ash of my parents, the soul of my sister.

"No," I said, but my voice was barely audible.

"You know I'm right," the governor continued, taking a step closer to me. I did not move back. "I remember you. The girl from the hospital. You were working your fingers to the bone to save the sick."

"You made them sick."

"But I cared about them," she said, and I remembered the way she walked the halls, giving comfort and hope to the patients. "Even if he hadn't been here in this cell, do you think the Emperor would have cared about the plague victims?"

The news sheets had mocked the Emperor's cowardice, true, but no one had been surprised by it. No one expected him to care about the dying poor.

"You're from the north," the governor pressed. "You know first-hand how unfair life is in the villages. I couldn't stop that as governor. I want to help *every* citizen of Lunar Island. But the laws are twisted and unfair, tipped to balance in the Emperor's favor. The rich stay rich. And your people . . ."

"Stay poor," I said, finishing the sentence in a whisper.

"You see, don't you?" Governor Adelaide said.

Maybe in the past, I would have believed what she wanted me to believe. But my eyes saw more now. My eyes saw the golden glow of my family's souls imbued within the metal of the crucible in my palm. My eyes saw the shell of my sister, fighting to protect me even now, even after she had died.

My eyes saw right through the governor. This wasn't about Lunar Island being a free nation. This was about her taking the Emperor's place.

She must have realized she was losing me. "Please," she said, her voice cracking.

"I have heard that word so many times in the last year," I snarled. "Mothers holding babies dead from the plague. Fathers watching their families wither to nothing but black and twisted limbs. Lovers pleading with Death. I am done with *please*."

"If you stand with me," Governor Adelaide said, "we would be unstoppable. I can give you this island's freedom. I can give you the whole Empire."

"You'll give me nothing," I spat. "I'll take what I want."

Something slammed into me from the back, making me hit the ground so forcefully that the breath was knocked out of me. Metal clanged against wood. I turned as Ernesta threw away the pieces of chair that Master Ostrum had splintered under the force of his sword after she had knocked me out of his range. She stopped the next blow with her shoulder, a sickening squelch filling the room as steel met flesh. I clutched my crucible, and white light stitched the gaping wound back together again as I healed Ernesta as quickly as I could. It drained me to use necromancy for healing, and I feared the moment she would be too far gone to save.

I turned to Governor Adelaide as she backed away from me. Her eyes tracked the battle; she relished in it. Master Ostrum and Nessie were both revenants, and while my sister was stronger, Master Ostrum was armed.

Master Ostrum lunged—not at Nessie, but at me. I scrambled back as Ernesta jumped between us.

If Governor Adelaide could not convince me to join her in her revolution, she would simply kill me and take my crucible—strong and powerful—for herself.

SIXTY-SEVEN

Grey

MASTER OSTRUM AND Ernesta battled, but Master Ostrum's focus was on killing Nedra, putting him in the more powerful offensive position. Ernesta could only defend.

Horror washed over Nedra's face as she realized the governor's plan. Master Ostrum had been more than just Nedra's teacher; he had been her mentor. Her friend. And now he was trying to plunge a sword through her heart.

The governor stood with her back to the Emperor and me. There was no escape from the small room, thanks to the undead guards. Governor Adelaide clearly believed the Emperor was nothing more than a weak child—and I couldn't much argue with that now—but she underestimated me.

I looked around me for a weapon, turning my back to her as I ran my fingers along the dark floor, hoping for a rock or something sharp. Before I could uncover anything, though, I felt the cold, sharp edge of a blade against my neck. I swallowed, my Adam's apple brushing against the knife, my skin scraped raw. Governor Adelaide yanked me up, forcing me around without removing the knife from my throat.

"Choose, girl!" the governor shouted. "Will you raise this boy after I kill him? Will it be the same to you?"

Nedra's eyes grew wide with terror. And Ernesta—whose actions were tied to Nedra's will—hesitated in her battle against Ostrum.

Master Ostrum struck immediately, swiping his sword against Nedra's back. Ernesta spun around, knocking the blade away. Nedra fell, cascades of blood soaking through her ripped tunic, but the cut had been superficial, thanks to Ernesta.

The knife bit into my skin. I was afraid to swallow, afraid to move at all.

Nedra watched us both as Governor Adelaide raised her arm, holding up Wellebourne's crucible. I marveled that such a tiny bead had caused so much death and war.

I felt Governor Adelaide suck in a breath—she was going to offer Nedra one last chance to join her or she was going to order Master Ostrum and the Emperor's guards to kill us both. But before she could speak—before I could think—I yanked my arm up and knocked my hand against the governor's wrist.

The iron bead flew into the air.

Cursing, Governor Adelaide shoved me aside, the knife sliding across my throat up to my jaw, thankfully avoiding my arteries. I clutched my neck and watched as Wellebourne's crucible soared into the air. Nedra stretched up her residual limb, as if she could catch the iron bead with the hand that wasn't there.

SIXTY-EIGHT

Nedra

MY SHADOW ARM could touch nothing but blood iron and souls. Fortunately, that was exactly what Governor Adelaide's crucible was made of. I snatched it from the air and wrapped my incorporeal fingers around the cold metal.

Governor Adelaide screamed at me, but Grey lurched up, grabbing her around the knees and knocking her to the floor. They struggled, giving me time to inspect the crucible.

I could see the golden threads of souls woven into the iron. Now that I held the crucible, I could feel them. It reminded me of my first night as a necromancer, when I'd dipped into my own crucible searching for Nessie's soul. I had pulled at the golden threads of light, and it had hurt my revenants. Their souls were linked to the iron.

I knew exactly what needed to be done.

"What are you doing?" Governor Adelaide screamed at me as she threw Grey off her.

I wrapped my shadow fingers around the golden threads of the souls in Wellebourne's crucible. And I *pulled*.

Cold washed over me. Wisps of my black hair had fallen free from my braids, and out of the corner of my eye, I saw them turn white as I struggled to wrench the souls of the dead out of Wellebourne's crucible. If it had been my crucible, I could have let the souls go with no effort at all. But I had not bound these souls to this iron, and breaking a connection I had not forged was far more difficult than I had imagined.

346

My shadow arm tensed. It felt stronger now, and I knew it was because I was letting my own life force drain in order to maintain a ghostly connection to souls that were not my own.

The souls swarmed inside the tiny crucible, reaching for me. They had not been given a choice. They wanted to be free. I strained harder.

The blood trickling down my back slowed. My heartbeat stilled. I was too weak even to shiver, despite the ice that seemed to engulf me.

My vision faded. The golden light disappeared. I still felt it, but all I could see was darkness.

The darkness moved like a living thing. It took a shape I almost recognized.

Deep, deep within me, I felt a hunger grow, a hunger I had almost been able to suppress. My mouth salivated, and something primal roared within my soul.

And something *snapped*.

My vision rushed back to me, blinding light forcing me to blink rapidly as I stepped back. Light filled the palm of my shadow hand, dripping threads of gold leaking between my impossible fingers.

Wellebourne's crucible was empty. Without the souls holding it together, it cracked in two, the pieces falling to the floor.

Governor Adelaide wailed.

Ernesta and Master Ostrum stopped fighting. Master Ostrum turned, looking to me, his eyes hollow.

I plucked out the golden thread of light that was his soul, and I let it go. His body crumpled.

Free.

"No." Governor Adelaide's voice was low pitched and sorrowful.

Thuds echoed from the corridor as I let all the souls go. The guards' bodies fell, empty, to the ground.

"It's over," Grey breathed, relief flooding his voice.

"No," I said, looking at Governor Adelaide. "It isn't."

"You destroyed my crucible," she snarled at me.

"But not the plague." I could release the souls, I could break the iron. But the curse still existed.

Governor Adelaide's eyes grew wide with horror. She tried to run away.

But she did not have her crucible to protect her anymore. And I had mine.

Power vibrated through me. I had never taken the soul from the body of someone living before.

I was shocked at how easily—how *naturally*—it came to me. My shadow hand pulled at the strings of golden light radiating around Governor Adelaide, and her soul squirmed, trying to wriggle free. I clenched my incorporeal hand.

Governor Adelaide's body froze. Her pulse thrummed violently in her neck, and her eyes darted wildly, but there was no other movement.

"Kill the necromancer," I said, bending down to pick up the sword Master Ostrum had carried. "Kill the necromancy."

SIXTY-NINE

Grey

NEDRA STRUGGLED TO raise the sword with one hand. I didn't know how she forced Governor Adelaide to be so still as she pressed the tip of the blade against the governor's chest.

"Ned?" I whispered.

"The plague still exists," Nedra said in a matter-of-fact voice. "I cannot stop it any other way."

I knew the rules. Nedra had been able to free the undead Governor Adelaide controlled, but she could not stop the plague.

Not while the governor was alive.

But I didn't want to see my Nedra become a murderer. I crossed the room and reached for her. Her hair had come undone from its braids. It was paper-white, but still soft and supple.

Her shoulders trembled with the effort to hold the sword steady at the governor's chest.

"There has to be some other way—" I started.

Before I finished the sentence, Nedra drove the sword into the governor's heart. The light left her eyes. Her mouth grew slack, a rivulet of blood leaking from one corner. The governor's knees crumpled, and her body fell forward, sliding along the blade of the sword until her chest slammed against the hilt.

SEVENTY

Nedra

THE PLAGUE WAS gone. The crucible was broken. The necromancer was dead.

"It's over," Grey said.

I looked down at the body of the governor.

Grey pulled me into a hug. He pressed my head into his shoulder, and all I could do was thank Oryous that we had both survived. But slowly, the rest of the world bled into our circle, like the blood staining the iron floor. Governor Adelaide's eyes were still open, watching us. Ernesta stared straight ahead, emotionless. The Emperor woke up, whimpering and covering his face to hide from the gore.

Grey let me go. His hands were sticky with the blood from my back, but he didn't seem to care. The cut was deep, but nowhere near deep enough to cause more damage than a scar.

"It's *all* over," Grey said again. His eyes drifted to my crucible.

I clutched it, staring at him.

"You destroyed Wellebourne's," he said. "You can destroy this one, too."

I closed my eyes. I could sense my revenants throughout the castle. They had fought for me. Some had families to go back to at the quarantine hospital.

I opened my eyes. But rather than look to Grey, I met Ernesta's blank gaze.

Letting go of my revenants meant letting go of Nessie.

I clutched my crucible in my hand—my hand made of flesh and bone. Unbidden, my father's voice filled my mind.

I want to keep you with me always, he had told me as we journeyed to the bay and my new life. *But I know I have to let you go.*

It wasn't just my sister. There was something of my parents within my crucible, too. I could feel them, faint but there.

"End it," Grey urged me. "You know it's not natural to be a necromancer. You know that these . . ." He glanced at Nessie. "They're not *normal*. Let them go back to their graves. Let them be at peace."

I moved away from him and headed to the door. Grey tried to pull me back, but Ernesta snaked between us, giving me space as I descended the narrow staircase. I stepped over the corpses of the Emperor's Guard, my feet smearing their blood, thick and dark, on the stone floor.

My revenants joined me, falling into line as I led the macabre parade through the deserted castle. Cold night air sliced through the open doorway leading to the city.

"Nedra," Grey called from behind me. I could hear the fear in his voice.

He pushed his way through the revenants to me. "Ned, please," he whispered. "Don't do this. Let them go."

I stopped but did not face him. "No," I said, my voice strong and loud, puncturing the silence. I cast one last look at him, then turned away. "They're *mine*."

My army of dead swarmed me as I descended into the night.

ACKNOWLEDGMENTS

BOOKS ARE STRANGE things.

The earliest seeds of this novel started after watching an interview with Charlize Theron on her portrayal of Ravenna in *Snow White and the Huntsman* and was influenced through many years of watching and reading Hiromu Arakawa's *Fullmetal Alchemist*. Later, a revolutionary subplot emerged thanks to Lin-Manuel Miranda's *Hamilton*. All art is a reflection of art loved.

This story evolved over the course of many years, shifting in focus and theme, influenced not just by the arts I loved, but the people I knew and the experiences I held. In the end, less than a page of text from the original manuscript has made it into this final book.

Huge thanks first to author Carrie Ryan, who, over a lunch of pad thai, suggested that I tell more of the background of Grey and Nedra's relationship. Suddenly what had been Chapter One shifted to Chapter Fifty-Nine. If you cried over Nedra's fate, please also direct your blame to Carrie, who said I couldn't *tell* Nedra's grief; I had to *show* it. If you're ever in Shelby, North Carolina, go to Joe's Place and LilyBean's Coffee House—books get rewritten there.

As you can surmise, this book went through many drafts, and at times I worried I'd never find the right way to tell this story I loved so much. My love to Lauren DeStefano, who encouraged me to keep writing "neccy," and Cristin Terrill, who helped me figure out the correct color of turnips. Shout-out to the Wordsmiths, who are all so supportive, but especially Jo Farrow, who let me turn her into a mule.

Angel Giuffria and Kati Gardner helped me make the character of Nedra ring true. They also provided me with a level of insight that I could not have otherwise brought to her. Any mistakes that remain are purely my own. I want to thank them both for their time and helpful notes.

The gorgeous map of the Allyrian Empire was drawn by artist and author Cat Scully, who gets as excited about beautiful skulls as I do, and who tackled this huge art project with so much enthusiasm that I knew it was in good hands.

I would not have the career I have without my agent, Merrilee Heifetz, who helped me quite literally make my dreams come true. Her notes on my early draft did require me to rewrite almost every-thing (again), but without doing that, I could not have found the right story. Thanks also to everyone at Writers House who guided me along the way, including, but not limited to, Allie Levick (who was the first person to notice North Brother Island, the inspiration behind Nedra's quarantine hospital), Rebecca Eskildsen (who helped me refine the map in a brilliant way), as well as Cecilia de la Campa and James Munro, who ensure my books travel all around the world.

Of course, I want to send special thanks to my editor, Marissa Grossman. This was a beast of a book, with more story than could fit between one set of covers, and editing it was surely no easy task. Her probing questions helped make this story shine and the world more real. Thanks also to Alex Sanchez for pushing me when I wasn't clear enough, and Samantha Hoback, Krista Ahlberg, and Ashley Yee for copyedits. Bridget Hartzler is wonderful and savvy, and I'm so lucky to work with her. My gratitude to Ben Schrank and the rest of the Razorbill team, all of whom are dedicated to making beautiful books.

When I wrote the first draft of this book, I had been thinking of how grief changes a person. I didn't expect to experience that change in the middle of developing the story. This is the last of my books that my father read before he passed away unexpectedly, Nedra's grief became my own. This book is dedicated to him, a gift he never saw. I will never not miss my Poppa.

My love to my mother and my husband and my son, who share my grief and joy.